Kathleen E. Woodiwiss, Johanna Lindsey, Laurie McBain, Shirlee Busbee...these are just a few of the romance superstars that Avon Books has been proud to present in the past.

Since 1982, Avon has been continuing a different sort of romance tradition—a program that has been launching new writers of exceptional promise. Called "The Avon Romance," these books are distinguished by a ribbon motif on the front cover—in fact, you readers quickly discovered them and dubbed them "the ribbon books"!

Month after month, "The Avon Romance" has continued to deliver the best in historical romance, offering sensual, exciting stories by new writers (and some favorite repeats!) *without* the predictable characters and plots of formula romances.

"The Avon Romance." Our promise of superior, unforgettable historical romance...month after dazzling month!

Avon Books are available at special quantity discounts for bulk purchases for sales promotions, premiums, fund raising or educational use. Special books, or book excerpts, can also be created to fit specific needs.

For details write or telephone the office of the Director of Special Markets, Avon Books, Dept. FP, 1790 Broadway, New York, New York 10019, 212-399-1357.

AVON
PUBLISHERS OF BARD, CAMELOT, DISCUS AND FLARE BOOKS

SAVAGE SURRENDER is an original publication of Avon Books. This work has never before appeared in book form. This work is a novel. Any similarity to actual persons or events is purely coincidental.

AVON BOOKS
A division of
The Hearst Corporation
1790 Broadway
New York, New York 10019

Copyright © 1986 by Georgia Pierce and Linda Chesnutt
Published by arrangement with the author
Library of Congress Catalog Card Number: 85-91178
ISBN: 0-380-75021-X

All rights reserved, which includes the right to
reproduce this book or portions thereof in any form
whatsoever except as provided by the U. S. Copyright Law.
For information address A Novel Idea, Ltd., 4830 North Glendale,
Wichita, Kansas 67220.

First Avon Printing, March 1986

AVON TRADEMARK REG. U. S. PAT. OFF. AND IN
OTHER COUNTRIES, MARCA REGISTRADA, HECHO EN
U. S. A.

Printed in the U. S. A.

K-R 10 9 8 7 6 5 4 3 2 1

To Johnnye Willett...because she cared.

Prologue

Arizona Territory—1875

The noon sun filtered through the lofty branches of the cottonwood tree. The black-clad horseman astride the ebony stallion gazed out at the vast panorama of pristine desert and the giant saguaros rising like monoliths against a robin's-egg-blue sky.

The leather saddle creaked as he shifted his weight, conveying his restlessness to the anxious horse. Barely able to contain his eagerness, the horse tossed his large, proud head and pawed at the hard-packed dirt in anticipation.

The stagecoach was seldom on time, but the rider was sure that if he had delayed his departure, the cursed thing would have come early. So he waited; the perspiration trickled into his eyes and blurred his vision of the desert wildflowers erupting in the valley below him.

As he mopped his forehead with his bandana, he heard a thunderlike sound in the distance. Through a thick cloud of choking dust, the stagecoach rumbled into view.

"It's about time," the rider muttered. Impatiently, he pulled worn gloves over his hands. Draping the bandana around his nose and mouth, he lowered the slouch felt hat to the rim of his sparkling blue eyes.

His nerves steeled, he gently pressed the heels of his boots into the horse's flanks and proceeded with caution down the steep, rocky embankment and concealed himself behind a large boulder. He heard the rapid tattoo of the horses' hooves and the raucous cry of the driver as his bullwhip snapped at the team of four horses, whose mouths were lathered from the breakneck speed.

"Okay, big boy, let's not keep them waiting," the rider urged his mount as he withdrew the Colt 45 Peacemaker from his holster.

"Now!"

The horse lunged forward, his powerful legs quickly overtaking the stagecoach.

Two familiar men sat on the bench, but the outlaw was undaunted by the shotgun the rifleman carried across his lap. One of the men, Slim, would remember him well from the first time he tried to defend his cargo. Slim had lost a good rifle when the outlaw's bullet blew the fine wood to smithereens. Pete, the driver, never was a problem. All he knew how to do was drive a stagecoach, and most of the time he didn't do that well. Both men valued their lives much more than the strongbox they were carrying.

The outlaw raised his gun and fired a warning shot into the air. As he drew alongside the coach, he had an eerie sensation that all was not well. Slim didn't appear as nervous as usual, and the driver was taking ing the team to a halt.

Slanting his eyes to the window of the coach, he gazed into the barrel of a gun propped on the ledge. His eyes met those of his opponent's in fierce battle, each daring the other to fire. As the wheel hit a deep rut, one shot was fired, then another, the blasts echoing through the narrow canyon.

For a brief second, the outlaw thought he was hit as the bullet whizzed by him like lightning and richocheted off a rock beside him. His ears rang like chapel bells while his stomach plunged to the toes of his boots. As he prepared to defend himself once again, he noticed the gun had disappeared from the window.

"Don't shoot!" begged the high-pitched wail of a woman.

"Stop the damn coach!" came a man's voice as it scored three octaves.

The stagecoach slowed and finally came to a stop. Both the driver and rifleman pitched their rifles to the ground, raising their hands so high above their heads they almost appeared detached from their bodies. There was complete pandemonium inside the coach.

"This man's bleedin' bad. He needs a doctor," a lady said in a terrified voice.

"All right, everyone, come out nice 'n' easy with your hands up," the outlaw ordered sternly, his voice muffled behind the bandana.

A woman stepped down, tears streaking her heavily

made-up face. From her gaudy attire and plunging neckline, it was apparent that her destination was the local town brothel.

The last person he expected to see next was Vern Hargrove, whose short, dumpy figure climbed unsteadily down from the coach. He was so obese it was difficult to determine where his layered chin ended and his bull neck began. The outlaw scanned his body, looking for some signs of blood, thinking... hoping ... Hargrove had been hit. But Hargrove's expensive brown suit, pinstripe vest, and wrinkled white shirt seemed intact. The fancy pearl buttons that ran down the middle of his shirt threatened to rain like hail if he breathed too deeply. It took all the control the outlaw could muster to keep from squeezing the trigger of his gun.

"Well, I'll be damned," the outlaw drawled. "If it ain't the big man hisself... Mr. Vern Hargrove."

Hargrove balled his fists and clenched them tightly at his sides. "You'll pay for this, I tell ya."

"No, Hargrove, you got it all wrong. You be the one who's payin'." The outlaw's laughter rippled against the bandana. "Now who's the unlucky bastard who took it on himself to play hero?" The outlaw glanced into the carriage at the man clutching his shoulder, his face hidden by the wide-brimmed hat.

"How badly hurt are you?" he asked with a trace of sympathy in his voice.

One long, muscled leg in a fine-tooled leather boot touched the platform, followed by the other. Stepping to the ground, the man straightened to his full height. The outlaw sucked in his breath as his eyes traveled from the booted feet to the glittering silver buckle at the waist of his low-slung pants. Damn, he thought in bewilderment, just how much farther up does he go?

The fierce glare of the sun hit the stranger's eyes as he shoved his hat back off his forehead. "Not so bad that the next time I see you I won't put a bullet between your eyes." There was no evidence of any pain in his deep, resonant voice. The sympathy the outlaw had felt moments earlier evaporated.

The stranger's cold eyes narrowed and his jaw twitched as he tried to control his anger. The outlaw knew he had the advantage, but he still felt uneasy as the stranger coolly confronted him. He was an imposing figure dressed in black pants, a soft leather vest covering a very white shirt, and a red bandana tied loosely around his neck. But what really drew the outlaw's attention was the gun belt slung low on his hip like an extension of his body.

The towering figure before him was handsome, but his features were typical of men he'd seen on Wanted posters who all seemed to pose with that same snarl on their lips. His eyebrows were dark and thick over somnolent gray eyes, now slitted against the sun. His nose was straight, and flaring slightly at the nostrils, the only evidence of his contained anger. A well-kept mustache snaked across his upper lip. His mouth was full and sensuous with a deep dimple on one cheek that, combined with the sneer, made his expression ruthless and extremely dangerous.

He was obviously a man who'd known physical labor. The sleeves of his shirt were rolled just above his elbow, showing the muscles bulging against the fabric of his shirt. Dark, crisp hair was visible through the open neck of his shirt, and his chest was broad, tapering down to a narrow waist.

The outlaw scanned the rest of his long, lean body in the tight pants. Yes, quite a specimen, he mentally observed, but a specimen to be extremely wary of in the future.

"Okay, mister, drop that gun belt. The rest of you do the same. Come on, Hargrove, I know you got that sweet little derringer tucked away somers."

Hargrove sputtered, but nonetheless tossed the derringer at the outlaw.

The injured stranger unbuckled the gun belt and dropped it to the ground, but his angry gray eyes never left the outlaw's face. His voice when he spoke was harsh, his words brutal. "I owe you one."

Motioning to the "lady of the evening," the outlaw directed, "After you make a dressing for his arm, bandage that smart mouth of his afore I silence him permanently."

The woman raised the hem of her skirt to tear off a strip of her petticoat, and the long length of her stockinged leg drew the attention of the men.

Beneath his bandana, the outlaw wrinkled his nose in distaste and looked up at Slim, whose arms were still reaching toward the sky. "Slim, ole buddy, how 'bout tossin' down that strongbox you be hiding up there?"

Hargrove stepped forward, his beady little eyes bulging out of their sockets. Waving his fists, he shouted angrily, "Don't do it, Slim, or you won't be ridin' shotgun for me no more."

"But Mr. Hargrove—"

"You heard me!" Hargrove shouted, glaring at Slim.

Slim shifted a wad of tobacco in his cheek, aimed straight ahead, and spat unconcernedly. The wad fell with a splat on the tip of Hargrove's boot. Hargrove looked up at Slim in disgust. Slim shrugged, as though it were an accident.

The click of the outlaw's gun turned Hargrove's face chalk-white. He was shaking in his boots so visibly that the outlaw swore he could hear his knees knocking together. So, Hargrove was a coward when he wasn't in control of a situation. That was why he paid other men to do his dirty work.

Slim simultaneously scrambled over the seat and began rummaging through the luggage. He lifted the strongbox and dropped it to the ground. It landed with a dull thud, barely missing Hargrove. Damn shame it didn't land on Hargrove's head, the outlaw thought.

"Ya want the mailbag, too?" Slim asked, cocking his brow.

"Hell no! Just who in tarnation do you think would be writin' me letters?"

Grinning broadly, showing several missing teeth, Slim hopped to the ground to stand with the others.

Shifting his weight in the saddle, the outlaw turned his attention back to the wounded man, who had removed his shirt. A thin trail of blood streamed down his sun-browned chest and arms, collecting in the thick mass of curly hair. Even that small amount of blood nauseated the outlaw, who had never shot anyone. He was grateful for the bright sun behind him and the bandana that concealed his face.

The woman carefully pressed the wound to staunch the flow of blood, and wound the strips of fabric around the man's shoulder. But the blood continued to seep through. Her hands lingered on his shoulder, and she leaned into him, her large breasts pressing into his chest.

"Sophie knows how to take care of a man, so don't you forget me when we get to Prospect City."

A slow, vexing smile deepened the dimple on the man's cheek as his eyes boldly stared at the full breasts spilling over the top of the woman's dress.

"I just bet you do," he said with a slow drawl.

The outlaw stiffened his back at the sensuous scene and looked the man in the eyes: cold, steel-gray eyes half-closed by the sun. A shiver ran up his spine as the stranger's eyes bore into him like shards of glass. He had the eerie feeling that this man could see straight through his disguise.

"What's your name, mister?"

The stranger's mouth mocked him with a rueful grin. "Why does it matter? Are you afraid of running into me again?"

The outlaw briefly assessed the size of the stranger. "Me... afraid? I wouldn't be in this business if I scared easy, now would I?" He hoped he sounded more convincing than he actually felt.

A faint scar ran down the man's chest and disappeared into the waistband of his pants. If he had survived that wound, he would more than likely live through this one. That thought had an unnerving effect on the outlaw.

Hargrove glared up at the outlaw. "His name's Barkley... Ashe Barkley, my new foreman at the ranch. He won't be forgettin' what you did to him, neither."

The outlaw didn't need Hargrove to remind him of that. He would just have to be extra careful in the future.

Ashe smiled scornfully. "If we hadn't hit that rut, you wouldn't be sitting so smugly in your saddle."

"We'll never know what might have happened, will we, Mr. Ashe Barkley? You could of been buried six feet under instead of takin' a little ole gunshot wound in the shoulder." Aiming his Colt 45 at the strongbox, the outlaw shot off the lock. "Now, Slim, if you'd be so kind as to fill up my bag here," he said, tossing a leather pouch to the ground, "I'll be moseyin' on up the road. 'Pears to me this fine-looking lady is just itchin' to nurse Mr. Barkley back to health."

Slim filled the bag and handed it up to the outlaw. "Anything else I kin help ya with?" He winked slyly, certain he saw the outline of a smile beneath the outlaw's bandana.

"Well, Hargrove, you done me real good this time. Guess you was thinkin' your hired man would protect you, didn't you? From the weight of this here bag, you must have struck it rich at the mines."

"Why you... you..." Hargrove sputtered, the blood surfacing to his bloated face. "That's the payroll for my ranch hands. They won't stand for this again, I tell you. They'll be comin' to getcha this time."

"They ain't had no luck so far. You managed to pay them before, so I guess you can do it again. A man with as much money as you got must have more stashed away. After all, you own everythin' in the whole town

... includin' this lovely lady. I just betcha she wouldn't mind workin' overtime to help you out."

At that remark, Hargrove's white shirt strained against his belly, threatening to spill fancy pearl buttons over the desert floor.

The outlaw looped the cord of his money bag around the saddle horn. Pulling a folded sheet of paper out of his shirt pocket, he tossed it to the ground in front of Hargrove.

"Sorry I can't stay around long enough for you to read it." With that, he pressed his heels into the flanks of his horse and quickly disappeared into the boulder-strewn mountainside.

Ashe Barkley bent down and retrieved the note. Hargrove had never allowed anyone to read the previous notes, but everyone at the ranch knew they must be dandies. The notes riled Hargrove so much that his ranch hands received the brunt of his fury for several days afterwards. Over Hargrove's protests, he read it aloud:

Read what I say, and be believin' it
What money's on board, I be receivin' it.
A constant burr in your britches I'll be
Until you hang me from the highest tree.
There's an old proverb I wish I'd said:
Money, like manure, ain't no good till it's spread.

"Shee ... it!" Slim said, doubling over in a fit of laughter.

"That's what the man said," Ashe supplied.

"Damnation, man!" Hargrove shouted, his big belly

puffed up like a feather pillow. "It ain't funny. It's downright insultin'."

Hargrove looked at all of them as an unrestrained guffaw of laughter broke among them. His face was livid with rage, and the veins in his neck bulged almost to the bursting point. Lifting his booted foot, he brought it down heavily on Slim's foot. Slim's laughter slid into a scream; and he hopped around on his good foot while he nursed the other. "Why'd ya go an' do that for, boss?"

"Nobody laughs at me, and you'd better remember it," Hargrove said in a harsh, raspy voice.

Ashe stuffed the note into Hargrove's pocket, saying, "Keep it with your other memoirs. Who knows, they may become classics someday."

Huffing and puffing, Hargrove stomped into the coach, the woman and Ashe following.

Slim climbed with difficulty on the bench beside Pete, and they snickered to themselves.

The stagecoach continued to Prospect City, rumbling and groaning almost as much as Hargrove. So much so that Ashe tilted his hat low over his eyes, feigning sleep. After a while, Hargrove began cursing the Poet Bandit in silence.

Each time the wheels hit a rut, Ashe winced at the pain in his arm. Damn that young scoundrel, he thought almost admiringly. Someone had taught him to shoot well. Although he hated to admit it, Ashe could have lost more than the temporary use of his arm. When he'd shot at the outlaw, his intention had not been to kill, only to maim because Hargrove wanted the bandit alive to suffer for all the previous insults he'd delivered.

Not only did the outlaw have a way with a gun, he also had an uncanny way with words. Ashe laughed to himself, wishing Hargrove would let him read the other notes stored in his safe. How long had it been since he had laughed like that?

That the outlaw possessed common sense was proven by the way he made his victims face the sun so they'd have less of a chance to identify him. Eyes too often gave away the identity of a person. Eyes also gave an enemy the advantage if they appeared uncertain or frightened.

Ashe sensed compassion in the outlaw, an uncommon emotion for one of his occupation. How many men would shoot a man, then turn around and ask how badly hurt he was? Would he have been so gracious had he known Ashe was out to get him and have a rope hung around his neck? Ashe grimaced at the thought. Somehow this man seemed different. He appeared to be a man you'd like to get to know instead of killing.

Rubbing his arm, Ashe knew it would be a while before he could aim a gun, let alone shoot someone with it.

The stagecoach came to a standstill in front of the hotel. News of the holdup spread rapidly, with Slim and Pete shouting to the people who lined the street and boardwalk. No one seemed surprised at what had become a routine event in Prospect City. More astounding would have been the news that the Poet Bandit had let a payroll go by, giving Hargrove just one moment of relief. But he had never failed to take it, so the townspeople just shrugged their shoulders and carefully concealed their amusement.

A musty scent wafted through the interior of the tunnel as the outlaw rode his horse through the narrow passageway to the light beyond. Once outside again, he dismounted, leading his horse down the rocky embankment to the valley below. Enclosed by tall canyon walls, the haven offered complete privacy from the outside world. A crystal-clear lake, supplied by a small waterfall that ran off the mountainside, lay within a field of short grama grass. An abundance of daisies hugged the water's edge, somewhat out of place in an otherwise arid landscape.

While the horse lapped at the cool water, the outlaw scrubbed at the white blaze on the horse's forehead until it disappeared.

The wide-brimmed hat was hastily removed, scattering hairpins into the grass. Hallie Parker removed the remaining pins and vigorously shook her head. A wealth of auburn hair flowed down her back, the bright sunlight touching it softly like a halo around her small cameo face.

Licorice, her black stallion, snorted and shook his enormous head, then nudged her playfully in the ribs.

Stroking the velvety softness of his nose, she smiled. "I believe, my friend, you enjoy these little escapades as much as I do. But I never expected to run into Vern Hargrove. It did my heart good watching him wiggle nervously beneath my gun." Her blue eyes flashed with excitement.

Kneeling down at the lake's edge, she cupped her hands and took a long drink of water, then filled them again and splashed her face to rid it of the dust and grime.

"Who is this Ashe Barkley?" she wondered out loud. It was a bad habit, but Hallie had to admit she found great pleasure in talking to herself.

She had seen many rough men in her lifetime. The small mining town of Prospect City was similar to other towns in the Arizona Territory. The majority of the men were prospectors, gamblers, cattle rustlers, and just plain drifters. Then there were the gunslingers who measured their worth by the notches in their guns. How many notches did Ashe Barkley have in his? But no, Barkley was only the foreman on Hargrove's ranch, not the hired protector of Hargrove's interests. It was quite by accident that he happened to be on that stagecoach. Or was it?

Sitting down, Hallie removed her boots and slid her feet into the cool water. She could almost smell the waterfall, and imagined how refreshing it would feel to stand beneath it.

Plucking a daisy, she rolled the stem between her fingers. She thought of another time when Hargrove had hired killers to do his dirty work, but she had never been able to prove it. But why bring another man in to get rid of the Poet Bandit when the town had willing men if the price was right.

Ashe Barkley. She had seen malevolence in his gray eyes as he stepped down from the coach. His voice was low and menacing, and what he didn't say had more effect on Hallie's nerves than the few words he had spoken. The silent, blazing anger in him spoke volumes. There was an air of authority in the way he stood towering above the others. He seemed to be a man who was the master of his environment.

Hallie gazed hypnotically at her reflection as it rippled across the glasslike surface of the water. Had ten years of living in a lawless environment affected her outwardly? She had tried to carry her scars within her, but the powerful thoughts of revenge she harbored assuredly must have marred the gentle planes of her face. But there were no deep lines etched there from constant worrying, only small lines at the corners of her blue eyes caused by years spent in the sun. Her sun-browned cheek was soft to the touch, not the leathery texture of most pioneer women.

She peered intently at her eyes mirrored in the water. They were unlike those of the woman on the stagecoach whose lids were lined thickly with a black kohl pencil and lashes brushed over repeatedly with black cream. Hallie's lashes were dark brown, tipped with golden highlights, framing pale blue eyes. A spattering of freckles across her upturned nose might have been partly hidden if she had access to the thick makeup the "lady of the evening" used. But artifice seemed so senseless in this wild, untamed country where a man needed only to see a woman to desire her.

She recalled Ashe Barkley's bold perusal of the whore who had flaunted herself so freely. Was this the type of woman a man like Ashe Barkley desired?

"Oh, pooh!" she berated herself. "Why should I care what kind of woman turns Barkley's cold blood to boiling?"

Wiping these unsettling thoughts from her mind, Hallie removed her clothing, allowing the lake to lure her to its depths. She waded to the shallow end and stood beneath the gentle spray of the waterfall. As she felt the water pepper against her breasts, she remembered how Ashe Barkley looked in admiration at the whore's large breasts, and for a brief second regretted her lack in that respect. It doesn't matter, she thought, thrusting her head beneath the spray of water, I don't want to draw attention anyway.

She relaxed and enjoyed a leisurely swim, wondering how much longer she would be able to keep her escapades a secret from her grandfather. As long as he spent his time at the mine, she could come and go without his questioning her whereabouts. Every day, all day, he slaved away at that worthless silver mine, seeking the mother-lode vein he was so certain existed. He had even been considering moving to the rundown shack at the mine, since it took so much of his time just getting there.

"Damn Ben Langley and his generous leftovers," Hallie swore out loud. Not only did he leave them a dried-up silver mine, but also a foulmouthed, overly talkative parrot named Sinbad. Maybe she shouldn't complain so. At least it gave Grandpa something to do, since Hargrove cheated him out of his own silver mine.

Ben and Hallie's grandfather had been friends for years. The story Ben told was that he got gold fever and, like so many other ship captains, left his ship anchored in San Francisco harbor while he struck out for the gold fields. When his search for gold proved futile, he heard rumors of silver in the Arizona territory, so he and Sinbad had drifted that way.

Meanwhile, Grady, Hallie's grandfather, had a lucky strike and built the ranch house, after which he invited Ben, his prospecting crony, to move in with him. Ben's mine had never paid off, but he kept on working it, thinking that someday he would be as fortunate as Grady.

When Hallie came to live with her grandfather, she took an immediate liking to the rough but gentle prospector.

"Ben, Ben, where are you now?" Hallie wondered. "Do you know what awaits you when or if you should return?"

The events that followed Ben's hasty departure had left her and her grandfather frightened for his safety.

Sarah Hargrove's body had been found at the entrance of Ben's mining shaft. With Ben up and leaving as he did, plus the damaging testimony of a prospector who claimed he heard Ben and a woman quarrelling that same evening at the mine, there was no doubt in anyone's mind that Ben Langley could have murdered Sarah Hargrove. That is, everyone but Hallie and Grady Parker. The townspeople assumed Sarah and Ben were having an affair and had had a lover's quarrel. Vern Hargrove had planted this seed of doubt and nurtured it until the people of Prospect City were certain that Ben Langley was a murderer.

What was still strange to Hallie was the disappearance of the unknown prospector who Hargrove said had overheard the argument. She was sure Hargrove had a hand in it, but to this day she couldn't figure out why.

Preoccupied with these thoughts, Hallie waded to the bank and sat on a large gray boulder to dry herself off in the sun.

Raking her fingers through her tangled hair, she wondered what other surprises awaited her before the end of the day.

After several minutes, her hair still damp, Hallie rose and retrieved her clothing from her saddlebag. Dressing in an outdated riding habit that had belonged to her mother, she ran her hand over the faded, threadbare jacket, remembering how lovely her mother had looked in this same attire. A warmth enveloped her that was not due to the warm, gentle breeze that played about her face and windblown hair.

"No matter what you may see, Mama, I'm a lady. Like you, I've had to wear disguises to survive," she whispered almost reverently, as though her mother were here in the quiet tomb of the canyon. "And I will survive. No one will ever take again what belongs to me or my family... and Vern Hargrove is no exception."

With that ultimatum, Hallie tossed her head regally and smiled through misty blue eyes that had long ago shed their quota of tears.

Chapter 1

Arizona Territory—1865

Hallie Parker, assisted by her father, James, stepped down from the stagecoach. Every muscle in her body ached from the cramped position she had maintained in the overcrowded coach. She breathed deeply, grateful to be where the air was free of the mingling scent of stale tobacco and unbathed bodies.

They had been traveling for months. Now they were near the end of their grueling journey. Her grandfather was expecting their arrival in Prospect City. At least, she hoped he had received the letter they had written months ago, telling him of their recent hardships and why they needed his help.

Hallie gazed up and down the dusty main street of Tucson at the low adobe structures with the fancy store fronts that lined the plank boardwalks. In front of her was a two-story building with a sign above it identifying it as the hotel she and her father would no doubt be lodging in that night. Several people milled around the hotel who were dark-skinned and black-haired, wearing large sombreros and colorful wraps. The pleasant smell of strong mixed spices drifted out the door of a small cafe nearby.

After their few belongings were assembled, Hallie and her father went into the hotel to arrange accommodations for the night. In their rather shabby room, Hallie fell across the bed, eager to feel the soft mattress beneath her. She was so exhausted she knew she would have no difficulty in falling asleep. A festive-sounding Spanish melody drifted in on a warm breeze through the open window.

"Nap if you like, sweetheart, while I try to find a horse and wagon and some provisions. We've still got a way to go before we reach Prospect City, and you'll need all the rest you can get. We'll get a bite to eat when I come back."

"Thanks, Daddy, I will." Plumping up her pillow, she remembered vaguely the conversation her father recently had with one of the passengers on the coach. If clothes were the mark of a gentleman, then this gentleman would surely pass the test. Not a scratch marred his shiny brown boots. His clothing was tailor-made, and there was not a flaw or speck of dust on his hat. She noticed the gold rings he flashed before the other passengers as he talked, entirely monopolizing the conversation. He was an extremely large man who, if he had been a gentleman, would have waited for the next stagecoach. Instead, he placed his bulky frame on the seat that was already occupied by her father, another man, and her. He was probably a Yankee, too, she had decided scornfully.

"Who was that rude man sitting next to you on the coach?" she asked her father as he was about to leave.

"Said his name was Vern Hargrove. Regretfully, he lives in Prospect City, so we'll probably run into him occasionally. He didn't mind bragging about owning half the town, either. When I mentioned I was Grady Parker's son, he had the strangest expression on his face." He was about to continue, but Hallie was sleeping peacefully.

Poor child, he thought, nodding his head dismally. It just didn't seem right bringing a thirteen-year-old youngster into such a desolate and untamed land. But what other choices did he have? His child already had lived beyond her young years, and he wondered if she would ever be able to forget the terrifying experiences she had suffered during the Yankee occupation in Atlanta. She still couldn't bear to be in a Yankee's presence—he could see it on her face as they traveled farther and farther west.

As he locked the door to their room behind him, he hoped her dreams were undisturbed by harsh remembrances.

"How long will it take us to get to Prospect City in this wagon?" Hallie asked just outside of Tucson.

"The hotel clerk said at least two days at the pace we'll have to go. It's a shame the stagecoach doesn't go in this direction."

Recalling her recent ordeal traveling on a coach, Hallie reassured her father quickly, "I'm just as glad it doesn't. I'd rather spend an extra day traveling like this than put up with that crowding again. I'll finally have a chance to look at the scenery, which I barely glimpsed on the way to Tucson."

Taking a roughly sketched map out of his pocket, James showed it to Hallie. "We've got several mountains and rivers to cross before we get to Prospect City. You may change your mind later."

James pulled the wagon to a halt and reached under the bench seat to retrieve a small package. Handing it to her, he said, "Open it. It's for you."

She ripped off the paper to reveal a small derringer, and she looked questioningly at him.

"It's for your protection, Hallie."

"But I don't know how to shoot a gun. And furthermore, what would I shoot?"

A worried look crossed his face. "We're in Indian country. You never know what might happen."

"But the man we ate with last night said that most of the Apache attacks were north of us now. They didn't harm us coming from Yuma."

James hoped his smile was more confident than he felt. He gripped her small hand in his. "I know, but for safety's sake, let me show you how to load it."

She watched in alarm as he slipped the bullet into the small cylinder. "Now, put it back under the seat where your hand can reach it in a hurry if need be."

As the wagon slowly continued on its way Hallie found herself eyeing the many grotesque giant cacti, terrified that behind each one lurked a savage. She canvassed the sandstone buttes rising from the dun-colored desert, expecting to see a wisp of smoke curling from their crests. Hadn't she read in her books that Indians sent messages that way?

The sun began its slow descent behind the mountains, splashing an unusual palette of lavender and pink across the silent horizon. A narrow dark ribbon of water broke through the desert, more like a stream than the river indicated on the map. Her father halted the wagon at its edge.

"We'll camp here for the night and pull out bright and early in the morning."

"Shall I gather some brush for a fire?" Hallie asked, leaping down to the ground.

"No fire, Hallie," he warned. "We'll have to make do without cooking. I brought plenty of beef jerky to hold us over."

That night, they slept beneath the star-bejeweled sky. An owl screeched into the dark silence, scaring Hallie. She pulled the blanket tighter around her small body.

In the morning, she saw by the circles beneath her father's eyes that he too had difficulty sleeping. After a quick bite to eat, her father reharnessed the mule and they once again set out on another long day of travel.

The stream, low from the lack of rains, presented no problem as the mule and wagon forded its rocky bed. As the day progressed without any sign of Indians, or anyone else, Hallie relaxed and climbed into the back of the wagon for a short afternoon nap.

The sudden change in the pace of the wagon shook Hallie awake. Sitting up quickly, she asked, "Why are you going so fast? Are we almost there?"

"Get back down, Hallie," James ordered.

Without another word, she slid down.

"We've got company," he said over his shoulder. "Or at least, we will be having company. They're about a half-mile ahead of us."

"Are they Indians?" Hallie asked, fear clutching her insides.

"Don't know. . . . Can't see them plainly enough. I'm pulling the wagon into the canyon. When we get out of their sight, I want you to get out and hide among the rocks on the mountainside." He held the gun toward her. "Take this, and use it if you have to. They haven't seen you yet, so they won't be looking for you."

Hallie took the gun with shaking hands. "What about you, Daddy?"

"I have the rifle."

"No, I don't mean that. How can you stand against them alone? You must let me stay and help."

James admired his young daughter for her courage, but he knew if their attackers were a band of Indians, neither of them stood a chance of surviving. "Maybe they're not Indians, just prospectors on their way to Tucson. Just do as I say. No matter who they are, Hallie, don't come out of hiding until I call you."

The wagon wheels lurched over the rough embedded stones into the narrow canyon.

"Hop out, Hallie!"

With tears in her eyes, Hallie leaned over and kissed her father. "Daddy, I love you."

"I love you, too." With a premonition of dread, he added, "If something should happen to me, sweetheart,

I think you're capable of finding your way to your grandfather's. You have the map and you know the direction. Just be careful."

"I'll see you later." That seemed more appropriate than good-bye. Good-byes could be forever.

With pistol in hand, Hallie leaped to the ground and scrambled up the boulder-strewn mountainside. She paused momentarily to watch her father stop below her and check his rifle. Hearing the sound of horses' hooves, Hallie immediately dropped down behind a rock, her heart hammering wildly in her chest. As the riders approached the wagon, she peeked out at them. A gush of relief took her breath away.

It was a party of three men, and they were definitely not Indians—unless Indians had exchanged their buckskins for trousers and felt hats which hid their faces. Hallie knew her father was feeling the same relief as she. The sound of their voices echoed off the canyon walls, and Hallie's finely tuned ears picked up every word of their conversation.

"Thank God," she heard her father say. "I thought you were Indians."

"Where ya headed fer, mister?"

"Prospect City. How much farther away is it?"

She heard a different voice say, "In that contraption, at least another five or six hours. We jest came from there."

Another man asked in a gruff voice, "You from these parts?"

"No," James said, "from Georgia. Came out to join my dad since the war and Yankees took everything I owned. You may know him... Grady Parker?"

There was a long moment of silence. Then: "Yeah, we heerd tell of him," a man said, laughing slyly.

Maybe they'll travel with us, Hallie thought with hope welling inside her.

"You traveling alone?" one of the men asked, glancing at the back of the wagon.

"Yes," was her father's reply.

Evidently, Hallie surmised, he still wasn't sure of the men's intentions.

"An awful lot of stuff for only one person."

She saw one of the men guide his horse around the wagon.

"Not really, when you've come as far as I have."

"Drop yore gun," the man said unexpectedly. "Where yore goin' ya won't be needin' it, mister."

Her father held on tightly to his rifle. The man who had done most of the talking motioned to the other two men. With three guns aimed at him, James had no alternative but to obey their command. He reluctantly tossed the rifle to the ground.

"I don't have anything of value, but take it all and then leave me be," he said angrily.

"I believe ya do have somethin' of value," the cruel man answered. "Yore daughter. Now, whar is she?"

Hallie stiffened. They couldn't know about her.

"I don't have a daughter. Like I said, I'm alone!"

"Check it out, Lem."

One of the men dismounted, then climbed into the back of the wagon. Unlatching one of the trunks, he swung back the lid and laughed loudly. Holding up a frilly lace petticoat, he asked, "Take a fancy to wearin' these, mister?"

"They belonged to my deceased wife," James said smoothly.

Pressing the barrel of his rifle into her father's stomach, the stranger said, "I don't believe ya."

The blast of the gun echoed through the canyon as Hallie witnessed the ghastly scene of her father bending over, his hands pushed into his stomach, falling headlong to the ground.

No, dear God, no... not again, Hallie screamed inwardly. Not my father too! Clutching the small derringer in both of her trembling hands, she tried to still them long enough to shoot at the men below. There was no way she could kill all three with only one bullet. Now she understood why her father had given her the gun. The sole bullet was meant for her, in case the Apache should come upon them. Oh Daddy, she cried painfully, I may not have been able to kill all three of those murderers, but I could have tried.

Their next words terrified her.

"You two scan both sides of the canyon for the girl while I go through his provisions to see if he may have more than he said."

Hallie frantically looked around for another hiding place. Several feet up the hill, a small opening sliced through the mountainside. Maybe, just maybe, she was small enough to get inside. Crawling like a snake on her belly, she felt the sharp rocks cut into her knees and elbows. But the pain was secondary to the fear of being slain like her father.

Reaching the opening, she turned onto her side, forcing her body sideways through the narrow slot. The length of her back and front raked the jagged rocks, bringing tears of pain to her eyes. She soon reached a wider path and was surprised to find a larger space, enough to take the pressure off her tortured body. Sitting against the cool, rocky wall, she pulled her knees to her chest, biting down on her knees to suppress the grief that tore through her. She heard footsteps outside the cavern and held her breath.

"Ain't no signs of her bein' around here nowhere," a man hollered. "Maybe the boss wuz worryin' about nothin'. He jest may have figured it wrong that the little gal was the man's daughter." Then, after a brief silence, he added, "Don't matter none, 'cause a rattlesnake or gila monster'll get her fer shore."

Hallie peered through the darkness. The thought of rattlesnakes had never entered her mind. And what in blue blazes was a gila monster? Nothing could be worse than what awaited her outside.

He probably just said all that to scare me out of my hiding place, she decided resolutely. Trying hard to put the terrifying words out of her mind, she caught herself listening for quiet sounds in the oncoming darkness. She was so scared that she could hear her heart thumping in her ears.

She remained in the cavern for what seemed like hours, watching the small shaft of light fade as evening approached. She turned the small gun over and over in her hand, wishing she could have helped her father. Once again, as with her mother, she could not identify the murderer. But this time a name lodged like a thorn in her memory... Lem.

Finally she decided that enough time had passed for her to safely leave her hiding place. She began the grueling task of inching her way through the vise-like passageway, leaving fragments of her torn and bloody flesh on the walls of the cave.

She crouched behind a boulder until daybreak. Her eyes searched the mountains and wagon trail. The only sound was the soft whir of a zephyr trapped within the canyon walls. Her eyes veered to the body of her father as she made a cautious descent down the mountainside.

His long, lean body lay chest down, his cheek against the dry earth. Kneeling beside him, she smoothed the chestnut hair from his forehead, utterly shaken by the loss of life's lustrous glow in his pale blue eyes.

After a long while, she dragged his lifeless body beneath the wagon, and found a blanket to cover him. It was then she realized her own dire situation. The men had taken no chances with the possibility of her surviving. They had removed all the food and water, leaving only the trunks containing clothing. She found her father's threadbare gray Confederate coat and covered the upper portion of his body.

It's ironic, she thought, that he should survive a war and lose his life because of three heartless murderers.

The mule!...

Her sudden thought was crushed as quickly as it was formed. They had taken that away also. She was trapped in a desert, dry except for that small stream they had camped at the night before. There was no chance for survival unless she either backtracked or chanced finding water in the general direction of Prospect City. Or someone found her before it was too late.

As night again pulled its darkness over the desert, Hallie sat propped against the wheel of the wagon, huddled in a woolen shawl that had belonged to her mother. She pulled it tightly around her small shoulders to ward off the cool breeze. A coyote howled mournfully at the bright yellow moon, making her aware she was not alone. Other night sounds coalesced, bringing with them the overwhelming horrors that can dwell in a child's mind. Even the cold metal of the gun that she clutched in her hand offered no sense of protection. If she slept at all that night, she didn't remember it. Early the next morning, she was awake to watch the sun's orange glow finger a mellow path across the gray-shrouded sky.

She murmured a short prayer, then said a silent, grief-stricken farewell to her father. Since she had no implements with which to bury him, she hoped someone would find his body before the desert swallowed him.

An eternity of blue sky and open space stretched out before her. An endless stretch of parched earth and towering red buttes brought foreboding thoughts to her young mind. The grotesque cacti, with their prickly thick arms reaching heavenward, seemed to mock her, daring her to venture among them.

The hours passed at a snail's pace as Hallie continued her trek across the desert beneath an unsympathetic sun. She licked at her dry, cracked lips, tasting the salty drops of perspiration.

The sunbonnet did little to protect her face from the fierce sun, and a blister soon formed on her nose. She had long ago removed the shawl, and found herself wishing for the night to hurry and relieve her with its cool breezes.

Her goal in the beginning of her journey had been a purplish-gray mountain in the near distance. It seemed so reachable at first, yet it seemed to retreat with each step.

She had to rest, if only for a minute. Sitting beside a cactus that did nothing to shade her, she removed her dusty boots. Dirt had found its way into the shoes and rubbed against her feet, forming bleeding blisters.

Water... if only she could find water. She could survive without food for a while. She had managed during the war when the Yankees stripped their cupboards bare. But their well had never run dry. When did she last have a drink? It was yesterday before she lay down for a nap... more than a day ago.

Maybe a short nap would help her to forget the dryness in her mouth and throat. Yes, then she would be somewhat refreshed to continue her journey. Lying down, she felt the warmth of the earth penetrate through her clothing, surprisingly soothing as it touched her battered and aching flesh.

She slept the sleep of a dying person, unaware of the coming of night or of the beginning of a new day. She drifted in and out of consciousness, but her mind rebelled against her better senses and swept her further into oblivion.

A tall, lithe warrior gazed down at the small figure lying on her side. He watched the slow rise and fall of her chest. If he left her here, she would be dead by nightfall. But what did it matter? She was a white child. He saw the tattered clothing, the deep gashes on her arms and legs, and the large blisters on her feet. In her hand, she held a small gun, her only possession except for a woolen shawl.

Raising his eyes to the cloudless blue sky, he saw the vultures soaring above him. They would not wait for her to die. As soon as he departed, they would sweep down upon her, and devour her alive. If she were a man, his decision would be simple: he would leave her for them to feast upon. He thought of his young sister, Doe Eyes, who was now afflicted by an unknown disease the white man had brought to his tribe. The medicine man could not cure her, and her death seemed imminent. The young white girl and his sister appeared to be near the same age. Would he wish such a cruel ending for Doe Eyes?

His decision made, the warrior swung his long leg over the back of the mustang and leaped to the ground. He kneeled beside the girl, removing the gun from her hand. Rolling her over, he stared intently at her sleeping face. She would be beautiful if it were not for the wounds covered with dried blood and the blisters on her nose. A reddish-gold curl fell across her sunburned cheek.

She needed water—and soon, if she were to live. Picking her up, he placed her across the blanket on his horse. Mounting behind her, he positioned her against his bare chest.

As he rode to the nearest water hole, he wondered if she were perhaps a survivor of an Apache attack. But few whites were spared by the Apache. They were either killed on the spot, or taken to their camp to be tortured.

How would his kinsmen react when he brought her

SAVAGE SURRENDER

into their tribe? Would they brand her as a slave and use her in sport? She had weathered the sun-dried desert, but would she be strong enough to survive the ultimate test, acceptance by his people? Her ability to survive alone was to be admired.

He led his horse to a small oasis secluded by a growth of mesquite and cacti. Dismounting, he gently lowered his captive to the ground beside the water. Placing her head in his lap, he leaned over and cupped his hands into the water, then brought it to her lips. The water dribbled over her lips and trailed down her chin.

Unconscious, but aware of the sensation of cool water, Hallie opened her mouth, running her tongue over her lips. Another trickle of water entered the parched recesses of her mouth, causing her to cough and sputter.

Water was the only thought that prevailed in the lethargic depths of her mind. She frantically reached out for the offered receptacle, grasping it firmly in her small hands; she gulped the life-giving liquid.

"No," a voice commanded, "too much make little one sick."

Hallie's mind was a maze of confusion. Who had the right to deny her this pleasure? She attempted to cry out rebelliously, but her words were cracked and unintelligible to her own ears. Forcing her eyes to open, she squinted into the sun, whose strong rays pierced her eyes like a thousand knives.

Turning her into his bare chest, the Indian removed the bonnet and stroked the dampened strands of her hair. "Rest, little one, then Sundog will give you more water."

She heard a voice rumble against her cheek as he spoke, and felt a knobby obstacle pressing into her temple. Moving her head from the intrusion, she opened her eyes and saw a strand of blue-chipped beads resting against a hairless, sun-browned chest.

Her eyes traveled upward and gazed into charcoal eyes staring back at her intently. His straight black hair was secured by an orange-and-brown woven headband. It took a few moments for his identity to register fully in Hallie's mind, and when it did, she fervently prayed to be carried back to welcome oblivion. Her whole body tensed in his arms and a small scream escaped her throat.

Sundog frowned, then offered her another drink of water. This time she stared in fright at him, her lips barely parting for the water he offered.

"Drink," he said softly. "Sundog means you no harm."

As Hallie lowered her lips into his callused hands, thoughts swept rapidly through her mind. He spoke English—did that mean he was friendly? Why had he given her water if he meant to hurt her? Maybe he was saving her now in order to torture her later.

The Indian dipped her sunbonnet into the water and began wiping her face with such tenderness that she stared at him in awe.

Sundog paused, and smiled at her puzzled blue eyes. Yes, she will be beautiful, he concluded, for she has eyes the color of a summer sky. Her face was small, but touched with softly defined features, high cheekbones and a short, upturned nose.

"Who are you?" Hallie asked suspiciously.

"I am Sundog, son of Chief Black Wing of the Apache."

Apache, Hallie thought with dread. Her worst premonition had been realized. She managed to ask, "Will you take me to my grandfather?" She hoped his prior kindness was a good sign that he would help her.

Sundog's face remained impassive. "You need to build your strength. You will come with me to my camp."

"And then will you take me...later?"

"No, little one, you now belong to the Apache."

Hallie's eyes blazed with the anger she was feeling. "I will never belong to the Indians, no matter how long you try to keep me." She tried to escape his grip, but she had no strength left for fighting. "You will regret the day you ever found me, for I will escape, I promise you. Even if I die doing it!"

Sundog admired determination and spirit in one so young. She would make a good wife for him one day— once he had tamed her and taught her the Indian ways. She would bear strong sons who would become brave warriors and leaders in his tribe.

"You are young and speak foolish words."

Rising, he leaned over to pick her up. She slapped him soundly across his face. Sundog's hand immediately flew to his cheek, but his features did not alter.

"Don't you dare touch me," Hallie warned, pulling herself to a sitting position. "I can walk by myself with no help from you...you savage!"

"Very well," Sundog said, walking to his horse. In one swift movement he mounted the horse. "Then walk."

Hallie's eyes darted left and right, seeking a place to run and hide. There was no place to go. In every direction, all she could see was sprawling desert. Sundog watched her, smiling to himself, and nudged his horse forward.

Looking back occasionally, he saw Hallie's careful steps, knowing how painful each step was. Her wrinkled bonnet, now dried by the sun, was perched askew on her proud head. The tattered hem of her dress tripped her frequently, but she managed to stay upright.

After an hour or so, Sundog glanced back, seeing Hallie drop to her knees. Dismounting, he walked back to her, frowning and nodding his head. "Do you wish to ride with me now?"

"No," she stated adamantly. "Go away and leave me alone." As she said the words, she slid to her belly.

Sundog stooped and picked her up. This time he met no resistance. She looked up at him with half-crazed eyes. "Do what you will with me now, but don't think I'll ever bend to your ways."

It was nightfall when they finally arrived at the camp. Hallie feigned unconsciousness. Her inner thighs were raw from the stiff woolen blanket, and every bone and muscle in her body felt broken and bruised.

She heard excited voices as the Indians milled around them but could understand nothing of what was said.

She felt herself being dragged off the horse and carried into a wickiup where several old women were waiting. Laying her down on a soft pallet, Sundog said, "These women will tend to your wounds while I speak with my father." Then he tossed back the flap of the tent and departed quickly.

There was a loud commotion outside, so loud that Hallie's eyes shot open, and she raised herself up on her elbow. An old squaw ran to the opening and threw back the flap.

"What is it?" Hallie cried, fearing the Indians were preparing to torture her mercilessly.

The squaw merely pointed to the night sky, where Hallie saw the fading path of a shooting star.

Why so much excitement over a shooting star? Hallie wondered gratefully. She lay down and closed her eyes again. She barely felt the hands tending to her cuts as she drifted in and out of sleep. When she awoke the following morning, she was surprised to find herself alone in the tent which was decorated with antlers, and strange masks. An assortment of bows hung on the side of the tent, alongside other objects she was unfamiliar with.

Sundog appeared with another Indian whose face was painted with bright red-and-white slashes. Antlers winged out from the side of his head, making him appear more grotesque. Painted on his fringed buckskin shirt was an amulet of a horned figure.

He gazed down at her. Any expression on his face was hidden beneath the layers of paint. He spoke to Sundog quietly using gestures and a language she did not understand.

"You are now called Bright Star Falling," Sundog told Hallie.

Hallie, who had not told him her name, said in

surprise, "My real name is Hallie Estelle Parker. Estelle means *star* in French."

Sundog said something to the strange-looking Indian. He replied in a quiet tone, then left the two of them alone.

Sundog sat down beside her. "Because of you, my sister, Doe Eyes, lives."

Hallie drew herself to a sitting position. "Because of me? What on earth did I do?"

"The medicine man said your entering into our camp at the time of the shooting star is an omen. The white man brought the disease to Doe Eyes. Her fever broke as the star shot across the heavens, taking her illness with it. You say your name means star. You were sent to us to save our princess."

Hallie's mouth dropped open. For several seconds she couldn't speak. "It's only a coincidence that this happened when it did. I'm glad your sister is alive, but it wasn't because of me."

Sundog brushed a stray curl from her cheek. "Because of the omen, you will be treated with respect. You are fortunate not to be marked and tortured as a slave."

Rising to his feet, he paused at the entrance of the tent. "Now you must eat to build your strength... Bright Star Falling."

As the days passed, Hallie regained her strength. The fierce sun had left her skin a golden brown, and put burnished streaks in the auburn mass. Her wounds healed, leaving only faint scars that would fade in time. It was the scars inside that would give her no peace.

The vision of her father being shot down in cold blood tortured her; her helplessness plagued her. She vowed to see his murderers punished someday.

Sundog gave no sign that Hallie would be released. She worried about her future and constantly planned her escape. The fortunate omen gained her time. Though she was not forced to labor with the squaws, she needed to learn their knowledge of how to survive in the desert.

She began to learn their language, and helped with the tending of the maize, or corn, which was used in one way or another at every meal. The cornshucks were used in making dolls for the children, and the young boys used the stalks as spears in their war games.

She learned to cook buffalo meat. It was boiled or roasted, or left to dry in the sun and then pounded with a stone. This was called pemmican.

The Indians wasted nothing. The hides of the buffalo had a variety of uses, from clothing to wickiups. The horns were used to make dishes, to make spoons, or to carry hot coals. The hair of the buffalo was used for wearing and making rope. Hallie was astounded by their ingenuity.

The Indians used various plants as medicines, and Hallie learned the purpose of each one. When she discovered that cacti held an unlimited supply of water and some that bore fruit, she berated herself for her ignorance and resolved to learn still more. All these things she stored in her mind for future use.

Sundog was pleased with Hallie's thirst for knowledge, but he was no fool. Knowing she planned to escape one day only increased his admiration of the young girl.

He watched a friendship blossom between Doe Eyes and Hallie, his sister's knowledge of English made them natural companions. Sundog hoped that this closeness would lessen Hallie's desire to try to leave him. Hallie eagerly demanded to learn how to shoot a bow and arrow and how to use a knife skillfully. Again Sundog understood her intentions. But, thinking that no amount of training in that respect would aid her in escaping them, he saw no harm in teaching her. He found she had quick reflexes and keen eyes, more so than some of the young boys who were training to be warriors. After observing how well she performed, he decided that—when she reached marriageable age—she would become his wife. Sundog was next in line to be chief of his tribe. By that time, he believed, Hallie would have resigned herself to the way of the Indians and would be proud of her new heritage.

Hallie was not treated as a captive, but she knew she was watched. Never was she allowed to roam unattended, which made any attempt of escaping futile. Her captivity remained a secret within the tribe. Anytime a white man was admitted into their camp, she was whisked away and hidden.

Hallie sensed that all was not well. Sundog was worried about something. He spent hours in council with the medicine man. One particular day when Sundog had been with the medicine man longer than usual, Hallie worked her way around until she was just beyond the flaps of the wickiup. She heard Sundog's angry voice. Easing closer, she listened, concentrating hard to follow the medicine man's calm words. "Sundog, I know what is in your heart for the white eyes. But it can only bring dishonor to the Apache. Have you never wondered about her abilities to master the skills of the warriors? Her spirit is drawing the strength from the tribe."

"No," Sundog replied, his tone void of emotion.

"It is true," the medicine man continued. "I do not speak falsely. I had a vision. In it our tribe was herded into pens. Our warriors were bound like oxen, turning the earth, planting the white man's crops. The children cried because their bellies were empty. Our women were used by the white man to satisfy their lusts." He paused to let the words sink in. "You are destined to be the next chief. Would you, could you bear to lead our people into such disgrace?"

Silence.

Hallie couldn't hear Sundog's reply. The medicine man spoke again. "You have made a wise choice. The stars have deemed her powerful. We do not want this power turned on our tribe."

A feeling of sadness washed over Hallie as she comprehended Sundog's decision. A moment later happiness superceded the sadness: she would be released.

There was a council meeting composed of the elders of the tribe, and they listened to the advice of the medicine man. This was followed by a tribal dance, unlike any Hallie had seen during her stay, which went on for a day and night. The Indians, dressed in bright-colored ceremonial attire, placed Hallie in the center of a large ring made of brush. They danced around her, singing and shaking rattles to the beat of a drum. The medicine man took a flaming torch, and as he danced around the circle, he lit the brush. Hallie was surrounded by a ring of fire as the medicine man sang a chant that only the Indians understood.

By the following morning, Hallie had collapsed to the ground with fatigue. Sundog carried her to the tent and laid her down on the pallet.

She gazed sleepily into dark eyes tinged with sadness. In a melancholy voice, he said, "Sleep, Star. Later you go back to your people."

Hallie's heart lifted with joy, but the pain she saw in Sundog's eyes touched her deeply. "You have been good to me, Sundog, and taught me well. I'll never forget you or your kindness."

Twirling her one long braid around his hand, he said in a tense voice, "You are young... so young, yet much older than your years. I will miss you, little one, and the times we have shared. Doe Eyes is saddened also."

Tears blurred her eyes. The time she had spent with the Apache had not been an unhappy one. Living with them, she had developed a sense of survival that she was certain would help her day-to-day. And she understood a little better why they behaved as they did towards her people.

"How am I to go, Sundog? Will I go alone?"

Sundog smiled solemnly. "A man known by your grandfather has been told of your release. He comes late in the day to take you home."

Home... Hallie tossed the word back and forth in

her mind. The only home she had ever known was gone, along with the hopes and dreams of a comfortable future.

Sundog left, and Hallie slept until dusk, to be awakened by Doe Eyes who had come to prepare her for the journey. She dressed in a beautifully beaded white buckskin dress that Doe Eyes proudly told her was created by her for her true sister. Hallie was led out of the tent to meet the man who would take her home.

Ben Langley sat on the ground, legs crossed Indian style, talking with Sundog and his father, Chief Black Wing. He was startled by the sheer beauty of the young girl. Her hair, thickly braided and hanging over her small breasts, was the color of the rain-washed buttes. Her carriage was proud—shoulders thrust back, chin held high in regal bearing.

Ben rose, and walked to her. "Ben Langley, madam, at yer service," he said, sweeping off his battered hat. "If you don't mind me saying so, you look like a princess in the Injun getup."

Hallie quickly assessed the man who claimed friendship with her grandfather. He was tall and lean, perhaps forty or so, with an abundance of curly black hair streaked gray at the temples; he appeared quite distinguished in a rugged sort of way. It was difficult to determine his facial features, for he sported a full but well-kept beard. A striking pair of piercing blue eyes continued staring at her in awe.

"They have treated me like a princess as well," she said, looking at Sundog with a smile.

Sundog stepped forward, lifting her chin with a sun-browned finger. "Though you leave us, Star, you will always remain in our hearts." He then placed her derringer in her hands. "Take this with you. Someday you may need it."

Doe Eyes, leading a mustang and a large roan horse laden with provisions, walked to Hallie and lowered her head to prevent anyone from seeing the tears that misted her eyes.

"Don't cry, Doe Eyes," Hallie said, embracing her friend. "My love for you as my sister will go with me wherever I go."

Ben watched the tender scene before him. Clearing his throat awkwardly, he said, "I'm thinkin' we'd best hit the trail before it gets too dark."

Hallie broke away from Doe Eyes, and reached up to stroke Sundog's face. "Good-bye, my friend." With those brief words of farewell, she mounted the mustang bareback and glanced around at what had been her home. The familiar smell of meat roasting over several small campfires drifted to her. She watched the squaws busy preparing the meal for their warriors. She saw the hides of the buffalo hanging between the posts to dry and heard the children laughing and playing games. She felt a wave of sadness to be leaving such a simple life. It would have been so easy to stay and so fortunate that she was forced to go.

As soon as she and Ben departed, Hallie had many questions to ask him, but one question outweighed all others.

"Mister Langley, did...did you ever find my... my father?"

Ben pulled back on the reins of his horse and turned

to her. "Yes, Hallie. A couple of prospectors found him and brought his body and the trunks of clothing to Prospect City. We buried him at the ranch."

"I was so worried that no one would find him before ... before..."

"I understand, child. You don't have to go on," Ben said, reaching out and placing his hand on her own. "What's important now is you. We never thought you could have survived after we looked for days on end for you in the desert."

"It wasn't Indians who attacked us. There were three men, and they just shot Daddy in cold blood. If I hadn't hidden in a cave, they'd have killed me, too." Hallie choked back the sobs in her throat as she went on to tell him the story. "All I have is a name to go by ... Lem. And so help me, I'll put a face with it someday. They'll wish I had never gotten away."

Ben knew by the determined look on her face that she meant what she said.

As they topped the crest of a hill, Hallie fought the urge to look back at the scattered wickiups and burning campfires. It was another episode in her life, and unbeknown to her, one that would mold her into the woman she was to become.

Chapter 2

Prospect City—1875

"Hargrove Mercantile... If we ain't got it... We'll get it!"

The bold words painted across the storefront renewed the anger Hallie Parker felt each time she encountered the hated Hargrove name. Snorting with disgust and muttering beneath her breath, she jumped down ungraciously from the buckboard. Her faded calico skirt billowed out around her. She smoothed it down, glancing around quickly to see if anyone had noted her hasty descent. Masking her anger, she drew a deep breath and very slowly counted to ten.

Draping the horse's reins over the hitching post, she walked briskly down the well-worn boardwalk, her back straight as an arrow and her head held at a defiant angle. Small wire-frame glasses perched on her dainty nose, and a dowdy poke bonnet covered her hair completely and was tied with a vengeance beneath her chin. Her steps were precise, and she nodded her head briskly in greeting, not stopping lest she be deterred from her objective. She pushed open the door of the mercantile store, and a bell tinkled loudly, announcing her entrance.

The room was dusty, and most of the items on the rows and rows of shelves had been there since the first day Hallie had ever come in. Old lanterns, used picks and shovels, and other relics of the prospectors long gone, scattered the floor. Muslin bags of flour, sugar, and dried fruits, and fabric for clothing, were stacked on the shelves. How Sam Franks ever found anything when asked for it, Hallie never knew.

As if she had conjured him up, Sam slowly shuffled his way to the counter. "Good day, Miss Hallie, what kin I help ya with this mornin'?"

"I need a half-dozen writing tablets."

"Ya on yore way to the mission?"

"Yes, Mr. Franks."

Sam bent over behind the long counter and retrieved the tablets,

"How's Grady?" he asked, placing them on the counter. "Haven't seen him in town fer a time. He still minin'?"

She sighed. "As long as there's a breath left in his body, I'm sure he'll be mining. It's in his blood... or so he tells me," she added, with another forlorn sigh.

"'Spect it is, Miss Hallie," Sam Franks said, shrugging his stooped shoulders, "'spect it is." Then his lined face lit up. "How 'bout some peppermint sticks for the young'uns at the mission?"

"Sorry, not today," she replied, taking the tablets and placing the money on the counter.

"Hell, Miss Hallie." Realizing his profanity, he quickly coughed and sputtered, "'Scuse me, Miss Hallie. Old Hargrove ain't gonna miss a few peppermint sticks," he said, handing her a sizable bag of the sweet, fragrant candy.

She thanked him for the candy. "I'm sure the children will enjoy it immensely."

Warmed by Sam Franks' unexpected gift, she left the establishment in a lighter mood, anxious to finish her errands and be on her way to the mission.

To avoid the Drinkalot Saloon where several unfamiliar men loitered about, Hallie crossed the street, the dust lapping at the hem of her skirt. A smile tugged at the corner of her mouth as she spied Pascal Fritts leaning with all the grace he could muster against the doorway of the telegraph office. If he shifted positions quickly without any forethought, he was apt to get tangled in his own long, reed-thin arms and legs. One wouldn't exactly call Pascal simpleminded, because he possessed the memory of an elephant. But on the other hand, he had not one lick of common sense, and he was totally lacking in grace. Pascal was also the town gossip, and always eager to share his bounty.

So as not to surprise him with her sudden approach, Hallie called out to him, "Good morning, Pascal. How are you today?"

Sure enough, as he shifted in her direction, he turned the whole of his body, nearly tearing his beak nose from his face as it raked the door frame. Hurriedly dragging a handkerchief from his pocket, he swiped at his red nose while rearranging his legs.

"Mornin' Miss Hallie, mornin'. Mighty fine day we're havin'. Won't be long till we'll be wishin' for these pleasant days, once we feel the full force of summer."

As his monologue droned on and on, Hallie became fascinated with his Adam's apple, watching it bob repeatedly against his stiff collar, the black string tie bouncing with a life of its own as his voice gained momentum.

"Mr. Hargrove's new foreman was shot, Miss Hallie—"

"Shot? Who was shot, Pascal?" she asked as his words penetrated her musings.

Pascal, delighted at Hallie's interest, plunged into his own step-by-step account of the latest stagecoach robbery. "Since Mr. Hargrove's men ain't found a clue or even so much as a trace of the brazen bandit that's been robbin' his stage, he's gone and hired hisself a bounty hunter as his new foreman."

"Bounty hunter?" Her face turned deathly white. Had Pascal not been so engrossed in his story, he would have noticed her pallor.

"Yes, a bounty hunter, but keep it under yore hat. I be the one that sent the telegraph to Phoenix to one Ashe Barkley."

Leaning over confidingly, he lowered his voice an octave or two. "I heerd tell he's killed fourteen men. They say he's so mean that the rattlesnakes skitter out of his way, not wanting to cross paths with him. I saw him in the Drinkalot Saloon the other day... and let me tell you... he's got about the coldest damn... 'scuse me, dang coldest eyes I've ever seen, look straight through you."

Hallie's mouth opened and her eyes widened at his tale. Pascal nodded and, seeing Hallie's intense interest, he went on to say, "Strange, cold man, strange..." He whispered, shuddering slightly to increase the drama. "He don't say a lot, but I got to admit he was right pleasant." A nervous giggle burst from his thin lips. "I mean, he didn't try to shoot me or nothin', just nodded his head when I spoke. I guess a woman might think him handsome, particularly since I saw the way Sophie, the new wh—, I mean the new lady in town, hung on to him like he was gonna disappear into thin air."

Hallie remembered Sophie well. The little hussy would have bedded him in the stagecoach if she'd had the chance.

"Why," Pascal continued, "the way Doc tole it, old man Hargrove had him take a look at Barkley's shoulder when the stage finally come into town. Doc probed and poked around while he was cleanin' that wound, and the whole time Barkley never uttered a sound. After Doc got him bandaged up, Barkley got up pretty as you please, pulled on his torn, bloodstained shirt, tossed Doc a ten-dollar gold piece, and left Hargrove standin' there without so much as a by-your-leave. Hargrove, as usual puffed up by his own importance, was disgusted at Barkley's display. He was swearin' viciously when he stomped out after Barkley."

When Pascal finally took the time to draw a deep

breath, Hallie quickly excused herself. Pascal's high-pitched voice stopped her.

"By the way, Miss Hallie, Barkley was askin' about good horseflesh. I tole him to go out to yore place. Tole him you and yore grandpa had some of the best horseflesh in these parts."

Hallie expertly guided the buckboard through the dusty streets, avoiding the numerous ruts with ease. The town buzzed with morning activity as the inhabitants went about their daily chores, calling out to Hallie as she passed. All admired the way she had stood by her grandfather when Vern Hargrove took the silver mine from him. Everyone had his own view of the card game that had cost Grady the mine, the one thing he cherished above all others with the exception of his granddaughter, Hallie.

Hargrove had kept harassing Grady until he wagered the mine. If Grady hadn't been so drunk, it might not have been such a disaster. But Hargrove had seen to it that Grady's glass was always full. The consensus was that Grady had been set up, since the other two players in the game had mysteriously ended up with plenty of money—and left town in a rush, never to be seen again. And there sat Hargrove with his greedy hands firmly grasping the deed to the mine.

Grady, a broken man, had left like a whipped dog seeking to lick its wounds. But no one would voice such an opinion, for fear that word would reach Hargrove's finely tuned ears.

The buckboard swayed in rhythm with the clip-clop of the horse as Hallie sat perched with her back straight.

Children ran helter-skelter through the street and across the boardwalk playing a loud game of tag. The storefronts all ran parallel with Main Street, with the exception of the two-story hotel that sat at one end. On the other end of town sat the white-frame church. There was the bootery where Hallie had her shoes made, and Mistress Martha's House of Stitches. Martha was the town's leading seamstress, and a widow for several years; Martha's husband had met his end in a freak mining accident. Rumor had it that Doc Nelson was sweet on her and had helped her get started in business.

As she passed the blacksmith shop, the sound of metal striking metal rang through the air. It combined with the other sounds, creating a cacophony of activity that passed in a blur before Hallie as she thought about all Pascal had told her.

So Hargrove had hired himself a bounty hunter, she mused. And to think he got shot before he even got his boots dusty. From the looks of him, he wasn't some bumbling cowpoke trying to make a name for himself by catching the Poet Bandit—unlike some of Hargrove's earlier attempts at unmasking the bandit.

A queer thrill raced through her as she recalled the slashing gray eyes that dared her to unmask and meet him face-to-face. With a feeling of dread, she prayed that Barkley would find a horse elsewhere, so he would not have to seek her out.

The whitewashed adobe mission came into view, backdropped by an azure blue sky. Hallie slowed the horse's gait with gently spoken words. Her heart swelled with pride as she gazed at the rust-colored buttes and sawtooth mountains that seemed hand-hewn by an overzealous sculptor.

Spring had come to the desert. Orange poppies dominated the rainbow of wildflowers that had sprung to life as though for Hallie's own pleasure. She took a deep breath of the warm spring air, enjoying the view, thinking of what might have been if fate had not crushed her future with a battle cry.

If it had not been for the war and envious Yankees, she would have her mother and father, their lovely plantation home in Atlanta, and perhaps a younger brother or sister. She would have been presented at elaborate balls in the latest fashions and found her place in the cream of Southern society. By now, she probably would be married to a plantation owner and have a child or two—instead of being a twenty-three-year-old spinster without hope of ever being married.

She had been too young at the beginning of the war to understand emotions such as hate. But with each progressing year, the tiny seed of hate sprouted and grew as she watched her mother and friends suffer the loss of their homes and loved ones.

Then Sherman broke through the Confederate lines, making his march across Georgia. The insufferable Yankees swarmed over everything the South owned. They were like bloodthirsty vultures, snatching with their greedy, clawed talons, caring nothing about the destitute people who were sucked dry. It wasn't enough that the Yankees defeated them in battles; they defeated the very core of their existence. Their hearts and souls were wrenched brutally from their already beaten bodies.

Her family was forced to sell some heirlooms for food. Her mother made the trip by wagon into Atlanta, and the unrelenting Yankees would not leave her alone. They leered at her and manhandled her until she had come home in tears, swearing never to go to the city again. She grew to hate her own beauty, and tried to conceal it by wearing disguises. She had her pride. No matter how destitute they were, her mother would become no man's mistress. She was a lady, a proud southern woman who would love only one man... and he would be coming home soon.

The war ended on Hallie's thirteenth birthday. There was no celebration, there was no decorated cake with candles. They were fortunate to have the charred remains of a room with a portion of roof to sleep beneath.

As each day passed, they would eagerly gaze down the dirt lane, hoping one of the passing men wearing the ragged gray coat would be James Parker. They had no idea whether he had survived the war, but nothing could snuff the flicker of hope that had given them the strength to go on.

One afternoon, Ella, their last remaining servant, hustled Hallie into the cellar. Her mother stood in the doorway with a gun, threatening an intruder as he tried to enter. Hallie could remember the silence, the damp, musty odor, and the knot of fear in her stomach as they waited for the man to depart. Her mother did not call, nor was there the sound of a shotgun blast. She sat huddled in Ella's arms for what seemed like hours until they forced themselves to leave their hiding place.

It was then they found her mother sprawled on the chipped marble floor, the skirt of her dress raised over her head. Ella screamed and grabbed Hallie to stop her from going to her mother. Wrenching her arm from Ella's firm grasp, Hallie knelt down beside her. She knew as she lifted the fabric from her mother's face what she would find. She had been violently raped, then strangled with her apron ties. The terror in her dead mother's eyes haunted Hallie to this day. There was no sign of the man nor of their shotgun. Hallie knew without a doubt if she had seen him just once, she would have searched the rest of her life for him to avenge her mother's cruel and needless death.

She and Ella dug a grave beneath the century-old oak and buried Estella Anne Parker. As they stood beside the grave, scattering rose petals on the earth's upturned surface, Hallie turned at the sound of dragging footsteps behind her and fell into her father's outstretched arms. Together they wept, then looked back at what remained of their home. There was not enough money or labor to rebuild it.

Everything they owned fell to the carpetbaggers, since they hadn't enough money to pay their back taxes. There was nowhere else to go but West, to join her grandfather in the Territory of Arizona. Ella, their faithful servant, was fortunate enough to find work at a nearby plantation that had not been damaged by the war because it had been used as headquarters for the Union. Ella had wanted to go with them to Arizona, but Hallie's father did not think she could survive the hazards of traveling such a distance. Selling the last of their hidden silver pieces, they began their long journey, never looking back as the rickety old wagon lumbered and creaked down the boxwood-lined lane.

* * *

Shouts of the children broke into Hallie's thoughts, and a smile quickly replaced the sadness on her face. As they raced toward her, they argued about who would sit beside her. Squeals of laughter erupted as a lanky, black-haired youth lifted a small, elfin-faced child to Hallie's side.

"Hello," she called out as the children scrambled into the buckboard.

Juan, the oldest of the eight children, guarded the youngsters with authority that belied his tender years as they made their way to the mission.

The padre, with unhurried steps, made his way toward Hallie, a smile bursting from his lips.

"Ah, Hallie, it surely is good to see you. It's as though you bring the sun with you every time you come." Clasping her hands, he gently patted them before releasing them. "Before you leave, come in and have a cup of tea with me. I have some wonderful news."

Entering the sparsely furnished room, Hallie bristled at the sight of the makeshift classroom. She wanted to cry out at the unfairness of it. Hargrove, that bastard, she fumed. It seemed everywhere she turned, she was reminded of his greed. How the padre did as well as he did with the scant amount of money he received was amazing. The eight children were orphans, and up until a few months ago had had only the barest of necessities. Only by the grace of an anonymous benefactor had their plight improved.

Hallie had taken it upon herself to teach the children.

Their thirst for love and attention was just as unquenchable as their thirst for knowledge.

As Hallie worked with them on their letters she found her mind wandering to other matters. The disturbing thought was how her chances of getting caught were narrowing each time, especially now that she had Ashe Barkley to contend with. He would be waiting for her at every turn in the road, his keen storm-gray eyes searching out any possible hiding place, discreetly stalking his victim until he had the advantage. Hallie was skillful with a gun, but she wasn't so certain that he wasn't better. Not because he was faster than she, but because he was a cold and calculating man, a man accustomed to killing for a living.

"Miss Hallie, is this good?"

Hallie welcomed the intrusion into her thoughts and slid her eyeglasses back from the tip of her nose. Glancing down at little Juanita's chalkboard, she smiled and nodded with a sigh. "You have your 'b' backward again. It looks like a 'd'." Six-year-old Juanita was the youngest but she learned quickly.

After an hour or so, the children began fidgeting in their seats and looking out the curtainless window at the cloudless blue sky. Hallie couldn't blame them for their sudden lack of interest, so she told them they were finished for the day. They straightened their desks, and with whoops of joy ran out the door to play.

Hallie sought out the padre before returning to the ranch. She found him in the small garden behind the mission, examining the young shoots just breaking through the turned soil.

"Will this year be better than last?" Hallie asked him.

Raising himself from a stoop, the padre turned in her direction. "It looks to be a good year. We were fortunate to have early spring rains."

"Is there anything you'll be needing from town when I come next time?"

"There are several things on my list, but I will have to take care of them myself. I should be asking what you and the children need," he said with a pleasant smile.

"What do you mean, Padre?"

Scratching his head in a puzzled way, he said, "Whoever has been leaving money on our doorstep gave us almost enough last night to build a new mission."

Hallie clasped her hands together in mock surprise. "Really? Do you still have no idea who our generous benefactor is?"

A frown creased his brow. "It is better not to dwell on his identity... or why he is being so generous in his offerings. I only hope he has come by it honestly." Then, raising and lowering his narrow shoulders, he continued. "If he has gotten it dishonestly, maybe he thinks God will forgive him his misdeed if he gives to those less fortunate."

Hallie smiled and placed her hand on his arm. "As always, you are right, Padre. We're better off not knowing."

Trying to cover her eagerness, Hallie stooped down to the garden, taking great interest in the trailing vines of the squash. "Do you think there would be enough money to have Jeb Smith build some individual desks for the children?"

"Ah... Hallie," he said with a laugh. "We have enough money to build twice that."

Hallie joined in the laughter. "Thank you, but eight will be plenty."

Hallie settled herself on the bench of the buckboard and adjusted the bonnet to shade her eyes. She flipped the reins lightly against the neck of her brown mare, and the squeaky buckboard leaped ahead, causing her eyeglasses to fall precariously close to the edge of her freckled nose. Once out of sight from the mission on the deserted road, Hallie removed the nonsensical wire-framed glasses, hiding them in the deep folds of her blue gingham skirt.

Everything Hallie did was calculated to conceal the real Hallie Parker. She had chosen to live this way until she succeeded in forcing Vern Hargrove from Prospect City. The money she robbed from the stagecoach was only a drop in the bucket compared to Hargrove's other vast holdings. It gave her much satisfaction to know she was getting under his skin.

Hallie smiled. Who would ever believe a twenty-three-year-old straitlaced spinster who took care of her grandfather would be capable of pulling off a stagecoach robbery? Or for that matter, could shoot straight as an arrow?

The quickened pace of the buckboard disrupted Hallie's thoughts. Dixie had a habit of racing to her destination when their home came into view. The sprawling, sun-washed hacienda merged with its surroundings, and from a distance it seemed a part of the fractured ridges hunched behind it. A narrow veranda built of hand-hewn timbers ran along the front of the house where they spent their leisure on hot summer evenings. A passageway connected the living quarters with the kitchen.

Hallie pulled the buckboard to a halt in front of the stables and was greeted by Luis, Maria's son, a large, hard-muscled young man whose energy was limitless.

"Buenos dias, senorita," he said, assisting her from the buckboard. "You come home early today."

"The children were in no mood for study today, and quite frankly, my mind was elsewhere, too." Rubbing Dixie's mane, she observed, "Guess Grandpa's still not home."

A wide grin spanned Luis' face. "Si, senorita, his belly called him home."

As she started to leave for the house, he called out to her. "I did not see you this morning before you left to tell you of our newest addition. Rebel is a new father."

Hallie's eyes brightened. Rebel was the wild stallion they had captured a few months back. Only in the last few weeks had he given up his fight and allowed Luis to mount his broad gray back.

"Marvelous! As soon as I get a bite to eat, I'll be out."

Hallie's heart was joyful at the news of the birth. The small amount of money Grandpa had invested prior to his downfall finally had begun to pay off. With Juan, Maria's husband, and their son's assistance, they had nearly tripled the head count of their cattle. Raising horses had been Hallie's idea, and in the beginning Grandpa had rebelled. Now he knew better than to complain. As Pascal had said, they had the best horseflesh available in the area, and the money they made from each one they sold made Grandpa proud of her endeavor.

Strolling through the courtyard, she picked a bouquet of spring flowers that grew along the flagstone path, and paused to breathe in the heady aroma. An unwelcome thought flashed through her mind. Just how in the world would she handle Ashe Barkley if he came to the ranch?

Hallie was pleased to see Doc Nelson sitting at the table with her grandfather as she entered the kitchen.

"Why, Doc," she said pleasantly, "what a surprise. It's a shame Martha couldn't come with you."

Maria placed a platter of fried chicken and a bowl of steaming vegetables on the table. "I said the same thing, mi niña. While your grandfather and Doc played checkers, the two of you could visit."

Doc chuckled. "Between her work and mine, we may as well live in different countries."

"It wouldn't make any difference if you were married to her," Grady said, passing the chicken to Hallie and Doc. "Take Hallie here. If she weren't runnin' here and there like she had a hot poker stuck to her butt, she'd be miserable."

"Grady Parker," Maria chastised, "watch your mouth."

Hallie giggled. "Why should he start now?"

Grady winked at his granddaughter fondly. "Why try improving a good thing?"

Hallie laughed and returned his wink.

After dinner, Maria and Hallie cleared the table while Grady poured himself and Doc a generous snifter of brandy. Doc meticulously set up the checkerboard. Hallie waited, counting to herself. When the men finally settled themselves to play, she waited for the words that would signal the beginning of the game.

"Gol'dang, Doc, why is it you always get to move first?"

"Them's the rules, Grady. Black man moves first," Doc assured him.

Hallie smiled. For as long as she had lived with her grandfather, every game he and Doc played began with the same question and the same answer. It had always puzzled Hallie why Grady and Doc didn't just exchange colors occasionally if black always moved first.

When she asked her grandfather why they didn't try her solution, he looked at her as though she were daft. "Now why would I go and do that? I've always been red, and Doc has always been black. That would be like changing course in midstream after all these years.... Bad luck to boot," he added as an afterthought.

Each man had his own set of rules and game plan. How they managed to complete a game surprised Hallie. But to a newcomer, it would appear as though it were the first game between them as they rehashed the rules.

"Crown my man, Doc," Grady bellowed. "By God, I've got you tonight."

"Just hold on a gol'dern minute, Grady, the game ain't over with yet," Doc retorted, capturing several of Grady's men in one move. "I'm just gettin' warmed up," Doc added with a grin.

"How the bloody hell did you manage that?" Grady questioned, eyeing the board in disbelief.

Hallie walked behind Grady. Leaning around him, she placed a gentle kiss on his rough cheek. "I'm going to lie down. It's good to see you, Doc. Good luck with your game. Good night."

"Don't be wishin' this varmit good luck. He cleaned me out last time," Grady roared.

"Who cleaned who out, you old coot? If my memory serves me, I was lucky to get out with my pants intact. I mean to change your winning streak, Grady. I'm goin' to teach this gol'dang cutthroat player a trick or two this time. I've been planning my strategy," Doc exclaimed.

"Humph," Grady grunted, not deigning to comment, only eyeing the board with determination.

Hallie fluffed up her pillow. Relaxing in bed, she flipped through her book of poetry. The men's voices carried through the house.

"You can't move the damned man backward, Grady. He ain't crowned."

"Did I move it? Hell no, I'm just studyin' my move ... plannin' my strategy, so to speak," Grady argued.

Hallie smiled as she extinguished the light. She would not read tonight. Her mind could not concentrate on the written words with the verbal ones reverberating through the house.

As far as she could remember, Grady had never

sought female companionship. Long ago she had questioned him about inviting various women out for dinner. "No" had always been his immediate reply.

"Don't you want to marry again someday? Grandma has been dead a long time."

His sparkling eyes had clouded over with grief. "I saw a few women in the years following your grandmother's death."

"And?" Hallie had questioned.

"Well, they just didn't come up to snuff."

Hallie never mentioned female companionship to her grandfather again.

As her eyelids became heavy, a familiar ache surged through her. Would she remain a spinster? Wasn't there someone somewhere for her? Someone who would come up to snuff?

Chapter 3

"Squawk! Something hot, something cold, a little brandy is good for the soul. Squawk, squawk!"

"Shut up, Sinbad, your mouth has a tendency to overload your brain," Hallie grumbled as she helped Maria clear away the dinner dishes.

The kitchen was Maria's domain, where Hallie strived to learn the secrets of Mexican cookery, but she never understood how a pinch of this and a pinch of that could produce such delicious, spicy hot foods.

The kitchen was large and homey, with a fireplace in the corner. Maria always cooked the evening meals in the early hours of the morning to avoid the heat during the day.

In the corner was her wood-burning cook stove where an iron teakettle sat permanently on its back surface. The individual cabinets where she kept their dishes and cookware were made by Jeb Smith, the local carpenter. He had also made the long pine trestle table where they ate their meals, except when it was too hot in the kitchen.

Hallie absently wiped the table, thinking about her grandfather. If she suddenly came up with the money he needed to run the silver mine properly, he would surely question how she obtained it. Though they sold horses and cattle occasionally, most of the profit was put right back into the ranch, except what they needed to pay the ranch hands and buy necessary supplies.

"Something is troubling you," Maria remarked offhandedly as she gazed at the girl she loved like a daughter. "I know you like the back of my hand, mi niña."

Hallie washed out her rag in a pan of water, wrung it out, and hung it to dry on a rack. "It's Grandpa, Maria. He's not well enough to be going to the mine every day. When he is gone for two or three days at a time, I worry something may have happened to him out there alone."

Maria rested her large brown hands on Hallie's shoulders and smiled at her. "Don't worry so, señorita. Things have a way of working out. Your grandfather will give up his harebrained notion of opening up that mine again."

"I don't think so, Maria. He seems hell-bent on having his own way," Hallie said in frustration.

Placing her hands on her wide hips, Maria said adamantly, "Hallie Parker, watch your mouth. Ladies don't swear. You've been around men too much, and needed a mother to guide you, instead of a rough old man and a ship's captain." Glaring at Sinbad who was watching them with his small, beady eyes, Maria said huffily, "And it doesn't help having that foulmouthed parrot around, either. Just look at him sitting so regally on that perch of his. I'd just as soon pinch his head off as look at him, but Grady would likely do the same to me."

Laughing helplessly, Hallie hugged Maria to her. "Your family and Grandpa have supplied all the guidance I need. I don't think you all have done such a bad job with me. And besides, if I were gentle, I'd never have survived in this harsh land."

Maria grumbled beneath her breath and continued cleaning the pots and pans. Hallie smiled at Maria's turned back. What would she ever have done without this proud Mexican woman? Maria and her family had been with her grandpa and Ben Langley years before Hallie had come to live with them. Working for the Parkers had enabled Maria to learn the English language.

She was a large woman, but one would not consider her obese. She was broad-shouldered and carried her five-foot-ten-inch height with the grace of a queen. Juan, her husband, was a large, rawboned man, and they had two sons whose physical strength equaled that of an elephant.

A bold knock at the door caused Hallie to turn quickly. Picking up her glasses from the table, she adjusted them on her nose, then smoothed her skirt. "I wonder who that could be?"

Maria shrugged her shoulders. "Could be one of my sons."

"And when did they ever knock?" Hallie asked,

opening the door. The blood rushed to her head as she immediately identified the caller. "Can—can I help you?" she asked, feeling a tremor run up and down her spine.

"Yes ma'am," came the rumbling voice of Ashe Barkley as he removed his hat, unleashing a mass of black, curly hair. "I was told in town that I might be able to buy a horse from a Mr. Grady Parker."

His manner was warm and friendly, not that of a man who could kill with the blink of an eye. Pascal had been overdramatizing as usual, Hallie thought.

"We do have a few horses, but my grandfather isn't here right now. Maybe I can help you, Mr. ... ?" She almost said his name. She had to be more careful than that.

"Barkley, Ashe Barkley," he supplied, running his gray eyes over her face almost caressingly.

Hallie felt her legs melt like butter in the sun, then she remembered who he was and gathered her composure.

"I'm Hallie Parker, Grady's granddaughter," she said, extending her hand. His handshake was warm and firm, and his grin was infectious. Hallie found herself smiling back at him, despite her attempt to remain unaffected.

"Won't you come in, Mr. Barkley? I'm sure you could use something cool to drink after your ride. Did you ride out from town?"

"No ma'am, from Hargrove's. I'm his new foreman."

Sinbad's keen hearing picked up the name Hargrove, and a stream of very understandable words

spewed out of his mouth. "Is that you, Hargrove?...
Squawk... squawk... Hargrove's a bastard... squawk!
Hargrove's a—"

"Hush, Sinbad, hush!" Hallie shouted. Grabbing the cage, she ran to the pantry and shoved the still squawking Sinbad inside and slammed the door.

She could still hear his muffled words: "Help!... squawk!... it's dark... squawk... who blew the lights out... squawk!"

She knew her face was beet-red, and her hands felt clammy. Leaning against the pantry door, she pasted an apologetic smile on her face. "I'm sorry, Mr. Barkley, Sinbad gets a little carried away at times. I would put croton oil in his water if I could get by with it, but Grandpa dotes on that fool bird. It belonged to his dearest friend."

Ashe tried unsuccessfully to hide his amusement, but he couldn't control his twitching lips.

"Damn bird," Hallie muttered under her breath. Pushing away from the door, she saw Maria with her hand clasped over her mouth, staring at Mr. Barkley.

"Mr. Barkley, this is my friend, Maria Valdez."

Ashe nodded affably. "Nice to meet you, ma'am."

"If you want to see the horses, I suggest we go to the stables." On her way out the door, she called back to Maria, "You can let that bird out now if you want to. If Grandpa comes home, he'll raise a stink, for sure."

Grabbing up her bonnet, she hurriedly put it on and tied the strings tightly under her chin.

Walking beside Hallie, Ashe slowed his steps to match her pace, forcing himself not to stare at the feisty Hallie Parker. Everyone spoke highly of her, and of how hard she worked to help her grandfather. From what he had learned, she ran the ranch while her grandfather spent his time trying to work a worthless silver mine. All and all, she sounded too good to be true, except that she was a staunch Yankee-hater. Luckily, he had acquired the proper drawling accent during the years he had spent in the south. Lord forbid that she ever find out where he was from and that he had served the Union cause. That, coupled with his working for Hargrove, would no doubt make him an enemy of hers also. If she did find out, she'd probably shoot him on sight... if she could even shoot, he thought, smiling at the notion, unaware that Hallie was watching him.

"I wonder, Mr. Barkley, what is it that you find so amusing," she said bitingly. "You have heard, no doubt, that it's delightful to laugh with someone, but altogether different to laugh at someone."

Stopping suddenly, Ashe placed his hands on her shoulders. "I assure you, Miss Parker, I was not laughing at you, only at my own circumstances."

The warmth from his hands surprised Hallie, and her stomach did queer things. Only when he released her did she wonder at her peculiar feelings. It must have been her not eating her dinner that caused the sensations.

The whinnying of a large gray stallion caught Ashe's attention, and he strolled to the rail fence. Propping one foot and his elbows on the fence, he gazed intently at the horse as it ran in a wild circle around the corral. "He sure is a beauty."

"Yes, he is," Hallie answered. "I think he knows it, too. See how proud he holds his head and tosses his tail high in the air. Of course, he has reason to be high-spirited today. He became a father two nights ago." Noticing how interested Ashe was in the horse, she added, "He really doesn't like the human race... he's wild and rambunctious; shifty, too."

"You don't see many horses of that color, either... kind of between silver and gray. Reminds me of silver ore," Ashe said, grinning at her. "What do you call him?"

"Rebel," Hallie replied, quickly pushing her glasses up on her nose.

That figures, Ashe thought, his eyes raking Hallie's stiff form. She's got that damn bonnet tied so tight, I'm surprised she can breathe. And I bet she's got on a corset laced tighter than hell. She'd have to. Nobody's waist is that small... why, my hands could reach around her. Nice figure, he thought, sliding his tongue across his upper lip, drawing Hallie's eyes by the bold gesture.

Catching herself, she snapped, "Did you come out here to gawk at me, Mr. Barkley, or are you really interested in buying a horse?"

The sarcasm was not lost on Ashe. Forcing himself to abandon his perusal of her, he laughed. "I definitely am interested in the horse."

Hallie wondered if she had been insulted, but didn't take the time to dwell on it. With a quick toss of her head, she retorted, "Very well, would you like to ride Rebel? You may find that you do not suit each other."

"Miss Parker, I assure you Rebel is a far cry from

any of the nags Hargrove offered to sell me. He won't part with any of his horses that are worth their salt."

"Could I be so rude as to ask what you're doing without a horse? It really doesn't fit—"

"Fit what, Miss Parker?"

The twinkle in his storm-gray eyes unnerved Hallie, and before she really thought about them, the words poured forth. "Your reputation has preceded you, Mr. Barkley. And, plainly speaking, I can't imagine someone like you being without a horse."

"It's only temporary, and to satisfy your curiosity, my horse was shot out from under me several weeks ago. My luck of late has been nil. Seems everyone has been taking shots at me."

"I heard," she replied, then glanced swiftly at his shoulder. "But you look none the worse for it." The color rushed to her face as she caught herself, and she turned quickly to Rebel. The abruptness of her movement caused the horse to snort and shake his head. Ashe said soothing words to the horse, never taking his eyes from Hallie, a question posed in their depths. He had not missed that sudden flush.

"Only grazed my shoulder. I've suffered worse."

"I guess a man in your business has to watch constantly over his shoulder."

"What would you know about my business, Miss Parker?"

She stiffened visibly at his abrasive question, and Ashe could have sworn he heard her spine crack in about three places.

Gracing him with her coldest look, she snapped, "Nothing, absolutely nothing, only hearsay."

Leaning negligently against the rail fence, Ashe raised one brown hand, and with his thumb pushed his hat farther back on his head. "Do I make you nervous, Miss Parker?" he asked, cocking a brow.

"Whatever do you mean?" If he says "Miss Parker" one more time, I'll scream, she thought. The way he draws out M-i-s-s as though silently taunting, spinster ... spinster. It grated on her nerves.

"Why, you're skittish as a colt," he mocked her discomfiture.

"I don't have the slightest idea what you are talking about." What was the matter with her? Just his presence seemed to still her tongue, usually so quick with a response to any situation. But with this big bungling animal, she seemed to flounder over what to say and her words caught in her throat. If I was exposed to him for long, I'd probably smother to death, she thought with self-reproach.

"Do you want Rebel or not? We have a few other horses you might be more interested in."

"No, Rebel will do nicely. I think we'll do fine together."

"I'm sure you will. Now, if we can settle on a price, our transaction will be completed. I'm sure you have things to do ... as I do," she said firmly.

"Why don't you unbend a little, Miss Parker? I'm not going to bite you," he said with a lopsided grin.

Hallie's heart raced. "I'm not in the habit of dealing with Hargrove or anyone associated with him. So if I seem uneasy in your presence, you surely can understand why. I'm certain you have heard about our dealings with Vern Hargrove." That statement stiffened her resolve not to be taken in by him.

"This has nothing to do with Hargrove," he assured her, "whatever you may think."

"I would think everything you did has something to do with Hargrove since you're on his payroll." She could see that her words had made him angry, because his cheek twitched as he ground his teeth together.

"Have it your way, Miss Parker, but bear in mind I have my reasons."

"Yes, I've heard you're out to get the Poet Bandit, to bring him down so Hargrove can make an example of him, so there will be no doubt in anyone's mind that no one goes against the powerful Vern Hargrove. Let's conclude our business, Mr. Barkley. It really matters little to me what you do."

Deciding there was nothing else to say to Hallie Parker to convince her otherwise, he turned his attention to settling on a price for Rebel. He watched her walk proudly back into her house and wished circumstances could have been different. Maybe they could have been friends. Lovers wouldn't be such a bad idea, he thought wickedly. If . . . he could get her to unbend a little.

Mounting his borrowed horse, Ashe led the great gray stallion away from Grady Parker's ranch. He looked forward to meeting Miss Parker again, and thought that the next time he would make a point of finding out what kind of woman was hidden beneath that spinster disguise.

Chapter 4

Hallie lifted her skirts to step up on the plank walk in front of Jeb Smith's carpentry shop. Next door, the Drinkalot Saloon was rip-roaring with activity even though it was still quite early in the day. Thinning her lips in distaste of men who had nothing better to do, she walked through the door of Jeb's shop. She heard the grating of the saw in the distance, and she made her way around several pieces of furniture to seek Jeb at the back of the shop. A cloud of sawdust hung in the air. Though the smell was pleasant, the fine particles caused Hallie to sneeze and her eyes to water.

A partially bald head popped up from behind a chest. His moon-shaped face was smudged with a mixture of sweat, dirt, and sawdust.

"Wal, Miss Hallie," he said, rising slowly to his feet and stretching his back, "what brings you into town?"

Hallie removed her glasses and dabbed at her eyes with her hanky. Between sneezes, she said, "I... ah ...I...achoo! Mr. Smith, can..."

Seeing her discomfort, Jeb Smith took her by the arm, leading her into the front area of the shop.

"I'm sorry," he sighed apologetically, "I'm so used to the dust, I forget my manners."

Stuffing her hanky into her reticule and replacing her eyeglasses, Hallie said, "I have a favor to ask of you, Mr. Smith."

"Shoot," he replied with a wide grin, showing a well-chewed splinter of wood between his crooked teeth.

"I need eight small desks for the orphans at the mission school, and I wondered how much you'd charge me to build them."

Jeb Smith smiled, thinking about what he had heard the townfolk say about how tight Miss Hallie pulled her purse strings. Had it not been for her, they said, Grady Parker would have lost every dime he had.

"Wal," he drawled, mentally calculating what he considered a fair price. After much haggling back and forth, a bargain was struck. At that point, Jeb Smith, mesmerized by her sparkling blue eyes, would have probably built them for nothing.

While in town, Hallie decided to buy some fabric for new curtains. As she crossed the street, a stray yellow dog began following her, sniffing at her ankles. She tried to shoo him away, but the dog trailed her until she disappeared into the shop. When she came out, her arms laden with packages, the dog got up from his resting place and continued after her. She did not have the heart to turn him away. "Poor starved thing. I'll just have to take him home with me," she decided.

As she waited for several wagons to pass by, Hallie heard a ruckus across the street. The saloon door swung open and slammed against the clapboard wall behind it. Out came two men, their drunken laughter vying with the sound of the horses' hooves and wagon wheels. The men leaned against the hitching post to support their reeling bodies. Hallie waited for them to get on their horses and leave, for her wagon was parked next to the saloon.

The men seemed not the least bit interested in leaving the vicinity. She recognized them as the O'Malley twins, both well-known for their trigger-happy fingers. It wasn't a proven fact, but the O'Malleys were thought to be murderers and cattle-rustlers. Folks avoided them, not eager to arouse their displeasure.

Squaring her shoulders and stiffening her spine, Hallie looked down at the sad-eyed dog and murmured, "We may as well take our chances, fellow." She began crossing the dusty street, her eyes riveted in the direction of the O'Malley twins.

They saw her. A mean, lewd grin spread across Clayton O'Malley's face. "Wal, wal, if it ain't Miss 'high and mighty.' Lookee thar, Clint," he called, waving a drunken finger. "Think she kin dance as well as she rides a horse?"

Hallie stopped in the middle of the street, her eyes widening as Clayton pulled his gun from his holster. Her heart plummeted to her feet as he aimed. The blast of the gun shook her as the bullet bit the dust within inches of her feet. The dog ran behind her skirts, whimpering.

"Clayton O'Malley," she shouted in anger, "put that gun away before you kill someone."

"Ah, come on, Miss Hallie. I'm just a-funnin' with ya. Surely ya kin take a little joke."

Hallie swallowed hard, hoping he had no intention of shooting at her again. Picking up her pace again, she watched him aim carefully as she approached. Another shot rang out. This time the bullet split the hem of her skirt.

Damnation, Hallie thought, dropping her packages to the ground. Two can play this game. Whipping open her purse strings, she reached for her small derringer. A thought suddenly occurred to her: My God, what am I doing? I could blow my whole cover.

Another shot almost hit the dog. To hell with the cover, she thought angrily as her hand grasped the cool metal of the gun. Before she could whip it from the bag, she heard a deep voice shout from somewhere behind her, "Drop your gun!"

Clayton O'Malley shifted his attention to his adversary and aimed his gun. Two shots were fired, one after the other. Hallie's hand froze on the cold metal of her gun as she saw Clayton O'Malley slump over the railing. His brother, Clint, shouting incoherently, pulled his gun from his holster, shaking it threateningly in the air.

Then a voice, cold and menacing, snapped, "I wouldn't do that if I were you. It won't put me out one bit to eliminate another man."

Hallie knew that voice. It had haunted her, invading her dreams at night.

She saw Clint O'Malley's eyes glaze over in anger and his gun freeze in front of him. Ever so slowly he lowered it to his side.

Pivoting around, Hallie saw Ashe Barkley standing outside the mercantile store. A wisp of smoke curled upward from his gun. His face was expressionless. Replacing his gun in the holster, he shoved back his hat, and removed a small pouch from his shirt pocket. He sprinkled tobacco on a square of thin paper and rolled a cigarette. Then, striking a match against the sole of his boot, he lit the cigarette, his eyes all the while never leaving Clint O'Malley.

Clint grasped the body of his brother beneath his arms and deposited him gently across the saddle of the horse. Mounting his own, he took the reins of Clayton's horse.

Ashe strolled casually toward Hallie, his long, muscled legs flexing against the fabric of his pants, his spurs jingling with each step.

"I hope incidents like this don't happen every time you come into town."

Hallie was wide-eyed with disbelief. How could a man kill someone and act so casual the next moment? The thought curdled her blood and left her speechless.

Clint O'Malley's voice interrupted. "I don't know who ya are, mister, but ain't nobody kills my brother and gets away with it." Then, narrowing his eyes at Hallie, he said with contempt, "It's all yore fault, lady, you and yore high falutin' ways. Clayton never meant ya no harm, but ya jest kept eggin' him on. Couldn't ya see he was drunk?"

Hallie said coolly, "That's what scared me most, Clint."

Casting them an angry look over his shoulder, Clint O'Malley led his brother's horse through town and disappeared. Anxious onlookers ran out of shops; the Drinkalot Saloon was empty for the first time since it burned down several years back. All eyes were fixed on Ashe and Hallie.

The reputation that followed Ashe Barkley to Prospect City was no longer a rumor.

Ashe sensed the sentiments of the townspeople. Word would get around about the shoot-out and every man who was quick with a gun would seek a gunfight with him. Some would be young and foolish, and no amount of talk would sway their intentions. They would die, just like all the others. And Ashe would be on the road again.

Sheriff Hastings came out of his office. Hallie always had wondered why Hastings had been hired in the first place. He did little to rid the town of troublemakers. The only time he took any action was when Vern Hargrove's interests were concerned. He had yet to get a lead on the Poet Bandit.

Coming across the street briskly, Hastings offered his hand to Ashe. "Jest want to thank ya fer riddin' me of a problem around here, Mr. Barkley."

Ashe ignored the man's outstretched hand. "Only one of them," was his cold reply. "Seems to me you should've been the one who took care of the problem. Do you always let drunkards harass women in town?"

Hastings' smile changed dramatically. He glared at Ashe and thrust his hand into his pants pocket. "I was busy."

Hallie knew he was lying, for he hated her as much as Hargrove did. If she had died, the O'Malley twins never would have been hanged for killing her.

Hastings quickly retreated to his office in anger. No man insulted him like that and got away with it. Hargrove would hear of this ... and soon.

Ashe stooped down to pick up Hallie's packages. A warm, wet tongue raked his cheek. Turning his head, he was greeted by another lick on his nose. For several seconds, Ashe stared at the sad-eyed dog that he swore was grinning at him.

Standing up, he wiped his cheek and nose on his upper arm. "Your dog?" he asked with a grin.

"No," Hallie answered, lifting her chin defiantly. "Do you shoot dogs, too?"

"Only two-legged ones."

"Oh." Hallie's stomach flip-flopped at his candor.

"Where's your wagon?"

"It's that one over there," she said, pointing toward the saloon. "The one next to the bloody hitching post." She bit her tongue for her crass reply.

Ashe smiled slowly, arching his brow as Hallie thrust her dainty nose into the air and walked regally toward the wagon. He watched the gentle sway of her calico skirt for a moment, then followed in her wake. Her scent drifted back to him, teasing his senses.

Crushing his cigarette on the ground, he tossed her packages into the back of the wagon. The bony dog looked up at him with pleading eyes. "Do you want the dog?"

"I suppose so. He could stand some meat on his bones."

Lifting the dog, Ashe set him down in the wagon and made his way to the front.

"Give me a minute," he ordered.

He walked across the street, ignoring the stares of the onlookers as he untied Rebel, led him to the wagon, and hitched his reins to the back.

When he placed one booted foot on the step of the wagon, Hallie was finally aware of his intention. Forgetting his wounded shoulder, she tried to push him from the wagon. Ashe's face turned pasty white.

He gritted his teeth at the pain she inflicted. He sounded more threatening than he intended; it took a considerable amount of effort to say the words through clenched teeth. "Keep-your-goddamn-hand-off-my-shoulder."

"Well! I never . . ." Hallie sputtered defiantly. Tucking a stray curl beneath her bonnet, she righted herself on the bench.

Grasping her hand that held the reins, Ashe climbed up and unceremoniously sat down beside her, his large frame pressed tightly against her thigh.

Angry blue eyes turned stormy. "Mr. Barkley, you are sitting on me." Wriggling her hips as though to shove him off the bench, she said waspishly, "Would you mind?"

"Yes, I would," came his stiff reply.

"Get off my wagon," she whispered in a snakelike hiss.

"Now, Miss Hallie, don't get so riled up."

"I said, Get-off-my-wagon!" Hallie's temper had reached the boiling point. Standing up, she began hitting him with her reticule, forgetting the hard metal derringer inside it. Without batting an eye, Ashe ripped the reins from her hand and slapped Dixie across her rump. Dixie, expecting a woman's gentle touch, felt the sharp sting and leaped forward in a mad dash. The sudden lurch caused Hallie to fall over Ashe's shoulder, her legs flailing in the air.

The townspeople stood in awe as the gunslinger and the proud Miss Hallie Parker careened through town as if they were headed for a fire. They would always remember Hallie beating Ashe's back with her reticule, and Ashe fighting the billowing skirt, attempting to save Hallie from further disgrace.

"Whoa," Ashe ordered, pulling back on the reins as they reached the outskirts of town.

Hallie stopped beating him when his hands gripped her hips and lingered there longer than necessary. Her face turned crimson. "You can put me down now," she said between clenched teeth.

"Such nice legs you have, Miss Hallie. Trim little ankles, well-shaped calves..." One hand caressed her thigh, making the blood rush to her head.

"Put me down, you... you—"

"Go ahead and say it," he mocked. "You'd be surprised how good it'll make you feel."

When she didn't answer, he roamed his hand over her derriere, caressing its fullness. Though she had on three layers of fabric, she felt her skin searing beneath his touch.

"Sonofabitch," she swore under her breath.

"Louder, I can't hear you."

"No!" she screamed at him.

Ashe restrained his laughter and released her, setting her on her feet. He had seen many a woman angry before, but nothing could come close to this wild woman standing before him. Wild and downright beautiful. Her bonnet was missing, and so was the thick knot on the top of her head. Thick wavy auburn hair, falling in every direction, nearly covered the upper portion of her body. Her eyes caught his attention, blue as the summer sky with long dark lashes like a furry caterpillar. Why hadn't he noticed them before? Then it dawned on him. She had lost her glasses in the fracas.

With her hand placed defiantly on her hips, she glared at him, not uttering a word.

He saw her eyes veer to her reticule beside him on the bench. He grabbed it. "No thank you, I've had my beating for the day."

"I hate you," she said, grinding her teeth together. "How dare you humiliate me in front of all those people. I'll never be able to go into town again."

"You brought it all on yourself, love."

"Don't call me *love*."

"Most women would love it."

"I'm not most women, Mr. Barkley."

"You certainly are. You're just a trifle late in discovering it, but in time you'll change your tune."

He saw her jaw twitching in anger; he saw her beautiful, full, kissable mouth; he felt the desire growing in his loins. "Oh hell, why wait."

Hallie was caught unprepared. Before she knew it,

he had pulled her down and across his lap, his strong arms wrapped around her like a boa constrictor. She tried to wrench away from him, but the movement only increased his determination.

His lips crushed down on hers, drowning out her urgent protests. As her one free hand pressed against his chest, he grabbed it, twisting it behind her back, enslaving her in his arms.

Suddenly the harsh pressure of his lips gentled, and much to her dismay, she found she liked the feel of his mouth touching hers. His tongue ran along her lips, teasing them, parting them. She tasted strong tobacco as his tongue searched the inside of her mouth. Her eyes flew open at the shock. How dare he kiss her like that!

Her innocent wiggling was Ashe's undoing. As her softness ground into his groin, his kisses became urgent and demanding. Hallie found it hard to breathe. Her head was swimming at his assault on her senses. In one final desperate attempt, she managed to pull her lips from his. She inhaled deeply.

"Took your breath away, didn't I?"

She saw the desire in his glazed gray eyes and snapped at him, "that's an understatement. You came closer to suffocating me, you bast—" She pursed her lips together.

"It'll come easier with practice," he said, tightening his arms around her.

"If I'm in your company much longer, it could become a habit."

"Which one a habit, Hallie? The kissing or the cursing?" Rolling his tongue in his cheek, he goaded her. "Have you never been kissed before?"

Hallie thought of the time when a drunk grabbed her on the boardwalk in town—the taste of the stale liquor on his lips and the foul stench of his body. That was the only time, but she would be damned if she would let Ashe Barkley know it.

"Of course," she replied huffily, sticking her nose in the air. "But not like that."

"Like what?" he taunted.

"It's indecent." She blushed.

"If you'd relax, you might find it quite enjoyable." Releasing her, he set her beside him on the bench.

Stiffening her back, she looked straight ahead. "It's time I went back to the ranch. This little game you're playing with me is sorely trying my patience."

Both sat in silence as the wagon made a slow journey down the road. Ashe feigned great interest in the vast terrain in order to lure Hallie out of her anger.

"Strange thing," he mused aloud.

"What's strange?" she asked looking his way for the first time.

"Those rocks that sit stacked on one another, sort of like children's blocks. In all these hundreds of years, they've yet to tumble down."

Hallie turned her eyes back to the road, saying scornfully, "If I'm lucky, they'll decide to fall on top of you on your way back to Hargrove's. If it weren't for Rebel, I'd pray hard for it."

"Damnit, woman, who's trying whose patience? Here I try my damnedest to carry on a decent conversation with you, and your vicious mind never stops working." Pulling Dixie to a halt once again, he turned in the seat to face her. "Do you realize I saved your life today?"

Reaching into her reticule, she found several hairpins. Coiling her hair back into a knot, she secured it with the pins. Taking a deep breath, she said very primly, "You did not save my life." She pulled out the derringer from her reticule. "Before you took it upon yourself to kill that man, I was about to do it myself," she snapped, waving the gun wildly in his face.

Ashe glanced at the gun, then back to Hallie. "Would you have killed him? Or should I ask, could you have killed him?"

Not wanting him to know she was an excellent shot, she shrugged her shoulders. "I'd have tried."

He stared at her for a long moment, a frown creasing his brow.

"Why are you looking at me so strangely? Every woman in this town carries a gun for protection against fast men—like you."

Toying with the reins, Ashe said, "You don't need a gun, love. Just hit him with your purse."

Slapping the reins, he gave Dixie the command, deciding to forgo any further conversation with Hallie Parker. When they arrived at the ranch, Ashe leaped down, not bothering to assist Hallie. He saw a glint of metal in the back of the wagon as he lifted the dog out. Reaching in, he picked up her little wire-rimmed glasses. He walked around to her side of the wagon and dangled them before her.

She reached out for them, but he pushed her hands

away and slipped them on her nose. "Just in case you decide to shoot someone."

Walking to his horse, he untied the reins from the back of the wagon and mounted. Hallie watched him until he appeared as a tiny dot on the desert. She smiled to herself, thinking: I didn't wear them the day I shot you, Ashe Barkley.

Chapter 5

For several weeks after Hallie's confrontation with the O'Malley twins, she avoided going to town. She took a different route to the mission for fear of running into Ashe again. And she wasn't eager to see the smirks on the townspeople's faces, either. Her encounter with Ashe was probably a legend by now.

Maria did not make matters any better. The day Ashe drove her home, Maria greeted her at the door with a suspicious smile on her dark face.

"Will we be seeing Señor Barkley often, mi niña?"

"Not if I can help it," Hallie said angrily, tossing aside her bonnet.

"He is one good-looking gringo," Maria said, urging Hallie to continue the talk. "Not many men like him around."

"Thank God for that," Hallie said with a shudder.

Her grandfather entered the kitchen. From the sleepy-eyed look on his face, she knew he had been napping.

He sat down at the table and ran a hand through his disheveled gray hair.

"What are we thanking God for?" he asked with a yawn.

Maria brought him a cup of rich black coffee; the aroma was so enticing that Hallie prepared one for herself and joined him at the table.

"The señorita, she comes home with that Señor Ashe Barkley. I tell her she is one lucky woman to find such a man."

Her grandpa's eyes narrowed beneath his unruly brows. "Stay away from that man, Hallie. Anyone who's got anything to do with Hargrove is dangerous to be around."

Hallie noted the desolate expression on Maria's face. "I know, Grandpa, believe me. He killed a man today."

Maria's eyes shot open, as did her mouth.

"Why'd he do that for?" he asked, then nodded his head and waved his hand in dismissal. "Don't matter none. A man doesn't have to have a reason to kill anyone anymore. That sorry excuse for a sheriff just sits in the saloon cavortin' with those same kind of men. I doubt if he'd know how to shoot a gun if the opportunity ever arose."

"Well," Hallie said hesitantly, knowing he would hear about it sooner or later, "he sort of had a reason, I guess. You might say he was defending me."

A broad smile erupted on Maria's face. "Then he can't be all bad, Señor Parker, if he—"

"Shut up Maria," her grandfather said with a scowl. "Tell me about it, child."

Maria puffed up and walked away to finish preparing dinner.

Hallie related most of her ordeal, but she was too embarrassed to tell him how she made a fool of herself in town.

Grandpa drained the last of his coffee and spat the dregs back into the cup. Leaning back in his ladder-back chair, he looked at Hallie several minutes before speaking. "I'm glad you weren't hurt, Hallie, but don't think he killed Clayton to save yore hide, gal. You may have been a good excuse for him to rid the territory of a cattle rustler. I hear tell Hargrove has had cattle stolen from his ranch lately, and that's part of the reason he hired Barkley."

Hallie's heart sank. Why, she didn't know. "What's the other part of the reason he hired Barkley?"

"To catch the Poet Bandit, what else?"

Hallie heard Maria gasp in the background. Hallie turned around in her chair and saw the strangest expression on Maria's face. It was almost as though Maria knew who the Poet Bandit was. But there was no way she could know.

Getting up from the table, Hallie walked to the back door and looked out at the purplish-gray mountains. "I doubt if Barkley will ever catch the Poet Bandit—he's much too crafty to allow that to happen."

"I pity the bandit if Barkley does catch him," Grandpa said, pushing back from the table. "Well, got to get back to the mine. Picked up a few more pieces of ore."

"Grandpa," Hallie said, turning to face him, "please give up this useless digging. Even if Ben did come back, he'd be no help to you. They'd hang him the minute he put his foot in Prospect City."

A sadness came into his eyes. "I know, child, but Ben was so sure he had a treasure in there somewhere."

"But your health won't allow you to do anything about it, so please quit fooling with it," Hallie pleaded.

"I have to continue. It gives me something to do." Then, kissing her cheek, he said, "If I have nothing to do around here, it will be the death of me, child. Idleness will kill a man in no time."

There was no arguing with him, so Hallie dropped the subject. After Grandpa left, Hallie thought of all he had said to her. What he said about Ashe Barkley was probably true. She would do well to forget about him. But the memory of his burning lips on hers was a constant reminder of how it felt to be thoroughly kissed. She chided herself for enjoying the kiss of a gunslinger and swore she would never get herself into that predicament again.

Each day seemed endless to Hallie. She worked more hours at the ranch, and rode with the men as they moved the cattle from one grazing pasture to another. Due to the intense summer heat, she spent less time at the mission during the week. When she did go to be with the children, she moved them outside to study beneath the shade of the cottonwood tree.

The Poet Bandit, too, had taken a break in routine— not because there were no stagecoaches to rob, but because of Ashe Barkley. Hallie decided if she discontinued her masquerade for a while, Hargrove would have to find other jobs for Barkley to do. Evidently that had happened, because she had not seen Ashe for more than a month.

But Hallie was still leery of Barkley, and was conscious of waiting for him to appear at any given moment. What damaged her pride the most was that she actually missed seeing him. She had never met a man she couldn't defeat in one way or another, but Ashe Barkley was indeed a challenge to her feminine wiles. It was a game of attack on his part and counterattack on hers. To date she had been the winner, but how much longer could she deny that he had captivated a part of her emotions that she couldn't control when in his presence?

Ashe had bided his time in stalking the invincible Miss Hallie Parker. After his disastrous attempt at lovemaking that afternoon on the way to her ranch, he had decided to let the situation cool before approaching her again. Her refusal of his amorous advances had not deterred him as it would most men. No woman had ever refused him, and he would be damned if Hallie Parker would be the first. It never entered Ashe's mind that he would be fighting his biggest battle since the war. Hallie knew more secret maneuvers than Grant and Lee combined.

Ashe had never needed an excuse to approach a woman. To the contrary, in the past, women most often propositioned him. With his reputation as a bounty hunter and gunslinger, he had been surprised that any woman would select him for a bed partner, but he theorized that men with a dangerous and adventuresome nature appealed to some women. Hallie Parker was different, and he knew now she wouldn't just fall into his arms.

Today as he rode to Hallie's ranch, he convinced himself that his excuse for seeing her was to inquire about Ben Langley. How he was going to bring up the subject without showing undue interest was unknown to him, for in actuality Hallie Parker was first in his thoughts.

Knocking on her door, he stepped back and removed his hat. He saw someone peering at him through a small peephole in the door. A large white eyeball with a dark brown iris stared at him for several seconds. If this were her big Mexican friend, he probably wouldn't make it over the threshold, especially if Hallie had told her of his ungentlemanly behavior. Maria is some bodyguard, Ashe thought humorously. Then again, Hallie most definitely guarded her own body well enough without anyone's help.

He heard the door unbolt, and was surprised to see it open without a question as to his intentions.

Maria, with a crisp, white apron tied around her large middle, smiled at him nervously, her big eyes flashing in all directions. "Qué pasa, Señor Barkley? What's the matter?" she whispered. "Has something happened to Señorita Hallie?"

Slightly alarmed, Ashe said, "No, not that I know of. I only came to pay my respects to Miss Parker. Is she not here?" He tried to look behind the tall, bulky woman.

"No, she has gone with my husband and son to find some missing calves. I thought when I saw you that something might have happened to her."

"May I come in and wait for her?"

Maria hesitated. "This is not wise, Señor Barkley." She nodded her head discouragingly, but stepped aside for him to enter.

Ashe immediately saw Sinbad eyeing him surreptitiously from his cage. "Is he dangerous?"

"Maybe... maybe not. We will only find out should he ever escape. He does not like the pantry overly well," Maria said jokingly, trying to calm her uneasiness.

Ashe laughed and walked into the parlor. As he looked around, he immediately felt warmth emanating from the room, which was not spacious or cluttered. A rocking chair and small divan occupied the space in front of a huge fireplace that boasted a thick handhewn timber above the yawning hole. A clock sat on the mantel, its brass pendulum ticking away the seconds. The mouth-watering aroma of fresh bread baking wafted from the kitchen into the room.

"If you're busy, Maria, don't worry about me. I'll just have a seat and wait."

Maria glanced at the clock on the mantel. "You should not have long to wait. Hallie will be in for her dinner shortly." Then, wringing her large hands nervously, she asked, pausing slightly between words, "Are you sure you will be pleasantly received, Señor Barkley?"

"I doubt it," he answered and strolled casually to the small secretary on the far side of the room, his eyes resting on a tintype that sat on the desktop. "Is this Hallie as a child with her parents?"

Noticing Maria's silence, he glanced over his shoulder.

"Si, the only picture we have of them all together. Hallie treasures it more than any possession she brought with her."

Ashe looked at the child's impish face smiling directly at the camera. Long, thick curls fell over her shoulders, small wisps framing a pair of big eyes. The photographer had managed to capture the numerous freckles that dotted her nose and cheekbones. She sat on her father's lap while her mother leaned in close to her father. The parents made a striking couple. The woman's fair hair was piled loosely on top of her head in soft curls; the father, barely smiling, showed his amusement in his eyes.

"Where are they now?" he asked, unaware of Maria's discomfiture.

Maria heaved a deep sigh. "They are both dead. We don't talk about it anymore around this house, for it brings such sadness to mi niña. Her life has been full of tragedies."

"And full of hate," Ashe supplied, not realizing his ill-chosen words.

Maria drew back at his words. "Not so," she spat at him, then quickly calmed herself. "There is not so much hate that there is no room for love in her heart. Love emanates from her like perfume from a flower. It is just that she chooses carefully whom she bestows it upon."

"What cause does she have to dislike me?" Ashe asked. "Or is it that she dislikes men in general?"

Maria placed her hands on her large hips and stomped

across the room. Planting her enormous frame within inches of Ashe, she shook a long brown finger in his face. "Now listen to me, Señor Barkley. Can you tell me why she should have a reason to like a bounty hunter? What she needs is a warm, gentle man in her life, one who does not make a living by killing. Murderous men have played a major role in her life. Most definitely, she does not need another one breathing down her neck."

Maria's rage surprised even her. She was breathless, and stood quaking in her shoes in the aftermath. What was it about this man that made her temper flare? No wonder Hallie always came in ranting and raving every time she met with him. And there he stood like a statue; no expression on his cold, handsome face to show her that one word of what she said had registered.

Ashe remained passive, and when he spoke it was without anger. "I won't deny that if there is a bounty to be collected, I'll do my damnedest to be the one to receive it. The only difference between my job and a marshall is that I don't have to wear a badge to do it."

Neither Ashe nor Maria was aware of Hallie standing at the opened door.

"Perhaps you should run for the office next time," Hallie said, surprising both of them. "Hastings is a poor excuse for a sheriff, except when it comes to tracking down an enemy of Hargrove's. But, of course, that's why he hired you, isn't it?"

Maria and Ashe turned to face her. Maria was scared that Hallie had heard her outburst, but was too shaken to ask. She shifted her gaze restlessly from one to the other. "If you will excuse me, mi niña, I will go check the bread." She left hastily, snatching up the bird cage before Sinbad could add more fuel to the fire.

Hallie strolled through the door, casually removing her hat and placing it on the hat rack. Ashe's eyes swept her slim figure in admiration. The severe knot that usually adorned the crown of her head was replaced by a long, thick braid that hung down the middle of her back. The homespun dresses he had seen her wear were replaced by tight-fitting pants. A pair of knee-length leather boots encased her long, well-shaped legs. Beneath a leather bolero, she wore a checked shirt, sleeves rolled to the elbows. A silver chain, partially visible at the open collar of her neckline, dropped between her breasts. The strangest addition to this attire was the gun belt she wore at her waist.

"I'm afraid a badge is too confining," he said, watching her as she unbuckled her gun belt and removed the gun from the holster. She didn't answer, but brushed by him to go to the desk. Opening the drawer, she pulled out a ramrod and soft cloth and began cleaning her gun.

"Did you find your missing calves?"

"All but a few. That tricky coyote we've been after got the poor things. He won't be sneaking off with them anymore." She placed the gun in the drawer and closed it.

"Then you really know how to shoot?"

Hallie hesitated before she answered. "Yes, of course. Shot him smack-dab between the eyes when he looked up from my calf he happened to be feasting on."

"I suppose it was at close range," Ashe teased.

His remark brought Hallie up short. Her pride took control of her common sense. "No, Mr. Barkley, he was quite some distance away." Realizing her error, she quickly retreated. "But perhaps luck was with me today and not with the coyote. I've had enough training to be able to protect myself if need be. Ben Langley taught me what I know."

"Ben Langley," Ashe repeated matter-of-factly.

"Yes, he was a friend of Grandpa's." Hallie walked away from the desk, sitting down on the arm of the divan. "He sort of took me under his wing when I first came out here ten years ago. Said a woman who lived in these parts needed to know how to defend herself." Hallie smiled as she recalled her first lesson with a gun. She rested her chin on her hand, her elbow propped on the back of the divan. "My first lesson was a disaster," she admitted, her eyes sparkling.

"Most are," Ashe consoled, recalling his own experience, marveling at this relaxed side of her. Her face had lost its tenseness; her voice was lighthearted and tinged with warmth. Of course, he reminded himself, she's in home territory and not completely alone.

"Ben thought he'd do it up right. He stuffed one of his old shirts and pants with straw and made a scarecrow for a target. He plopped a gun in my hand, saying, 'Shoot the son of a bitch, Hallie, shoot to kill.'"

Ashe knew by her unusual choice of words that she was completely caught up in the memory. He was enthralled by her childlike radiance and her delight in the story.

"Well, I stood there with my hand wrapped so tightly

around that gun, you'd have thought I was trying to choke it. Aiming it, I closed my eyes just as I squeezed the trigger. The blast nearly knocked me off my feet."

For the first time, Hallie looked up at Ashe and was pleased to see his interest.

"Did you miss your target?"

"Some might say I didn't," she exclaimed, laughter threatening to overset her. "I was mortified when I saw twigs of straw falling from the crotch of the scarecrow's pants." Hallie's eyes shot open in shock when she realized what she had said and to whom. She clamped her hand quickly over her mouth.

"Go on," Ashe urged, stifling his laughter at the look on her face.

Clearing her throat, she hesitantly continued. "Ben was ... just as ... surprised as I was. He ... he stood there with his eyes popped out and his mouth wide open. I looked up at him and said, 'Ben, I forgot to tell you I am left-handed.' Ben said, 'Don't matter none, gal, I think he's done for anyways.'"

Ashe's laughter was full-throated. "Your Ben Langley must be quite a character. I'd like to meet him one day," he said, deliberately baiting her. Any information concerning Hargrove's past could be beneficial to him in his quest for revenge.

Hallie's face assumed a polite expression. "I'm afraid that's impossible. Ben disappeared after ... after ..." She looked curiously at him. "Surely you've heard the talk—especially since you work for Hargrove."

"Yes, I've heard the talk. Do you believe Ben Langley is guilty?"

Hallie got up and waved her arms. "No, Ben didn't

do it," she stated unequivocally. "I'd bet my own life on it."

"Sometimes when someone who means a great deal to us is accused of a crime, we don't want to believe he is capable of committing the crime. You evidently were very close to the situation, Hallie."

"Not to the situation—to the man. He in some ways took the place of my... my father," she replied unsteadily. "No one will ever convince me that he is a murderer." Quickly changing the subject, she went on, "I need to check on one of my horses before dinner. She's past due in delivery, and Juan's not here today to see to her."

"Do you mind if I come with you?" Ashe asked, knowing by the expression on her face that she would rather he leave. "I had a reason for coming out here today, and we could talk about it while you tend to the mare."

"Very well, if you'd like," she gave in, seeing no way to politely discourage him. But she was out of the parlor and opening the door before he was aware she had gone.

She quickened her steps to keep her distance ahead of Ashe; however, he stayed discreetly behind for the sole purpose of watching her walk in the tight pants. The heat rising within him had nothing to do with the extremely hot day.

As he entered the long corridor of the stable, Ashe saw Hallie disappear into one of the stalls. He noticed that most of the stalls had occupants.

The stable was immaculate. Of course, everything Miss Parker did had to be the best. He wondered if she would be the best in other things... particularly making love. With this thought, he joined her in the stall.

Hallie was stroking the chestnut mare's nose, whispering softly to her. "You're going to be fine... just fine, girl. It won't be much longer."

She looked at Ashe with worried concern. "Juan thinks it may be a stillbirth. There's been no movement in a week."

"That's a shame. Is the father as fine a breed as the mother?"

"You should know. Rebel's the father."

Hallie's heart skipped a beat when Ashe smiled. Oh, if he weren't so blasted handsome, I would be able to ignore him, she berated herself. She returned her attention to the mare.

"Rebel seems to get around, doesn't he?" Ashe commented. "If you should require stud services, I'm sure we can work out something."

Hallie flushed; she knew that mating the horses was not what he had in mind. "Rebel's services will not be required, Mr. Barkley. There are others just as capable... and they are not quite as arrogant and uncivilized as he."

"Sometimes it takes a spirited stallion to tame a feisty, willful mare," Ashe countered.

Damn him, Hallie cursed inwardly. Why is he taunting me this way? Thrusting her nose into the air—a habit Ashe was tiring of quickly—Hallie whipped past him like a whirlwind. Ashe reached over her shoulder, gripped her nose, and turned her around. "If that freckled nose of yours gets any higher in the air, it'll scrape the ceiling."

She slapped his hand away, visibly trembling with anger. "Just what was your reason for coming out here today, anyway? To humiliate me further? Did I not make myself clear that day in town when you manhandled me in front of all those people? If not, then I'll try again." The condescending smile on his mouth increased her fury. "It may come as a shock to you, Ashe Barkley, but I was raised a lady, and I had a good teacher. My mother." She caught her breath. She had never talked to anyone about Estella Parker except Maria. That was a private memory which he had no right to intrude upon.

A gentleness touched the hard planes of Ashe's features. "Do you want to tell me about your mother?"

Hallie lowered her eyes to hide the sadness. With her boot, she nervously raked a path through the scattered straw on the dirt floor. "No, Ashe, I can't. All I will say is that I loved her. And I doubt she'd approve of *you!*"

He didn't stop her as she left the stall. For a few moments she stood motionless in the aisle, then walked to an empty stall across the way. Ashe followed her. He watched her as she retrieved a pitchfork and began filling a small cart with straw.

"Can I help you?"

"No, I'm perfectly capable of doing this myself."

Her guard was up again, and it infuriated Ashe.

"If you're the lady you claim to be, you'll allow a man to help you when he offers."

Hallie stabbed the pitchfork into the ground and

turned to meet his angry face. "Oh for God's sake," she moaned, "do it and then please be on your way."

Ashe finished filling the cart. "Now, where do you want me to carry it?"

"Outside the stall we just left. We may need it tonight."

Hallie watched him lift the heavy cart effortlessly and pull it across the aisle. His strides were long and purposeful. She gazed in awe as the fabric of his pants strained against the flexed muscles of his thighs. She thought of the strength of his arms and how she felt the day he had held her tightly.

Dropping the cart handle, he brushed his hands off on his pants. "Now, is there anything else I can do for you, milady?"

Hallie didn't trust her tumultuous emotions and was quick to reply, "No, thank you. Please leave now."

"Not until I tell you the reason I came out here today."

"And what could that be? Is Rebel giving you problems?" she parried insolently.

"No, Rebel and I are getting along just fine. I wish I could say the same for us. My intention was to apologize." A crooked smile lifted his mustache, the dimple deepening his cheek.

She shot him a suspicious look. "That doesn't quite suit your character, Ashe. But, I suppose I should be grateful for even that much," she said, her tongue innocently wetting her lips. "Which time are you apologizing for?"

"All but one," he answered, smiling down at her.

Her pouting rosebud mouth was tempting him to

smother it with his own. He could almost taste her sweetness. His stomach drew into tight knots. She was so alluring; her tongue challenged him with its playful antics.

His voice was seductively low. "Seems like I gave something to you the other day that you didn't want. I've come to retrieve it."

A frown creased her brow. "You've given me nothing but trouble."

Ashe's hand left his side and reached for the heavy braid that draped over her breast. Hallie lowered her head, watching him wind it around his large hand and stroking it with his thumb. It was as though her hair were alive. Uncertain of his motives and the unsettling emotions he was stirring within her, she stepped away from him.

"No, Hallie, don't pull away from something you want," he said, gripping the braid and bringing her body to rest against his hard chest.

She protested weakly, "How would you know what I want, Ashe?"

He tilted her chin upward, his thumb caressing the contour of her lips. "Believe me, I know," he said softly. "I'm not going to take from you what you don't want to give, Hallie."

Lowering his mouth, he felt her grow tense in his arms. "Relax," he crooned, brushing his lips lightly across her cheek, then to the lobe of her ear.

His warm breath sent shivers up and down her body. She tilted her head to the side as his teeth bit lightly at her earlobe, then trailed down to the crook of her neck.

Take it slowly, Ashe warned himself. Let her catch up with her emotions. His mouth rested on the pulse of her throat, feeling the erratic beating of her racing heart. He felt her lean into him, felt her softness against his hard flesh.

As she turned her head, her face brushed the coarse growth of beard on his cheek. His steel-gray eyes met hers, and she saw in them the duskiness of gathering clouds before a storm. They trapped her, mesmerizing her with their unpredictable desire. The air grew pregnant with her anticipation. She wanted him to kiss her, needed his hard male strength to comfort her. She had never wanted any man before, but she wanted Ashe Barkley. Perhaps it was because she had never allowed a man to touch her mind, her body.

"Why are you doing this to me?" she murmured throatily.

"Because you want me to."

Slowly, deliberately, he lowered his mouth, his lips moving over her cheekbone and down to linger at the corner of her mouth. "Tell me to stop, Hallie, and I will."

She was caught up in a vortex of emotion, rendered senseless by his power of persuasion. She moved firmly against his body, breathing, "No, I want you to kiss me."

"God, Hallie..." He kissed her gently, stroking her shoulder. Her lips quivered beneath his gentle exploration of her mouth. Her heart beat so rapidly in her chest, she thought it would leap from its stronghold. He lifted his lips from hers to gaze into her eyes. He kissed her again, and she returned it fiercely, wanting to put an end to his teasing. His lips were hot as a branding iron. There was a savage urgency in their conquest, but Hallie's lips were burning no less. She answered kiss for kiss, her hands moving of their own accord to the nape of his neck, her fingers twining in the coarse, thick hair.

Ashe broke the kiss, rubbing his chin against her cheek. "You feel so damn good," he whispered shakily, as though his breath were not coming easily.

Hallie touched his face, her finger tracing his hairline, his ear, and down the line of his cheek. "You, too," she murmured.

His muscular body pressed full against her slenderness. He became aware that the hand still clutching her braid now rested in the valley between her breasts. He felt their soft fullness crushed around his hand and ached to caress them. He imagined his mouth covering them, his tongue teasing the rosy peaks to exquisite tautness.

He kissed her possessively, pressing his mouth firmly against hers as though she intended to run away from him. His knuckles moved against a knobby object, and he remembered the chain he'd seen earlier. He closed his fingers around it and drew it from beneath her shirt.

"What's this?" he asked, noticing the beautiful craftsmanship of the necklace. On the end of the long chain was a large silver disc embedded with turquoise stones.

Hallie smiled up at him, desire still apparent in her eyes. "A friend gave it to me many years ago. I'll tell you about it someday... but not now."

Ashe dropped it into her blouse. Finding that comfortable soft spot between her breasts, he recaptured the braid as an excuse to rest his hand again in its fullness.

"I agree," he said huskily and once again tasted the sweetness of her mouth.

Hallie sought his lips, exploring their hot, soft fullness. She trembled at the tickling sensation of his mustache beneath her nose; savored the taste of tobacco on his lips, the roughness of his cheek as it rubbed her tender flesh. Never had she felt so alive. Every delicate nerve ending in her body burned like wildfire.

She felt herself being lifted up, and momentarily she gazed into Ashe's desire-filled eyes. She asked no questions when he lowered her to the bed of straw in the corner of the stall. All she wanted was the feel of his sinewy, rock-hard body against her own, his lips taking hers with their sweet savage assault.

He anchored her beneath him with his long leg draped over her thigh. Desire surged through her, unfamiliar but acceptable. His tongue penetrated her lips. This time she didn't rebel, but parted them willingly, accepting and pleasuring herself with his heated intrusion. Her tongue met his daringly, and skimmed lightly over the evenness of his teeth, then into the deepest recesses of his mouth.

Ashe's imagination blossomed to its fullest. No longer was it his tongue invading her, but that part of his body that ached to find fulfillment in her womanly softness. The pressure of his mouth increased, his tongue leaving no part of her sweet mouth unexplored. His desires raced, snapping his last shred of control.

God, how I want her, he groaned silently with overwhelming passion. His hand enveloped her full breast, kneading urgently. He tossed the chain behind her neck to give him unimpeded access to her lovely breasts. He felt her struggle beneath him, but he was too carried away to stop his efforts. He wanted her skin next to his. His fingers adroitly unbuttoned her shirt and found their way to the silky mounds beneath.

Hallie moaned into his mouth, then pulled her lips free of his. She thrashed her head back and forth in the straw, trying to find the courage to ask him to stop tormenting her this way.

He brushed his palm lightly over the tip of her breast and felt the pebble hardness of its peak. Aroused by her desire, he gently rolled her nipple between his fingers, causing shuddering sensations in her loins. She whimpered, and he drowned out her protests with his mouth. She arched her back. He taunted the other breast in the same manner, bringing her under his seductive powers.

What's happening to me? Hallie screamed inside. She never intended for her desires to run away like this. It was wrong to give in to this man. You are like Sophie, she berated herself. Ladies don't let men take advantage of them this way. But God, how good it feels.

His hands moved to the front clasp of her pants. An alarm went off in her brain. She pulled her lips from his, her eyes wide with fright.

"No, dear God, don't Ashe," she cried softly. "I can't... please."

Her hands pushed at his as he skillfully unbuttoned

her pants. The harder she fought him, the more insistent his other hand became on her breasts as he manipulated her pain-pleasured nipples.

"Stop, you little fool," he groaned hoarsely, "I'm not going to rape you."

An animallike scream welled up inside her. "Then what are you doing to me!"

"What you were meant for, Hallie," he said, stopping long enough to gaze into her luminous, passion-filled eyes. Her expression was an intermingling of anger and aroused passion.

She tried to act indignant, but she was in a mild state of shock at what she almost had allowed to happen. It wasn't all his fault. She was as much to blame as he.

"I'm through playing games with you, Ashe Barkley," she said, pushing him aside and sitting up.

Ashe rolled to his side, the pain in his loins so great it hurt with the effort. He looked across at her and said slowly, "I don't know how to play games, Hallie, but you seem to be an expert."

There was an awkward silence. Ashe rose to his feet and turned from her. But Hallie had seen the unmistakable evidence of his desire and was amazed how easily a woman could arouse such passion in a man.

She struggled to find the right words. "Ashe...I never meant for this to happen, believe me. I don't know what got into me."

He said, "Don't you? You seduced me, Hallie."

"I what!" she screamed. "Don't you have things

confused a bit, Ashe? You came here with that thought in mind, did you not?"

"Yes, but I never expected to have the tables turned on me," he said. He turned to her with his bold grin. "You're damned hard to figure out, Hallie. First you beat me with your purse, then you fall willingly into my arms. What can I expect the next time?"

He watched the rapid rise and fall of her breasts beneath her unbuttoned shirt. All the time he had delighted in fondling those creamy mounds that were partially visible to him now, he had never actually seen them. But he had marveled in the feel of them—small, yet full and soft. He recalled how they seemed to swell in his hands as he aroused her with his urgent caresses.

Hallie stood up, placing her hands on her hips, which parted the blouse further from her breasts. "There won't be a next time, Mr. Barkley."

Ashe felt his breath quicken in anticipation. "Oh yes, there'll be a next time, Miss Parker. I'll make damn sure of it."

His eyes were snagged on her open shirt as though he could will it to disappear.

"I'll avoid you like the plague."

"You've already tried that, but it didn't work."

Hallie frowned and unconsciously looked down where his eyes were boldly fastened. She gasped in mortification, turned and quickly buttoned her shirt.

"Damn you," she hissed, shaking the straw from her hair. "Just go!"

Ashe laughed at her discomfort. "I've already touched the forbidden fruit you'd rather no one knew existed. You're a warm-blooded temptress, Hallie, and

I aim to get a fuller taste of your delectable charms another time."

"No man has touched me in such a manner and no man ever will again," she hissed at him.

"I did," he said matter-of-factly, "and I will again."

Picking up his hat, he walked casually into the corridor, leaving her in her fury. Turning, he grinned and raked his eyes boldly over her body. "Button your pants, Hallie. I'd hate to see you trip over them." Then he laughed outrageously. "Maybe it wouldn't be such a bad idea after all . . . to catch Miss Hallie Parker with her pants down for once."

"Go to hell, Ashe Barkley!"

He slapped his hat against his thigh to remove the straw. "Thanks, but no thanks. I've already been there and I find the climate here quite similar."

Hallie could think of no other words to throw at him. She could only stare at him in fury. She heard his footsteps fade; then she sat down in the straw to regain her composure before she went into the house.

As Ashe untied Rebel, Maria came out on the porch. "Where is Hallie? Supper is ready."

"She's still in the stable cooling off," Ashe said, mounting his horse.

"What you mean, Sēnor Barkley?"

He grinned at her. "Well, Maria, you were right after all. I wasn't pleasantly received."

Looking questioningly at him, she asked, "What you say to her?"

"I told her I'd be back." Then he added, "Among other things."

Maria rolled her large brown eyes. "You are one

crazy hombre, sēnor, muy loco." She watched Ashe depart, then called out to Hallie to come to supper.

Oh mi niña, he is such a man. If only things could be different. She shrugged her large shoulders in despair.

Chapter 6

The heavy ornate door leading into Hargrove's study was half-opened, and the aroma of an expensive cigar drifted into the large foyer. Ashe glanced up the winding staircase and down again to the marble floor. Each time he stepped into this house, he was sickened by the lavish display of Hargrove's wealth.

Hargrove's home reminded Ashe of those glorious old Southern plantations he had seen during the war. It seemed out of place sitting on red dirt surrounded by cacti and barren mountains.

Before he knocked on the open door to announce his arrival, he studied Vern Hargrove's large sausage figure which was sprawled comfortably in his fine-tooled leather chair behind a massive walnut desk. His booted feet rested on the desk as he leaned back in his chair, puffing idly on a cigar that matched his size. His overly thick lips formed smoke rings while his beady eyes followed the smoke ascending to the high ceiling.

A sneer curled Ashe's lips. Bastard, he thought. Acts like a damn king, sitting on a throne and issuing orders to peons. With that thought, he strolled leisurely into the room, not bothering to knock.

Hargrove immediately choked and lowered his feet to the floor, noticeably embarrassed at having been caught daydreaming. He pounded his fist on the desk, jarring the fragile porcelain lamp that threatened to fall off the corner.

"Damn your hide, man, don't you know to knock before you enter?"

Ashe smiled crookedly and sat down in a plump Queen Anne chair, his long legs stretching out before him. "You asked me to stop by when we finished the branding. What is it you want this time, Hargrove?" He pulled a tobacco pouch from his vest pocket and casually rolled a cigarette.

Hargrove's mouth sliced into a mean grin, the mammoth cigar wedged like a giant toothpick between his teeth. "We're gonnna have to get down to serious business, boy. Gotta hell of a lotta cash coming to me from the mint in San Francisco."

Ashe took a long draw on his cigarette. "Don't you always?"

"Not the size of this one. If the Bandit got wind of this, he could retire for life. That silver mine that Grady Parker lost to me years ago has finally paid off," Hargrove said brazenly. "I got me one of them new machines that dig down deep . . . and what it cost me paid off."

Ashe was in no mood to hear Hargrove's boasting. He let his eyes stray to the portrait that hung over the fireplace mantel. He concentrated on the woman who seemed to reach out to him with her haunting gray eyes.

"Why'd the two of you never have children, Vern? Seems to me a man as affluent as you would want a son or daughter to inherit your fortune one day."

Ashe examined Vern's face as he awaited an answer. He had most assuredly struck a sore spot. Vern's face turned livid with rage. "It ain't none of your damn business."

Ashe rose and walked across the room to gaze intently at the portrait of the small, frail woman with the faint, melancholy smile.

Why would anyone kill such a woman? Ashe wondered. "Did she always look so sad?" Ashe asked, looking over his shoulder at Hargrove who seemed rather nervous.

"No, not always. She was a beautiful woman when I married her, but don't let her innocent face deceive you," Hargrove said maliciously. "She was any man's woman."

"I find that hard to believe, Hargrove."

Hargrove angrily ground his cigar in the ashtray. "It's true. The whole time we was married, I knew what she was doing; but I stayed with her, hopin' she'd change her ways. After a while I ignored it, and considered myself lucky she didn't have some man's bastard. Ben Langley was just one man among many that she consorted with."

A muscle twitched in Ashe's cheek. "Are you sure they were having an affair?"

Hargrove smiled diabolically. "Sure I'm sure. Why else would she have sneaked off to that mine? They must have had a powerful big argument for him to murder her. 'Course, he didn't have no right to kill her. She was my wife, after all. If I had caught him, I'd have killed him with my bare hands. Even though she weren't no count, she was mine... and nobody takes what's mine."

"Why didn't you just divorce her when she didn't change?"

"What? Divorce?" Hargrove seemed utterly appalled by Ashe's suggestion. "And sully my reputation? I'm an important man, Mr. Barkley, and what man wants it to be known that he married a whore?"

Ashe chuckled humorlessly. "If she'd bedded that many men, Hargrove, I'm sure her insatiable appetite for men was well known by everyone."

Hargrove's eyes nearly bulged from his head. "Let's drop the damned subject. I didn't call you in here to give you my life's history. Now sit down and let's discuss my plans for gettin' this money in here without that brazen bandit gettin' his paws on it."

Hargrove closed the door to the study and took his seat. "What I say to you goes no further than this room, you hear?"

Ashe leaned back in his chair. "That's what you pay me for, isn't it, Hargrove?"

Hargrove stared hard at Ashe. The man's quiet, deadly demeanor caused him to feel uncertain and uneasy. He had yet to trust Ashe and wondered if he ever would.

The second Ashe stepped out of Hargrove's house and saw several of the ranch hands eyeing him awkwardly, he had an uneasy feeling that something was wrong. Then he saw Jake Olsen standing at the door to his bunkroom with a malicious snarl on his upper lip.

Olsen was one man Ashe tried to keep his distance from if at all possible. He was a great rock of a man, barrel-chested, and weighing close to three hundred pounds, all of it hard muscle. He didn't like Ashe, and he went out of his way to pick fights. On several occasions Ashe had come close to calling him out and ending it once and for all. But Olsen was known for his brute strength, and Ashe was not ready to have his face smashed in. And Olsen would definitely choose his fists over a gun.

Now it appeared that Ashe was forced to be in the man's company for at least three days. Hargrove had chosen Olsen and two other disreputable men to bring his shipment from San Francisco. Ashe was to meet them in Tucson to make the trip on in to Prospect City. Lem McPhail and Farley Adsit weren't regulars at the ranch. Hargrove based them in San Francisco to handle his dealings there. All three had been in Hargrove's hire since Hargrove first came to Prospect City. Rumor among the ranch hands was that Hargrove only used them for special assignments... and what signified special assignments Ashe thought he probably could guess.

When Ashe was within ten feet of Olsen, Olsen moved his massive frame in front of the door to block Ashe from entering his room.

Ashe ignored the man and stepped onto the porch.

"Excuse me," he said undauntedly. "You're blocking my way."

"That was my intention, Barkley," Olsen said, an evil sneer curling his thin lip. "We got things to talk about."

Ashe shoved his hat back and narrowed his eyes. "As far as I'm concerned, we have nothing to say to each other. You dislike me for some unknown reason, and frankly speaking, I don't give a damn. Now back off before I decide I like you even less," he said, nudging Olsen's massive body with his shoulder so he could enter his room.

Olsen placed his large hand directly on Ashe's chest, shoving him back. "You're steppin' in where ya don't belong."

"That's my damn room, and I'm stepping in," Ashe said curtly. "I've had it with your threats, Olsen. If you want a fight, I'll oblige you."

"You wouldn't stand a chance, Barkley, and after this trip we're makin' for the boss, I'll prove it. And there's one more thing," Olsen said, stepping aside slightly. "If anyone gets the bounty on the Poet Bandit, it's gonna be me. Hargrove is offering a pretty penny for his capture, and I'm gonna be the one to get it. I've worked here longer than you, and I don't like someone movin' in on my territory, understand?"

"Maybe you should talk to Hargrove about it, Olsen.

Evidently he gave up on you a long time ago." Ashe pushed him aside, and opened the door to his room.

"Just one minute, Barkley."

Ashe turned, noticing that several of the men who had been wandering back and forth paused at Olsen's order.

"What is it?" Ashe asked, casually leaning back against the doorjamb. "I'm tired as hell and don't have time to waste on you."

"This shipment we're bringin' back..." Olsen said quietly. "If that bandit should happen to make an appearance, you watch them guns of yours. He's mine."

"He belongs to whoever gets him first, Olsen. You read me?"

Olsen glared menacingly at Ashe, his large chest swelling at Ashe's remark. His voice bellowed in rage. "You won't live to spend your bounty, Barkley. If you collect it."

Olsen checked Ashe's face to see if he had gotten his message across, but it remained expressionless.

"And you, mi enemigo, will not live long enough to see me enjoy my reward," Ashe said, resting his hand on his holster. "Don't think for one second that it wouldn't give me great pleasure to blow your pockmarked face to hell. Stay out of my way, for it's mighty tempting at this time."

Ashe entered his room and pushed the door closed with a briskness that belied his anger. As he freshened up for supper, he heard a rap on his door. Opening it, he saw Bart Jordon, the oldest cowpoke at the ranch, solemnly standing there.

"Mind if I come in? Got somethin' to say I figger you might be needin' to know."

Ashe smiled and stepped back. "Sure, come on in."

If Bart had something to talk about, Ashe definitely wanted to hear what it was. Bart was not one for saying much, but when he did, it was generally worth listening to.

"Jest thought you needed to know that the last foreman, Sam Carter, died in his sleep."

Ashe raised his brows. "And I assume it wasn't from natural causes."

Bart took off his hat, which was as weatherbeaten as Bart himself. "Not unless a bullet between the eyes is considered natural. Found him right there," he said, pointing a finger, "in that same bed you're sleepin' in now."

"Did you catch the murderer?"

Bart's scraggly eyebrows met in the middle as he frowned. "No. But we have our own ideas as to who done him in." Scratching his nose, he continued, "Me and the boys don't know you none too well, Barkley, but it seems only fair to warn you you're treadin' on dangerous ground. Foremen don't last very long around here."

"Thanks, Bart, I get the message loud and clear."

Turning, Bart went to the door, then hesitated. "If I was you, I'd sleep with a loaded pistol under my pillow. I hope you be a light sleeper. Carter wasn't."

The door closed behind Bart, and Ashe stared at it for several seconds, narrowing his eyes in deep thought. No matter what happened, Hargrove would be his... when the time was right.

* * *

That night after supper, Ashe lay on his bunk trying to sleep, but his mind was a jumble of thoughts. He thought of the woman who had intruded into his life. What the hell did he see in the Yankee-hating, strait-laced Miss Hallie Parker?

Now there's a question I can answer, he thought in amusement. She's damn beautiful and about as easy to control as the weather. Ashe had never dealt with a self-righteous virgin, but most certainly, that afternoon in the stable had removed all barriers when she willingly accepted his loveplay. Almost willingly, he thought, smiling into the darkness.

He sensed in Hallie a tremendous inner struggle to maintain her rigid reserve. She seemed torn between allowing her passions to flow freely and damming it up inside her. Just from that one taste of Hallie in the throes of desire, Ashe knew he wanted to be on the receiving end of the pure sweet passion that would pour from her like a raging river out of control if she ever chose to release her emotions again.

What would he do with her if he won his conquest? Not if . . . when . . . he corrected his thoughts. Most assuredly, he would have to change his method of approaching her. Though she looked fragile and helpless, Hallie Parker was the most strong-willed and cocky woman he had ever run into. He had managed to bring Rebel under partial control. But he doubted gentle words and soft caresses with the promise of a lump of sugar would ever make Hallie give in to her desires.

Running his finger across his mustache, he closed his eyes, thinking delicious, sensual thoughts of Hallie

Parker stripped of her spinster trappings and lying warm and naked beneath him.

Sweat trickled between Hallie's breasts as the noon sun beat down relentlessly on her and her magnificent black steed. With every step, she bemoaned the fates that had placed her in this predicament. She had ridden to the mine yesterday to try to talk her grandfather into giving up the idea of moving into the lineshack. Luis had taken the buckboard, loaded down with things to make Grady more comfortable, to the mine. Hallie had ranted and raved, but nothing would change Grady's mind. "Lass, how do you expect me to ever do any good at the mine if I only give it a lick and a promise? If I stay at the ranch, it takes me a half a day just to get to the mine. Then when I get going good, it's time to start back home," he said in exasperation. "If I stay at the mine for a spell, my chances for a strike are a hell of a lot better. I want to put machinery in here and really get down to business. Ben had his heart set on working the mine. When he comes back here, I want to have something to show him."

"Grandpa," she said sadly, "Ben can't come back here—not until his name has been cleared."

"If I can make the mine pay off, I can hire one of those fancy lawyers to get to the bottom of Sarah's murder. We both know Ben is innocent. We just have to prove it before Ben comes riding in here and they hang him without giving him the benefit of a fair trial."

"Grandpa, don't you think you could make more money if we really worked the ranch? We could raise more cattle and horses. I'd help, Grandpa. I would work with you," she pleaded.

How could she tell her grandfather she was already checking on a lawyer who would help her clear Ben's name?

"No, Hallie. The ranch is your love, not mine. The way your eyes light up after you've stayed up all night helping to bring a new foal into the world; the way your heart pounds and your palms sweat when it takes its first wobbly steps. That's the way I feel when I find a good chunk of ore. Blood rushes through my veins like it's trying to break free, and I too break out into a cold sweat. Can you not understand, Hallie? How I love it? It's my strength. Take it away and you might as well plant me six-feet deep." His eyes implored her to understand.

"I understand, Grandpa, truly I do. I just don't want you to move up here. Who will take care of you?"

"Juan's son Miguel will be here with me. He's a pretty fair cook, so we won't starve." He laughed, patting her on the back. "It's not like I won't be around. I'll be coming home every couple of weeks for supplies. And you'll be all right. You have Maria and Juan. If you need me, send someone to fetch me," he said with a smile, knowing he was finally wearing her down.

Finally giving in to his pleas, she hugged him fiercely and promised to try to accept his decision. She spent the night at the lineshack. Across the room, her grandfather snored peacefully while she tossed and turned on a lumpy, hard mattress.

As she lay awake, visions of steel-gray eyes haunted

her. Warm, sensuous lips had sought hers until, exhausted, she drifted to sleep in the strong embrace of one Ashe Barkley.

She had expected to be home long before now, but Licorice had lost a shoe and she couldn't bring herself to ride him. His foot was swollen and he was limping. Her own feet were faring no better. Her boots were definitely not made for walking mile after lonely mile.

"Not much farther, boy. We'll rest when we get to that tree up ahead," she promised.

Licorice snorted and his ears perked up. Glancing around, Hallie noticed a billowing cloud of dust. Several riders bore down on her. She grabbed her glasses from her saddlebag and buttoned her blouse.

As they drew closer, Hallie cringed. Hargrove was leading the pack, his generous bulk spreading like raw dough over his saddle.

"Well, saints deliver me, if it ain't Miss Hallie out here all by her lonesome. Guess you ain't gonna be so uppity when you're out here leading a lame horse," he sneered.

Angrily, Hallie spat at the ground beneath Hargrove.

"What's the matter? Didn't you have the guts to shoot the horse?" Drawing his rifle, he cocked it and aimed at Licorice's head. "Well, it don't bother me none. I'll do the honors."

Hallie couldn't move. She stood motionless, gaping at him until a cold, determined voice broke in, "I don't think so, Vern."

Turning, Hallie saw Ashe Barkley with one arm propped casually over his saddle horn. His rifle rested in the crook of his arm, pointing directly at Vern Hargrove. The dangerous glint in his storm-gray eyes left no doubt in anyone's mind of his intention.

"You'd go against me, Barkley?" Hargrove stormed.

"If need be. If that's what it takes to save good horseflesh," he answered coldly.

A chill ran up Hargrove's spine. "Hell, a lame horse ain't good for nothin'. All you can do is shoot him. Quit pointin' that rifle at me," he sputtered, lowering his own. "Have it your way, but let me tell you a thing or two. You work for me. I pay your wages. Don't you ever point a gun at me again, 'cause I'll kill you."

"Mighty big words for a man looking down the wrong end of the barrel."

The words struck their mark. Digging his heels into his horse's flanks, Hargrove turned, the other riders following suit. He called back over his shoulder, "That's one skirt you won't be gettin' under, Barkley. I'd say she's plannin' on takin' her virginity to her grave."

With that final insult, Hargrove was off, leaving a cloud of dust in his wake and a very red-faced Hallie humiliated beyond words. Her mortification was soon overcome by her anger.

"Bastard," she hissed, gazing at the retreating riders. She was unaware that Ashe had dismounted—until strong hands clasped her shoulders and gently turned her. He cupped her chin and lifted her face. "I'm sorry, Hallie. He was just running off at the mouth."

Her large blue eyes searched his face. He seemed sincere, and he had helped her. Gone against Hargrove to help her, she corrected herself. The corners of her mouth twitched into a full-fledged smile.

Ashe's heart turned over.

"Sticks and stones..." she recited, her eyes dancing. "Thank you, Mr. Barkley. It seems I'm once again in your debt."

"I'll call it in one day." Smiling, he turned to Licorice and lifted the horse's fetlock, examining the hoof. "A bad stone bruise. When did he lose his shoe?" he asked, gently rubbing the horse's leg.

"About two hours ago, I guess, though it seems more like ten."

"So you've had a long walk."

"A very long walk. I'd like nothing better than to sit and rest my poor abused feet."

Abruptly lifting her into his arms, he placed her on Rebel's back. "You ride on up there to the shade of that tree, and I'll lead Licorice. We can rest awhile, then I'll see you back to your ranch."

"You don't have to do that. I'm quite capable of getting home on my own," she snapped, ruffled at his high-handed manner.

Ignoring her outburst, he asked, "What kind of a fool name is Licorice? That's candy. With a Dixie and a Rebel and that damn Sinbad... and Lord knows what else, how did you ever come up with Licorice?"

Tossing her head, she answered softly, "I didn't name Sinbad."

"Thank God for that! You'd probably have called him Lee. By the way, what did you name the stray dog, Jefferson Davis?"

Hallie had the grace to blush.

Throwing back his head, he laughed royally. "See what I mean?" he choked. "Why Licorice?"

As they reached the spreading limbs of the paloverde tree, Ashe's arms gently helped her from the horse. Taking a blanket roll from his horse's back, he spread it on the ground. "After you," he indicated with a sweeping gesture of his arm.

"Thank you." Smiling hesitantly, she lowered herself to the blanket. "I named him 'Dawg'."

Ashe laughed. "Now tell me why Licorice?" he asked, lying down beside her and stretching out his long legs.

"I spent some time with the Indians when I was a child. When I was brought back to my grandfather, he and his partner, Ben, spoiled me terribly. Every time one of them went into town he invariably brought me licorice. They were so pleased with their gift that I didn't have the heart to tell them I hated licorice. I would thank them very graciously, then try my level best to get rid of it without getting caught. Hence the name Licorice—sort of a tribute to their loving kindness. And I do love my horse, so it's no longer a lie that I love licorice," she answered, her eyes twinkling with mischief.

Ashe propped himself up on an elbow, his eyebrow cocked in puzzlement. "What's this about the Indians?"

Hallie, surprised that she could talk so easily with Ashe, recounted her experience.

"This necklace you asked me about..." she said, reaching down into her blouse to remove the heavy medallion. "Sundog gave it to me. It's a good-luck charm."

"You're just full of surprises, aren't you?" he commented.

You don't know the half of it, she thought, quickly turning her head away lest he discover the blush that stained her cheeks.

"Did you get a look at the men who killed your father?"

"No, just a glimpse of their backs. They were too far away," she said angrily. "It's been so many years now since it happened, I doubt if I could ever find them, so I've given up."

Removing her hat, she repinned the strands of auburn hair that had worked free from her usual severely knotted hairstyle.

"Why do you bind your hair up like that?" Ashe asked, watching her movements.

"It gets in my way, otherwise." Turning to face him, she went on, "I've bent your ear enough for one day. Tell me about yourself, Ashe."

A shadow veiled his eyes, barely discernible, except that Hallie was looking straight at him. It was gone so quickly that she wondered if she had imagined it. His jaw became set, indicating that she had struck a nerve.

But she persisted. "Where are you from?"

Removing his hat, he raked his fingers through the curly black hair. Cushioning his hands behind his head, he stared pensively through the lofty branches of the tree. He took so long to reply, Hallie began to wonder if he had heard her at all.

As if the words were pried from him, he finally said, "Everywhere... nowhere."

Her puzzled eyes searched his face. "Everyone is from somewhere," she countered.

"Does it matter, Hallie?"

"No, I guess not. I was just wondering," she said, looking into his gray eyes. A surge of fear raced through her. Suddenly her dilemma struck her full-force. What in the world was she doing out here miles from nowhere with a notorious bounty hunter? She drew her knees toward her to stand when Ashe's hand closed over her shoulder. "Don't go."

The seductive tone of his voice made her recall his actions in the stable. "I need to. Maria will be worried."

"Are you sure that's the reason? You seem frightened all of a sudden. I'm not going to hurt you."

"No, but you're not going to reveal anything about yourself, either. You seem to keep everything bottled up. Your insides must be like a raging volcano," she snapped.

"Not that I've noticed." His smile was slow, deliberate. "What would you like to know, Hallie?"

His smile confused her. What manner of game was he playing now?

Puzzled, she asked, "Why did you go against Hargrove on my behalf? Won't you lose your job?"

"It matters little to me whether I lose it. He sought me out, not the other way around. I won't stand by and watch anyone mistreat an animal... or a woman."

She asked hesitantly, "Would you have shot him, Ashe?"

"We'll never know, will we?" he answered, shrugging his shoulders. Reaching for a loosened wisp of her copper hair, he wrapped it around his fingers, gazing intently at his hand.

"Are you really a bounty hunter?"

Raising his head, he met her look unflinchingly. "I've collected a few bounties."

"Are you here to collect the bounty on the Poet Bandit?"

"I work for Hargrove, and if the opportunity arises for me to get the so-called Poet Bandit, then I'll get him. Let there be no doubt about it."

Fear churned against the walls of Hallie's stomach. Her hands became damp with perspiration. "Maybe the opportunity won't present itself. Could be that the bandit has retired," she said hopefully.

"If he doesn't want his neck stretched, I'd say that would be the wisest thing for him to do. Hargrove is really changing his tactics this time," he said.

Hallie's interest perked up. "What do you mean by 'this time'?"

"Hargrove's got a lot of money coming in from San Francisco. He's not sending it on the stagecoach for fear of being robbed. So he's hiding it aboard a freight wagon that's bringing in machinery for the mines. Who would bother to rob a freight wagon? He figures he's outsmarted the Poet Bandit at last."

Hallie missed the sly smile that tugged at the corners of Ashe's mouth. Her mind was scrambling over the information that Ashe had unwisely laid in her lap. So that bastard Hargrove thought to outsmart the "Poet

Bandit." Well, we'll see who outsmarts whom, she thought gleefully.

Suppressing the urge to burst out laughing at her newfound knowledge, she capitulated, "Smart man, Hargrove."

"I never thought I'd live to hear you say anything good about Hargrove," Ashe said. "Are you sure you haven't been in the sun too long? Here, let me see if you're feverish," he said, leaning over to place a hand on her forehead.

Hallie laughed and asked impishly, "Well?"

"No, you don't seem to have a fever."

Inside, Ashe ached to hold her in his arms, to be consumed by the fire her presence always kindled. But his mind shouted out to him, go slow, don't push. Because if you push, she'll be forced to push back. So, strapping his desire with bands of steel, he tweaked her nose and leaned back on his haunches, never taking his eyes from her.

"If you feel rested, I'll take you home."

"Yes, I'm fine, and I do need to be getting back," she replied with a touch of disappointment.

Drawing her to her feet, he was struck once again by her uncommon beauty. Her skin was the color of honey. Large, questioning blue eyes were framed with thick dark lashes. Noticing the absence of her glasses, he scanned the blanket until he discovered where she had laid them. Picking them up, he asked with a smile, "Do you need these? You're very careless with them."

"No, it's too hot. Every step I took, they would slide down my nose," she replied, placing them in the pocket of her shirt.

Positioning her on Rebel, Ashe gathered Licorice's reins and mounted behind Hallie, drawing her close against his chest. The clean smell of her hair surrounded him. Drawing deep breaths of the sweet fragrance, he rested his chin on her head.

"We'll take it slow, Hallie. I don't want Licorice to be in pain than necessary."

His voice was husky, causing tremors to cavort along Hallie's nerve endings. Quickly banishing her wayward thoughts, she asked, "What was Hargrove doing out this far from his ranch?"

"A wild stallion has been giving Hargrove trouble. He lost several mares to that devil, and thought he had the corral fixed where nothing short of a tornado could tear it down. But when that stallion appears, snorting and rearing his mighty head, those mares would go through fire to get to him. I'll have to give him credit— he's a smart devil," he said laughingly.

"Last night everyone was asleep when I heard this terrible ruckus. When I got to the stables, that white devil had done his damage, and along with that, he had several mares following in his path. I got a glimpse of him, and he's something to behold."

"So the Poet Bandit isn't the only one after Hargrove," Hallie mused under her breath.

The sun beat down relentlessly, sapping Hallie of her remaining strength. Her long walk had taken its toll, and soon she was slumped against Ashe, sleeping peacefully. Her head lolled from side to side, her exhaustion apparent.

Resting his large hand against the side of her face,

Ashe positioned her head against his chest, while his now-softened gray eyes leisurely studied her.

As the ranch came into view, he shifted restlessly in the saddle, the ache in his loins abating not one whit.

"Hallie," he whispered, not wanting to startle her.

But startle her he did. She came awake with a jerk, and her head cracked against Ashe's nose with a dull thud.

Blood spurted. Dragging a handkerchief from his pocket, he quickly covered his nose. "Damn, Hallie, you're a dangerous woman."

"I'm sorry, Ashe, you startled me," she said in embarrassment as she eyed his injury with concern.

When they reached the house, Hallie dismounted hurriedly and called for Maria. With much reluctance, Ashe put himself into Maria's capable hands.

"This really isn't necessary," Ashe grumbled. "I've suffered worse injuries than this."

Keeping a wary eye on Hallie, Maria soon had Ashe ensconced on the sofa, his head tilted back and cool cloths resting across his nose.

With a frown marring her brow, she turned to Hallie. "Qué pasa? Did you strike Señor Barkley?"

"Nothing is going on, Maria. It was an accident."

"Then if you think you can take care of Sēnor Barkley, mi niña, I will finish my chores in the kitchen."

"Thank you, Maria, he'll survive."

Kneeling beside him, Hallie removed the cloth from his face. "I think the bleeding has stopped, Ashe. Does it hurt?"

"Only when I think about it."

"Then don't think about it. Think about something else."

"What would you have me to think about, Hallie?"

She was unnerved by his smile. "Think whatever you will, but I have chores to do. I believe you know the way out."

Before she could move, Ashe's arm snaked out and trapped her against him. "You have a bad habit of doing that, Hallie."

"Doing what?" she asked, feigning ignorance.

"Of darting off every time something comes up that you don't want to talk about."

"That's not true, Ashe. We've talked about a great number of things. I'm not in the habit of baring my soul to every stranger who comes along."

"Is that what I am, Hallie . . . a stranger?" His brow rose in question.

"Not anymore. You know more about me than anyone except Grandpa and Maria." She fidgeted in his embrace.

"I want to know what you have stored in here," he said, placing his hand over her heart.

Sadness etched Hallie's face as her mind raced over a kaleidoscope of pictures in her heart. With a slow, pensive smile, she answered, "There's nothing there, Ashe."

"I don't mean to bring you sadness, love. I want you happy with a heart bursting with joy." His hand had found its way to the nape of her neck, his fingers massaging the tautness of her muscles gently.

"Grandpa brings me happiness even if I do have to

fight like a bear to gain an inch with him. The ranch makes me happy."

"That's not the happiness I am referring to; someday I'm going to show you." Shrugging his shoulders, he added, "I didn't mean to be maudlin. Maybe it's the loss of blood." With one smooth movement, he stood, bringing Hallie to her feet. "I should be going. I don't want to wear out my welcome."

Hallie followed him to the door. Just as he stepped through, he turned, and with the boldness that was common to him, he winked. Why it bothered Hallie, she didn't know. But for some reason it made her insides feel giddy and brought a tremulous smile to her lips. Without a thought, she winked back, then blushed furiously. She could hear Ashe's laughter as he mounted his horse.

Chapter 7

The team of six horses trudged slowly through the pass. The wagon they were pulling was heavily laden with mining machinery and food supplies. One man sat on the bench, his elbows propped on his knees, the reins held loosely in his hands. Two men rode alongside the wagon, one of them occasionally scouting ahead for any surprise that might await them.

Ashe Barkley sat astride his large gray stallion, keeping the tail of the wagon in sight as he canvassed both sides of the canyon walls. Every nook and cranny was a possible hiding place for the Poet Bandit, so he kept his senses alert. If his plans succeeded, he would finally have his chance to unmask the bandit. But he wanted to find a way to do it privately without the other men seeing him. He hadn't exactly figured out how to accomplish that.

Hargrove had taken no chances. The three men who

guarded his cargo were hired gunmen. It mattered little to them if the bandit died, even though Hargrove had specified he wanted him alive. But today, Hargrove and the three gunmen were not expecting the bandit to appear on the scene. They thought the money was well hidden in bags of flour where no one would think to look if they were held up. It was inconceivable to Ashe that the Poet Bandit would manage to pull off this robbery.

Suddenly there was frantic movement around the freight wagon. The men jumped from their horses shouting obscenities while Lem leaped down off the bench, joining the others behind a boulder.

Ashe dug his heels into Rebel's side, and as he neared the wagon, he was astounded to see one arrow after another sailing down from one side of the canyon's crest.

"Get back, man!" Lem shouted. "Injuns are all over that damn hill!"

Ashe took shelter behind a rock, his eyes searching the top of the canyon as the arrows rained down on them intermittently from several angles.

"More'n likely it's that scoundrel Geronimo and his band of renegades," one of the men called to Ashe. "Must be at least ten of 'em takin' potshots at us."

Ashe squinted into the sun as he gazed upward. "Can't see a one of them. Of course, Apache are sneaky bastards, and kind of creep up on you when you're not looking. Seems like they're playing games with us."

"Yeah?" Lem asked. "Well, I fer one ain't fer stickin' my nose outta here to find out."

As abruptly as the arrows began, they stopped. It was so quiet in the canyon, a single pebble sliding down the mountainside could have been heard.

"Damned varmints!" Olsen whispered loudly. "They's just itchin' for us to show our asses. Farley, why don't you show 'em who's boss? You've kilt a few of 'em afore."

"Yeah, but only when I'm lookin' straight at 'em ... and they ain't armed."

Ashe decided to give it a try. He edged his way around the boulder and made a dash toward the wagon. Immediately, arrows flashed around him, too close for comfort. Crouching down beside the wagon, he lifted his rifle barrel, scanning the canyon once again.

"Them sneaky bastards," Lem shouted. "They intend to pick us off one by one."

Once again stillness prevailed. The three anxious men behind Ashe were breathing rapidly, with an occasional nervous clearing of throats. Even Ashe felt uneasy, not understanding what the sneaky Apache were up to. Supposedly the wagon carried nothing of value except the horses.

Ashe glanced around quickly, noticing that Rebel and the other three horses were wandering aimlessly in the canyon. He reasoned that they had an edge over the Indians because they had rifles, if the Indians had guns, they wouldn't be using bows and arrows.

That theory was ruined when Farley got brave and tried to make a run for his horse. Bullet after bullet bit the dust at Farley's heels as he chased his horse. Caught in the open with no shelter, he shouted in terror, "Hot damn, I'm daid, I know I am!"

Another bullet buzzed by his ear. Farley seemed to disappear within his clothing, sucking in his rear end and stomach at the same time. As the next bullet rang out, Farley's hand slapped his forehead; he reeled and fell to the ground. All three men stared, their mouths gaping. It was the first time Ashe had seen fear in Jake Olsen's face.

"Lem was right," Olsen said. "They mean to get us one by one. They're just takin' their sweet damn time in doin' it."

At least a half hour passed before anyone decided to test the Indians again.

"Cover me," Ashe whispered to Olsen and Lem. "I'm going to get across to those rocks and work my way to the top. If any of them show their faces, blow it off."

Ashe carefully eased out from behind the wagon in a crouch. He was met with blessed silence. With his rifle aimed at the crest of the hill, he cautiously maneuvered his way to the first point in his plan, using the cacti and boulders as a shield.

Maybe they were just waiting for him so they could kill him face-to-face, he thought, but he kept pressing upward, the tension mounting within him.

He made it to the top with no problem and slowly slipped in and out between the rocks, searching above and below for the wily Apache. There was no sign of them, but from the scattered hoof marks in the dirt, there must have been several of them. Where they had gone was the question now.

Ashe slowly made his way back down the mountainside, dodging the prickly thorns of the cacti that grew in abundance along the way.

As he walked over to Farley, he said to Lem and Olsen, "They're nowhere around; you can come out now."

Kneeling down to turn Farley over, Ashe saw a black eye shift upward in his direction. "Is it safe to breathe now?" Farley asked, his face as white as a sheet.

"You son of a bitch," Ashe hissed. "I thought you were dead."

Farley's voice quavered. *"You* did!" he said with mortification. "I thought for sure I'd met my Maker."

No bullet mark, no sign of blood was visible on Farley's skinny body. Ashe realized that Farley had passed out stonecold in sheer terror. He almost choked, stifling his laughter.

"I doubt, Farley, it was your Maker you'd be meeting. More than likely the devil himself."

"Yeah, you're probably right," Farley said, rising to his feet. Seeing the stunned faces of Lem and Olsen, he added, "Never could lie worth a damn nohow."

"What happened?" Lem asked. "You decide to play daid or somethin'? Smart thinkin' on your part, Farley."

"Somethin' like that," Farley's eyes shifted to Ashe, daring him to say otherwise.

"Think Geronimo's done through takin' potshots at us?" Olsen asked, gazing around the area warily.

"Geronimo! Hell, Olsen," Lem said derisively.

"Yeah," Farley said, "if that had been Geronimo,

our butts woulda been in the ground . . . like about six feet deep."

"We'd better round up our horses and give it another try," Ashe said, whistling for Rebel.

After everyone mounted and Lem had repositioned himself on the bench, they continued through the pass. Olsen rode a short distance ahead while Ashe stayed behind the wagon. Farley stayed beside the wagon, so close that he seemed attached to it.

As they rounded the bend, Olsen pulled back tightly on his reins; his huge roan stallion reared up nervously.

"Get on up here," he shouted back at them. "Damn Injuns got 'em one after all."

Ashe dug his heels into Rebel's flanks and raced ahead of the lumbering wagon. Nearing Olsen, he spied a man lying facedown on the ground with an arrow protruding from his back. Panic surged through him, for the familiar figure that lay lifeless on the ground was the crafty bandit.

Damn you, Hallie Parker, Ashe cursed silently, recoiling in anger. I knew you'd get it sooner or later, but not by a damned Indian.

Olsen was unaware that the Poet Bandit lay at his horse's feet. His main interest at the moment was keeping an eye out for the Indians.

Ashe leaped to the ground beside the bandit. As he started to remove the arrow, he immediately knew something was amiss. The arrow was between the armpit and back. Like a flash of lightning, the bandit rolled over and Ashe heard the click of guns. Two colt 45's were aimed at Ashe's gut, and a pair of glittering blue eyes glared at him from over the rim of a bandana.

"Back off, Barkley!" The voice was deep, and had Ashe not known it belonged to Hallie Parker, he would have thought a young boy was speaking.

Ashe was too shocked for words. That brazen vixen had set them up from the very beginning and they had fallen for it royally. No wonder the arrows came from the same place each time. She had moved all over that damn mountaintop like a wild dust devil to make them believe there were several Indians. Though Ashe didn't enjoy the two guns aimed threateningly at him, he had to admire the bandit's ingenuity.

Olsen, seeing the mask, put two and two together and inconspicuously raised his rifle. His action was not missed by the bandit. A sharp retort split the air, and Olsen's rifle flew from his hand, pieces of wood flying into his face.

"Don't you try that again or you won't be seein' the morrow," the bandit said brusquely and eased to his feet, his eyes never leaving the two men.

Hearing the gunshot blast and seeing the masked bandit, Lem stopped the wagon several yards back. Both he and Farley brought up their rifles, but the bandit's menacing voice removed any notion of shooting.

"I got me two guns here aimed at your pals' heads. You shoot, and they are deader'n a doornail. Just drop them guns and get that wagon up here now before I blow you all to smithereens. The same goes for you two," the bandit ordered, pointing his gun in the direction of Olsen and Ashe.

After everyone had dropped his weapon, the bandit let out a shrill whistle, summoning a large black stallion with a white blaze from behind a mass of rocks. Snorting and dancing, he made his way to his master.

Ashe grinned, for he knew the horse was Licorice in disguise. Just like the bandit. She had thought of everything. But one thing she didn't realize was that Ashe recognized her. That would be his secret until the right moment came to confront her. Now, she was one woman against four men and for him to reveal her identity could endanger her life.

"Sorry, but we ain't got nothin' on this wagon you'd be interested in, bandit," Lem said. "'Course, could it be you're taken up minin' on the side?"

"I just happen to know better, mister," the bandit said cockily. "Hargrove tried to pull one over on me today, but as usual, he lost. Now dump all them bags in there to the ground."

Lem's ugly face appeared so innocent the bandit knew he was lying. "Ain't nothin' in them bags 'ceptin' flour and meal."

"Ain't, huh?" the outlaw pointed his gun at Lem. "Then it won't hurt you none to prove it."

Lem looked at the other three men for confirmation.

"Do as he says," Ashe said. "Hargrove's money is not worth any of our lives."

Olsen's eyebrows furrowed. He shifted his bulky weight in his saddle. "How'd you find out, bandit? This was a secret that only us four and Hargrove knew."

"Seems you have an informer in your little party. How else would I know?"

The four men eyed each other suspiciously, which the outlaw found amusing. "'Nuff talk. I ain't got all day."

Farley got off his horse and climbed around the machinery in the back of the wagon to assist Lem in tossing out the muslin bags. As the flour sacks hit the ground, puffy white dust clouded the air.

The bandit, not taking his eyes off the men, reached into his saddlebag and tossed several leather pouches to the ground. "Fill 'em up."

Ashe took his Bowie knife from its sheath, and with one quick slash ripped open the first bag. Embedded within the flour were several stacks of bills tied together. With each successive bag, the pile of money grew. Ashe began stuffing it into the bags, and when he finished, he handed it to the bandit.

"No," the outlaw said. "Put 'em in my saddlebag."

Ashe did as he was told, his eyes sweeping over the slight figure in the baggy trousers.

Hallie, though she appeared reckless and unconcerned, was as uptight as a coiled spring. Ashe's hand had inadvertently brushed her thigh as he placed the pouches into her saddlebag. The brief contact reminded her she was a woman, no matter the unusual circumstances of the moment.

"Lem," Olsen said gruffly, "Hargrove ain't gonna like this one bit. He's gonna ask why four men couldn't overtake the bandit."

Hallie's stomach leaped to her throat. Lem! How long had she waited to hear that name? Anger welled up in her like an erupting volcano. Were these the same three men who had murdered her father, or was it merely a coincidence that this man's name was Lem? Waves of anxiety rolled over her mind like a tumbleweed on an open field.

Without thinking, she asked angrily, "Lem, do you know what a gila monster is?"

Lem looked puzzled at her question, as were the other men. "'Course I know what a gila monster is. What fool don't who's from these here parts? Why'd you ask a dumb question like that fer?"

What the hell is going on in Hallie's mind? Ashe wondered tensely. She seems to have gone mad. He saw a tremendous fury in her eyes, then it quickly changed to a faraway, meditative expression. Come back, Hallie, he wanted to warn her. Don't let them catch you off guard or I've lost you forever.

"Bandit?" Ashe asked louder than was necessary. "Are you through with us?"

Hallie's mind snapped back to reality. She was frighteningly aware of how close she had come to losing control of the situation. "I reckon so," she drawled, nonchalantly withdrawing the familiar folded sheet of paper and tossing it to Ashe. No one moved as Ashe bent and quickly stuffed the note into his shirt pocket. Without another word, the bandit mounted, and pulled the reins to the right; the horse lowered his black head in their direction as an actor would do after a successful performance. The black-clad bandit and the black stallion blended as they raced through the narrow canyon.

Ashe, seeing Olsen hurriedly dismount, tried to delay Olsen while he gathered up his own guns. "Want your rifle?" he asked, knowing Olsen would instantly take off after the bandit.

"Hell no! It'd do me no good now," Olsen spat, remounting his horse.

Lem and Farley hurriedly retrieved their weapons. Lem said, "Let's go get him."

"No," Ashe said hastily and mounted Rebel. "You stay here with Farley and protect the freight."

Olsen grunted, and veered his horse in the direction of the bandit, leaving Ashe in a cloud of dust. Fortunately for the bandit, Olsen's three hundred pounds of rock-hard flesh slowed his horse some, but the distance between Hallie and the men decreased rapidly. Olsen pulled his gun from his holster and shot wildly.

Racing by Olsen's side, Ashe watched him carefully aim his gun at Hallie's small back. Just as Olsen pulled the trigger, Ashe bumped Rebel into the side of Olsen's horse, causing Olsen's arm to shift and the bullet skew away from its target.

The bullets whizzed past Hallie. Suddenly, a sharp piercing pain ripped through her shoulder. A burning sensation encompassed the upper portion of her body. Leaning low in the saddle, she urged Licorice on faster. Blackness threatened to overcome consciousness. Fear mushroomed and hung suspended like a storm cloud.

Each step the horse took jarred her body, causing blood to run down her arm, streaking Licorice's mane.

"Damn you to hell, Barkley, you done that on purpose!" Olsen shouted over the thundering hooves as Ashe sped by him.

Over his shoulder, Ashe shouted back, "I told you it was each man for himself."

Ashe riveted his attention to Hallie, and saw that Olsen hadn't missed his mark after all. He could barely distinguish her small form from that of Licorice's large black body as she slumped forward on the horse's neck.

He would never know what caused him to look back at Olsen. Perhaps it was the instinct that came from serving in the war, and making his living as a bounty hunter. The premonition that a gun was pointed at his back woke every nerve ending in his body. He drew his gun from his holster faster than the blink of an eye and he turned. Balancing his hand on the crook of his arm, he fired. He saw Olsen's gun drop to the ground and Olsen, still sitting like a mighty oak in his saddle, clutch his chest as the blood flowed through his fingers and spread across his shirt.

"You must have eyes in the back of your head, man," he rasped before his eyes glazed over and the mighty oak was felled.

Hallie slid from the saddle and led Licorice through a thicket of paloverde to the cave entrance. Holding her shoulder, she stumbled to the water's edge. Dropping to a large flat rock, she cradled her arm and rocked gently to and fro, the tears rolling down her face. Blessed darkness overcame her, releasing her from the pain.

"Damn fool woman."

The harshly spoken words penetrated Hallie's consciousness, and with reluctance she opened her eyes.

"You," she groaned.

"Hell yes, and you'd better thank your lucky stars it is."

"You son of a—"

"Tsk, tsk, is that any way for a lady to talk?" he drawled.

"You shot me?" The question hung in the air.

"If I had, you'd be dead," he said with a calm that sent chills up Hallie's spine. "Here, let's get you out of that shirt so I can take a look at your shoulder." He reached for the front of her shirt.

"I can manage," Hallie snapped, pulling away from him.

"You're going to have to take off the damn thing. It's torn and bloody as hell," he persisted.

She dodged his knowing gaze. "I don't have anything on underneath."

"I don't mind," he said.

"I didn't think you would, but I do. Turn your head."

Amused by her modesty in the face of both her pain and unmasking, Ashe complied.

Removing the shirt was harder to do than Hallie anticipated. Some of the blood had dried, gluing the fabric to her wounded shoulder. Wincing, she pulled at the material, but it clung tenaciously to her skin. Whimpering, she tugged again.

Ashe whipped around and came to her aid, and soon had Hallie red-faced and naked from the waist up. Grabbing the discarded shirt, she covered her breasts hurriedly.

"Store that damn pride for a while, Hallie. I've got to take care of your shoulder. Before you came to, I got a pretty good look at it. You've lost quite a bit of blood. Fortunately, it's a clean wound." There was a wealth of tenderness in his words.

"If you'll look beyond those rocks, you'll find clothes and towels," she said, pointing in the direction of her cache. She smiled weakly.

"You came prepared, I'll have to say that for you," he said in surprise.

Bringing the bundle, he pulled out a clean shirt. Ripping the sleeve from it, he dropped it to her side. "Here, put this on before I forget that you're wounded," he said with amusement. Noting Hallie's fumbling attempt with the buttons, Ashe pushed her hand aside and buttoned the shirt with practiced ease.

"Ashe," she hesitated, "if you didn't shoot me, who did?"

A deep frown marred his brow, he answered absently, "It was Jake Olsen, Hargrove's hired gunman, trying to make a name for himself by bringing down the Poet Bandit."

"Well, if you found me, surely he can do the same. He'll probably bring Hargrove with him."

Frightened now, she struggled to stand until Ashe's words stopped her.

"He's not going to be bringing anyone anywhere."

Again the coldness of his voice frightened Hallie. "What do you mean?"

"He's dead, Hallie. Do I have to spell it out for you?"

"You . . . you killed him."

"Don't push, Hallie," he said with frigid finality. "What's done is done."

"Just like that you killed a man? Don't you feel any remorse?"

"Should I?" he asked, shrugging his shoulders. "He would have killed you or me."

Shaking her head, her voice faltered. "I guess I should thank you, but since I've known you, you've killed two men. The one I witnessed, you did with such callousness. Then you waltz in here and tell me you've killed again."

"My God, Hallie, what did you expect me to do?"

"I didn't expect you to do anything," she snapped. And why did he? To protect the bandit from killers, she thought suddenly. To protect *her!* She looked at him in utter amazement. "You knew! But how? You knew I was the Poet Bandit?"

"You became careless, Hallie." The grim set of his mouth revealed nothing. "I've seen some damned fool stunts in my time, but this takes the cake. One tiny bit of fluff against four armed men."

Puffing up indignantly, she spat, "It wasn't *too* damn foolish. I got the money, didn't I?"

Laughing at the memory of the men believing they were under attack from a renegade band of Indians, Ashe relented. "Yeah, okay, you got the money; but you almost lost your life in the process. Mighty high stakes if you ask me. By the way, why didn't you wear your goodluck charm? It might have come in handy today."

"I forgot it," she replied weakly. "How did you know it was me, Ashe? Did I say something to give myself away?"

"No. It's what you didn't say that puzzled me. When you make a living with a gun, you notice things quicker." He added harshly, "You have to, if you want to stay alive. The dead giveaway, if you must know, was your left hand. After you shot me, I noticed how you held your gun. Then, while relating your story to me about you and Ben, you mentioned you are left-handed. The gun and gun belt you wore looked strangely familiar to me. You also showed you knew how to use a gun when you said you'd shot the coyote that had been carrying off your calves. The pieces began to fall into place. I'd heard things in town about your grandfather and Hargrove." A smile touched his full lips, and Hallie's heart plummeted.

"It's for sure you can't go home until your shoulder begins to heal... unless your grandfather is in on your unlawful activities, which I doubt. Has no one ever seen through your spinster ruse?" he asked, rising to his feet.

"People usually see only what they want to. I just helped them to see what I wanted them to see."

"I know what I see," he said with a grin.

She ignored that remark. "My grandfather knows nothing about this, and neither does anyone else. Since I had planned to go to the mine today after I took care of Hargrove's money, Maria won't be expecting me any too soon. It is not unusual for me to strike out by myself." She smiled secretively. "And Grandpa didn't know I was coming. Should Maria ask me why I was gone longer than usual, I guess I'll just have to tell her the truth. The only reason I haven't taken her into my confidence is because I hate to worry her."

"Got it all figured out, haven't you? What are you going to eat?"

"As you said, I came prepared. Look in that sack."

She pointed toward the same boulder where her clothes had been. "See what I mean?" she asked as Ashe opened the cloth sack. "Maria sent the food for Grandpa and me, and she has a generous hand."

His eyes scanned the assortment of food: hard cheese, bread, coffee, cornmeal, and fruit pies. With a lazy smile, he lifted his eyes to hers. "I'll have to admit you seem to have left nothing to chance."

"That's where you're wrong. I didn't plan on getting shot."

"No, I guess not." Turning away, he said over his shoulder, "I'll see to the horses and get a fire started ... if you want to lie down." With that, he strode quickly from her sight.

What manner of a man is he? Hallie wondered. No barrage of questions, no condemnation—only help. He seemed to have figured out the answers for himself and accepted them, offering her his protection in unspoken words.

Ashe had gathered kindling, and when he had the fire burning brightly, he saw to the horses.

Taking a bottle of tequila from his saddlebag, he uncorked it and took a long pull of the fiery liquor. Walking to Hallie, he handed the bottle to her, saying quietly, "Drink."

"I don't drink."

"You'd better start. I've got to take care of your shoulder, and you're going to need all the comfort you can get."

She took the bottle from his outstretched hand, and tilted it toward him in a mock toast. "To comfort," she whispered, lifting the bottle to her lips, taking several large swallows. Tears sprang to her eyes and gasping for breath, she wheezed. "Damn!" A burning sensation progressed from the back of her throat to the pit of her empty stomach. She clasped her hand over her mouth and swallowed rapidly until the feeling dissipated. She raised watery blue eyes to Ashe, who watched her with an amused smile.

"Good girl," he said, reaching for the bottle.

Warmth spread through her, and when Ashe gave her back the bottle, the liquid went down smoothly the second time.

Ashe watched her closely. Squatting down beside her, he spread a blanket and coaxed her to lie down.

Giggling, she told him, "But I'm not sleepy yet."

"No, you're drunk, love."

"Me?" she slurred, ramming her hand within inches of his face. "How many fingers am I holding up?"

"One, Hallie."

"Are you sure?" she asked, examining her hand.

Leaning over her, his voice was hoarse as he whispered, "I'll be gentle, Hallie."

She watched as he slowly pulled a linen towel from her bundle and ripped it into strips. Dipping a large piece into the water, he began bathing Hallie's shoulder with a gentleness that surprised her. When he poured the tequila into her wound, she fainted from the fiery blaze of pain that seared her shoulder.

Ashe worked quickly while she was unconscious, soaking a strip of fabric in the liquor, and securing it to her shoulder with more strips. Hallie's body jerked spasmodically as her body tried to draw away from the source of pain.

Stretching out beside her, he drew her close, rocked her gently, and whispered soothingly until her whimpering ceased and she rested peacefully.

Chapter 8

The muted red robes of twilight merged into the dark shadows, turning the evening to night. The moon rose, scattering rays of light across the couple who lay together beneath its glow.

Ashe stared into the night, alternating cool, wet cloths on Hallie's dry hot skin while mulling over the questions plaguing him. He shook off his disturbing thoughts. Nothing mattered but caring for Hallie. Everything else could wait. Why it mattered so much to him, he didn't analyze.

She sure is a feisty thing, he thought. All spunk and fire. She wears her pride like a second skin.

She began tossing again, and Ashe drew her to him. Weak blue eyes met strong gray. She whispered hoarsely, "I don't feel so good, Ashe."

"I know love, but the worst is over. Go back to sleep, I'm here."

"I'm thirsty, Ashe, may I have some water?"

"Sure," he answered gently. He lifted her head and gave her a sip from his canteen.

Afterwards, Hallie seemed to rest better. Ashe lay listening to the night sounds—the hooting of an owl and the mournful wailing of a coyote. The sound of falling water nearby finally lulled Ashe to sleep.

Morning came and Hallie wasn't as feverish as she had been during the night, but she was still warm to the touch. Throughout the day, Ashe kept a close watch over her, periodically bathing her with cool water from the lake, or giving her a drink when she requested one. Her vulnerable smile of gratitude made his heart beat erratically.

Resting against a boulder, he reached for his tobacco, dragging out the note that Hallie had intended for Hargrove. He rolled his cigarette, lit it, and took a deep drag. Unfolding the note, he read:

I ain't easily misled, you thievin' old coot
Once again, I be a-receivin' your loot
Secrets are deceivin' so I ride alone
Ain't nobody's silence I trust but my own.

Just how many times do I have to teach you
A fool I ain't, and I am out to beat you.
Thief robbin' a thief don't make me no sinner
Leave no doubt in your mind—I am the winner.

Chuckling with delight, Ashe folded the note and returned it to his shirt pocket. I'll be sure Hargrove gets this, he thought in amusement. Hallie, Hallie, what am I to do with you? he wondered as he watched her sleep. Her unbound hair lay like a veil around her shoulders—shimmering like gold as the light reflected off it, Ashe thought, craving to run his hands through it.

Undeniably, the war had left its mark on her, too. The boldness with which she had sought revenge was astonishing. Her small shoulders carried a large burden. If it was in his power, he vowed, he would help to ease her load.

Lying down beside her, Ashe rubbed the long burnished strands of hair between his fingers as he drifted off in a much-needed sleep.

Blue uniforms surrounded Hallie, no matter that she slapped out repeatedly at the misshapen forms; they kept closing in on her. She gazed into leering faces that floated before her, elongated apparitions that changed before her eyes like clouds tossed by an angry wind. They tormented her with eerie laughter as they reached out for her.

Her shrill scream penetrated the still morning air, waking her from the horrible dream. Opening fear-filled eyes, she looked into Ashe's concerned face.

"It was only a bad dream, Hallie." He pushed tangled strands of hair from her face. "How do you feel?"

"Sore." She grimaced.

"That's to be expected."

"I fainted, didn't I?"

"Either that or you passed out from too much tequila," he said dryly, and she groaned, remembering.

"What were you dreaming about? You must have been fighting Indians."

"No, Yankees," she retorted.

"Well, whichever, you sure do pack a wallop. I'll be black and blue for a week."

She gazed at him skeptically.

"I was trying to hold you down so your shoulder wouldn't start bleeding again, and ward off your blows at the same time. Do you think my eye will be black?" he asked with a grin, tilting his head for closer inspection.

"I'm sorry. I was seeing Yankees coming at me from all sides."

He thought of what she'd think of him if she knew he was a Yankee and shuddered. Later, when she trusted him more, maybe he'd tell her. Maybe.

The day progressed aimlessly. Hallie lay on her blanket and watched Ashe. His effortless movements were graceful, sensual. She watched him as he added wood to the fire. The muscles rippled in his broad back, teasing the tightly stretched fabric. Buckskin breeches hugged his long legs and firm behind. Hallie thought of something her grandfather had once said: not enough rear end to make a dying man a bowl of soup. That surely applied in Ashe's case. Scolding herself, she quickly glanced away. Damn, Hallie Parker, what's gotten into you? You're eyeing him like the main course of a condemned man's last meal. The color gushed to her cheeks as she pondered her wanton thoughts.

"Do you think you can manage a few hours by yourself?" asked Ashe. "I thought I'd go back to the ranch and check in. I don't want anyone wondering about my absence. I'll bring back a few supplies and let it be known that I won't be around for a day or two."

Hallie was amazed at how easily he had taken over. "Really, all this isn't necessary," she protested.

He ignored her as he saddled up and drew the straps firmly around Rebel's belly. "I'm a right fair cook, but we don't even have a coffeepot. I'd have come better prepared had I known we were going to be here a few days."

"I'll be fine. Don't think you have to stay here with me. I appreciate what you've done for me, but I don't need a nursemaid."

"I insist."

"You insist on what? Being a nursemaid?"

"If that's what I have to do," he answered with a gleam in his eyes as he strapped his gun around his waist.

Hallie wondered why he seemed so determined to take care of her. One minute he was her enemy, and the next, her daring protector. Warmth coursed through her. Not such a disagreeable predicament, she concluded with a smile.

After Ashe bade her to take care and made his silent departure, Hallie slept, her dreams centering on the man who had given her the warmth and security she hadn't felt since she was a child.

When she awakened, her shoulder was considerably better; but after several days without bathing, she felt dirty and sticky. The soft melody of the nearby waterfall beckoned her. Looking at the position of the sun, she figured she had at least a couple of hours before Ashe's return.

Gingerly, she got to her feet, testing her arms and legs. "Well, they're still working," she muttered.

A long, cool soak in the lake being her goal, she gathered a linen towel and a sliver of soap from her cache. The towel was damp. She surmised that Ashe must have bathed earlier while she was sleeping.

She carefully removed her clothing, and taking the soiled garments with her, she waded into the water. After scrubbing her clothes, she draped them over the rocks for the sun to dry.

As she sank down in the blue depths, her naked skin felt soothed and refreshed. She soaped herself leisurely and relaxed, lying back in the water, floating idly, the sun warming her cool body. Her mind drifted with her body as she watched the fluffy white clouds cavorting overhead.

Closing her eyes, she could almost see Ashe's quick gun hand moving, discharging his brand of punishment. The image changed quickly to his slate-gray eyes caressing her; softly spoken words eased her pain. Bunching her hair into his large hand, he kissed her lips, draining her strength with his passion.

Ashe Barkley was no man's fool, she thought, admonishing herself for her passionate daydreaming. He was a man who kept a tight rein on his emotions.

The sound of the waterfall came closer, and as she drifted toward it, a fine mist sprayed over her. Shaking off her thoughts, she rose to her feet and awkwardly soaped her hair, wincing painfully as she tried to move her injured shoulder. Then she stood beneath the curtain of falling water, luxuriating in it as the dirt rinsed away.

Ashe entered the tunnel and came out on the other side. He gazed down on the makeshift camp, and, failing to locate Hallie, his eyes moved to the stream. The sight brought him up short, and he softly muttered, "Goddamn." Unable to tear his eyes away, he stood mesmerized. An ache shot through his loins. He knew there would be hell to pay for witnessing the scene before him.

Hallie stood naked under the tumble of water, the peaks of her full, firm breasts taut from the coolness, her slim waist smooth and glistening.

Wet... Ashe thought, running his tongue slowly over dry lips, his mouth suddenly parched as he viewed the goddess before him.

With hair tangling over her face, Hallie didn't see Ashe as she made her way to the shallow edge of the stream. Draping her hair over her good shoulder, she raised her eyes and met Ashe's stare head-on. Stunned, she stumbled back into the depths of the water to hide her nakedness.

"You sneaky bastard, how dare you slink in here without making your presence known," she shrieked, trying unsuccessfully to cover her breasts from his hot gaze.

"If the truth be known, love, I was struck dumb by your beauty."

"I thought you were going to be gone for several hours."

"I have been. I thought you might be worried because I took so long. I rode like hell to get back, only to meet with your caustic tongue."

"If you would be so kind and turn your head away, I'll get out of the water. I'm beginning to shrivel up like a prune."

"You've nothing to hide that I haven't seen already. ... Is this what you're looking for?" he asked, picking up the towel and letting it hang loosely from his fingers.

"I can't think of a name bad enough to describe you," she ground out angrily, as she stomped out of the water and grabbed the towel from him. "You're no gentleman!"

"Well, it's plain to see you're not, either ... Mr. Poet Bandit."

Hallie wrapped the towel around her slim body, dismayed by how little it covered.

"Do you think it was wise to get your shoulder wet?" he asked with concern.

"I couldn't help it, and I couldn't stand being so dirty."

"If you'll let me, I'll change your bandage," he offered. "That one's dripping wet."

While Hallie dressed—which was a slow process with only one good arm—Ashe built up the dying fire. He cleaned and skewered a rabbit he had killed on his way back, all the while watching Hallie as she fumbled with her clothing.

She'd bust a gut before she'd ask for my help, he thought, sweeping to his feet. By God, I'll help her whether she wants me to or not.

Pushing her hands aside, he tied the ribbons of her

chemise and helped her dress in a riding skirt and shirt. He was standing so close, Hallie could feel the heat radiating from his body. She could smell the faint aroma of tobacco, and the musky, masculine scent of him. His shirt was only partly buttoned, exposing the dark hair that matted his chest. She could see the pulse beating in his throat, and her fingers ached to touch the spot.

Raising her head, her eyes slammed into his. Lifting his hand, he softly stroked her cheek, trailing his fingers lightly across her parted lips. She stood entranced, unable to move as his fingers stroked her face

Unconsciously, her tongue darted out to wet her lips. That was Ashe's undoing. Her moistened lips looked too inviting. He had no other thought than to taste the sweet, warm mouth before him.

Lowering his head, he trailed the same path with his tongue that hers had only moments before. With a low growl, he drew her to him, his mouth possessing hers in a hungry assault. She swayed against him, wrapping her good arm around him, encouraging his exploring mouth and accepting his tongue, welcoming it as it teased her own. She answered his advances as he withdrew his tongue, her own dancing over his lips to enter his warm mouth as they sparred. His mouth did wonderful things to her. His teeth gently nipped, then his mouth tugged at her tongue, sucking, releasing, teasing.

Oh my God, what am I doing? her mind raved. Of its own volition, her body arched against him. She moaned into the softness of his lips.

Drawing her bound arm from between them, she

placed her hand on his cheek, feeling his warmth. Releasing her mouth, he turned his head, capturing an exploring finger into his hot mouth, tugging at it, his tongue flicking the pad of her finger and releasing it. She ran it over his kiss-swollen lips, wondering at these new sensations and the boldness she felt in his arms. A shudder ran through her body.

"Are you cold, love?" His voice was husky with emotion. "Come over by the fire, your hair is still wet. I'll help you dry it."

Hallie moved closer to the warm fire. She was frightened by her swirling emotions, yet at the same time curious about her reactions to Ashe.

The aroma from the pot of coffee on the fire filled the air. The rabbit was turning a golden brown. Hallie's mouth watered; she was starving.

Ashe prepared her plate and handed it to her. Sitting across from her near the fire, he couldn't concentrate on his own food for watching Hallie eat. She didn't pick up the meat and eat it. Instead, she pulled the meat from the bone with her fingers, then very slowly put the meat to her mouth, trailing it across her lips. Her tongue darted out to capture the succulent juices that escaped. It was a sensual process that arrested Ashe's attention. Damn, he groaned inwardly as he felt the familiar tightening in his loins.

Her words finally struck a cord, and he mentally shook himself.

"I'm sorry, I didn't hear you. I was ... thinking ... about something else." Now she has me stammering like a lovesick schoolboy, he chastised himself.

Smiling softly in the waning light, she repeated her

statement. "I only said you made good your visit. Plates, coffeepot, clean cloths for bandages, soap... and a rabbit to boot." Then gazing over at him with a noticeable frown, she asked, "Was anything said about the man you shot?" She shuddered at the thought.

"Yes, they found his body, but don't worry. I explained the circumstances to Hargrove and he seemed satisfied. At least the Poet Bandit doesn't have a murder pinned on him."

"How did you manage that, Ashe?"

"That bastard, Olsen, tried to shoot me in the back. After he winged you, he turned his gun on me. We'd had words before. He was a cruel bastard, Hallie, and Hargrove knew it; that's why he was hired. But Hargrove is not one to worry overmuch about anything that doesn't put money in his pockets," he smiled, then tossed the cleaned bone into the fire, "so the matter is closed."

Leaning forward, Ashe added on a serious note, "Hallie, I want you to promise that you'll stop this foolishness. You very easily could've been killed. It was only a stroke of luck that I happened to be there."

Tilting her chin rebelliously, Hallie snapped, "It's not foolish. It's my grandfather's money. Hargrove stole the mine from him. I'm as sure of that as I am of the sun rising on the morrow, but I just can't prove it."

"So you've set yourself up to ruin him. Don't you realize that you'll be the one hurt? You can't ruin him, Hallie. You're just an itch he can't scratch. Aggravation, but nothing crippling. He's like an octopus, his arms reaching out far and wide. He has investments in a variety of things. His wealth is great, and it's going to take more than a few robberies to ruin him."

"Yes, Ashe, I know he has tremendous wealth, but he's stolen most of that. What he didn't steal belonged to his late wife, Sarah."

Ashe sat very still for a moment before he asked, "Did you know her very well?"

"No, not well. She was very quiet and seemed so sad. I've never seen anyone who looked so miserable." Hallie lay back, resting on her side. "She was very beautiful, and that sadness seemed to intensify her beauty. I'm not in the habit of telling tales, but I've always heard Hargrove dealt harshly with her. Maybe that's why she was so sad. I don't guess anyone will ever know now."

"You're probably right," he answered, thinking of the portrait he had seen of Sarah Hargrove. The sadness that lined the hallways of his heart he pushed away, denying its presence as he gazed mutely into the fire.

Hallie, too, was remembering. Revenge... she mustn't let anything stand in her way. Tears sprang to her eyes. She swiped at them in annoyance as she thought how futile were her attempts to ruin Hargrove.

Their thoughts drifted and sadness lingered. They were alone in the emptiness, empty in their loneliness ... until suddenly they were in each other's arms. Who made the first move, they would never know, never care. All thoughts of revenge and grief scattered swiftly as their lips met, simultaneously, explosively.

Hallie's blood soared through her veins as Ashe's mouth seduced hers. Her lips parted, welcoming his searching, probing tongue. Ashe had never tasted anything so luscious, so inviting. Sweet, glorious surrender. Her arm spanned his back, her hand caressing as it moved to the nape of his neck, burying her fingers in the mass of black hair.

Ashe cupped her chin with a warm hand, his thumb gently stroking her delicate cheekbone. His lips, curious to know more of her, roamed at random across her face, leaving a fiery path.

Settling at last at the throbbing softness of her temple, he groaned low. "I'm going to make you mine, Hallie."

"I know," she whispered.

Gently, he lowered her to the blanket. She watched as he unbuckled his gun belt and laid it aside. Fear of the unknown surged through her. Noting her apprehension, Ashe lowered himself beside her and drew her to him.

"I'll be gentle, love," he whispered. His lips once again sought hers. He kissed her until she was breathless, and aching for his touch.

Nimble fingers loosened the buttons of her shirt and untied the ribbons of her chemise, drawing them from her, the riding skirt followed. A rush of cool air enveloped her. She drew away shyly, embarrassed by her nakedness.

"No, love," Ashe coaxed. "Don't shy away from me. You're beautiful."

His words soothed her hesitation. His eyes swept over her naked splendor, devouring her. Her hair draped like a shimmery mantle, partially covering full, ripe breasts. A single bud, taut with desire, was visible between the long strands of burnished hair.

Tremors raced through him. He had to taste the ripe fullness exposed to him. Lowering his head, his hot mouth locked onto the taut nipple. Brushing her hair away, he caressed the other, exciting moans of pleasure from her.

Drawing away, he gazed down into dark, sultry eyes, passion clearly smoldering in their stormy blue depths. His mouth dipped once more to place a passionate kiss on her swollen lips. She caught his tongue with her teeth and gently bit the intruding member. His eyes widened at her play, and he moaned hoarsely into her mouth.

She ran her hands over his chest, tugging at his shirtfront. With pleasure, he shrugged out of it. His boots required more attention; and with reluctance, he released her to shed them. Standing, he pulled impatiently at his pants, then stood naked before her, the firelight illuminating his masculinity.

"You're beautiful," she whispered.

He laughed huskily. "I've been called a lot of things, but never beautiful. You're the beautiful one," he murmured reverently, his voice thick with passion.

A jolt of pleasure shot through her at his words, and she opened her arms to welcome him.

With slow, sensuous movements, he alternately kissed and brushed his lips and tongue over the soft curves of her body. Hallie was burning, her need escalating as she clung to him, urging him on.

She gasped as his hand trailed between her thighs and his fingers entered her warm softness. Moaning urgently, she arched up to meet his hand. "Please," she implored, her voice breaking on a sob as she clutched frantically at him. "Please love me."

"I do... I will," he groaned huskily as he shifted upward. Guarding her injury with care, he kissed her slowly and moved between her thighs.

His entry was slow and smooth, but he cautioned her lovingly of the pain to come. She bit her lip to keep from crying out, digging her nails into his back. His mouth moved over hers and quieted any sound she made as he plunged deeply. He waited for the pain to subside, and whispered loving words of passion Hallie had never heard.

Slowly, he began moving against her. Once again her nervousness was overcome as her desire mounted. She met him thrust for thrust as he filled her again and again. They climbed until their passion soared end over end, like a billowing wave, crashing ashore on the sands of contentment.

"Damn," Ashe whispered, awestruck, rolling to his side, taking Hallie with him. Never had he experienced such fulfillment.

"I don't know what it is about you, Hallie Parker, but I think I'll have some more."

They made slow, passionate love, and Ashe lay back exhausted, swearing that once again the "Poet Bandit" had won.

As Ashe lay sleeping, Hallie watched the slow, even rise and fall of his chest. In the sparse flickering of the firelight, his face appeared strong and angular, even in sleep. The dark, full mustache only enhanced his handsomeness. Reaching out her hand, she gently touched it, and then his full lips, wondering at his purpose for being in Prospect City. Was it simply to capture the "Poet Bandit"?

She did not feel sleepy, but it was only minutes until she was curled peacefully against Ashe, sleeping deeply. The moon made its ascent and hung precariously over the mountain as though it were reluctant to disappear over the horizon. Sparkling stars flirted shamelessly with the hills as they stood like mute sentinels.

Light, feathery strokes brought Hallie from her deep sleep. Looking into Ashe's face, she saw passion burning in the depths of his gray eyes. Raising her hand, she caressed the strong line of his jaw, her fingers coming to rest on his mouth. Lightly biting the tips of her fingers, he groaned and drew her to him. His mouth sought hers, and once again their passion flared and burned brightly as they explored, slowly, lovingly, until they became one. When at last their desire was spent, they lay contented for a time in each other's arms.

Then, suddenly scooping Hallie up in his arms, Ashe carried her to the water's edge, and slowly lowered her into the cool water.

Delighted laughter echoed as Hallie and Ashe bathed each other. Ashe was careful of her wound and extremely sensual in his play. On occasion, Hallie's boldness would strike her and she would blush to the roots of her auburn hair. But Ashe was quick to note her feelings and would coax her further with his audacious behavior.

Sitting on a large rock, Hallie rested between Ashe's long legs as he gently brushed her tangled hair. The hypnotic strokes of the brush and the rhythmic fall of the water relaxed her almost to the point of sleep.

Ashe's voice broke through her reverie. "Hallie, something has been puzzling me. You sat astride Licorice commanding those men like a drill sergeant when suddenly something happened. I was afraid the men would notice your detachment and overpower you, but luckily they didn't." Laughing, he added, "I guess it was because you had them shaking in their boots."

Drawing from his embrace, she turned to face him, sadness etching her countenance. Taking a deep, shuddering breath, she said, "Echoes from the past, Ashe. I believe Lem, the man on the buckboard, was one of the three men who killed my father as we traveled from Tucson to Prospect City. The second day of travel, we saw riders approaching. My father made me hide in the rocks until he could find out what the men wanted." Her voice quivered as she continued, "After they shot him, they searched for me. I couldn't see their faces, but I could hear them. One of the men was named Lem, and I remembered his voice. That day someone called him by name. It was as though I had been jolted back in time and I was the little girl hiding in a hole in the mountainside. They were talking about rattlesnakes and gila monsters." She shuddered. "Can you imagine what the word *monster* does to a frightened thirteen-year-old? I'm convinced they were sent by Hargrove. No one else would have known that my father wasn't alone. He wasn't robbed, just shot in cold blood. They took everything that would have helped me to survive... even the mule."

"God," Ashe ground out fiercely, enraged by the cruelty of it. "It still amazes me you survived."

"I wouldn't have if Sundog hadn't found me after I'd wandered around on the desert in search of water. I was unconscious, and he took me to his village and cared for me."

"What makes you think it was Hargrove? You didn't know him at the time, did you?"

"My father became acquainted with him on the stagecoach from Fort Yuma when we were coming out here. They talked, although, as I remember, Hargrove did most of that. A boastful man; I disliked him on sight." She laughed weakly. "Because he took up so much room. I was squeezed between my father and another passenger while he spread his generous bulk out comfortably."

"Hallie, I don't mean to keep bringing up unpleasant things, but why would Hargrove want to kill your father?"

Jerking from his embrace, she accused, "You don't believe me, do you?"

Grasping her hand, he drew her back to him. "I'm just trying to straighten it out in my own mind. I know what a bastard Hargrove is. Now tell me why you think he had your father killed."

"I want you to know, so you will understand why I hate Hargrove. Grandpa thinks Hargrove killed my father so it would be easier for him to take the mine. My father was a very intelligent man, and Hargrove knew he wouldn't have stood a chance of getting the mine if my father lived. Hargrove had planned a long time on one day owning the mine. Dealing with an old man—especially one who loved a good game of cards and the taste of aged brandy—was easier than dealing with my father. I have to say that losing the mine cured Grandpa. The only cards he plays now is solitaire or a friendly game of gin rummy."

"What are your plans now? You don't have to continue your masquerade as the Poet Bandit."

"I shouldn't have to now; that was some haul. The mine must be doing great." She hesitated a moment, then she continued, "I don't want you to think I'm money-hungry, Ashe. I'm not. My needs are simple. A large chunk of the money will be donated anonymously to the mission. Those children have needs. I don't want them turning into thieves. As for the rest of the money, I have a special use for it."

"You won't tell me what that is?"

"No." She smiled, taking the edge from her firm reply.

"And that's as it should be," Ashe said, caressing her face. "We all have our secrets." He kissed her lightly, and she wondered about the secrets he harbored.

Drawing from his embrace, she searched his face for any clue that might reveal those secrets.

"Such deep thoughts, love. Is that frown for me?" he asked, running his fingers over her brow.

"No, I was only thinking. I need to be getting home. Maria will begin worrying if I don't return soon. My shoulder is much better, and I think I can manage without her noticing... if I'm careful."

"You know best. I'll get the gear together."

Standing, he turned from her, his mask back in

place, his features emotionless. All at once, as if what happened between them did not exist. Tears burned her eyes.

"Ashe," she choked.

"Yeah." His voice was strangely cold.

"What about us?" she asked, moving hesitantly toward him.

Hauling her into his arms, he whispered huskily, "I don't know, love, honest to God I don't. Let's give it time. That's something we both need."

His mouth found hers, pillaging the warm softness, bringing moans of pleasure from her. Once again he took her, only this time, it wasn't the gentle lover, but the violent gunslinger. She soared, meeting him thrust for thrust until they were carried away by a whirling eddy of endless desire.

Ashe rode with her until the ranch came into view. Hallie was reluctant to have him come any farther. Ashe kissed her soundly and turned, heading Rebel in the direction of Hargrove's ranch. She watched as he faded into a speck in the distance; then with gentle words, she prodded Licorice toward home.

Chapter 9

"Miss Hallie," Pascal called from across the street, "a letter come for ya this mornin'."

Hallie waited for several wagons to pass, and then made her way to the telegraph office. Walking down the narrow boardwalk, she tried to avoid several men lounging on benches outside the stores who purposely extended their legs to block her way. Rather than start a scene, she stepped off the boardwalk, ignoring their gibes and lewd grins.

"Pay 'em no mind, Miss Hallie," Pascal said, politely taking her arm and leading her into the telegraph office. "They's just some drifters who don't know a lady when they sees one."

"You said you had a letter for me?"

"Yes, ma'am, sure do." Pascal pulled an envelope from the slotted cabinet behind the counter. "Now why would you be needin' one of them fancy lawyer dudes?"

Hallie's mouth dropped open. She grabbed the letter from his bony fingers. "You didn't read my mail, did you, Pascal?"

Pascal's feelings were noticeably hurt. "No, I wouldn't do nothin' like that. It's just got one of them fancy return addresses."

Oh damn, Hallie cursed silently. Now Pascal the Mouth will spread all over town that I've hired a lawyer. She had to think fast.

"It's nothing urgent," she said smoothly. "It's just some legal advice Grandpa asked me to get for him so he could write a proper will."

"Grady been sick?" Pascal asked with concern, and came around the counter to her side.

"No, but he's nearly seventy and wants to make sure I'm taken care of if something should happen to him."

"Well, glad to hear that. Grady's been 'round here longer'n anybody else I know."

"Yes, and I hope he'll be around years longer." Hallie smiled to herself, knowing that today she wouldn't be the subject of Pascal's wagging tongue. Turning to leave, she said, "Good day, Pascal."

As she stepped forward, she heard a ripping sound and looked down to see Pascal's foot anchored to the hem of her skirt. Slowly raising her head, she realized he had no idea what he had done. Carefully tugging at her skirt, she asked, "Pascal?"

"Yes ma'am?"

"You're standing on the hem of my skirt."

He gazed down, and the color rose above his starched white collar and up into his face. His Adam's apple seemed lodged in his throat. He gulped. "So sorry... so sorry," he managed and hastily removed his foot. With a thin, nervous smile, he said, "Good day, Miss Hallie."

Outside, Hallie found a private spot, anxious to read the letter from Ira Delaney, a lawyer she knew from San Francisco. He and her father had become friends during the war. He too had left the South after the war, taking his family with him to California. Hallie had written him, following her release from the Indians, to tell of the fate of her parents. Now she was asking for his help in clearing Ben's name. At the time she had written him, she felt no urgency to find the men who murdered her father. But that was before the "Poet Bandit" had encountered Lem. "Lem" was a common name, and she heard it often, but until her last robbery, she had never been able to place a voice with the name.

After reading the letter, she put it into her reticule. Delaney had convinced a well-known San Francisco private investigator, Stephen Bradshaw, who was reluctant to take Hallie's case, that she was capable of paying for his services. He was willing to come to Prospect City to make a preliminary investigation, even though the murder of Sarah Hargrove had happened months ago. He should arrive within the month, but could not provide a definite date.

She had more than enough money now to hire this Stephen Bradshaw. What could be more fitting than to spend Hargrove's own money to find the murderer of his wife?

The stagecoach came to a halt in front of the hotel. As usual, the activity of the townspeople came to a standstill as they paused to gaze curiously at the passengers who were disembarking. Only the drunks and gamblers who frequented the saloon remained completely oblivious of the arrival of the weekly stagecoach.

Hallie laughed to herself, thinking that the townspeople probably were waiting to hear if the Poet Bandit had struck again. Disappointment was evident on their faces as Slim shook his head and said, "Seems like the bandit has found hisself greener grass to graze on. Ain't seen hide ner hair of him in weeks."

Everyone's attention was drawn to the sole passenger who was being assisted from the coach by Slim. A young woman gazed shyly around the town, shielding her eyes from the fierce glare of the sun. She reminded Hallie of the porcelain doll she had as a child: petite, fragile, and dainty. She was wearing a daffodil-yellow dress, the skirt made fuller by the layers of lace-fringed petticoats that were revealed as the breeze gently wafted around her ankles. The bodice was modestly inset with an overlay of delicate lace and molded alluringly to small breasts and an extremely tiny waist. Perched atop her long, bouncy blond curls was a matching bonnet that framed an exquisite heart-shaped face.

Consciously, Hallie lowered her eyes and frowned at her drab brown taffeta skirt and plain white blouse.

"Now I wonder," Pascal murmured from behind her, "what a purty little gal like that is doing in a place like this."

Hallie glanced over her shoulder at Pascal, who was awestruck by the young woman's beauty. He loosened his tie and stretched his scrawny neck, trying to see over the gathering crowd of men blocking his view.

Squaring her shoulder, Hallie replied curtly, "I'm sure it won't take you long to find out, Pascal," and continued down the boardwalk to her wagon. The men she passed gave her no thought: they were like hungry wolves feasting on their next meal as they pushed and shoved, trying to be first across the street to make the lady's acquaintance.

The saloon door swung open as she walked directly in front of it, and two drunks staggered through, knocking Hallie headfirst over the railing.

Two large hands grabbed her hips to prevent her from falling. Hallie was livid with rage, thinking one of the drunks was taking liberties with her. Turning and swinging her lethal recticule in one swift movement, she slammed it into her tormentor's stomach. She heard his gasp and drew her arm back to strike him over the head while he was doubled over, but she arrested her hand in midair as she recognized her victim.

Slowly Ashe lifted himself to a partly upright position. He glared at her with rock-hard eyes, his efforts to control his temper evident by the furious working of his jaw.

Hallie lowered her arm and clenched the purse strings in her suddenly moist hands. "Ashe, I didn't know it was you," she said beseechingly.

"Thank God for that," he growled, "your aim most likely would've hit the target."

Hallie's face quickly reddened, and inadvertently she glanced down to below his belt buckle.

Ashe smiled crookedly. "Don't worry, no harm done."

Her eyes shot up at his suggestive remark. Ashe took her by the elbow and propelled her down the boardwalk and around the corner of the saloon. Placing her against the clapboard wall, he braced his hands on either side of her head, fencing her in.

"Why is it every time I'm in your most charming presence, you somehow manage to injure me in one way or another?" His eyes were mocking her, but there was no anger in his voice.

"I thought you were one of those drunks pawing at me. Where did you come from so suddenly?"

"Unfortunately, I followed them out of the saloon. If the truth were known, I didn't know whom I was saving. All I could see was a fluff of petticoats and two pretty legs dangling in the air."

"And that's all Ashe Barkley needs to see to save a damsel in distress." Then, remembering the young woman, she continued, "I know another damsel who will be in distress if all those men keep vying for her attention at once."

"Am I needed elsewhere?"

Ignoring his bold remark, she said softly, "You once said I was pretty even in my spinster clothing."

He felt he was melting in the luminous glow of her blue eyes. "Even lovelier without," he retorted rakishly, and trailed his finger down her neck to rest on her collarbone.

Hallie wrestled with her emotions. "But do you really think of me as a lady, especially since I let you ... I mean...." She couldn't say the words.

"You are a lady with class, Hallie, but you are a woman too. I would not want you to be such a lady that you forget that." His hand dropped to cup her full breast, and he felt her quiver beneath his touch as his thumb caressed the aroused peak.

Her lips parted as she saw the desire flicker in his storm-gray eyes.

"Kiss me, Ashe," she implored with a shiver of unleashed passion.

Removing her eyeglasses, he stuck them into his shirt pocket and wondered what had come over her. Anyone passing by could see them if they looked this way, yet she didn't seem to care about propriety. The urgency of her request sparked a fire in his loins that had waited to be rekindled for too long.

His mouth brushed teasingly across hers, his tongue trailing along the wetness of her lips. He curbed the passion within him, wanting the kiss to last for an eternity. The humdrum sounds of the bustling town dimmed and Hallie only was conscious of what this man's hands and mouth were doing to her.

But Ashe was aware of their surroundings; and, not wanting to jeopardize Hallie's reputation, he drew her protectively into his arms. Not breaking the kiss, he searched out an alcove nearby. Raising her slightly off her feet as he embraced her, he carried her to the privacy of the nook. Still holding her, his hand lowered and cupped her buttocks, pressing her softness into his hardness.

Their lips met time and again in sheer abandon, their wild desire superseding caution.

Ashe groaned with pleasure at her unrestrained passion, wishing fervently they were back at their hidden canyon lake where they could give in to their desire. He had so much to teach her of the joys of lovemaking, and he wanted her to join him as they climbed step by step to ecstasy.

A sudden clash of metal, and a cat's screaming meow startled them from their embrace. Two scrawny cats darted past them and disappeared around the corner.

Hallie giggled. "Do you realize where we are?"

Ashe looked at the overturned cans, and the odor of rotten garbage assailed his nostrils. "I'm rapidly beginning to realize. Seems we've intruded into someone else's territory."

"You certainly choose strange places for a rendezvous, Ashe Barkley," Hallie said, bringing her arms up and locking her hands at the nape of his neck. "But I doubt anyone would dare disturb us...except of course, all the starved animals in town." She purposely ran her long fingernails along the base of his neck.

A lopsided smile tugged at the corner of his mouth. "Keep that up and you may reap the consequences that starvation entails, my love."

"Oh?" she replied coaxingly, and pressed her breasts sensuously against his chest.

Ashe swiftly unbuttoned her blouse and, slipping her blouse off her shoulder, he trailed numerous hot kisses down her neck and between the valley of her breasts. Swirling his wet tongue around each taut peak, he felt his anticipation growing.

Hallie's entire body weakened as his mouth and tongue assaulted her. He was lifting her into his hardness, easing her skirt slowly up to her thigh. His hand began untieing her pantaloons, and she felt his warm, callused fingers stroking her bare skin. And then Hallie came to her senses.

"Stop, Ashe!" She tried to slide out of his embrace, but his hands pressed her with determination against his throbbing flesh.

Hallie panicked, and she kicked her dangling feet into his shins. He released her and she backed against the wall, wildly ashamed of her behavior. She studied his passion-filled face. Did he think so little of her that he would have taken her in an alley like a trollop off the streets? But wasn't that what she deserved? After all, she had been the instigator.

Turning, she pressed her forehead against the clapboard wall, her hands clenched into fists.

"Hallie," Ashe said, gripping her shoulders, a worried frown creasing his brow, "I'm sorry. What else can I say?"

Gathering her composure, she turned quickly and adjusted her blouse. She crossed her arms across her chest, sighing deeply. "There is no reason for you to apologize. I don't think I should see you again." So I don't give way like this again, she added silently, not caring where I am, or who might be watching.

Ashe arched a angry brow. "Just like that! Have you forgotten how much you enjoyed our lovemaking?"

Hallie pushed past him, kicking an empty can in her path. Pivoting, her skirt whirling about her ankles, she said with undue calmness, "That is my problem, Mr. Barkley." She stalked off, leaving Ashe staring after her nonplussed.

"Damn," he cursed, and vented his temper on the overturned trash can.

Hallie heard a violent clatter as she rounded the corner and walked hastily toward her buckboard. She untied Dixie's reins, and was about to step into the buckboard when someone called her.

"Hallie, wait!"

Peering over her shoulder, Hallie saw Martha standing outside her sewing shop, waving anxiously at her, an excited smile on her face. Hallie stepped down from the buckboard and hurried to her. "Good afternoon, Martha," she greeted. "It's seldom I see you outside your shop."

"I know, but today is special. If you aren't in a hurry, I would like you to meet my niece who arrived just today."

Hallie wondered briefly if the young woman she saw getting off the stagecoach earlier was Martha's niece. "I would be delighted to meet her."

Martha beamed. "Then please come inside and join us in a cup of tea."

The narrow aisle of the shop was flanked by long tables with an assortment of fabrics stacked neatly on the surface. At the back of the small shop was the room where Martha did her sewing. Since Martha was the only seamstress in Prospect City, the light from her shop could be seen in the wee hours of the night. When her husband, Frank, had died in a freak mining accident, Martha was left penniless. Knowing how skillful she was with a needle and thread, Doc Nelson had generously offered to help her out by financing the House of Stitches. Now he was able to court her openly, but their times together were few and far between. While Martha worked into the night to complete orders, Doc Nelson spent late hours across the street at the Drinkalot Saloon. His usual excuse when he'd had one drink too many was, "I shouldn't have set her up in business; I should have married her."

Lifting her skirts, Hallie followed Martha upstairs to her living quarters above the shop. She had visited Martha here on several occasions. As always, when Hallie entered the apartment she was amazed to find no sewing clutter. A mixed bouquet of freshly cut flowers sat on the small table in front of the open window, its fragrance permeating the room.

"Have a seat, dear," Martha invited. "I'll tell Clara you're here. She's freshening up a bit." She disappeared into the spare bedroom.

Hallie sat down at the dining table where Martha had placed a tray of sweet cakes and apple tarts. As Martha and Clara stepped into the room, Hallie was once again startled by the beauty of the young woman. She had removed her bonnet, and her shimmery blond hair fell over her shoulders. Her face was radiant, a rosy glow suffusing her creamy complexion which had never been touched by the sun. Large, dark brown eyes examined Hallie as she awaited the introductions.

"Hallie," Martha said, "This is Clara Gentry, my niece. Clara, Hallie Parker."

Hallie rose from her chair and offered her hand to Clara. "I'm delighted to meet you, Clara."

"It is indeed a pleasure to meet you," Clara said exuberantly. "For a while I thought I was the only young woman who dared to travel to this part of the country. I'm glad to find someone else seems to have made the treacherous journey unscathed."

Only Martha noticed the brief sadness which etched Hallie's features. "You've come a long way?"

"Yes," Clara answered, "All the way from Kentucky."

"If you two will excuse me," Martha intervened, "I'll get the teakettle hot." She headed for the kitchen, and Clara and Hallie sat down at the table to chat.

"It seems we are neighbors in some respects," Hallie said. "I'm originally from Atlanta, Georgia."

"What a small world," Clara declared, taking a bite of the tart. "How long have you lived here?"

"Close to ten years. What brings you here, Clara?"

Clara's voice wavered. "My mother, Aunt Martha's sister, died a few months ago."

"I'm terribly sorry. Were you left alone?"

"Not entirely. My brothers have families of their own, so I just sold our home and moved out here. My father died right after the war, so there was no one to manage our farm. I hadn't seen Aunt Martha since I was a small child. She and Uncle Frank never had any children and spoiled me terribly." Leaning forward, she whispered, "She's much thinner than I remembered. Has she been ill?"

Seeing Clara's concern, Hallie explained how hard Martha had worked since Frank had died.

"Then maybe I can help lighten her load," Clara said brightly. "She doesn't know her niece is quite experienced in the art of sewing. Living in a household of men and being the only girl, I had to learn quickly. My mother and I had our hands full."

"You didn't by chance make the dress you're wearing, did you?" Hallie asked in admiration.

"Yes. Do you like it?"

"I've never seen such beautiful workmanship," Hallie replied.

"Now, Clara," Martha said, entering the room and overhearing their conversation, "I did not invite you here to live with me to put you to work. When you wrote to me, telling me of Nancy's passing, you never mentioned you sewed."

Clara giggled. "You never would have allowed me to come here and help you out if you had known. Please, Aunt Martha, I want to help...really I do."

After Martha poured their tea, her eyes ran swiftly over Clara's pretty dress. "Well...only if you'll take the time to enjoy yourself."

Hallie pursed her mouth. "Should you not listen to your own advice, Martha? With Clara working with you, maybe you can have your evenings free every now and then. I'm sure Doc would like that, too."

Martha's eyes twinkled. "He does get quite frustrated with me at times. But he's hardly the one to criticize. We've had many a meal interrupted when he gets called away to tend to the sick. Of course, I can't get angry with him over that."

"Could we have Doc for dinner one night?" Clara asked anxiously. "I would love to meet him."

Martha's hand flew to her forehead. "Oh dear, I forgot I invited him tonight. That was before I knew you would be arriving today. I didn't prepare a thing."

Clara rose from her chair. "Then let's get out the pots and pans. I'm a rather fair cook, too."

"I really need to be going. You wouldn't want me in your kitchen. Maria certainly doesn't want me in hers," Hallie said, picking up her reticule.

"Who's Maria?" Clara asked.

Hallie laughed. "My friend who also has been my grandfather's housekeeper for years."

"Your parents are still in Atlanta?"

"My . . . my parents are both dead." Taking a deep breath, she tried to smile, but sadness still lurked in her eyes. "I'd better be on my way. I'll stop by the next time I'm in town."

"Please do, Hallie," Clara said softly and extended her hand. "Thank you so much for coming by."

As Hallie descended the steps to the shop, she smiled and thought: It won't be long before Clara's doorstep is crowded with men wanting to court her, Ashe Barkley, too, most likely. She ignored the twinge she felt at the thought.

When Hallie finally began her journey home, she did not leave unnoticed. Ashe Barkley stood beside Rebel and argued with himself whether to follow her and give her the eyeglasses or keep them until she sought him out to retrieve them. On the other hand, he knew she'd never venture to Hargrove's ranch.

He remembered wondering what he would do with Hallie Parker after he seduced her. Since he had accomplished what he had set out to do, he should be able to carry on as he always had. There were too many women available to allow one little bit of fluff to get under his skin. She was unlike any woman he'd ever known, and he didn't know how to deal with the unsettling emotions that rioted within him. He thought of a line in one of her Poet Bandit poems: "A constant burr in your britches I'll be...." It was intended to irritate Hargrove, not Ashe Barkley. But now she was a burr in his britches, and kept sinking deeper and deeper into his aching flesh; he didn't know how in hell he was going to rid himself of the gnawing desire that ate at him twenty-four hours a day. It seemed as though the tables had been turned on him.

Reaching into his shirt pocket, he pulled out her eyeglasses. She didn't need them in order to see, but was she so blind she couldn't see what she was doing to him? In the separate identities she so painstakingly established, he found something that drew him back to her time and again. He was amused by the humor and wily personality of the Poet Bandit; he admired the proper Miss Hallie Parker who possessed the intelligence and determination to survive in a man's world; and he desired the woman who concealed her heart and soul within a thick shell, occasionally giving him a glimpse of the real Hallie Parker. Never knowing which of these vibrant personalities would emerge, he found his pursuit of Hallie interesting and pleasurable, but she seemed about as attainable as a star. He'd reached out and touched that star once—what had caused her to suddenly distrust him?

Ashe replaced the eyeglasses in his pocket and, sliding his booted foot into the stirrup, he swung his long leg over Rebel's back. Trotting slowly out of town, he watched the buckboard ahead of him with the stiff, proud back of Hallie Parker behind the reins. No, now is not the time, he thought, branching off in the direction of Hargrove's ranch.

* * *

"Señorita Hallie," the children said gleefully as she stepped down from the buckboard. "Hola!" Taking her by the hand, they led her through the door to the classroom. Eight shiny new desks now sat in the small room instead of makeshift tables. Hallie felt their excitement. She ran her hand over the smooth, unmarred surface of one of the desks. Tears came to her eyes when she noticed a larger desk at the head of the room with a vase of mixed wildflowers sitting on top of it. She walked down the narrow aisle to it and found a note from Jeb Smith, the carpenter, lying on its surface. "Just my way of showing appreciation for what you are doing for these children."

Little Juanita came to her side and yanked on her hand. "Qué pasa, Señorita Hallie?"

"I'm just so happy, it makes me cry," she sniffed, smiling down at Juanita. Taking a daisy from the vase, she asked, "Did Mr. Smith send the flowers, too?"

"Oh no," Paulo proudly stated, "we picked them for you to say thank you."

Kneeling down, Hallie opened her arms, hugging and kissing each child. "Now, let's try our new desks."

Hallie, with her back to the children, printed two short words on the blackboard for them to identify. She heard their eagerness to answer, and turned smilingly. Her smile quickly disappeared when she saw Ashe Barkley leaning against the doorjamb. She attempted to ignore him by looking at Paulo, whose hand was raised. "All right, Paulo, can you tell me the first word?"

A wide grin spanned his impish face. "Love. L.O.V.E."

"Very good," Hallie answered, trying to remain calm.

Anna Maria was bouncing up and down in her seat. "Let me tell the other, Señorita Hallie, por favor."

Hallie looked at the other children, who gazed at her with pleading eyes. "You'll all get a turn, so don't fret. All right, Anna Maria, your turn."

"Blue. B.L.U.E."

"Correct. Now who can make me a sentence using both words?"

Ashe pushed away from the door and ambled down the narrow aisle, his heavy boots thumping against the hard-packed dirt floor. The children stared at him questioningly as he patted each head in passing.

What's he up to now? Hallie asked herself as he sauntered up to her, took the chalk from her hand, looked her squarely in the eyes, and grinned rakishly. Turning to the blackboard, he wrote: "I love your angry blue eyes."

Hallie felt the color rising in her face. She prayed the children were unable to decipher all the words, but their stifled giggles told her otherwise.

Straightening her spine, she thrust her chin at him and pasted a mock smile on her mouth. "Perhaps you should be the teacher, Mr. Barkley. You do have a way with words."

His dark brow winged upward as though considering her proposal. He shook his head. "The Poet Bandit might be a better choice."

The children were so quiet that Hallie almost forgot

they were in the room. They seemed bewildered by the conversation.

"Mr. Barkley, what reason do you have for interrupting my class? If it is to tell me how angry my blue eyes are, then you haven't seen the worst of it."

"Would you come outside with me for a moment? I have something to give you."

"All right." Then, turning to the children, she said nervously, "Read tomorrow's lesson in your primer. I'll be back in a few minutes."

Ashe followed closely behind her, feeling the smoldering flame of desire that Hallie always seemed to arouse in him. Too many days had passed since he had seen her, and his dreams were full of her naked splendor. Even dressed like a spinster, she was desirable. To cool his ardor, he had begun to frequent the brothel. Sophie had failed miserably in squelching the flame Hallie had kindled.

Outside the doorway, she turned to face him. "Once again you have managed to humiliate me," she lashed out, shaking an irate finger in his face. "Now, why are you here?"

"You, of course," he replied, running his eyes over her crisp white blouse, then back to her face. "I do love your angry blue eyes." He removed her eyeglasses from his shirt pocket and placed them on her upturned nose.

"I thought I'd lost them," she conceded, remembering the moment he had removed them to kiss her.

He chuckled. "I've never met a woman who possessed so many personalities. Frankly speaking, I like the one with whom I spent those glorious days and nights. Was that the real Hallie Parker, or are there a few more I've missed along the way?"

Hallie toyed nervously with the string tie at her throat. "I really don't know," she said in a remote voice. "It's been such a long time since I've known her that even I wonder who she is."

Ashe tilted her chin up, and her eyes met the warm desire in his. "Then let me help you find her again so we can get reacquainted." He shoved his hat back, making her aware of his handsome sun-browned face.

"I don't think that's a good idea, Ashe. Things are better the way they are now."

He brushed his finger across her lips as though to silence her. "Don't run away from me again, Hallie. What we had in those three days went beyond our sexual experience. We crossed a new horizon by casting aside the ill feelings between us. I had hoped to gain your trust, and as for my behavior in town the other day, it was uncalled for."

She raised her eyes to meet his. "I still don't know you well, Ashe—but it's myself I don't trust, not you."

Ashe sensed the turmoil churning within her. "Don't shut me out." Leaning forward, he brushed his lips across her forehead. "Avoiding me will not solve the problem, Hallie."

Hallie heard the children, and from the noise, she knew they were getting restless. "Ashe, this isn't the time for this discussion. I need to go back to the children. Was there any other reason you came to see me?"

"Yes. I was worried about your gunshot wound. Is

it healing properly, and did you have any problem explaining your absence for those three days?"

"It's tender, but healing just fine. No one knows about my injury, and my absence went unnoticed."

"Good," he said, thrusting his hands deep within his pockets. "I guess you'd better go back in while we can part on friendly terms."

Mounting Rebel, Ashe tilted the brim of his hat in a polite farewell and pressed his heels gently against Rebel's flanks.

As he disappeared, Hallie felt a sinking within her heart. She had tried to end their relationship, but he wouldn't take no for an answer. Did Ashe love her or did he only enjoy making love to her? If she openly expressed her love for him, would he turn away from her? He did not seem the type of man to settle down and become a family man. Regardless of the answers, it was too late for Hallie already. Should Ashe Barkley leave Prospect City, which she was well aware he could do without a moment's notice, he would take her heart with him.

Chapter 10

The gray clapboard building, which was the Prospect City Hotel, stood like a sentinel at the end of Main Street. Curtained windows overlooked both sides of the street. A long porch ran the length of the building, complete with weatherbeaten rockers and narrow flower boxes overflowing with primrose. The wide steps leading to double doors that stood ajar were Hallie's destination as she smoothed the shimmering fabric of her skirt and adjusted her lightweight shawl.

A message had been delivered to the ranch that afternoon; Stephen Bradshaw had arrived on the noon stage. He had invited her to join him for dinner. The hotel dining room was renowned for its home-cooked meals, and as everyone knew, it was the only respectable place in town to discuss business and have a good meal. It was a place a lady could join a gentleman for dinner with impunity, and a place Hallie Parker felt comfortable entering unescorted.

She was really upset with Bradshaw's high-handed behavior. He should have found a way out to the ranch and introduced himself. Hell fire, she was the one paying his fee. He had taken a room at the hotel (a room she might well be paying for!), sent her a message confirming his arrival, and invited her to join him for dinner. Though she was anxious to meet him, she felt this business relationship had already gotten off on the wrong foot by her coming to him. She had a thing or two to say to Mr. Stephen Bradshaw.

She entered the hotel and started across the lobby, her temper escalating with each step. Just as she reached the counter, someone called her name. Turning, she came face-to-face with a captivating smile.

"Miss Hallie Parker, I presume?" he asked, extending his hand. "Stephen Bradshaw at your service. If you will allow me, our table is ready."

Nodding her head in astonishment, she clasped his arm as he led her into the dining area.

So much for anger, she mused, her ill thoughts evaporating as he drew her chair out for her, then seated himself.

He was a tall man dressed in an expensive three-piece pinstripe suit. A shock of gleaming red hair capped a very handsome face. Sparkling blue eyes assessed her as her own examined him. She was glad she had taken such care with her appearance.

Gone was the matronly bun at the nape of her neck. She had brushed her hair until it gleamed with rich highlights, then secured the sides to the back of her head to tumble at will over delicate shoulders. The wire glasses were gone, and her eyes sparkled. She wore a dress Clara had painstakingly made for her of the palest blue satin, which fit her tiny waist snugly, then flared out into yards of shimmering skirt. A square neckline hinted at the fullness of her breasts. No ruffles or flounces distracted from the beauty of the wearer; her mother's cameo resting against her creamy throat complemented the deceptively simple design of the dress.

"What a surprise to find that I am in the employ of such a lovely lady." Stephen Bradshaw's eyes twinkled in merriment.

"Thank you for your lavish compliment, but I assure you it won't gain you an extra cent," she countered tartly.

Draping his hand over his heart, he shook his head in mock sorrow. "You wound me deeply, Miss Parker. Beauty is in the eye of the beholder, and I behold loveliness, wit, and a way with words that would delight the most indifferent admirer."

Her laughter bubbled up spontaneously as she allowed herself to enjoy his outrageousness, and she relaxed.

"I believe, Miss Parker, that we will do splendidly together."

"Mr. Bradshaw, may I be so bold as to inquire— do I hear a touch of Southern drawl?"

His features became stoical for a brief second, then a wide grin split his handsome face. "Yes ma'am, you sure do. I intend to return to the South someday, but it isn't feasible at this time. But someday..." A faraway look crossed his features.

"Someday. I know what you mean, Mr. Bradshaw," Hallie whispered, patting his hand. "I am originally from Georgia."

"Well, I'll be damned," he drawled, "this calls for a celebration." Cocking a fiery red brow, he asked, "Would a glass of wine be suitable?"

"The occasion calls for no less," she replied seriously.

As the serving girl poured sparkling red wine into crystal glasses, Stephen ordered their meal, and Hallie gazed around the small dining room. Several men seated at a table midway across the room stared in curiosity at her and her companion. Pascal Fritts was seated among them. She could see the questions flit across his face as she nodded politely in his direction.

Within the blink of an eye, he was on his way to her table. Hallie prayed he was watching where he was going. It was apparent he had only one thing on his mind, and that was assuaging his curiosity. She couldn't have endured the embarrassment if he had tripped and landed headlong on their table. Luckily, he made the journey without mishap, owing only to the wide aisle between the tables.

"Good evening, Miss Hallie. How are you?"

"Hello, Pascal. I'm fine, thank you. And you?"

"Jes' fine," he mumbled, glancing at her companion.

"Pascal, have you met Stephen Bradshaw?"

Stephen stood, clasping Pascal's outstretched hand.

"You ain't from around these here parts, are ya, Mr. Bradshaw?" Pascal inquired, trying to figure out the connection between Hallie and Bradshaw.

"No, I came from San Francisco. Miss Parker has

long been a friend of my family. I had some business in the area, so I decided to renew our aquaintance."

Hallie smiled. Words slid over his lips like water off a duck's back. She couldn't help but be amused and she appreciated his discretion concerning the true purpose of his visit.

Excusing himself to return to his table, Pascal turned back one last time. "Miss Hallie, you sure do look different tonight. I don't exactly know what it is, but, well... maybe it'll come to me." Shrugging his thin shoulders, he left their table.

Hallie, not wanting to be rude, hugged her arms round her middle and bit her lip until she could contain her laughter. She raised dancing blue eyes to Stephen's face as he asked, "Stalwart gentleman, isn't he?" Stephen's smile was warm and friendly as he raised his glass to Hallie. "To friends, Hallie," he said, touching their glasses.

She answered, "To friends. May they be true and long-standing."

"Amen," he replied, drinking deeply from his glass. "It didn't bother you that I stretched the truth about our friendship to Mr. Fritts?"

"On the contrary, I was delighted. By this time tomorrow, everyone in town will know the story of my old friend coming to town."

"I need you to tell me everything you know about Ben Langley. Even little things that seem unimportant to you might just be the key I need. And Hargrove—tell me anything you can about him. I have some background on him already. He's not unknown in San Francisco."

The serving girl brought their food and departed with a shy smile for Stephen. There were large steaks dripping in their own juices and potatoes fried to a golden brown, accompanied by fresh green peas and piping-hot bread.

Cutting into the steak, Hallie glanced at Stephen. He was staring boldly at her. Startled, she asked, "Is something wrong, Stephen?"

"No, not really. You are very beautiful, Hallie. I don't think I have ever met anyone quite as lovely as you. Have you ever thought about leaving this one-horse town for the big city?"

A blush stained her cheeks and she was quick to note, "Why, you'll turn my head with your flowery compliments if you're not careful. My grandfather is here and he's the only family I have. I couldn't leave him. I haven't told him about your expected arrival. If you want to know the truth, I haven't told him anything. If it's all right with you, I'd just as soon this be our business."

"Unless you choose to divulge the reason for my presence, I can assure you that my lips are sealed. You're the boss, remember?"

Hallie then told him everything she could about Ben Langley and Vern Hargrove. Sometimes the bitterness would surface and she would push her food aside. Each time Stephen would push it back with a witty comment, and she would smile and resume eating. When she finished her meal, she declined the offer of dessert. She sipped her coffee while Stephen had a large helping of peach cobbler dripping with rich cream.

"Where in the South are you from, Stephen?"

"Columbia, South Carolina, a beautiful place—at least, until Sherman burned it." His features suddenly became cold, and hatred leaped from his eyes.

The blood drained from Hallie's face, and the words she was about to speak lodged in her throat as she saw Ashe Barkley standing in the doorway of the dining room. His stance was as bold as everything else about him, and his presence commanded attention. Every head turned in his direction.

He spotted her and his long strides closed the distance between them in an instant. The muscles flexing in his jaw seemed as lethal as the gun strapped snugly to his thigh.

"Evening, Hallie." He switched his attention to Stephen. "You're a little far from home, aren't you, Bradshaw?"

"The home you refer to is no more. You Yankee bluebellies saw to that. You all wanted to make sure we went to our knees. I just didn't realize you would kick a man while he was down and then ride roughshod over his broken spirit."

"I know it's been said before," Ashe reminded Stephen coldly, "but war is hell. I wanted no part in the destruction and burning of homes. I only wanted the damnable war over. I was sickened by the loss of so many lives and the rape of a beautiful land."

Hallie's breath left her in a rush, and she whispered, "You're a Yankee, Ashe?" Placing trembling fingers over her lips, her face a deathly white, she moaned hoarsely.

"Not only a Yankee, Hallie, but a deadly bluebelly. Captain Ashe Barkley," Stephen spat.

Ashe saw the pain on Hallie's face and cursed the rotten luck that had brought Bradshaw to Prospect City. She wasn't ready to hear this—she didn't love him enough yet to forgive him his past. He watched as hatred began to burn in her eyes, and he flinched to hear it in her voice.

"Get out of my sight, you lying bastard," she hissed. "The sight of you sickens me. To think I called you friend! You, of all people, should know how I hate Yankees."

He started to turn away, but he knew he had to try to salvage something. "No, Hallie, that's where you're wrong. I didn't tell you because I knew you wouldn't understand." With that, he was gone.

Her war memories overcame her with the force of an avalanche, as she let her hatred have full rein, even while her apparent attention was on Stephen.

They remained at the table talking until it was obvious it was long past closing time.

Stephen told her as much as he knew about Ashe's exploits in the war. Although they fought on different sides, Stephen knew Ashe Barkley's name well. The man was revered, his courage and daring had moved him swiftly through the ranks. His reputation struck fear in the most stalwart fighter. It was almost as though Barkley didn't care if he lived or died. Stephen had heard this time and again when Ashe's exploits were related. Stephen had prayed he would never come face-to-face with the legend. His prayers hadn't been heard, he told Hallie as he took her to Martha's apartment.

She had asked Clara if she could spend the night.

As it turned out, she didn't have the strength to drive back to the ranch, after these revelations.

Clara welcomed her with open arms. She suspected something was troubling Hallie from the vacant look on her normally vibrant features. But she said nothing, not wanting to pry. The constant tossing and turning and the smothered sobs Hallie tried to hide in the fluffy pillow told Clara volumes. She wondered what the man's name was. Without a doubt, a man was the cause of Hallie's pain.

Ashe groaned as the raucous sound of noisy children drifted through his window. With a sharp, indrawn breath, he swung his legs over the edge of the bed. Taking cautious steps, he crossed the room to the washstand, his head pounding with each step. He picked up the pitcher of tepid water on it and liberally doused his head.

Dripping wet, he scanned the room quickly, taking in the disheveled appearance of his clothing, and the half-empty bottle of whiskey resting precariously against his pillow.

"What the hell," he muttered angrily mopping his head with a towel. Picking up the bottle, he drank deeply, relishing the burning pain as he sank once again onto the bed.

Cushioning his arms behind his head, he let his thoughts run rampant as he drank his breakfast of brain-numbing liquor.

That bitch, that fiery, feisty bitch. Why the hell should he take the blame for the whole damned war? She could have her milk-faced Stephen Bradshaw. What in God's name was he doing in town anyway? It seemed to him somebody said last night in the saloon they were old friends.

"Old friends, my ass," he muttered violently.

He remembered Bradshaw well. Ashe and his unit had been patrolling for snipers when they had come upon a deserted campsite. He had positioned his men, and they had waited... waited for hours in a mist of drizzling rain, straining their ears for any untoward sounds, Ashe himself sitting perched in a tree until his legs were numb with pain. And their waiting had paid off; the only problem was that they were outnumbered two to one.

They had the advantage of surprise, however, and they had attacked swiftly and violently. The ensuing battle was bloody and fierce, and when it was over, Ashe's unit triumphed, and Stephen Bradshaw was one of the unlucky bastards captured. Bradshaw had little to say, but the hatred was evident—not that Ashe could blame him for that. Had their positions been reversed, Ashe no doubt would have felt the same. He felt a reluctant spark of admiration for the man who had survived prison camp, which at best had been a death trap. Survival had been the name of the game, and apparently Bradshaw had come out a winner.

A soft rap on the door interrupted his thoughts. When he didn't respond, the door creaked open and Sophie peeked around the frame. She smiled brightly and entered the room, blatantly ogling his nakedness. Ashe pointedly drew the sheet over himself.

"Didn't realize you were such a late sleeper, but then it was almost dawn before you agreed to take a room. That was some game. You must have come away with a bundle." Her eyes scanned the room until they came to rest on the scattered bills and gold pieces piled on a scarred chest next to the bed.

"I haven't counted it... if that's what you mean."

"No, I just thought I'd check to see if you need anything." Lowering herself to the edge of the bed, she ran her hands over the firm muscles of his thigh. "I guess the other players thought you'd be too drunk to play a winning game. They realized their mistake quick enough, I reckon, after you cleaned them out." Her hands became bolder when Ashe didn't seem to mind her advances.

"Can I get you anything, Ashe?" Her voice was filled with innuendoes as she gazed at him with warm brown eyes.

"You might get me another bottle of that rot gut whiskey, if it's not too much trouble."

Her touch left him cold. Without insulting her outright, he eased himself from the bed. Drawing on his pants, he raked a handful of money from the chest. Picking up her hand, he placed the money in her palm, closing her fingers around it. "This should take care of the bottle."

"She must have dug her claws deep, Ashe." Sophie stared at him in amusement.

Anger flashed across his features, and with a muttered curse he draped his gun belt around his waist, buckling it with a vengeance.

"Forget I said anything. It's none of my business," she said rapidly, stuffing the money in her bodice. "I just don't like seeing you trying to forget whatever it is eating at you by drinking."

"You're right, Sophie."

"I am?" she asked in astonishment.

"Yeah, it's none of your business," he answered coldly.

Drawing herself up, she replied stiffly, "I'll have your bottle sent right up." Eyeing him warily, she gathered her skirt in her trembling hands and flounced from the room.

His overly bright eyes were the only indication of the large quantity of liquor Ashe had consumed. He sat at the table in a relaxed position, his cards held loosely in his hand. There was a dangerous air about him. He hadn't spoken a half-dozen words, except when it was his turn to wager. His clipped responses had discouraged conversation. The other men at the table fell into an uneasy silence.

Clint O'Malley pushed through the saloon doors. All movement stopped as the other customers eyed him warily. He never failed to cause trouble when he had too much to drink, and he had obviously come to drink. He always seemed to single out one individual and ride him as hard as he could until fights broke out or a fast draw ended it for the unlucky bastard. The large ornate mirror behind the bar had been replaced more than once because of the O'Malley twins, and Clint seemed to have grown meaner by the day since his brother's death. His eyes narrowed and sparked with burning hatred when he saw Ashe.

The men at Ashe's table didn't miss the dangerous

yellow flecks in Ashe's cold gray eyes, nor his free hand sliding beneath the table to rest on his gun. They were more than relieved to see Clint O'Malley divert his attention to Sophie.

Making his way to the bar, he whispered loudly in Sophie's ear. "How's 'bout me and you gettin' us a bottle and goin' upstairs for a while?" Not waiting for her answer, he draped his arms around her, his hands kneading her buttocks as he drew her close. Sophie reached for the bottle and led him upstairs.

A short while later, O'Malley descended, a smug smile on his face.

"That sure as hell didn't take long, O'Malley," one of the miners called out. "You been takin' lessons from rabbits?"

One could have heard a pin drop until suddenly O'Malley threw his head back and laughed. "Yeah, Gus, you know me, pick 'em and stick 'em."

Everyone drew a sigh of relief and began talking again.

Pascal Fritts sat quietly at a small table with Doc Nelson, discussing the upcoming celebration that took place annually in Prospect City.

O'Malley's voice rang loudly through the room, his voice slurred slightly as he pounced on his chosen victim. "Pascal, come 'ere and have a drink with me."

Pascal swallowed nervously, and he answered in a nervous, high-pitched voice, "Me?"

Doc watched with sympathy as Pascal made his way to O'Malley's side.

"Yes, O'Malley?"

"Ya got any tidbits to share with us?" O'Malley asked, shoving a drink at Pascal.

"Well, me and Doc was just discussin' the big celebration comin' up."

"No, no, that's not what I mean," O'Malley interrupted. "I want to know who's sleepin' around this week. Ya do keep up with it, don't ya?"

"Why, Mr. O'Malley, I would never repeat such a thing," Pascal said with indignation.

"Pascal, I believe yore lying. Everybody in town knows yore just like an old woman, carryin' your tales to anyone who'll listen. Well, I'm listenin'. See, ya have everyone's attention," he said with a sweeping gesture of his hand.

Pascal gazed about the room, all eyes rested on him. O'Malley didn't notice the marked pity in those eyes.

"I'm waitin', Pascal. What's it gonna take?" An ugly sneer spanned O'Malley's face. Grabbing Pascal by the collar of his shirt, he shoved him roughly against the bar. "Damn ya, ya scrawny excuse for a man."

"Leave him be." The coldness of the voice swept through the room, chilling the spine of more than one patron.

"Well, damn my soul, if Ashe Barkley ain't come to your aid, Pascal."

"It'll be more than your soul if you don't unhand him."

"And when has yore word become law around here, Barkley? From what I hear, you've been nursin' a bottle all day." Pushing Pascal from his side, O'Malley turned his full attention on Ashe. Those standing nearby began moving nervously away.

"I'll bet ya can't even stand up. Ya'd best leave well enough alone or they'll be carryin' ya out on a slab."

"I've never been one to pass up a sure thing, O'Malley. This is one bet you lose," Ashe replied, rising smoothly to his feet.

"Ya man enough to collect, Barkley?" O'Malley sneered.

"I hate to disappoint you, O'Malley, but you don't have anything I want."

"Ya'd be singin' a different song if I had Hallie Parker. I'd like to see yore face if I tumbled her right before your eyes... You know, that's somethin' to think about. I bet she'd really put up a good fight. I like that in a woman—if ya know what I mean."

"Shut your goddamn filthy mouth, you son of a bitch."

"Ya gonna shut it for me?" O'Malley asked with contempt, reaching for his gun.

No one saw the gun leave Ashe's holster. One second it was there, then in the blink of an eye it had cleared the leather. Once again Ashe Barkley had ruled in favor of death.

Returning from the general store, Hallie and Clara were pushed aside as several miners rushed past.

"What's all the commotion about?" Hallie called out to one with a slower gait.

"Ashe Barkley done kilt the other O'Malley twin. A faster gun hand I ain't never seen. O'Malley never knew what hit em. Never even got his gun raised. Can't say as I'm sorry, good riddance if you ask me."

Hallie looked as though she'd seen a ghost. Bracing

herself against the storefront, she asked, "Is Ashe all right?"

"Fer as I could tell, it didn't bother him none. O'Malley had lit in on Pascal when Ashe stepped in. Then O'Malley had a few choice words to say about you, Miss Hallie. That did it. Barkley shot him clean through the heart."

Hallie's ears were ringing and a strange buzzing sound whirled around in her head. Not again, her mind screamed, Oh my God, not again.

"You all right, Miss Hallie?" A concerned voice pierced her mind, and with great effort she nodded her head.

"Thank you," Clara said, speaking for the first time. "I'll see that Hallie rests for a while, and she'll be fine. I think it's just the shock."

"Good day, ladies. I'm anxious to hear what the sheriff has to say."

Clara steadied Hallie, and got her as quickly as she dared to her room.

Hallie stretched out on the bed, her mind in a turmoil as she sifted through what the miner had told them. What could O'Malley have said about her to cause Ashe to kill him? Maybe the miner had it all wrong. That thought was her salvation as she pictured Ashe dealing his own brand of punishment. A man that lives by the gun dies by the gun, he'd said. The words seared her mind. Tears streamed from her eyes and into her hair.

Clara caught her attention as she placed a cooling cloth on her face. "Does this sort of thing happen often, Hallie?"

"Not as frequently as it used to. But one time is more than enough."

"I don't mean to pry, Hallie, but may I ask if you are grieving the killed or the killer?"

"Not O'Malley. He was rotten to the core."

"The other man is Ashe Barkley, right?"

"Right."

"Do you care for this Ashe Barkley?" Clara asked shyly.

"No, I hate him," Hallie answered emphatically.

"It seems strange to shed such tears for a man you hate."

"Well, I hate him...Oh Clara," she sobbed, "I don't know what I mean. I hate the way he makes me feel. He's a Yankee, and I hate Yankees. They destroyed everything, my life, my home, my family. He lied to me...well, maybe he didn't lie, but he made such a fool out of me."

"Well, if that's the case, maybe you should know I'm a Yankee, too, Hallie," Clara said, rising to her full height.

"No, you can't be."

"Oh, but I am. I haven't sprouted horns or a pointed tail, but I'm definitely a full-blooded Yankee. Do you think only the South suffered because of the war? Are you so immersed in self-pity that you can't see that other people suffered too? Or do you hide behind this hatred because you can't face the truth?"

Hallie shook her head angrily, denying Clara's words. But she had to acknowledge them finally, and she answered guiltily, "I never thought about people in the North suffering." Then she broke down and told Clara about her mother's death, the ruination of their beautiful home, how they had to forage for food, how they had buried what valuables they could and sold them as the need arose, and finally how she had to leave her beloved mammy behind when she and her father left Georgia. As the story unfolded, Clara held Hallie offering what comfort she could, her tears mingling with her friend's.

When Hallie finished her story, Clara told hers. She had been raised in Kentucky, but her family was torn apart by the war, one brother swearing allegiance to the South while the other vowed to support the North. There were also two younger brothers left at home who were too young to fight in the war but old enough to take sides, and they fought continually. There were the tears her mother shed as she begged and pleaded with God to send the older boys home safely. Her father aged before her eyes, endlessly walking his fields, hoping to catch sight of his sons returning, and then finally dying of a broken heart.

"My brother who supported the South came home. The other one didn't. The saddest part was when he discovered they were in the same skirmish on different sides. My brother will go to his grave wondering but never knowing if one of his bullets killed my brother Michael."

"I'm sorry, Clara, truly I am."

"I know, Hallie, but you've got to understand that you can't live in the past. Don't let your pride get in the way of your happiness. You have your whole life in front of you."

My whole life, Hallie thought. It seemed like forever. But she was not sure if even that was enough time to forget—or forgive. It wasn't something that would just go away. She would have to make conscious choices and abide by the decisions.

And, if Clara were right, listen to her heart as well as her mind.

The lone figure leaned casually against a gray boulder, his look menacing as he watched with interest the approaching riders.

Hallie's hair streamed behind her, and she outdistanced her companion by a length. She called out to him, her spontaneous laughter echoing through the canyon. Drawing on her reins, she slowed Licorice until Stephen Bradshaw drew up beside her, his words unclear to Ashe as he watched the pair. He surmised they must have been to the mine to visit her grandfather. No telling what else they'd been doing, he thought sourly. Bradshaw sure as hell spent enough time dogging her every step.

He had seen Hallie and Bradshaw in town several times together, always in deep conversation as though their meeting was more business than pleasure. Ashe wondered what Hallie was up to. Any more of her harebrained schemes, and she would end up getting hurt again or something much worse. He was sure she hadn't confided in Bradshaw about her unlawful activities. Something was going on, and he sure as hell intended to find out what it was.

As he watched the pair, they split up, Hallie heading in the direction of the ranch and Bradshaw heading toward town. Ashe mounted Rebel, and keeping Bradshaw in sight, followed at a leisurely pace. On the outskirts of town, he caught up with Bradshaw.

"I know you don't have a hell of a lot to say to me. But I'd like to give you a little friendly advice—Hargrove is a vindictive man, and he's aware of your snooping around. He may not kill you outright, but I can guarantee he could, and would, make your life miserable."

"Are you threatening me, Barkley?" Stephen's voice dripped with contempt. "Could it possibly be jealousy rather than concern for my welfare that prompts your advice?"

"I don't pretend to know what's going on between you and Hallie. And I don't particularly care. The issue is your safety, if you plan to remain in Prospect City."

"If that's all you have to say, I'll be on my way," Stephen snapped, reining his horse away from Ashe.

"Don't say you weren't warned, Bradshaw. Just be sure you always have one eye over your shoulder."

Ashe watched as Stephen galloped away, a flicker of admiration in his eyes. Had Hallie hired Bradshaw to find her father's killer? The trail would be stone-cold by now. It was unlikely that anything would surface to implicate Hargrove. But what if she'd hired him to clear Ben Langley's name? If that was the case and Langley was indeed innocent, then Bradshaw was in more danger than Ashe had at first thought. If Hargrove found out what Hallie had done, wouldn't he be more likely to single her out than Bradshaw?

"My God," he muttered angrily, "she's done it again." With nagging dread, he turned Rebel toward Hargrove's ranch.

Chapter 11

Prospect City had come into existence because of the mining boom. There were townspeople who could remember well when buildings replaced tents, finally giving a sense of permanence to those who had made the town their home.

One day each year, the miners and the townspeople would hold a celebration commemorating Prospect City's beginnings. It was an event that had something for everyone from sack races for the children to a challenge boxing match for men who wanted to prove their physical prowess.

An enormous amount of food was prepared, with each family contributing a picnic basket and shopkeepers donating tables where this abundance of food was spread out for all to enjoy.

A haunch of beef, slowly roasted over a deep pit of hot coals the whole night, its enticing aroma a welcoming signal of the oncoming celebration.

The festival was a release from the humdrum chores of daily life and one of the few times a year that neighbor met neighbor equably and their women could enjoy each other's company and the welcome break of talking about "female" topics.

It was the social gala of the year and everyone looked forward to it with anticipation.

In addition, some of the women prepared pies, cakes, and other sweets to be auctioned off, with the proceeds going to the orphanage, the only fund-raising event of the year.

On the evening prior to this annual event, Hallie anxiously waited for Maria to finish her chores for the day. The instant she saw Maria depart, she made a quick dash from the stable to the house. Feeling as though she were an uninvited guest in her own home, she opened the door to the kitchen and entered Maria's domain.

The kitchen was spotless, the pots and pans hanging neatly from an iron rack above the long scrubbed top pine work table.

She intended to bake an apple pie for the auction.

Donning one of Maria's aprons—which was large enough to wrap around her waist threefold—she gathered all the necessary ingredients for making an apple pie, all the while wishing she had paid more attention to Maria's instructions.

While dried apples stewed slowly on the cookstove, Hallie mixed the pie crust. Then, remembering she had forgotten to add the cinnamon to the apples, she sorted through the various spices, smelling each one until she identified the one she sought. She added it and let the mixture cook awhile longer before dipping her spoon into the mixture to taste the result. She decided it needed a touch more cinnamon.

Sinbad, who was kept in the kitchen, followed her every movement. Unable to keep his opinion to himself any longer, he squawked, upsetting Hallie's concentration.

She shook her finger menacingly at him. "If you dare mention I was in here this evening, I'll wring your orange neck." He immediately buried his head beneath his wing, almost as if he understood her threat.

Distracted by his antics, Hallie grabbed the closest spice jar and sprinkled it liberally into the stewing mixture. The spicy sweet aroma wafted through the room as she replaced the pot lid, and Hallie thought that anything that smelled that mouth-watering good just had to taste delicious.

Finally, she meticulously placed a latticework of dough across the surface of the pie, delighting in her handiwork. Before she slid it into the oven to bake, she remembered that Maria always sprinkled cinnamon on top, and she did the same.

As the pie baked, she began the task of cleaning the kitchen, finding as much flour on the floor and on herself as she had used in making the pie. She sang as she washed and dried the dishes, and melted into the domestic scene around her, imagining herself married and cooking meals for her husband and children. It touched an alien place in her heart with a deep yearning she had never known existed.

Pulling the apple pie from the oven, she set it on the table to cool. The crust was a toasty brown, and she resisted the urge to pinch off a piece to sample it.

She wondered which lucky man would bid on her pie. This was her first year of entering anything in the auction, and that in itself would surprise everyone. She took the pie with her to her bedroom, and hid it in her chifferobe to forestall Maria's discovering her illicit use of her kitchen.

Grady Parker, dressed in his finest woolen trousers and a crisp white shirt, stepped up on the platform to deliver the welcoming speech. For as long as Hallie could remember, Grady had been asked to do the honors, since he was among the first miners to settle in Prospect City.

Standing at the front of the large crowd with Maria and her family close beside her, Hallie listened intently to his words and watched the animated gestures of his arms and hands accenting risqué jokes, the same jokes he had told for years.

Unconsciously, she searched the crowd for that familiar face, but it wasn't there. In the weeks since her heart-crushing discovery that Ashe Barkley was a Yankee, she found herself expecting some kind of confrontation with him that would end her anguish. He had hurt her with his deception, and she felt she had been made a complete fool; and the resulting fury and pain burned like a fiery torch in her heart. The same thought tumbled over and over in her mind: she had given herself willingly to a despicable Yankee.

The crowd applauding at the end of Grady's speech

brought her thoughts back to the present. Everyone shook Grady's hand as he moved through the crowd, anxious to hear how the prospecting was coming along.

Hallie saw Clara and Martha behind a long table readying the baked goods for auction. They were fenced in by a group of men and she wondered if their mouths were watering over the delicacies or over Clara's extraordinary beauty. She wove her way through the crowd to ask if she could help in any way.

"No, everything is taken care of," Clara said, then winked impishly. "Do you think if we yelled fire, we could clear a path out of here?"

"You couldn't move them from this spot unless the Drinkalot Saloon was on fire."

"You look very pretty today," Clara went on. Hallie could wear anything and look good, Clara thought, admiring the pale coral dress that brought out the auburn highlights in her unbound hair, which was tied back with a matching ribbon. The scooped bodice did not hide the gentle swell of her breasts and the creamy texture of her skin.

"It's old, really, but I've not had many occasions to wear it."

By this time, Hallie was feeling like a caged lion. "I don't know about you, but if you're game I'm ready to rake a path through these men and see what else is going on around here." Clara was agreeable, particularly since two women were making their way behind the table to relieve them. As she and Hallie came around the table, the prospectors congenially formed a path for them. Knowing that every square inch of their bodies was under intense scrutiny, they tamed the gentle sway of their hips as they hurried past the men.

Stephen Bradshaw greeted them at the end of the line, and Hallie noticed immediately that his gaze rested solely on Clara. She quickly introduced them, and after a few polite words, she excused herself, leaving the two of them to become acquainted on their own.

Her attention was drawn by the auctioneer who raised his gun and fired a shot into the air to silence the crowd so he could begin auctioning the baked items.

She wished that this particular event did not require the donor to put her name on her contribution. I know it's a good pie, she told herself. She remembered how delicious it smelled as the aroma of the cinnamon floated from the oven. Deciding firmly that she worried over nothing, she anxiously waited for her own name to be called.

Clara's item was called up; it sold for the highest price ever paid for a baked item, and Stephen Bradshaw was the purchaser. A shy smile glimmered across Clara's lips as his name was announced.

"Miss Hallie Parker!" The auctioneer's voice drummed like thunder in Hallie's ears. She clenched her clammy hands into the folds of her skirt.

"An apple pie, pleasing to the eye, but no doubt more pleasing to some hearty man's stomach," the auctioneer droned. "Do I hear a dollar for such a tasty morsel?"

An unfamiliar voice rang out from behind her and then the squeaky voice of Pascal Fritts entered the bidding. The crowd cheered Pascal on until his competitor reluctantly backed down.

"Going once... going twice..."

"Twenty dollars," a new voice thundered.

Everyone, including Hallie, turned and stared in astonishment at Ashe Barkley seated defiantly in his saddle as Rebel sidestepped anxiously beneath him. He had evidently just arrived.

Pascal's Adam's apple bobbed convulsively in his long, thin neck. He gazed worriedly around the crowd.

"C'mon, Pascal, ya ain't gonna let him outbid ya, are ya?" one of the prospectors yelled

Pascal's bulging eyes rested momentarily on the gun that was strapped to Ashe's thigh, and the perspiration coursed down his face like a waterfall.

"Going one... going twice... sold... to the man on the gray stallion."

A faint, roguish smile barely touched the corner of Ashe's mouth, unperceived by everyone except Hallie. Ashe's stone-hard eyes clashed with her stormy blue ones.

Swinging his long, muscled leg over Rebel's back, Ashe dismounted and made his way through the crowd to claim his prize. Stopping abruptly beside her, he jeered, "I hope it's worth the money I paid. My curiosity got the best of me. I had to see if you do as well in the kitchen as you do in... other things."

The crowd was dwindling, leaving Ashe and Hallie alone in front of the table, her apple pie had been the last item sold. Thrusting it into his hands, she spat, "Take it! If I'd known my efforts would have been wasted on you, I'd have poisoned it."

He studied her briefly, removed the cover from the pie, held it to his nose, and then replaced the cover.

"Well?" she asked angrily.

"Well what?"

"Aren't you going to taste it after you spent so much money?"

"I always save the best for last," he said with a half-smile.

Hallie was tempted to snatch the pie from his hands and grind it into his arrogant, handsome face. Instead she whirled, and in a most unladylike way, stomped down the dusty street.

She headed toward the long line that had formed waiting for lunch, only to find she had lost her appetite. Nothing tempted her. Not even the bowls of fresh summer beans, corn, squash, sweet potatoes, or the hot Mexican foods of every variety, or the succulent roast beef arranged on the table.

She located Grady, Maria, and Juan at the end of the line and joined them. She was dismayed to see Ashe, who had suddenly come up behind them.

"Now I know why you were behaving so suspiciously yesterday, señorita," Maria said with a knowing smile. "But you seem very displeased that Mr. Barkley bought your pie. Don't you know the quickest way to a man's heart is through his stomach?"

"Frankly, Maria, his heart is the least of my interests. If I'd known earlier that I'd have such easy access to his stomach, Ashe Barkley would be regretting right now that he bought my pie."

After filling her plate and finding a shady spot beneath the overhang of a building, Hallie looked around to see where Ashe was. Unfortunately, he was too close for comfort. She almost choked on a bite of beef as she saw him watching her with amusement.

Attempting to put Ashe out of her mind, she thought of her conversation with Stephen a few days before. He was having no luck in his attempt to gather information. People would clam up when he casually brought up Vern Hargrove's name or anything concerning him. There was a fear in them that Stephen sensed ran deep. The money he offered on the side did not tempt them. Rather, it made people more suspicious of him. A few of Hargrove's ranch hands followed him discreetly when he rode out to the mines to question a few of Langley's prospecting buddies. He was beginning to believe Hallie was right about Langley; if Langley was guilty, why was there such an interest in his own activities? Someone knew the truth, but finding him was like searching for a needle in a haystack.

The departure of Grady and Juan broke her thoughts. Turning her attention to Maria, she said, "I haven't seen Luis today. Where are he and Consuela?"

Maria smiled radiantly. "Consuela had back pains last night and did not come to the celebration for fear of having their baby on Main Street. If you think you can do without me tomorrow, I'd like to stay with her tonight."

"Of course. It's no problem. Luis has frequently delivered colts, but delivering his first child is another matter, and he may need you."

Maria nudged Hallie in the ribs, motioning toward Ashe with her eyes. He was eagerly slicing through the apple pie with his Bowie knife as he cast a greedy smile toward Hallie. Hallie waited in anticipation as he cut a generous slice and bit into it.

He chewed only once. The expression on his face was one of pure agony.

Hallie was too shocked for words. Ashe frantically spewed the contents from his mouth, his hands groping blindly for the tall pitcher of beer beside him. Coughing and sputtering, he tossed his head back and quickly drained the entire contents. His hands clutched his throat, his face contorted in agony.

"Surely it can't be that bad," Hallie said, grasping Maria's arm in trepidation.

"Madre de Dios, what did you put in that pie, mi niña?"

"Apples, sugar, and cinnamon—that's all."

"That man acts like he just got a mouthful of a whole hot chilli pepper. Are you sure it was cinnamon?"

Hallie recalled how she had sniffed out the cinnamon, and how Sinbad's squawking had interrupted her. Was it possible that, because of her annoyance, she had picked up the wrong bottle?

"Oh my Lord, no wonder he's going crazy! Maria, I might have used red pepper instead of cinnamon."

Ashe, unable to endure the pain that continued to burn like molten lava in his throat, grabbed the empty pitcher and ran to the barrel of water that was positioned between Hallie and him. He ladled water into his pitcher and gulped it down, but nothing seemed to take the raw burn from his mouth and throat. His teary eyes focused malevolently on Hallie, and he clenched his fists at his sides to keep himself from plowing them into her startled face.

"Oh, senorita, he is as red-eyed as a raging bull. You must have added enough hot pepper to blow up Prospect City."

Slowly, Hallie drew her legs from beneath her and rose to go to Ashe and apologize, but he turned abruptly from her and returned to where he had been sitting. Picking up the pie, he turned back and walked with precise, deliberate steps toward her.

Hallie stared helplessly at the man towering over her, blanching at the blazing anger in his eyes.

He sucked in a ragged breath between clenched teeth, and when he spoke, his voice was deadly calm and raspy. "How in the hell did you know?"

"Know what?" she asked meekly.

"That I'd be the crazy fool who'd buy your damned loaded pie."

Hallie, appearing braver than she actually felt, answered cheekily, "I did not know you'd buy my pie, but you should feel honored to be the first man to ever taste a pie baked by Miss Hallie Parker herself."

"You're a damned witch," he wheezed, massaging his aching throat. "You wouldn't have dared do that to any other man in this town but me."

She arched her brow. "Perhaps I am a witch." Then, feeling very reckless, she said with a devilish smile, "While I was making my pie, I had the eerie sensation someone was in the room with me. A vision came to me—an apparition I guess you'd call it—of a tall, dark man with cold gray eyes, hovering near the stove, enjoying the sweet, rich aroma of the cinnamon. As

I watched him, a wavering blue uniform came into view, and it suddenly dawned on me..." She paused for additional effect.

"Damnit, Hallie," Ashe cursed beneath his breath, "come off of it."

"No, no." Hallie waved her hands in front of his face. "You were the one who said I am a witch. I'm only verifying your statement."

Ashe stoically crossed his arms over his massive chest. "Go on then," he said caustically.

She looked around, no one but Maria was within earshot. Her words rolling one over the other, Hallie quickly finished, "It was a sign... a sign warning me that some Yankee bastard was going to buy my pie, so I smothered it with hot chili peppers." She waited a brief second to see what effect her words would have on his passive, implacable features. As the redness crept up his neck and on to his scowling, bloodthirsty face, Hallie spun around and grabbed an astonished Maria by the arm. Maria shrugged apologetically as Hallie hustled her away into the crowd. She saw Ashe drop the pie facedown on the ground and squash his boot heel into its remains.

Hallie didn't understand most of the garbled Spanish words that Maria repeated over and over, but knew she had not heard the end of it.

The weather turned threatening with the musky, lingering scent of a gathering storm. Clouds moved across the sky as though undecided which direction to go. Some of the late afternoon contests were scheduled closer together, and crowds rushed from one end of town to the other so as not to miss any events.

The tables were moved back into the shops and the street was cleared for the horse race. Beer and whiskey flowed freely, and the men's spirits elevated as quickly as their moneybags deflated.

Hallie went to Clara's room to dress for the horse race. It would be an easy win this year, she thought as she brushed her hair until it gleamed; she coiled it at the nape of her neck. She wondered if Ashe would ride Rebel in the race. She hadn't seen him since the pie episode an hour or two ago, and she hoped he had gone back to Hargrove's ranch.

Everyone was assembling for the horse race when she emerged wearing a long riding skirt, colorful shirt, and a bolero, and joined the riders lined up at the end of Main Street. The spectators who couldn't see well enough from the boardwalk climbed into their wagons. Agile children shimmied up the support posts of the overhead awnings for an unobstructed view.

At the sound of the gun, the horse race was on, with Hallie's horse running third, but she was not worried. She knew how to win, and held Licorice back as one horse after another sapped its strength to get ahead. She pulled back on the reins to keep Licorice under control. His numerous jaunts with the Poet Bandit astride had given him more training than any of the other horses in the race.

Hallie felt there was only one horse to beat in order to win, and that was Vern Hargrove's. He was barely in the lead, and the second horse was close on his heels.

Hallie leaned down and caressed Licorice's mane and said, "Remember, Licorice, we're running after the stagecoach. We're going after Hargrove again, but this time he's going to know who beat him."

Licorice's ears seemed to perk up at her words as though he sensed what she expected from him.

Noticing she was gaining slightly on the two leaders without increasing her own speed, she leaned over Licorice's mane and nudged him with her knees. No further command was necessary. Licorice felt the reins loosening against his bit, and with a burst of energy previously held in check, he sprinted ahead, his hooves appearing to barely skim the parched earth beneath him.

The large, sinewy muscles of her stallion rolled and quivered against Hallie's thighs. His midnight coat glistened, and the strong scent of sweating horseflesh assailed her nostrils. Licorice was exerting all the physical and mental force he possessed to take the lead. He was running neck-and-neck with Hargrove's steed. Hargrove's man lashed his horse repeatedly. Hallie silently cursed him as long welts surfaced on the horse's flanks, his mouth foamed and his steps faltered. It wouldn't have surprised Hallie if the poor animal fell on the spot and died instantly.

It was a two-mile race around the town, and the finish line was in sight, a bright red banner waving them in. Hallie lay almost full-length across Licorice's back and was ecstatic as she left Hargrove's horse and rider in a choking cloud of dust.

The crowd cheered as Hallie and Licorice flew over

the finish line. Her wide-brimmed hat slapped against her back; her hair, loosened from its knot, streamed out behind her like a red-gold banner caught by the wind.

Chapter 12

Hallie led Licorice into the livery stable to rub him down.

"See," she said, brushing his coat with gentle strokes, "Hargrove's no different from anyone else. He can be beaten, and we proved it."

"The only thing you've proved, Miss Parker, is how downright stupid you are."

Hallie, aware of the identity of the intruder, blatantly ignored his presence behind her.

"You'll regret the day you tried to make a fool out of me."

Hallie turned to face him and regarded him with insolence. "I didn't make a fool out of you, Hargrove. You were born that way."

A few men who happened to be in the stable tending to their horses stopped abruptly at Hallie's careless words.

"You connivin' little bitch," Hargrove growled, a fiendish sneer curling his upper lip, "I shoulda shot that damn horse of yours that day when I had the chance. Maybe then you'd remember who is boss in this town."

"Are you quite through blowing off steam?" Hallie snapped. "I don't have time to listen to your idle threats. Get your pompous ass out of my sight and accept your loss like a gentleman for once."

Hargrove took a quick, deep breath, momentarily stunned by Hallie's audaciousness.

The men nearby were taking great pleasure in watching a mere woman openly insult the man whom they had cursed time and again among themselves, never daring to say it to his face. Seeing the rage in Hargrove's eyes as he focused his attention on them, they hurriedly finished what they were doing and left the livery stable. Hallie Parker was obviously one woman who could take care of herself without their help.

When they were alone, Hargrove immediately took advantage of the situation. He towered over her and gripped her arm, his large, fat fingers biting into her flesh. "So ... there's spirit in the little woman. Let's see if you have it when there ain't nobody around to protect ya."

"You don't scare me, Hargrove, you only make me sick to my stomach." Hallie tried to jerk free, but his grip tightened painfully. "Go ahead. We both know you're stronger than I am."

She watched him flinch, and the hate and anger she felt for this man gave her the courage to taunt him further. "Is that what you did to Sarah? Squeezed the spirit from her soul and left her a shell of a woman?

I'm not like Sarah, by God, and I won't let you manipulate me or terrorize me with your threats."

He stared at her with a strange, distant expression in his eyes. His grip on her arm loosened and she pulled away. "I take it I've made my point clear to you, Hargrove."

"Yeah, ya made it clear all right, but you're a fool ... and so's your friend Stephen Bradshaw. If he keeps stickin' his nose in where it don't belong, he's likely to get it blown off."

Turning, he walked to the entrance of the stable, tossing his final words over his shoulder. "Do I make myself clear ... Miss Parker?"

His words shook her. Was Stephen getting too close to the truth? He was definitely stirring up something with his investigation. He was sitting on a stick of dynamite, with some desperate individual—Hargrove perhaps—watching his every move ... waiting until the appropriate time to light the fuse. She might be responsible for endangering Stephen's life. With that thought, she hurriedly left the livery stable on Hargrove's heels to find Stephen and tell him of Hargrove's dangerous words.

She found him in a cluster of men near the boxing ring. Each man was placing bets on the boxer he thought would win in each separate match. Not wanting to interrupt him, Hallie paced impatiently on the boardwalk behind them until Stephen noticed her harried face and quickly joined her.

"By the look on your face, I take it you don't care for gambling, Hallie."

"We gamble on something ... or someone ... every

day of our lives, Stephen. As it stands now, it appears we are gambling on your life."

Stephen's eyes narrowed. "Are you trying to tell me something I don't already know?"

She related the scene between her and Hargrove and waited for his reaction.

"Hargrove's a bigger fool than I thought," he said explosively.

"But your life is hanging by a thin thread. I think we ought to halt the investigation for a while."

Stephen grinned. "It'll cost you money."

"The money is not important, Stephen. I don't want your death on my conscience for the rest of my life."

"What about your life, Hallie?"

"Mine?" she asked, her eyes blinking in rapid succession.

"Yes, yours. We've been seen together time and again. Don't you think that anyone with any sense at all would be suspicious?"

Hallie's senses sharpened to a fine pitch. She stared mutely at Stephen's serious face.

"Am I still fired?" He placed his hand on her arm. "Hallie, this is what I do for a living. Sometimes it gets rough, I'll be the first to admit. You don't ever get used to it, but you accept having someone continually breathing down your neck."

His words sounded familiar to her, almost the same words Ashe Barkley had said. "I never thought the investigation would come to this, though."

"It always does when you're close to the truth."

* * *

The remaining events rapidly took place one after another, in view of the rapidly darkening sky. The final event of the day was the boxing match, which was Hallie's least favorite event. She usually left the celebration just as the boxing began. Not this day. Stephen Bradshaw had joined Clara and her, and without dragging them outright to ringside, he kept drifting closer to the roped-off area.

"Ladies, I do believe I'm the envy of every man here."

"Whatever are you talking about?" Clara asked with pleasure.

"Why, the men are just green with envy. The two most beautiful women in Prospect City are on my arm and all these men know it. I tell you truly I've seen more than one unfortunate man catch a sharp elbow in the ribs from an observant wife."

Hallie and Clara laughed uproariously at Stephen's outrageous compliments.

Silvery gray eyes followed Hallie's every move. Ashe leaned inconspicuously against one of the few remaining trees in the city, his hat pulled low over his eyes, a cigarette dangling loosely from his lips. Exhaling a mist of gray smoke, he crushed the cigarette beneath his boot, and, pushing himself away from the tree, he scanned the crowd until his eyes rested on the figure of Hargrove surrounded by his cronies. He made his way toward them.

"Any of these boys good enough to come away a winner, or do they just beat each other to a bloody pulp?" he asked Hargrove.

"Not to speak of. They just do it for the hell of it.

Usually when the time arrives for their match, they're too drunk to care. For the most part, it's just a lot of blood ... bloody noses and busted lips. Not too much damage, but enough blood to keep the crowd happy. What about you, Barkley?" Hargrove asked, his interest suddenly perking up. "Are you any good with your fists?"

"I can take care of myself," Ashe said shortly.

"I'd be willin' to make it worth your while if you could beat any man of my choosin'."

"How much?" Ashe asked indifferently.

"Does five hundred sound like a fair price?"

"Sounds like a hell of a lot of money, to my way of thinking," Ashe answered, wondering whom Hargrove had in mind.

"Yeah, but I get to pick your opponent, and you have to beat him to collect it."

"Sounds fair enough to me. Just let me know when. I'll be around." And with that, Ashe disappeared into the crowd.

It was all Hargrove could do to keep from rubbing his hands together in glee. It had been so simple. He didn't have much use for Barkley, but he had even less for that Stephen Bradshaw nosing around and asking a lot of questions. The only problem facing him was how to get Bradshaw to agree to the match. Shouldn't be too hard, he thought. He had heard there seemed to be bad blood between the two men, if he could credit Pascal's tales. Either way he would come out a winner. If Barkley beat the hell out of Bradshaw, it might be easier to encourage him to leave town. If the fight went the other way, he would still come out ahead because he wouldn't have to pay Barkley.

He rubbed his hands together in anticipation. Nothing could be better. He'd teach that snoop Bradshaw a lesson, or wipe the arrogance from Ashe Barkley's face. Or both. That was worth five hundred dollars! One of his men handed him a pistol. He lifted his arm, and a gunshot rang through the air, bringing a hushed stillness over the milling crowd, as they watched Vern Hargrove climb into the boxing ring. "Ladies and gentlemen, let me have your attention. We have an additional treat for you all. I'm sure many of you know my foreman, Ashe Barkley. Well, he has consented to fight any man of my choosin'—I might add, for a sizable purse."

Murmurs of consternation greeted this announcement, and a restless shifting of feet as the crowd awaited the name of the man he chose.

Hargrove's piercing eyes scanned the crowd, finally settling on Bradshaw. "How about you, Bradshaw? You got the guts to go against Barkley?"

Hallie blanched and grabbed Stephen's arm. "Don't do it, Stephen, please don't."

"This is just the opportunity I need, Hallie. I can beat the living hell out of Barkley with no complaints from anyone."

Eagerly Stephen made his way to Hargrove's side. "What's in it for me, Hargrove? You don't expect me to take a chance in getting my brains knocked out for nothing. Sweeten the pot, and I just might be interested."

"A hundred dollars, win or lose. You can't do better

than that." Hargrove usually wasn't so generous, but he really wanted this match to take place, and he was fearful that Bradshaw would back out unless he made it worth his time.

"Couldn't we get a little sweeter? How about two hundred?" Stephen asked, cocking a brow. He could tell Hargrove was becoming nervous, and relished the thought. "I'll do it for two hundred, or you can stand up here and let Barkley smash in *your* face. You can't let the people down now that you've promised them a fight."

A cheer went up from the crowd, and Hargrove angrily felt the tables had suddenly been turned.

Doc Nelson was given the job of refereeing the fight, to eliminate one fighter from absolutely beating his opponent to a pulp. Only basic, existing rules were applicable in these annual matches. The ring was in the center of Main Street, and a cowbell of undistinguishable origin was used to start the fight. The rounds were supposed to last for three minutes, but more often than not, they lasted longer.

In the past, the bell-keeper had been known to become so engrossed in the fight, he would forget to ring the bell. Or the crowd would become so loud and boisterous, the fighters couldn't hear the bell when it rang. A gunshot was then allowed to end that round of fighting.

Ashe took off his gun belt and carefully laid it aside. As he stripped off his shirt, the muscles rippled across his broad back. When he turned around, Hallie sucked air deep into her lungs. He was gorgeous, she thought, remembering how it felt to run her fingers through the dark hair that matted his chest. He seemed unconcerned about the match, but Hallie knew better. She could see the muscles flexing in his jaw, which was the way he showed tension.

Sophie's high-pitched voice called out to Ashe, "I'm pulling for you, Ashe. Drinks are on the house if you win, honey."

Hallie would have slapped her if she had been close enough to reach her. "I'll bet that's not all that'll be on the house if you win... honey," she mimicked just loudly enough for Ashe to hear.

A teasing smile lit his features as he deliberately nodded in Sophie's direction.

The men in the crowd applauded as they voiced their approval. The cowbell clanged raucously, drowning them out. Clara gripped Hallie's hand in fear. Hallie switched her gaze to Stephen. He too had removed his shirt, revealing a chest that was broad and firmly muscled. Flaming red hair also covered the length of his chest, and disappeared into the waist of his pants. The sight of him half naked did nothing for Hallie. All she had to do was glance at Ashe, and her blood raced riotously through her veins.

Facing each other, the fighters circled, their arms held close to their bodies, waiting for an opening. Stephen landed the first blow, a straight shot to Ashe's stomach. Returning quickly, Ashe parried another attempt and delivered a short, punishing jab to the side of Stephen's head. Stephen staggered backward. Regaining his balance, he charged at Ashe. Stephen's right arm shot out, but Ashe turned, catching only a glancing blow to his chin.

The cowbell rang loudly. Each man returned to his corner covered with a thin sheen of perspiration. Too quickly, the bell rang again to resume the fighting. On and on it went. The men seemed equally matched. Stephen's nose was bloody, and Ashe sported a cut lip. But Stephen's punches were becoming erratic, and Ashe dodged them with ease.

Stephen made his final mistake when he whispered through clenched teeth, "Yankee bastard."

Ashe saw red. The words Stephen uttered sounded too much like "uppity bastard," words he had lived with in his heart for as long as he could remember. He was damned if anyone else would ever get away with calling him that again. He had pulled his punches, not wanting Hargrove to gloat over arranging the fight. But damn it, enough was enough. He drew back his arm, releasing the anger brought on by Bradshaw's slur. Catching Bradshaw beneath the chin with a deadly uppercut, he snapped his head upward. Simultaneously, Bradshaw sank to the ground, out like a light. The crowd went wild, applauding and stomping their feet.

Ashe nursed his bloodied knuckles, paying no attention to the boisterous spectators. Waiting until he was sure Bradshaw was all right, he picked up his shirt and shrugged it on, not bothering to button it. He tucked it into his pants, then strapped on his gun belt.

Bradshaw seemed little worse for wear as he was helped up by Clara Gentry.

He seems in capable hands, Ashe thought, swinging his long legs over the rope in search of Hargrove as he accepted congratulations.

Scanning the crowd, he looked for Hallie, but she was nowhere in sight. She obviously couldn't take it, he thought scornfully, as he approached Hargrove.

"I believe you owe me," Ashe reminded him gently.

"Easiest money you ever made, I bet," Hargrove sneered.

"I wouldn't say that."

"You tellin' me killin's easier?"

"I don't end up with a busted lip—that's all I'm telling you."

Hargrove drew a wad of money from his jacket pocket and rapidly peeled off the bills and handed them to Ashe, who carelessly stuffed them into his pocket.

"Ain't ya gonna count it?"

"I don't believe you'd try to cheat me, Vern. There's not a man living who's ever cheated me." The coldness of his words left no doubt as to their meaning, and Vern Hargrove's thick lips became bloodless.

Ashe turned away, disgusted.

Hallie quickened Licorice's pace, having no desire to be caught in the middle of the desert in a storm. She had left the boxing match in a hurry—not so much because of the approaching storm as the private storm that was building inside her. Try as she might, she could not hate Ashe Barkley. She had wanted to soothe his wounds as Clara had Stephen's, but how could she touch him without remembering the way his skin rippled across his back as she caressed him during their lovemaking?

She breathed a sigh of relief as the ranch came into view. The gray sky hung suspended over the desert like a giant tarpaulin ready to split its seams from the weight of the rain collected on it. She rushed Licorice into the security of the stable and took care of his needs.

As she strolled down the corridor of the stable, she noticed the nervous snorting and whinnying of the horses. Stepping outside, she saw the cause of their anxiety. No longer was there a gentle breeze, but a dusty wind so strong it threatened to lift her from the ground. Storms were a common occurrence during the hot summer months. They sometimes struck with such fierceness that the horses went wild with fright.

Holding her bandana partially over her eyes to keep out the dust, she ran against the force of the wind as she made for the house. Once inside, she leaned back breathlessly against the heavy door, listening to the eerie sound of the wind howling like a coyote through the breezeway.

The cast-iron bell on the front porch was caught in the vortex of the storm, its incessant clanging deafening to her ears. Grandpa had put the bell there for her safety when he left for the mines, so that if she ever needed help, Juan and Maria—who lived within earshot—would come to her aid.

Leaving her position at the door, she sat down on the divan and watched the brass pendulum of the clock swing back and forth. She wished she had the company of the old stray dog she had found in town, but Grandpa had taken a liking to the poor bag of bones and had taken him to the mines. Only Sinbad was left, and he was probably squawking in the kitchen.

She felt fidgety and on edge. Finally she rose and

lit the lantern on the table. She paced back and forth around the living room until it became pitch-black outside. Taking her gun from the desk drawer, she went into her bedroom. She tried to light her lantern, but the wind coming through her open bedroom window snuffed it out.

Damn, she muttered, going around the bed to close the window. The curtains danced from the force of the wind. Rain splattered the floor and dampened Hallie's clothes as she struggled with the window. Slamming it shut, she lit the lantern and changed into a thin cotton nightshirt.

She pulled back the bedcovers and slipped the gun beneath her pillow; then she lay down between the cool sheets and picked up a small leather-bound book of poetry to divert her attention from the lightning that zigzagged menacingly around the house. A flash split the sky, striking a nearby target. She tried to ignore the cracking sound, but the sizzling bright flashes seemed to touch the house at every point; the thunder seemed to shake the foundation.

Hallie couldn't hear the repeated pounding on the front door or the voice calling her name behind it. But Ashe was frantic that something had happened to her. Desperately he tried to knock down the door, but it was bolted.

"Open up, Hallie," he shouted futilely.

When he received no answer, he ran around the porch to the door off the breezeway. The wind was so strong he nearly lost his hat before he opened the door and rushed in, forcing the door shut behind him. There was no sign of her in the living room. His heavy-booted feet thumped across the wood floor. Opening the door to one of the back rooms, he was brought up short. Hallie sat comfortably in bed, a kerosene lamp on a table beside her, a small leather-bound book in her hands. Hearing the floor creak, she quickly brought the sheet up to cover her breasts, which were barely concealed beneath the thin nightgown she wore.

My God, she screamed silently. In the shadows, all she could see was a tall, dark form in her doorway. Easing her hand beneath the pillow, she pulled out her gun, pointing it at the stranger. "Whoever you are," she said undauntedly, "state your name or meet your Maker."

"Ashe Barkley, ma'am, at your service," Ashe replied smartly, stepping into the light, an amused grin on his face.

"All the more reason to shoot you," Hallie retorted waspishly.

As Ashe started to move forward, he heard the click of her gun. "Are you all right, Hallie?"

"You'd better ask yourself that question, Ashe Barkely."

"Damnit, Hallie, put that gun away. I didn't come out here to ravish you. God forbid if I ever entertained such a thought."

"Liar," she hissed, putting the gun back beneath her pillow. "Every time you come around me, you seem to have that thought in your mind. Why did you come all the way out here, anyway?"

She saw the flicker of the light mirrored in his eyes as he said, "I was worried that you might have been caught in the storm." He smiled rakishly. "But it seems you fared better than I." Without an invitation, he sat down beside her on the bed.

"I thought your bout in the boxing ring would incapacitate you for a few days," she retaliated sarcastically.

He grinned. "The blows I received on my head can't compare to the damaging effects your pie had on my stomach. If I didn't know better, I'd think you really had planned it." His eyes caressed her. Hallie gripped the sheet tighter around her breasts. "You may be a witch, Hallie, but you use other forms of wizardry on a man—like casting a spell on him and creating demons within him that torture him mercilessly when he dares to think of you."

Hallie was mesmerized by his tender words, and reached out to caress the bruise on his cheek and down to touch the blood-encrusted cut on his lip. There was a tinge of sadness in her voice as she spoke. "If only we were not worlds apart, Ashe, then perhaps I could drive some of those demons out of your soul."

"Worlds apart because I am a Yankee," Ashe said, rising from the bed and moving to the window. Gazing at the streaks of lightning in the darkness outside, he said, "I lost my brother to a Confederate bullet, Hallie, I held him in my arms while the life drained from his body. I have reason for hating the South probably more than you have reason for hating Yankees. The lives that were lost on both sides were more valuable than the destruction of property suffered by the South."

Hallie's throat ached with the tears she tried to hold back. Her voice was raw with emotion. "What about the rape of the South's women and the death that more often than not followed that violent act?"

Ashe turned and frowned at her eyes overworn with grief. "What are you trying to say, Hallie?" Ashe came to the bedside and gazed down at her distraught features. "I'm not the only one harboring demons, am I?"

"No," she croaked. "I've carried this one within me for years." Looking up at him, she let a single crystalline tear spill over the rim of her eye. "Ashe, my mother was raped and murdered."

Her words were punctuated by a crack of thunder and lightning and struck a sympathetic nerve in Ashe's heart. He sat down beside her and unfolded her fingers from their tight grip on the bedsheet. "By a Yankee."

It was a question that required no answer, but Hallie felt a strong impulse to release the hate from her heart. "I used to think that, but once Clara asked me if I actually saw the man." She watched his fingers stroke the palm of her hand. "I didn't."

Raising his warm gray eyes to her tearful blue ones, Ashe replied, "Even so, Hallie, Yankee or not, all men are not rapists."

Gulping back the tears, she said, "I know but it will always be there to haunt me. I can't help that, Ashe. God help me, but I can't." No longer capable of holding back the tears that had been dammed for years, Hallie broke loose with heartrending sobs.

Drawing her into his arms, Ashe tried the only way he knew to soothe her. He kissed her forehead and wiped her tear-streaked cheeks. "Go ahead, love, cry till all the tears are swept from your heart. I know how much you need to spill them."

Rocking her back and forth, Ashe kissed away her tears as rapidly as they were shed. He whispered comforting words and offered soft caresses. He had never felt so helpless in his life, knowing that no amount of comforting words would ever remove the pain from her heart.

The sheet fell away from her as Ashe pulled her thinly clad body into the haven of his arms, exposing the smooth, creamy bare arms that wrapped around him and gentle swell of her breasts that pressed shudderingly against him.

She felt his wet shirt against her cheek, thinking it was her tears that had soaked it. Lifting her face from his chest, she dabbed at her eyes with the corner of the sheet.

"Do you feel better now?" Ashe asked huskily.

"Somewhat," she admitted, sniffling; she wondered why she had told this man the haunting secret of her past. "Can I ask you something, Ashe?"

"Only if I can choose not to answer," he replied.

"Why did you fight Stephen?"

"I was mad as hell, and Hargrove offered me the perfect opportunity to vent my anger."

"Why? You yourself said the war is over."

His features stilled as his eyes raked her face. "Guess."

Rising to his feet, he felt the water dripping off the brim of his hat. Tossing it onto the bedpost, he asked nonchalantly, "You wouldn't by chance have something of your grandfather's I could put on until these dry out, would you?"

"That could take all night!" she protested and leaped from the bed.

He grinned rakishly. "I know."

His eyes swept over her caressingly. Her nightgown was damp from being pressed against his wet clothing. The light from the lantern behind her silhouetted her shapely figure beneath the transparent gown, increasing his desire.

"You can't stay here, Ashe." She was stunned by his proposition.

Ashe began unbuttoning his shirt. "Have you ever made love during a rip-roaring storm?"

Hallie was watching each button as he released it from its buttonhole. "Of course not. You should know that better than anyone." The last button was unfastened, and his hand dropped to the gun belt at his waist. "If this was the whole idea behind your coming out here, then you'd just better hightail it back to your own bed."

Anger sizzled in his eyes as he rebuckled his gun belt. Plucking his hat from the bedpost, he walked out her bedroom door into the living room. "I'm sorry I wasted my time riding out here in the storm just to make certain you were all right."

As he opened the door, the rain and wind gushed in with a violent force, molding Hallie's gown to her slim body. Not wanting him to make the trip back to Hargrove's ranch in such bad weather, she tried to smooth their differences. "Ashe, you can sleep in the stable if you like. There's food for Rebel in the storage room."

"Thanks, but no thanks," he replied sharply. "I think I would rather take my chances in the storm."

"Are you hungry?" Hallie asked meekly. "I could fix you a bite to eat."

Raking his eyes over her boldly, he said, "Food is the last thing on my mind."

Chapter 13

After Ashe departed in anger, Hallie continued her pacing about the room. Damn him for making me feel guilty, she swore, stopping at the window. If he gets struck by lightning, it won't be my fault. I offered him a place to stay and even a meal, but no, he had other things on his mind. Serves him right if he gets sick.

As she started to climb back into bed, she realized how the damp gown clung to her body like a second skin. No wonder Ashe wanted to stay the night with me, she thought angrily. She removed the wet garment, tossed it to the floor, and put on a dry gown before getting back in bed. Just because they had made love didn't give him the right to continue seeking her bed. It had been a mistake and, though she hated to admit it, a wonderful experience. But she couldn't allow it to happen over and over again at his whim. There was no future in that kind of relationship. She had the ranch and her grandfather to take care of. Ashe Barkley was a bounty hunter, a man who drifted from town to town reading the Wanted posters. What reason did he have to stay around Prospect City? He already knew the bandit's identity.

He had never mentioned turning her in for the reward. Perhaps he felt that taking her virginity was compensation enough for losing the reward money.

The rain increased in intensity, large drops of water finding their way through the chimney in the living room to rat-a-tat-tat monotonously on the stone hearth. Closing her eyes, she tried to concentrate on the rhythmic beat to block the sound of the rolling thunder from her mind.

Her thoughts continued to drift to Ashe. He was probably cursing her with every breath. She could have offered him Grandpa's bed, but she doubted Ashe would have been satisfied with that arrangement either.

She couldn't understand her feelings about Ashe. She enjoyed his lovemaking, but how far beyond that did her feelings for him go? Did she truly love him, or only love the passion he had awakened within her? She did not have experience with other men, so there was no way to make a comparison.

She was once again startled by a rapid crackle of lightning. Dear God, much more of this and I'll end up sleeping in the stable with the horses, she thought. The last time they had a storm of this intensity, the horses nearly tore down their stalls.

Another flash of lightning struck the cast-iron bell, reverberating it like a hammer on an anvil. She heard the piercing screams of the horses over its raucous clanging. That was all it took to send Hallie fleeing out the door into the heavy downpour, heading for the stable to tend to the frantic horses.

Visions of Hallie in the wet gown—and awareness that she was so close yet so far away—did nothing to squelch the desire burning within Ashe. He had given up the wild notion of riding back to the ranch, deciding instead to spend the night in Hallie's stable with the intention of leaving before she awakened, fighting back the urge to go back into her house and take her and be damned.

Restlessly Ashe roamed the corridor, calming the nervous whinnying of the horses. But no sooner would he get them all settled than a vicious peal of thunder would send them into another frenzy.

When he heard the wild clanging of the bell, Ashe darted out of the stable, giving no thought to his state of undress. The heavy rain pounded his naked flesh, and with each flash of lightning, his vision of Hallie running toward him became a reality. She fell into his strong arms, and she circled her arms around his neck and buried her face against his chest as he carried her into the shelter of the stable.

Her damp gown rubbed against his bare chest, making him quicken his steps to seek an empty stall. There was no light to guide him, so he felt along the wall until he found an open doorway.

Gently placing her down on the bed of straw, he eased down beside her, murmuring, "You're all right now, Hallie, I'm with you."

Bolting upright, she groaned in aggravation. "That's

what's bothering me. Had I known you were here, I would have let you tend to my horses."

"I have tended to them and soothed them to the best of my ability. Why don't you just admit it, Hallie?"

"Admit what?"

"The storm frightened you too."

"You would like to believe that, wouldn't you, Ashe Barkley?" she snapped. "That way you would have a good excuse to soothe my nerves and..."

Ashe chuckled. "Make love to you? I don't need an excuse to do that."

Hallie's heart somersaulted as he gently pushed her down into the bed of straw and lay down beside her. Placing his arm beneath her head, he held her close to him, the length of his naked body pressed against her. Her heart pounded wildly in her chest. Was he waiting for her to reach out for him? she wondered, turning her head toward him in the darkness. They listened to the rolling thunder and nervous whinnying of the horses.

Stalling for time, she said, "Listen to it. Sounds like the end of the world, doesn't it?"

"Let's hope not, love. I've just started living."

His words rang over and over in her mind. The man who lay naked beside her had done more than merely kiss her. The storm did not frighten her; Ashe Barkley frightened her. He had the power to control her mind and body—and what was worse, he knew it.

"Ashe?"

"Hmmm?"

"Are you not afraid of anything?"

He found her hand and brought it to his mouth,

brushing his lips across the open palm. "We all harbor some fear, Hallie."

"You don't seem to be afraid of dying, so what fear could be worse than that?"

She rolled over in his arms and felt his warm breath on her face as he whispered sensually, "The fear of living another day without you in my arms like this."

The question Hallie longed to ask lay silent on her lips. Did he desire her only for their sexual interludes, or was there a deeper meaning in his words?

She circled his ear with her fingertips and, hoping to cover the seriousness of her statement, she said lightly, "The Bible says it is a sin to lust. Do you lust for me, Ashe Barkley?"

Her gentle caressing of his ear caused Ashe to tremble inside. "Guilty as charged, Miss Parker." Then he asked, "What about you?"

Hallie shifted in his arms and gazed into the darkness, listening to the drum of thunder that equaled the rolling pounding of her heart. "I don't know," she answered truthfully. "Lately, I've wondered if I wouldn't have been better off if I'd never known what it was like giving myself to a man. Fantasies are less difficult to cope with than reality."

"Fantasies don't give fulfillment, love," Ashe said, caressing the satin skin of her shoulder. "Fantasies leave an ache inside you: a need so strong that it seeks an outlet for release."

"But," Hallie supplied softly, "the ache becomes greater once you've found that release. If you'd never come into my life, Ashe, then I could have lived up to my old-maid image. I almost made it—just a few more years, and no one would have even noticed if I'd discarded my disguise... or even cared."

Ashe smiled. "With a face and body like yours, it wouldn't have taken long for some man to discover your hidden charms. I knew what you were concealing, the first moment I met you."

"You couldn't have," Hallie said in irritation.

"I have a very good imagination, my love. But I don't want fantasies. I want what I can feel and taste." His hand left her shoulder and crept to the nape of her neck, his fingers entwining in the wet, silken tresses that squeaked and smelled of fresh rainwater. "Something like this."

"Ashe, I didn't come out here for this." She jerked her head, feeling the tightness in her scalp with his fingers caught in her hair. Her pulse beat rapidly in her throat as his lips trailed over her face, teasing the corners of her mouth.

Taking her hand, he guided it to his male hardness. "I want you, Hallie, and just holding you won't ease the ache that throbs here."

He held her hand in place, and she could feel the heat of his arousal. "No good can come from this, Ashe."

"Don't say that when you know better."

A bolt of lightning struck somewhere nearby, and the horses snorted frantically. The wind whistled through the cracks and crevices of the stable, and the rain pelted the roof like an avalanche of large stones.

Hallie's senses reeled, and her body trembled against Ashe's. Her hand unknowingly squeezed his rigid member as the thunder and lightning played haphazardly around them. Ashe drew in his breath and quelled the urge to cry out at her innocent foreplay, her overzealous hand creating a maelstrom within him that was quickly surpassing the raging storm outside.

A horse in the stall next to them battered his hooves against the wall.

"The horse..." she said breathlessly, her palm kneading Ashe with each succeeding word, "I've got to soothe him before he hurts himself or tears down the stall."

Ashe spoke as calmly as he could between gritted teeth. "Don't worry about him, Hallie. He's all right."

She bolted upright again, her weight pressing down on him as the horse banged his massive bulk against the wall of his stall. "He's in pain."

"Damnation, Hallie, calm down," he growled. "If I get up and kick the hell out of this stall, will it help *my* position any?" Then, with as much patience as he could muster, he said, "I'm the one who needs soothing."

His words made her realize what she had been doing to him, and she removed her hand as though she had touched the hot surface of the stove. "I'm sorry, Ashe."

"Don't be sorry," Ashe replied, pulling Hallie down on top of him so the warm, wet length of her melted into him. "Now, you may continue where you left off, but with a little less enthusiasm; I'm not made of iron."

Hallie pressed her palms against his chest. "No, Ashe, this was a mistake," she insisted. "I didn't know what I was doing."

"Yes, it was a big mistake, and one that only you can correct, love. You don't squeeze, yank, and knead that part of a man without following through. So forget your spinster inhibitions and finish what you started."

Ashe couldn't see her face in the dark, but he could almost feel the heat generating from her body.

"I'm waiting, love," he said softly, pulling her hands from his chest so that she collapsed against him.

"Then you'll wait forever, Ashe Barkley. If I had known you were out here, and stark naked to boot, I'd have—"

"Gotten here sooner?" he asked casually as he slipped the narrow straps of her wet gown over her shoulder. In an instant, the gown was tossed aside.

"Damn you, Ashe Barkley," Hallie said, failing to smother her laughter. "Why do you always twist my words to suit your needs?"

"If I didn't take the initiative, you for damned sure wouldn't."

His hand roamed with feather lightness across her back and down to the narrow indentation of her waist. "It's been weeks of sheer torture for me. All I've done is remember our time together. Don't tell me you have forgotten how much pleasure we gave to each other."

Hallie lay against him, her head in the crook of his neck. The crinkled hair of his chest teased her sensitive breasts. How much more of herself could she give to this man, knowing that someday he would drift on to another town and find another woman to quench his seemingly insatiable lust? Whom would she turn to on those lonely nights when memories haunted her dreams? It would have been better never to have known the ecstasy he so successfully fulfilled in her. Oh, why had he broken through the defenses she had built to avoid pain such as this?

"Hallie," Ashe murmured softly into her hair, "though I can't see you, I've memorized every delicate satin inch of your body. I want you, Hallie... I need you so much it hurts."

Lifting her face, she brushed her lips across the coarse stubble of his cheek. "I want you, too, Ashe. But what am I to do when you leave Prospect City?" There, she'd said it, and by the way his breathing seemed to hesitate at her question, it was one he dreaded answering.

"Who says I'm leaving?"

"And why wouldn't you? The Poet Bandit no longer rides, and there are bounties to be collected elsewhere in the Territory."

He glided his hands up her back and beneath her hair. "I've yet to collect the bounty on the Poet Bandit ... and I plan to." He felt her body go rigid against him.

"Oh!" she exclaimed furiously, pushing her palms against his chest to free herself from his embrace. "One more time for the road, huh? Well, no dice, Mr. Barkley, I'm not so easily taken."

Ashe chuckled and rolled her onto her back in the prickly straw. Pinioning her hands above her head, he said, "I'm going to marry the Poet Bandit. Night after night of pure bliss—that should keep the bandit so satisfied and exhausted, she'll never again feel the need to terrorize Hargrove. That's worth more than Hargrove could ever pay me."

Ashe was as surprised at his declaration as Hallie.

He had never intended marrying Hallie, or any woman for that matter. But if that was the only way to have her, then damnit, he would do it and suffer the consequences. One thing for certain: there would never be a dull moment. He would always wonder which Hallie Parker he would bed at night and which one he would wake up with each morning.

"Marriage! Me marry you?" Struggling against him, she arched her hips to propel his rock-hard body from her own.

He took advantage of her open thighs and thrust his knee between them. "Yes, Hallie, you're going to be my wife whether you like it or not. I'm going to do the honorable thing and marry the woman whose virginity I took."

"The honorable Ashe Barkley," she mocked. "A gunslinger, bounty hunter, and a Yankee—and he feels honor-bound to marry the woman he disgraced. Well, don't feel so obligated, because I've told you I feel no guilt over what I've done. So go ahead and turn me in. I'd rather hang than be blackmailed into marriage."

Ashe smiled at her adamant refusal, then lowered his mouth, kissing softly the pulse that beat erratically at her throat. "No, love, I don't relish seeing a rope hanging around such a beautiful neck," he muttered hoarsely. "And think what you'd miss, Hallie." His mouth moved up her neck and across her cheek, resting on the corner of her mouth.

"Nothing you can do will make me change my mind," she argued, feeling his tongue circle her lips.

"Nothing, absolutely nothing, so remove yourself from my body."

"Not before I prove to you you're wrong."

With her hands still pinned above her head, he probed her lips apart with his determined tongue, only to feel the barrier of clenched teeth. "All right, vixen, have it your way. There are other ways to mellow your refusal, ones you've yet to discover."

Ashe brought her hands to her sides, holding them down with his larger ones.

"Then you plan to rape me?" she asked unflinchingly, and lay stone-still.

"Only your senses, love."

Slowly, deliberately, his lips began a fiery journey down the creamy column of her neck, gliding over her shoulders, and to the sensitive space joining her arm and chest.

Hallie trembled slightly, humiliated that she should respond at all to his caresses. As his lips and tongue trailed down her side and across her satin, taut stomach, Hallie bit into her tongue to keep from moaning. The muscles of her stomach tightened and released when his tongue circled her navel and gently probed its depths. Sporadic shivers ran between her legs, and she gasped at the delicious warmth surging through her.

Ashe felt her body grow pliant. No longer was she pretending she was unaffected by his touch. She twisted beneath him, muttering vague curses, and he wondered if she meant them for him or for herself.

Every inch of her body felt as though it had been touched by light raindrops that continued to pelt and tease her skin even as his lips and tongue sought other forbidden places.

Then the supreme ecstasy of his wet, warm mouth trailing over her hips and inner thigh wore down the last remnant of her composure. Her hands struggled for release from beneath his powerful grip, but Ashe was oblivious to her efforts.

"Let me go, Ashe ... please," she cried, raising and lowering her head, arching her hips to thrust him from her.

Ashe slid up her body until his mouth crushed her own. Finding her lips parted, he thrust his tongue between her teeth and tasted her mouth as thoroughly as he had her body.

Breaking the kiss, he said, "I'll let you go, but don't fight me, Hallie. Will you promise me that? There is so much pleasure I want to share with you if you'll allow me."

Hallie's pulse raced, and random thoughts skittered through her mind. "But I already know the joys of lovemaking."

"No, you know only the final act of love," he said, breathing in the rain-washed scent of her hair. "Trust me, love."

He kissed her again, and she responded shyly at first—as though she somehow knew what his expectations were. Her hands were free now, and she caressed each rippled muscle in his back and ran her fingernails lightly down the side of his back, joyfully feeling his flesh undulating beneath her tender gestures.

Taking her hand, he guided it downward between

them to touch his pulsating member, and rejoiced when he felt her warm, trembling hand enfold it.

His hungry mouth covered her breast, taking the taut rosy peak into its depths, seemingly to devour it wholly. She arched her back and pressed into him, dazed by excitement as he pulled at the sensitive peak, his desires running rampant with a demanding need. Hallie's hand worked rhythmically with the spasms that raced like lightning through her body.

His hand met hers between their bodies as his fingers sought entrance into her moist womanly softness. He stroked and caressed her, the sensitive nodule now erect with desire. She writhed against his hand, her mind dizzy with anticipation and her body jolting with the passion that blossomed from Ashe's expert and tender love play.

He lifted his sweat-soaked body from her and, kneeling between her thighs, he ran his hands caressingly down her long, tapered legs and back up, cupping them beneath her hips.

"Now... please," Hallie cried hoarsely, reaching out blindly in the dark for him.

He raised her hips, and she waited for the onslaught of his first violent thrust, but was shocked to feel his warm breath caressing her.

"No, Ashe... no," she whispered, but it was more like an urgent request than a refusal.

"Yes, love," he groaned hoarsely.

She didn't know if it was agony or bliss that gripped her senses. Her body was thrown into convulsive shudders that seemed to crescendo in intensity. Ashe, sensing her needs, moved from between her thighs and lay down beside her, rolling her full-length onto his hard-muscled body. Positioning her over him, he held her hips and arched up, plunging deeply within her.

She felt his fullness inside her. Sensing the surging, aching desire of his manhood, she answered him by giving in entirely to her own needs.

He moaned within his throat as he felt her body tighten and throb around his hard member. Grasping her hips, he rotated slowly and sensually. The sensation in his loins was so pleasurable, he could no longer restrain himself. Thrusting upward, he drove aggressively into her eager warmth again and again. They cried out together as violent shudders swelled an burst, releasing a flood of ecstasy that obliterated the tempestuous storm surrounding them.

Hallie lay awake in the warmth of Ashe's embrace, watching the subdued light of dawn slanting through the crevices in the stall. She couldn't recall when the turbulence actually ceased, for her dream had been as tumultuous as the storm. She had envisioned herself on Licorice's broad back with a black scarf masking her face. Her hands were bound tightly behind her, but it was the coarse, prickly loop around her neck that woke her with a violent jerk.

Now as she felt his soft, warm breath on her shoulder and his hard, muscled chest against her back, she wondered if this man, who had taught her the joys of being a woman, could ever settle down. In her heart, she was sure he couldn't, but how many ways had her heart been deceived?

She gently lifted Ashe's arm from around her waist so as not to wake him, and rolled from his side, wondering how she had slept with the straw pricking her naked flesh. Draping her nightgown around her, she rose and gazed down at Ashe's sleeping form. His mouth was partly open, and she felt the urge to kiss him awake and have his lips do the same wonderful things to her they had done the previous night.

Leaving him asleep, Hallie padded softly through the corridor, hearing only an occasional snort and whinnying from the horses. Luis, she hoped, would stay home today, if Maria was correct in assuming he was about to become a father. She wondered if the baby had been born during the storm. Then another thought occurred to her, and her legs nearly folded beneath her. Could she possibly have conceived a child while Consuela was giving birth to another? Was that Ashe's intention? Get her with child so she would be forced to marry him?

The sun still lay low in the horizon, dispersing a gossamer palette of pastel colors. A vaporous mist hovered over the rain-washed earth, yet the ground appeared dry. The sultry breeze that stirred the air was suffocating, causing light perspiration to bead on her brow as she made her way to the house, noting the sad condition of her once beautiful flowers. Their rainbow-colored petals had been beaten to the ground by the force of last night's wind and rain. Because her attention was on the flowers, she did not see the object in her path, and her toes crunched painfully against it. Looking down, she saw the large cast-iron bell with a wide crack running its length. She pushed it aside and continued toward the house.

The door was open; in her haste, she had failed to close it behind her last night. Except for a small puddle of water in the doorway, there was no other rain damage. She went into her bedroom; she located and pulled the copper tub into the middle of the room.

After several trips back and forth filling the tub with the heated water, Hallie shrugged off her nightgown and stepped into the tub. The lukewarm water lapped gently at her body as she relaxed her head against the rim and closed her eyes. She relaxed thoroughly for a moment, forcing her mind to become blank. Then errant thoughts crept in. Why was Ashe forcing her to marry him? He had no room in his life for a wife. Was he now wondering how he could reverse the situation without making a fool of himself? Surely Ashe must care for her in his own way if he said he wanted to marry her. Her own feelings about him were just as muddled. She enjoyed their verbal battles; she was drawn to the dangerous, feral aura that emanated from him like an intoxicating drug; she was obsessed with the mere contact of his hand on hers, and the way his eyes caressed her sensually. Was this love?

Did Ashe experience these same emotions, she wondered. And was he, like her, frightened to admit them? She would give him another chance to beg off by refusing his proposal again. His threat to turn in the Poet Bandit was a blunder on his part—she would test him by flinging his ultimatum back in his face.

Immersing her hair in the water, Hallie washed it in a concoction of yucca root and lemon juice, one of the many useful things she had learned during her stay with the Indians.

A frothy lather covered her hair, and she hummed a happy tune. Raising one leg, she ran her wash cloth from toe to thigh, and then lifted the other leg.

This was the pose that met Ashe's hungry eyes as he quietly opened the door to her room. So engrossed in what she was doing, Hallie didn't hear him enter. Rising to kneel, she reached over the tub for the pail of fresh rain water she had prepared. Tossing her head back, she began pouring the water slowly over her hair to rinse out the soap, which immediately ran into her eyes. They started to burn and she rubbed them futilely while blindly searching for a towel.

Ashe feasted on her nakedness for a moment, feeling desire once again pulsate in his loins. A few remaining soap suds dwelled on the peaks of her breasts, reminding him of the last remaining snow drifts on a mountain crest.

Then he walked quietly to the tub and picked up her towel, but a creak in the floor gave away his presence.

Barely opening her burning eyes, Hallie snatched the towel from his hand and wiped her eyes, at the same time trying to cover her nakedness. "Don't you know to knock before you enter?" she asked angrily, stepping from the tub.

Ashe smiled. "I didn't think it was necessary. After all, I've seen you unclothed before, and we are going to be man and wife."

She glared at him, as she tossed on a robe. "I'm

not married to you yet, and I think we need to discuss this matter further before we take such a drastic step."

"I don't see the necessity for any further discussion." Placing his booted foot on the bed railing, he rested an arm casually across his knee. "I'm going to have you, Hallie, and there's no way you're going to back out of it."

Her arms akimbo, she sashayed over to him, a defiant look on her pert face. "And if I don't, will you turn me over to Hargrove?"

Ashe's smile faded; his eyes turned deathly cold. "No, but I'd hate for your grandfather to learn of your foolish shenanigans."

Hallie felt a ringing in her ears, and shook her head to clear it. For several seconds, she studied his face in disbelief. "You wouldn't dare."

Standing straight up, Ashe placed his hands on her shoulders. "Oh, but I would, and you'd better believe it."

Pivoting in anger, Hallie paced back and forth in front of him, waving her arms in extreme irritation. "Why are you doing this to me? You know I don't want to be married to you. I've got Grandpa to take care of and a ranch to run." Her voice rose and ended in a cry. "I can never leave my home."

"Hallie, Hallie," Ashe chided softly. He walked over to her and tucked a wet lock of hair behind her ear. "Do you think I'd take you away from all this?"

"You're a drifter... and a ... killer," she wailed.

Ashe winced at her words. "I never notched my gun after I killed a man. It was only a job, a job I had to do to make a living. Since the men I killed were killers of innocent people, it made my job as a bounty hunter easier to endure. And as for my being a drifter, Hallie, even drifters want to settle down someday."

She wanted to ask him why he had chosen her, but the words wouldn't come. Instead she asked, "Wouldn't it be more to your liking to keep a mistress?"

Ashe grinned wickedly. "Would you be willing?"

Hallie's mouth dropped open at the insult. "And have you saddle me with a child and go traipsing off to another woman?"

"You may already be carrying my child."

Hallie reddened. "Believe me, I've thought of that."

"Then what other choice do you have?"

"I could at least wait and see; and until that time, you keep your hands off me so I don't get pregnant in the meantime."

A vague, inscrutable expression touched his features, and he turned from her as though he was hiding something.

"We'll marry as soon as I can make the arrangements, no matter as to the state . . . of your condition."

His words left no room for arguments. Hallie drew a deep sigh, sat down on the edge of the bed, and looked down at her folded hands. He had her in the palm of his hand and knew it. She would rather die by hanging than cause her grandfather any suffering by the revelation of her lawless activities.

"Very well, Ashe," she replied stonily. "You hold all the right cards at the moment. But even the best of gamblers lose on occasion. You could find me a very unwilling wife and regret the day you ever set eyes on Hallie Parker."

"It's a chance I'll just have to take, and I've taken them all my life." Rocking back on his heels, his hands clasped behind him, he continued: "There's one more thing that has to be done before we take our vows, and that has to do with Bradshaw."

Hallie's chin thrust up. "What has Stephen to do with this?"

"That's what I'm asking you, Hallie. I know the two of you are up to something, so spit it out."

"It's my business and no concern of yours. You are not yet my husband, Ashe Barkley, so I owe you no explanation."

Hallie trembled with rage. Grabbing the plump feather pillow, she hurled it with all her might at his stone-hard face. Tiny feathers scattered the air, lighting with defiant contrast on Ashe's blue-black hair.

"You little hellcat," he grated. Hallie ducked expertly as the half-filled pillow came soaring back toward her and slammed into the headboard of her bed. The pillow quickly deflated to a worthless rag as a multitude of downy feathers swirled around the room like snow.

The tension mounted to a suffocating stillness, their breathing was shallow and forced as each waited for the other to make the first move. A feather rested on the tip of Hallie's nose and she resisted the urge to sneeze.

Ashe took one step forward. Hallie took two back, trapping her legs against the bed. She compared her situation to that of a tiny mouse watching a great sleek cat slowly stalk his prey with quiet but precise steps.

Yellow flecks glittered in his feral gray eyes, and his thin-lipped mouth set in grim determination.

"Don't you... don't you come near me." Hallie bounced back on the bed on her bottom, and rolled over, scrambling to the opposite side of the bed. Once again feathers scattered the air, creating a useless barrier between her and her stalker.

"Tell me, Hallie, what Bradshaw means to you," Ashe ground out.

Hallie was hemmed in, the door was behind Ashe, and at the foot of the bed was the tub, the water obscured by soap scum. Edging her way down the length of the bed, she hedged, "He's only a friend, a business friend."

"I'm a friend, too, Hallie." His voice was deadly calm.

"You don't exactly look like one now," Hallie said, curling her fingers around the bedpost, her peripheral vision on the tub beside her. "I've said I'll marry you, so go away and leave me alone."

Tired of the cat-and-mouse game, Ashe made the next move, and began inching his way around the foot of the bed. Hallie darted like an agile, startled doe toward the rim of the tub with Ashe in hot pursuit. She dipped her cupped hands quickly into the water, and swamped him with a healthy splash of water. Thinking she now had the advantage, she made a run for the door. Her feet continued their flight long after she was lifted from the floor and brought back against a wet, massive chest, while muscled arms tightened around her waist. She kicked at his shins and her wet hair stung his face as she whipped her head from side to side.

Ashe tumbled her facedown on the bed, the weight of his knee pressing into her back. Grasping her flailing arms, he brought them behind her, anchoring her hands to the small of her back.

"Now, Miss High and Mighty, I've got you right where I want you, and by God, if you don't answer me, I'll rip that damn robe off you and take you right now."

Hallie craned her neck to glare at him between the strands of hair draping her face. "Barbarian!"

"In fact, I think I'll do just that since you won't cooperate."

Flipping her over on her back, he pinned her hands beneath her and held her legs down with his hard-muscled thigh. In the struggle, her half-secured belt had come untied, and her robe was completely open, baring her beauty from head to toe. Ashe drew in his breath. "Ah, God, Hallie," he moaned, "why are you being so damned difficult? If it's Stephen Bradshaw you want, then tell me. At least do me that favor."

A big blue eye peeked at him between the wet strands of dark auburn hair. Was it jealousy that caused him to behave like an animal? Hallie wondered with satisfaction. How far could she go in tantalizing him into admitting it without making him lose control and do as he wished with her? Never one to admit defeat, she decided to test fate and suffer the consequences later.

"If that should be my wish, would you be willing to free me from my promise?"

"Only if you weren't carrying my child would I

release you. No man will ever have what belongs to me." His voice was grave and deadly.

Hallie's heart constricted with despair. He was concerned only about the child she could be carrying; he had no love for her.

"Does a child mean so much to you?" she asked, feeling the tears burning behind her eyes.

"Yes, if it's mine. I won't have a child of mine go through life believing another man is his father."

Hallie felt defeated, drained. She had sought words of love from him, but had received instead harsh-spoken words of reality. What had she expected from him? she thought with remorse. She had woven a world of fantasies around this one man and dreamed of marriage to him in her most secret thoughts. But the reality was—he desired her, he did not love her.

Her voice trembled slightly as she spoke. "There's no need for you to hold me down. Release me, and I'll tell you why Stephen Bradshaw is here."

Ashe loosened his grip on her and rolled to his side. Hallie draped the robe around her to cover her nakedness and sat propped against the headboard. "I hired Stephen to help me find the murderer of Sarah Hargrove."

"I figured as much. You still believe Ben Langley is innocent."

"Yes, and so does Stephen. No one knows why he is here, not even Grandpa."

Ashe mulled over that tidbit before he spoke again. "His life is in danger, Hallie, if Ben is indeed innocent. People are suspicious of his questions, and from what I hear, he's willing to pay well for information. But money won't make them talk. Send him back to San Francisco unless you want his death on your conscience." Then, he added, "Unless, of course, there are other reasons why he's here."

A frown etched her brow. "What do you mean?"

"Has business turned into pleasure?"

Hallie stiffened. "It's a pleasure doing business with him," she said, turning his words around. "He's a very likable man, and a gentleman to boot. More so than most I know."

Ashe rose to his feet and brushed the feathers from his wet clothing. "Fire him."

"Fire him!" Hallie exclaimed. "After all the trouble I've gone to... you want me to fire him! You have no right to make that demand of me. I'm the one paying him—not you."

"And it may cost you more than money before it comes to a head," he said very seriously. "His life means nothing to me, but your life does."

For a brief moment, Hallie's hopes soared, and she checked his face for some sign of feeling, but his features remained impassive.

"But he's on to something. I know it, he knows it, and evidently you do, too, or you wouldn't be so concerned."

Sitting down beside her again, he ran a finger down the length of her arm, and arched a dubious brow. "I'll relieve Bradshaw of his duties and I'll find your murderer."

Hallie's eyes shot open at his suggestion. "But you work for Hargrove."

"Are you afraid I'll tell Hargrove what you've been

up to? I don't have to tell him—he already knows. With Bradshaw off his back, he may think you've given up your search."

"It seems to me he'd be grateful to find the man who murdered his wife," she said huffily. "And it's not Ben Langley."

"Perhaps he'd rather kill the man himself." Then, seeing the downfallen expression on her face, he continued, "Look, Hallie, I don't like Hargrove any more than you do, believe me. He's still out to get your friend, Ben Langley, for the murder of his wife; if you try to protect Ben, then you're in his way. An accident could happen, and no one would be the wiser."

"All right, all right." Hallie gave in, and leaped from the bed to pace around the room while she decided how to handle things. She stopped abruptly. "I'll take Stephen off the case. It is possible that Ben will never come back—he could be dead already, for all we know."

That idea had never entered her mind until that moment. Turning to face Ashe, she paled. "What if Hargrove has killed him already?"

Ashe strolled to her side, placing his hands around her waist. "I've thought of that too, love. The only way we'll ever know is if Ben comes back."

Chapter 14

Grady Parker, not at all pleased with the news of Hallie's upcoming nuptials, stomped and stormed throughout the house. Hallie followed, trying to calm him down.

"A damn gunslinger... my granddaughter marrying a gunslinger! What in tarnation is this world coming to when your only living kin stands up to your face and tells you she's marrying a man you've warned her against repeatedly from the first mention of his name? Have you gone daft, girl?"

"Grandpa, I'm trying my best to control my temper, but you're rapidly wearing it thin. Don't you realize you're talking about your future grandson-in-law?" Hallie coaxed, emphasizing the word *grand* as much as she dared.

"Lord knows I'm aware of that. You don't have to rub it in."

"Grandpa," she entreated, quick tears gathering in her eyes.

Gentling his words, he embraced her. "Hallie, honey, I don't mean to hurt you. Just give me a little time to adjust. Hell, I've just had the shock of my life." Tilting her chin, he searched her face. "Do you love him? That's the most important thing."

She looked him straight in the face and replied, without hesitation, "I do, Grandpa, I love him very much."

"Very well, then, you're the one who has to live with him. I just hope he doesn't make you a grievin' widow."

Pleased that her grandfather seemed to accept her forthcoming marriage without so much as a tantrum, Hallie hugged him tightly and whispered softly, "You'll love him, Grandpa. He's a good man, regardless of what you've heard about him."

"Don't rush it, child. I'm capable of only one step at a time right now."

"That's all I ask, Grandpa. Maria is ecstatic about the news. She's already planning a feast. You'll have a chance to talk with Ashe tonight. I've invited him to supper."

"Supper—Ashe is comin' to supper. Hargrove... Hargrove's a bastard," Sinbad's raucous voice interjected. Had Grandpa not been in the same room, Hallie would have severely chastised the bird.

"Ben, squawk... you home, Ben?"

Hallie turned with a jerk. A chill ran up her spine. She half expected to see Ben lounging in the doorway.

It had been so long since Sinbad had mentioned Ben's name.

"Ben... I'm starving... Ben's struck it rich."

"Shut up, Sinbad," she whispered angrily. A premonition of danger surged through her. It was almost as if Sinbad sensed something. It was eerie, and she didn't like it one bit, coming on the heels of her bargain with Ashe Barkley.

Ashe opened the door to his bunkroom and paused in the doorway, his eyes scanning his meager belongings. A bedroll, toiletries, and a few items of clothing were his only possessions, but that was all he had ever needed or wanted. Easy enough to bundle up and take with him into a new life.

As he deposited them by the door, he saw old Bart shuffling slowly toward him.

"Heerd tell you was leavin'. Thought I'd jest drop by and say good-bye and offer my congratulations. Mighty fine little gal yore gettin' hitched up to."

"Thanks, Bart, can't say I'm sorry to be leaving this hell-hole," Ashe said, hoisting up his bedroll. "Don't see how you could stand being here as long as you have."

Bart bent down and picked up Ashe's duffel bag. "Wal, I warn't always here, but then I got too old to mine and never found enough ore to amount to nothin' anyhow."

Bart followed him to where Rebel was waiting and watched him strap his gear to Rebel's back. "Don't guess Hargrove was too happy to see you leave."

"I think he was more upset that I was marrying Hallie Parker than he was about my leaving."

When Ashe turned around to bid Bart good-bye, he saw a worried frown on Bart's face.

"Got something on your mind, Bart?"

Bart shifted a wad of tobacco in his jaw. "Jest wonderin' how come you be the one to get Miss Parker fer yore bride instead of that Bradshaw feller. From the way folks was talkin', they expected him to be the one."

"Lucky, I guess," Ashe said, grasping the pommel and sliding his boot into the stirrup.

"Afore ya go, I got to say somethin' to you," Bart whispered, slyly looking around for listeners. "I'm gettin' old, and maybe tomorrow I won't be wakin' up."

Ashe waited, frowning. Bart said in a low, raspy voice, "Bradshaw's been around askin' the boys questions about Sarah Hargrove. They ain't lying when they say they don't know nothin' about the murder. What worries me is the safety of your bride-to-be."

Ashe removed his foot from the stirrup. "This isn't a good place to talk. Let's go into the bunkroom."

When they were inside, Ashe demanded, "What about Hallie's safety?"

"It's plain to me she hired Bradshaw to go snoopin' around. You remember that foreman feller, Sam Carter, I told you about, the one who was murdered afore you come here?"

"Yeah, I remember."

Bart shifted the tobacco wad to the other cheek. "Sam was the one who seen Ben Langley and Sarah

Hargrove together the night she died. Saw em arguin' and her cryin' and all. Well, being new and all, he thought he'd get on the boss's good side by tellin' him what he seen. He come to me later scareder 'n hell, wishin' he'd minded his own business, tellin' me he needed to talk to somebody. Well, we was interrupted before he finished his story.... That night he was murdered."

"Did Langley see Carter?"

"No, he said Langley didn't see him hidin' behind the rocks that night."

"What does any of this have to do with Hallie?"

"Maybe nothin', maybe somethin'. She was real close to Ben, and she's still tryin' to save his neck, the way I see it. The thang is, it looks to me he's guilty as sin, and that's why he took off. The girl could get caught right in the middle of somethin' and get herself hurt. I don't think Ben would ever hurt her, but she's put a lot of faith in that man." He patted his heart. "It's here where she's gonna be hurtin'."

"Do you think that perhaps Sarah's death was accidental?"

"Dunno," Bart said, shaking his head. "Didn't know him real good, but folks say Langley had a helluva temper. Could be he jest let it get the best of him and then..." Bart slammed his fist into his hand.

"What about the prospector who supposedly heard Ben and a woman arguing that night?"

"I don't think he ever existed," Bart said, then lowered his voice. "Hargrove probably made up that rumor to cover up the foreman's death. He couldn't tell anyone that Sam was the snoop 'cause that would've raised too much suspicion about Sam's death."

"So you think Hargrove killed Sam," Ashe concluded.

Bart was quick to deny that. "Hargrove ain't kilt nobody that I know of."

Ashe knew immediately what Bart was implying. Hargrove's money could buy him anything... even someone's death.

"Anything else, Bart?" Ashe was eager to leave, but he wasn't eager to face Hallie with the facts he'd just discovered.

"No, jest wanted to get this off my chest. Been botherin' me lately. Jest keep it under your hat, cause I wouldn't want Hargrove to know I've been talking to you."

"Thanks, Bart. I won't say a word to anyone," Ashe said, going to the door. "Let me know if you hear anything else."

"Sure thang," Bart said, staying behind in the room after Ashe mounted and departed for the ranch.

Ashe rode Rebel at a slow gallop, needing the time to decide what to do and how to approach Hallie. Bart was right in assuming Hallie's reaction if she ever discovered Ben was a murderer after she had trusted him and even tried to save his life. It would be a long time before she would ever trust another man—himself included. He had hoped for Hallie's sake that Langley was innocent, but now he had his doubts.

Taking extra care with her appearance, Hallie brushed her hair vigorously, letting it hang freely down her back and curl softly over her shoulders. She could hear Ashe talking with her grandfather, and prayed that her grandfather wouldn't try to intimidate him. From their boisterous laughter, they seemed to be getting along well.

Squaring her shoulders, she entered the room. Both men turned in her direction.

"Well, I see Grandpa has shown you where he hides his brandy. Not everyone is given that privilege."

"I assure you, I've enjoyed it immensely," Ashe commented, winking rakishly at her.

Blood rushed to her face as she wondered if his words held double meanings. Before she could reply, Maria entered, announcing dinner.

The table was covered with a gleaming white tablecloth, and a variety of food that would have tempted the palates of the most fastidious eater: Sopa de Aguacati—a thick avocado soup, tamales steeping in a hot pepper sauce, frijoles, and a medley of summer vegetables, and after, flaky apple turnovers dusted with sugar and ground cinnamon, and rich black coffee. Ashe took a bite, and grinned at Hallie. "Now this is cinnamon, my love."

Her eyes raced to his, and seeing the humor there, she smiled thinly. "I've asked Maria to label the bottles."

Sipping his brandy, Grady eyed Ashe with curiosity. "Where do you and Hallie plan to live, Ashe?"

"I had planned this for a surprise for Hallie, but your question deserves an answer. I've bought the ranch that joins your western boundary. It is a sizable spread, and there's a sturdy house on the property. Your neighbor claimed Hargrove tried to buy his place several times, but it's apparent he doesn't have much use for Hargrove, either, so he sold it to me."

"Ashe, it's none of my business, and you can take my suggestion or not, but this place belongs to Hallie." With a gruff laugh, he continued, "I didn't want the same thing happening to this ranch that happened to mine. I don't believe Hargrove could entice Hallie into a crooked card game."

Getting to her feet, Hallie stood behind her grandfather's chair, her fingers gently massaging his shoulders. "You're right, Grandpa, I can't bear the sight of Hargrove—much less endure his presence across a table."

"Before you go on a rampage about Hargrove, let me finish. There's no reason why the two of you shouldn't live here. The house needs some work, but nothing the two of you couldn't handle. I'm not here often, but I sure would hate to see the place abandoned."

As Ashe opened his mouth to speak, Grady held up his hand. "No, don't give me your answer now. Think about it. You and Hallie talk about it. I'll only add that it sure would be nice to think about you two raising your family here." Sniffing loudly, Grady excused himself. "I've had a long day. If you two don't mind, I'm going to bed."

Time sped by as rapidly as the fluttering of a hummingbird's wings, and soon Hallie was unpacking the dress that had been her mother's wedding gown. The once pure white fabric had faded with age to a mellow ivory. Clara and Martha volunteered to alter it, and as Hallie stood before them for the final fitting, both women were awestruck. They thought she looked breathtaking, ethereal, as though she were an angel of the highest realm. Pleased with their reaction, Hallie hugged herself tightly, secretly thankful she wasn't doomed to remain a spinster after all.

Laughing happily, Hallie plunged the pitchfork deep into the mound of straw that had been a bed of love only nights before. Just as she lifted the fork, a piece of paper drifted to the floor. Leaning over, she scooped it up. Looks like a letter, she thought, but how... Ashe must have lost it the night of the storm.

Tingling sensations shot through her. She had thought of little else since that night. Only by placing a tight rein on her emotions had she been able to go about her daily activities and wedding preparations.

Drawing the creased page from its envelope, she scanned the contents briefly. Catching her breath, her blood running cold, she reread the letter slowly, trying to understand the words that threatened to shatter her fragile heart.

July 11, 1875

Mr. Barkley,

I was most distressed to learn of your mother's death. Sarah Hargrove was a gentlewoman, and to discover that her life was destroyed by such force is almost more than I can bear. Not only was I her solicitor, but a personal friend for many years. Long before your birth I called her my friend.

I hope you will change your mind about your inheritance and accept it in the light that it was given... to a dearly loved son from a grieving mother.

Godspeed in finding the man who killed her so needlessly.

Respectfully,
William James

The words tumbled through Hallie's mind like tumbleweeds in a dust storm, pelting her from every direction. If Ashe is Sarah Hargrove's son, then that makes him Vern Hargrove's son also. Doesn't it? her mind screamed. He doesn't carry Hargrove's name. Was Sarah married before? If so, why hadn't Ashe come to Prospect City to his mother?

Oh my God, she groaned as another turbulent thought assailed her mind. If Ashe were seeking Sarah's killer, that would place Ben in even worse straits. She knew he hadn't killed Sarah, but Ashe didn't... unless he believed her after the many times she had argued with him. No wonder he had been so adamant about her dismissing Stephen, assuring her that he would find Sarah's killer. She never dreamed that her plan to save Ben might be the very one that would place his life in the balance.

Hallie finished her chores with a heavy heart, and planned what she would say to Ashe.

Later that night as she was sitting on the porch enjoying what little breeze there was, she suddenly saw the most magnificent stallion she had ever laid eyes on. He came bearing down on the corral at breakneck speed, snorting and whinnying loudly as though he were calling to his mate.

His white coat was just visible in the darkness as he reared up and pawed the air, his call unmistakable. Her horses lunged at the corral, knocking the fence down as though it were no more than matchsticks.

Hallie could taste the dust the horses were stirring up in their attempt to free themselves.

Suddenly she jumped to her feet, shouting, "Stop it, you bastard, those are my horses."

The stallion turned at the sound of her voice and, raising his proud head, he whinnied angrily. His eyes blazed red in the darkness, and his upper lip curled back dangerously, displaying strong white teeth.

Running into the house, Hallie pulled on britches, shirt and her boots. Then, grabbing up her rifle, she ran back outside, cursing the stallion's temerity. Grabbing a bridle, she lifted it over a very skittish Licorice and, mounting him bareback, she raced from the ranch. She could barely make out the stallion as he stood on a small rise pawing the air. Then he was off like a shot.

She followed in a dead run, knowing the chances of capturing her horses were slim. Her unbound hair whipped about, stinging her face as she turned, trying to avoid the choking dust.

That arrogant beast reminds me of Ashe, she thought. Takes what he wants and to hell with the consequences. He was a wily devil—she gave him credit for that. He was heading straight for the canyon. Following him through the rocky crevices would be difficult in broad daylight, but to attempt it at night was foolhardy. But she would be a bigger fool if she didn't try to reach her mares before it was too late.

She wasn't prepared when Licorice stumbled. As he tried vainly to right himself, he unseated Hallie.

She fell with a thud, her last thought, as the darkness reached out to enfold her, "You devil, you've won..."

Ashe sat by Hallie's side, laying cool cloths on the angry protrusion at her temple. She lay so still, her color deathly white. Ashe's heart hammered in his chest and perspiration beaded his brow. Lowering his head, he gently kissed her forehead.

Leaving her room, he stormed out at Maria, "Hell fire, Maria, how long is it going to take Doc to get here?"

"Soon, señor..." she whispered, noting how distraught Ashe was. He must love her niña very much, she thought.

Ashe paced the floor as he waited, thinking back to the past several hours. He had been eager to see Hallie, and had set out early for the ranch. When he arrived and saw the wreckage, he knew immediately what had transpired. Tracking the horses had been short work. When he saw Licorice standing by the inert form sprawled on the ground, his heart soared into his throat. Racing to her side, he gently lifted Hallie's head. For one brief second, she opened her eyes and whispered, "Please don't kill Ben."

Wondering at her strange request, he lifted her in his arms and eased onto Rebel's back, bracing her head against further jolts.

Maria met him in the yard, wringing her hands, tears pooling in her eyes.

"She's not—"

"No, she's had a nasty lick on the head. You'd better send someone for Doc Nelson." Ashe had placed her on her bed and reluctantly left the room while Maria sponged her off and pulled a soft white nightgown onto her still form.

Ashe's thoughts were dispelled as Doc Nelson puffed into the house, his face beet-red. "Juan tells me Hallie has been hurt. Where is she?"

Ashe led him to Hallie's side, and he gingerly touched her temple. "Let's get her out of that gown and I'll check her."

Maria paled. "I've already checked her," she said rapidly. "No broken bones, only a few scratches."

"Then why the hell did you send for me?" Doc snapped.

Ashe was puzzled at Maria's attitude until a notion struck him like a bolt of lightning. Hallie's shoulder. The scar was still visible, and Doc would know immediately that it was from a gunshot. The conclusion he would draw could be shattering for Hallie.

Stepping in quickly, Ashe pressed Doc for his opinion. "We need advice on how to handle her head wound. She hasn't moved since I brought her back."

Doc examined her head more thoroughly, this time lifting her eyelids, first one, then the other. "I'd say she's suffering from a mild concussion. There's really nothing you can do except keep her warm and flat on her back. Don't try to wake her, but let her come to on her own."

Maria, trying to appease Doc for her earlier outburst, offered to make dinner for him. He was quick to take up her offer, and they left the room. Ashe settled himself by Hallie's bed, drawing her hand into his own, never taking his eyes from her recumbent figure.

Hallie drifted in a semiconscious fog. A light up ahead drew her attention, and she struggled to reach it.

Opening her eyes, she saw Ashe leaning over her, the concern etched in his features as he reached for her. As he closed his arms around her, Hallie sobbed quietly, unnerved.

Finally, the tears ceased and she lay limp against him. He dipped a cloth in the bowl of cool water, wrung it out, and placed it against her eyes.

"You've got a red nose, do you know that?" he teased.

"I never was one who could cry prettily. My eyes swell and my nose turns red."

"It sure is a pretty red nose," he answered, kissing it lightly. "You took a tumble, Hallie. You've got a lump on the side of your head the size of a goose egg."

"Is Licorice all right?"

"He's fine, love. He was the reason I found you so easily. He was standing beside you like a faithful friend."

"Before you start telling me how foolish I am, I want you to know I already realize that. It was stupid of me to go chasing off after a wild stallion in the middle of the night. I was so angry—that hateful bastard came storming in here like some primitive beast, screaming and pawing the air, and my mares couldn't wait to get to him."

"If you promise to rest, I'll see if I can find any

trace of them." He leaned close; his warm breath caressed her face. "Get well, love, you've a wedding to attend."

As Hallie's eyes swept over him, all liquid and sultry, he felt the familiar ache of desire sweep through him. His common sense, struggling with the desire leaping through him, finally won out when he glanced at the injury on Hallie's head. One didn't make love to one's future wife when she lay suffering from a concussion. Restraining his desire, he straightened to his full height, and with a mischievous smile saluted her. "Later, love."

Hallie slept peacefully, not waking until Maria hustled in carrying a supper tray.

"With Senor Barkley's tender love and my good cooking, we'll have you up in no time." Heaving her enormous breasts, Maria continued quickly as though she had rehearsed the words often. "I must speak with you about something that has troubled me for a long time." Squaring her broad shoulders, she sat down next to Hallie. "I have kept my silence until I can bear to keep it no longer. I am aware of your role as the famous Poet Bandit."

Hallie tried to keep her expression impassive as she raised her hand in protest, but Maria hurried on, "No, mi niña, it is no use to deny it. Do you think I would disclose the fact after I have tried to protect you for so long? I had the devil's own time convincing Doc not to examine you."

Hallie looked up at her, puzzled.

"Your scar, Hallie. Do you think I have lived in this

savage land where the gun is law without being able to recognize a gunshot wound?"

"I'm sorry, Maria, I would never have intentionally worried you. It would seem my charade was not as secret as I thought. Does Juan know?"

"No. The others would have no reason to suspect you. It is only that I am with you more than anyone else. The pieces just fell into place. Your secret is safe with me. You are a wild rebel, mi niña. I hope Señor Barkley can tame you ... or love you so desperately you will no longer have a thirst for revenge."

"I can assure you, Maria, that the Poet Bandit lives no more. I have no desire to be shot at again, or even get caught. Besides," she said trying to appear haughty, "I'm to be married."

"Can't be soon enough to suit me," Maria muttered.

Being bedridden for several days gave Hallie time to think—too much time. She was plagued with questions about the letter she had found, and she continuously rehearsed ways to broach it to Ashe.

Suddenly he was standing in her doorway, dusty and tired. He had spent his time searching for the mares and repairing the corral fencing. His eyes searched her face, and he asked, "How are you feeling, love?"

This tender concern, coupled with the revelations in the letter, made it impossible for her, in her overwrought state, to approach the subject calmly. She burst out: "I found the letter, Ashe. I know you're Sarah Hargrove's son."

"I know, love."

Stunned, Hallie stared at him. "How?" she whispered.

"I knew the only time I could have lost it was the night of the storm. I figured you found it. You've been acting like something was eating away at you. I've been wondering when you'd bring it up." Cocking his brow at her, he said, "It still doesn't change anything, Hallie. You're going to be my wife."

Removing his hat, he ran his fingers through his ebony hair as though he was tired of the whole situation. He eased down on the bed beside her, and cupped her chin in his large hand. "Are you upset at becoming a bastard's wife, especially Sarah Hargrove's illegitimate son?"

"Illegitimate." The words were torn from her. "I don't understand, Ashe."

With a ragged breath, he released her to pace the floor. He paused at the window and ran his fingers down the edge of the curtains. Whipping them aside, he gazed out the window, not seeing the miles of open range or the towering buttes in the distance. He saw a drunken Sam Barkley wielding a vicious bullwhip. The memories washed over him, and once again he felt the hot shards of pain.

He had grown accustomed to the beatings and the harsh words inflicted upon him by his drunken father. He seemed to be the only one of the eight children his father singled out to bear the brunt of his cruelty. The brutality was worse after the death of his mother. But he had schooled himself not to show emotion when he was beaten. Otherwise, he angered his father, who thrashed him even more.

He had been quick to learn and a hard worker, but nothing he did pleased Sam Barkley. They had been poor farmers, but several times a year a messenger had brought money. No one seemed to know why or where it had come from, but each time Sam Barkley would go on a drinking binge.

But the last time, Sam had been particularly mean, and Ashe had made up his mind he wouldn't take any more abuse. He and his older brother Vance had decided to leave and join the Union army, make their mark, and help bring the war to a quick end.

In March, 1862, he had become Private Ashe Barkley, a "hated" Yankee. But he was able to live with it because it was different, it was tangible. He had known what he was fighting and why. With his father, he had never understood, and had not been able to put his finger on the cause.

He turned to face Hallie. "You once asked me where I came from. Are you still interested?"

At her softly whispered assent, he began, "I was born in Boston, Massachusetts. For most of my life, I thought my parents were poor farmers. Can you imagine the shock when I found out that my real mother was a wealthy society lady?

"My brother—or at least I thought he was at the time—told me what he knew of my heritage as he lay dying on the battlefield. When he was a small child, he had hidden in the closet one night when a beautiful lady came to our home. She was very grateful that our mother, who had been highly recommended to her, had agreed to help in her most desperate hour of need. She was at her wit's end and didn't know what else to do, and her fear for the future of her unborn child was uppermost in her mind. She stayed until the baby was born. Every year after that, money arrived to be used for the child's care... more than sufficient, if Sam Barkley hadn't gotten meaner with the passage of time and drunk more and more." Pain was evident in his eyes as he gazed at her. "I was that child, Hallie."

Hallie said nothing, but waited for Ashe to dispel the ghosts that tortured him.

"Answers... I had a few. Sam Barkley was not my father. I finally understood Sam's attitude toward me. After all those years, it was like a blind man suddenly regaining sight. I had a name and a person to search for... Sarah Ashton Hargrove, my mother.

"I buried Vance beneath the bloodsoaked earth in the Tennessee mountains, and fought to the end of the damnable war. And then I was determined to find my mother and know why she had done what she had. I had to know about my past before I could plan my future.

"I had no one to answer all the questions that plagued me, so after the war I returned to Boston. My mother's solicitor answered some of my questions, but there were still many gaps. For a while I decided I didn't care. If she didn't care, why the hell should I? So I drifted. It wasn't intentional that I made a name for myself with a gun. It just happened. I didn't give a damn one way or another whether a bullet got me or mine got some poor bastard. The bounty money was secondary."

Dragging his hand through his hair, he continued in a ragged voice. "I knew for a long time where she was. As I look back, I can see that, without being aware of it, I continually drifted closer to where she lived." He walked to the edge of the bed. "Then, out of the clear blue sky, Hargrove approached me. He wanted the Poet Bandit stopped at any cost. Hell, I thought, now's my chance. I'll ask her straight out why she gave me up." Shrugging his shoulders, he added, "I'm sure you realize I was too late."

"What about your father, Ashe?" Hallie asked softly.

"I have no idea who he is. I do know it isn't Hargrove. I've wondered if my father abandoned her, or maybe he never knew about me. He could have died before she realized she was pregnant." He clenched his jaw. "God help me, Hallie, but I don't think she was a whore."

"Nor do I, Ashe," Hallie answered quietly.

"Perhaps it was a tragic love affair. My father could have been a married man. Damn it, Hallie, I just don't know." Dropping to the bed, he massaged his temples, as though the ache was more than he could bear.

"You've kept all of this bottled inside yourself for so long. Why didn't you tell me sooner?"

"Hell, woman, it isn't exactly dinner-table conversation. I don't want pity, just some answers. Can you understand?"

"I'm willing to try if you'll be open with me in the future. My only concern is your peace of mind. It matters little to me the circumstances of your birth. A name doesn't make a person. It's what's in here that counts," she said, placing her hand over his heart. "You once asked me what was in my heart. I tell you truly, there's more there now than ever before." She hugged him tightly, seeing the vulnerable boy who had been desperate for approval and love.

* * *

Keeping Hallie in bed was tantamount to holding back an approaching storm. Finally, to everyone's relief Doc pronounced her fit; all that remained of her injury was an angry bruise.

Now plans for the wedding could proceed, including the invitation to all her friends in town to attend the wedding. She would have it no other way. However, any wedding was an event for the townspeople, and many planned to go who were not specifically invited.

They were being married in the small church in Prospect City. The preacher was a short, quiet man of undetermined age. His wife, on the other hand, was a stout, robust woman who kept in tow their passel of children. Hallie liked the man, and he seemed nice enough when he wasn't preaching hellfire and damnation. His favorite sermon was about sins of the flesh. It never failed that, when he really got fired up, shouting to the congregation about lust being the devil's handmaiden, Grady would jab Hallie in the ribs and roll his eyes toward the front pew where the preacher's children were seated like stairsteps.

Hallie had made arrangements to dress at Martha's for her wedding. Clara's excitement soon had Grady scurrying to the Drinkalot, promising to return in time to escort Hallie to the church. Clara hovered over her like a mother hen, making sure not one small detail was overlooked. For luck, she had something old, her mother's wedding dress; something new, a gauzy confection of a camisole; something borrowed, a dainty ribbon for her hair from Clara; something blue, seductive lacy garters.

Standing inside the doorway of the church, Hallie gazed down the narrow aisle at the man who awaited her. He was dressed in a charcoal gray three-piece suit and a dazzling white shirt that contrasted handsomely with his gleaming black hair. She couldn't read anything in his expression as he watched her. Her palms were damp and her mouth felt as though it were full of cotton.

The organist began playing the "Wedding March," and Grady clasped his granddaughter's arm as he led her down the aisle. Every head turned, watching in reverence as Hallie made her way to the altar.

Breathtaking was the only word to describe the bride. Her lustrous hair had been drawn away from her face, and Clara's ribbon wove through a single braid that rested in the multitude of curls that swept her back and shoulders. Her well-defined cheekbones were flushed with color, and her lips—full and inviting— were soft pink as she ran her tongue nervously over them.

The high collar of her wedding dress hugged her creamy throat, and the bodice molded the soft curves of her breasts while dainty lace insets showed a hint of satin skin. Long sleeves billowed to her elbows, then fit snugly to her wrist with tiny pearl buttons running from wrist to elbow. Yards and yards of the delicate fabric made up the skirt.

As Ashe's firm warm hand clasped hers, Hallie looked into gentle gray eyes. Drawing from his strength, her nervousness melted away and she stood regally beside the man who had chosen her for his wife.

The ceremony was brief. Ashe's voice rang with

commitment as they promised to love, honor, and cherish as long as they both lived. Ash produced a narrow gold band and slipped it on her finger. And then he placed his warm mouth on hers, and kissed her gently.

Afterwards, in the garden behind the church, the guests celebrated. Fiddles and banjos were brought out, joined by a single battered guitar played by a shy cowhand, who sang bittersweet lyrics in a plaintive voice. One song led to another, and soon the added sound of the harmonica had the people squaring off with partners as a lively foot-stomping song ripped through the air.

Hallie accepted kisses from those eager to congratulate the bride, disappointed as Ashe was continually pulled from her side. He accepted the congratulations and the many slaps on the back with a friendliness that Hallie hadn't seen before. She also noted the various bottles that passed among the men. Ashe sampled each, taking a long pull of the gold-colored liquor. The women sought the shade, and caught up on the latest gossip when they weren't being swept away for a lively dance.

Clara, bubbling over with happiness, hugged Hallie tightly. "I'm so glad you two worked out your differences. He's the handsomest man I've ever seen," she whispered.

Stephen was more restrained as he tendered his best wishes; he offered his hand to Ashe and Ashe accepted it.

Ashe drew Hallie into his strong embrace. She was in heaven. His clean, masculine smell teased her senses.

The strong smell of liquor didn't escape her either

when he whispered hoarsely in her ear, "I'm ready to have you to myself. If one more man tries to put his lips to yours, I won't be responsible for my actions."

Satisfied by his threat, she asked sweetly, "You're not jealous, are you, Ashe?"

Jealous. The word struck a nerve. He had never thought he could care enough about anyone to succumb to jealousy. But the word perfectly described the emotions he felt when one of the men approached Hallie. "Hell yes, I'm jealous," he groaned. "How would you feel if every woman from miles around hung around my neck slobbering over me?"

As Hallie pondered the question, the familiar high-pitched voice of Sophie halted their dancing. Her perfume reached them before she did.

Long arms clasped Ashe in a bear hug, and her mouth inched closer. "Oh, Ashe, honey, what have you done?" she demanded. "I must kiss the groom, at least." As Sophie placed her generous lips over his, Hallie saw red—deep, glowing, fiery,—no doubt about it . . . red. Clenching her hands, she tapped her foot as the kiss seemed to go on and on.

Drawing Sophie's arms from his neck, Ashe pulled away. "Sophie, have you met my wife?" he asked, laughter twinkling in the depths of his eyes.

When Sophie finally left them, Hallie looked sheepishly at Ashe. "In answer to your question, I know what you mean, and I don't like it at all."

Smiling deliciously at her, he stroked her cheek with the back of his hand. "Then let's get the hell out of here."

"Fine with me," she answered as he pulled her along, making hurried farewells.

Ashe swooped Hallie up in his arms and carried her to the hotel. Her laughter was muffled as he placed wild kisses over her face. He dumped her unceremoniously onto the bed, and her skirt and petticoats flared over her head, her long legs flailing air as her shoes fell off. Warm hands captured her legs, stilling them.

Pushing her skirts from her face, she watched Ashe's face as his hands remained beneath her petticoats. Stroking her legs, he ran his hand over her thigh and down again to her ankle. Feather-light sensations darted along the inside of her leg. She drew in her breath as quivers ran through her.

"These garments are in the way, love. I want you naked before me." His voice was deep and husky, and he growled low in his chest as his mouth sought hers.

Lying beside her, he loosened the braid and watched the strands untangle, mingling with the other curls that tumbled over her pillow.

"If you lie here quietly, I will bring water for a bath."

When it was ready, he pulled her to her feet and began unbuttoning the numerous pearl buttons that ran down the back of her dress.

"Did I tell you how beautiful you looked today? You took my breath away."

"Thank you, Ashe. You looked pretty handsome yourself."

"You'll turn my head if you're not careful," he teased.

Taking her hand, he undid the buttons at her wrist, his fingers sliding beneath the fabric to caress her arm. Hallie watched in wonder as Ashe painstakingly loosened every tiny button. Each touch sent her blood racing.

His hands lingered as he eased the dress from her shoulders and down over her hips. When he untied her petticoats and pantaloons, they slid smoothly to the floor. She stood before him in her gauzy chemise and stockings held up by the lacy blue garters.

Sucking in his breath, he knelt before her, running his hand once again over her legs. As he rolled the garters and stockings from her legs, he stopped periodically to place his warm lips on various parts of her legs, his tongue teasing her sensitive skin until she felt she would melt to the floor. Tossing the stockings aside, he stood up and clasped her bare buttocks, drawing her to him and burying his face in her sweet-smelling hair. She pressed against him, her body aching with need. Her lips moved over his throat, and she could feel the throbbing of his pulse. The pounding of her heart matched his as her hands roamed at random over him. His lips sought hers, and once again they discovered new delights.

Ashe removed the last remaining garment. He lowered his head, and his tongue teased one taut nipple while his fingers kneaded the other.

Hallie moaned, and Ashe picked her up and lowered her carefully into the bath water.

Leaning her head back against the rim of the tub, she watched as he hurriedly pulled off his own clothing. The light flickered over his golden body, emphasizing the lean hardness of his torso.

Picking up a bar of soap, he dipped it into the water. Very slowly, deliberately, he bathed her, tantalizing her with his suggestive exploring. Cupping his face in her hands, she kissed him deeply, moving erotically against his hand.

Her body was aching for relief. "I need you, Ashe, now," she implored.

"Not yet, love," he whispered, kissing her lightly, and helping her out of the tub. Her body sparkled with droplets of water. He dried her slowly with a linen towel. His fingers stroked her womanly softness. A cry escaped her lips, and she fell back upon the bed.

He moved his hands and mouth over her body, bringing spasms of pleasure to her sensitive skin. His warm breath caressed her as he whispered words of passion that only heightened her desire. His hot mouth sought once again to pleasure her in the wildest, most exciting ways.

Her fingers tangled in his hair, as she ecstatically tossed her head from side to side, the wild mane of auburn hair shrouded her. At last Ashe swept it aside, his mouth closing over hers.

"Oh, Ashe, what you do to me," she groaned.

"No, love, it's what we do for each other."

He molded her body to his, and her hands caressed him, fondled him, until he growled deep in his throat.

She skimmed her breasts over him, and leaned over him. Her mouth slid across his firm stomach and up his sides. Her hair enveloped them as she teased him with her love play. Her tongue slid across his chest lightly, flicking his nipples. She rotated her hips against him, feeling the rigid maleness of him. Lowering her hand, she touched him fleetingly, then with confidence she clasped his hot maleness.

With a hoarse groan, Ashe rolled her aside, and positioning himself above her, he plunged deeply with his first thrust. Hallie moved with him, accepting his length, glorying in it. It was as though she were the sun, and he the moon. They blended, melted, then exploded in a canopy of shooting stars.

Their bodies were still entwined as Ashe rolled to his side. Replete, she lay against him, drowsily snuggling closer to the warmth of his body.

His voice was deep with emotion. "I love you."

Her eyes leaped open and her sleepiness disappeared. Astonished, she asked, "You do?"

"I damn sure do," he answered, gently ruffling her hair.

"Your love is returned twofold, Ashe."

"What more could a man ask, my love?"

Snuggling closer, they wondered at how fate had thrown them together. Hallie's hand brushed her abdomen. Was it too soon to tell Ashe of her suspicion? Would he be pleased that his seed had found fertile ground? If she was right, she was already carrying the fruit of their love.

She drifted off to sleep, never knowing when Ashe placed his hand over hers and smiled into the darkness.

Chapter 15

The white stallion's whereabouts continued to plague Hallie's thoughts. There were few ranches—besides Hargrove's—in the immediate area which stocked horses, and she wondered when the stallion would decide to strike again.

To appease her, Ashe suggested they take a few days off from the ranch chores and search the hills for the mares the stallion had successfully hidden for the past few months.

Packing enough provisions to last them for several days, they left early one morning before the sun rose. It was most likely the stallion had journeyed north into the wooded mountain region where water was plentiful and vegetation was abundant.

They traveled a full day in the hot, baking sun to reach the base of the mountain. As twilight neared, they made camp at a stream beneath a canopy of tall ponderosa pines. As Ashe unpacked their provisions, he watched Hallie stroll along the bank of the stream.

She called back to him over her shoulder, "We'll have plenty to eat tonight. The stream is full of fish." She picked up a stick and whittled the end of it to a fine point. Removing her boots and rolling up her denims, she waded knee-deep into the stream. She stood as still as a statue, her spear poised at the surface of the water. With a quick, light jab, she plunged it beneath the surface and up again to reveal a sizable trout.

Smiling, she tossed the fish to the bank and speared another in a split second. "If you'll get us a fire started, I'll clean and cook them."

Chuckling, he rose from the bank where he had been sitting, and nodded in amazement. "Where'd you learn to do that?"

Running the blade of her knife skillfully down the belly of the fish, she said, "Another lesson taught to me by the Indians."

"But you were only a child," Ashe said as he gathered scraps of wood. "I thought you lived with them for only a few months."

"True," she said almost wistfully, "but each day I lived with the hope of escaping. Learning their ways quickly was my only chance of surviving if I had escaped."

"You said Sundog was good to you."

Hallie looked up from what she was doing. "No matter how I felt about Sundog, Ashe, I did not belong with the Apache. I think he somehow knew that each time I requested him to teach me their ways, I planned to leave them." Then she smiled and said, "The bow and arrows I used in my last robbery were made by me when I lived with the Apache. They are not as fine and accurate as those made by them, but they served their purpose well that particular day."

Ashe smiled back at her while thinking: What other knowledge and skills lie buried within this woman's mind that emerge only when she chooses to let them?

After the fish sizzled for a short time over the hot coals, they sat away from the heat of the fire and talked intermittently as they pulled the flaky, moist meat from the bones, eating with hearty appetites. When Ashe was finished, he lay down on his side, gazing intently at her as she picked her bone clean.

"Am I doing something wrong?" she asked, and tossed the bone into the fire.

His hand reached out and stroked her arm. "You're like no other woman I've ever known... or hope to know, Hallie Barkley."

Hallie focused on his hand, her voice quiet and solemn. "I can't change the way I am, Ashe. I hope you realized when you married me that being domestic is not a role I am accustomed to. I can't cook, sew, do needlework, or any of the other things a woman is supposed to do for her husband."

Ashe took her hand and, rubbing his palm, noticed a few calluses. "Can't or won't?"

"I've never desired to learn these things until..." She paused and looked into his warm gray eyes. "Until I met someone to do them for. Now I'm afraid it's too late for me to learn."

Pulling her down beside him, he tweaked her nose.

"I think you could do anything you set your mind to. The truth is, I can't imagine you doing any of those things anyway. There is only one trait you possess, my love, that I find hard to accept."

"And what is that?" she asked, amused.

"Your insatiable thirst for independence. A man likes to feel he's protecting his woman, taking care of her special needs whether in or out of bed."

"Would you have me meek and simpleminded, running to you over every minor incident?" she asked placatingly.

Ashe laughed and kissed her forehead. "Hallie, there are no minor incidents in your life. And you tackle them without giving one moment's thought to the dangers."

Rolling over on him, she rested her weight on his chest. "You've managed to pull me through a few of them. So, see, I do need you after all."

Ashe stroked her back and loosened the knot of hair at the nape of her neck. "I doubt it. You've managed to stay alive all these years without me."

"And now I wonder how," she said, lowering her lips to his. Her hair tumbled over her shoulders and wispy strands teased his face.

A few moments later they undressed and bathed together in the cool mountain stream. The sky altered from lavender to indigo blue. The moon, peeking through the high, shady branches of the pines, spilled mellow moonbeams across the water. Exhausted from their long day of hot and dusty travel, they lay together beneath a single bedroll, their warm bodies touching intimately, breathing softly in unison. A bright shooting star streaked across the heavens as they slept.

In the early morning, as a fine mist hovered over the water before the sun rose, Ashe woke Hallie by kissing her parted lips, then moved down to swirl his tongue around the rosy tips of her breast. Her sleep-filled eyes opened to see the thick crown of blue-black hair, his face buried between her breasts torturing her once again in the most exquisite way.

A singing trill of a bird, the gentle play of water lapping at the shoreline, and the cacophony of the chirping crickets harmonized with soft moans of pleasure as the new day broke through the night.

Journeying around the base of the mountain, Hallie and Ashe hoped to locate a path of some sort that would indicate the stallion might have traveled that way. They found several routes up the mountain, ones used by deer and small game, but nothing denoting the traffic of a herd of horses.

Hungry and tired, they stopped along the way and ate a light lunch of beef jerky and fruit.

"There's no way you and I can bring them back alone. We'll need several men, and I'd bet Hargrove has several mares in with the herd," Hallie remarked at one point.

"It's ours I want back," Ashe replied sternly. "Hargrove can do his own searching."

Hallie looked up the mountainside, remembering a story Sundog had told her about this particular mountain. "The Apache think this mountain possesses certain magical powers. They used to go to the top to pray. The medicine man would sing sacred chants relating to the mountain, and no one else was allowed to sing them. Sundog said that all the winds on Earth originated there on the crest of the mountain."

Ashe wondered at her solemn expression. "Do you believe it was magical powers? Are you afraid to go to its top?"

"I don't believe in magic as such. Perhaps the night they took me into their tribe, their belief in magic saved my life."

Ashe leaned over and kissed her. "Then I too should be grateful for their beliefs. Without them, I wouldn't have you now."

"There's something I have wanted to ask you," Hallie said, feeling the moment right to bring up the subject. "If I had chosen not to marry you after you threatened me with exposure, would you really and truly have told my grandfather?"

The tiny crow's-feet at the corner of his eyes creased as he smiled. "You're damned right I would have, and your grandfather would have welcomed me with open arms if he'd known everything you had been up to."

"But it would have killed him if he ever knew," she protested.

"It would have killed him quicker if his granddaughter had been captured—or died."

Chewing on the tough beef jerky, Hallie said lightly, "Well, it makes no difference, for I would have married you eventually anyway."

Surprise skittered across his face. "So I went to all that trouble for nothing?"

Hallie slowly raised her head and gazed at him with

luminous blue eyes. "We're going to have a baby, Ashe."

A radiant glow suffused his face, but was quickly replaced by a slight frown. "I wish you'd told me earlier. We'd have forgotten about tracking down the horses."

"Don't start pampering me now, Ashe Barkley," Hallie said, her voice rising an octave. "I've not been sick a morning yet and I don't plan to be, either."

"I had a feeling you were pregnant. I wondered when you'd tell me," he said, his eyes focusing on her breasts. "A man notices little changes here and there. You'll just have to take it easier when we get back to the ranch."

Rising to her feet, Hallie said in irritation, "I'll see Doc Nelson and let him tell me what I should and shouldn't do, Dr. Barkley. But for now, I'm going to look for my horses with or without your help."

Turning abruptly, she started to walk toward Licorice, but was stopped by firm hands on her shoulders. "You've got to realize it isn't every day a man is told he's going to be a father. Perhaps I've overreacted."

Turning in his arms, she placed her cheek against his chest. "I'm sorry I got so angry," she said compromisingly. "This is all new to me, too, you know."

"I know, love." He bent down and picked up her hat, and placed it on her head. Smiling, he said, "Let's see if we have any luck in finding your horses."

They searched until all hope was lost of finding them before nightfall... if at all. As they prepared a campsite, Ashe noticed a shiny object lying in the short grass. Dismounting, he walked over and picked it up.

"What is it?" she asked.

"A heavy silver bracelet with turquoise embedded in it."

He gave it to her, and she turned it over in her hand to inspect it. "It's an Indian woman's jewelry, but what's it doing here?"

"You said the Indians come here to pray. Maybe she lost it."

A frown etched her brow. "I suppose so, but most of the Indians are on the San Carlos Reservation now, except for Geronimo. Rumor has it he comes to the reservation for a short time, then flees back into Mexico where he preys on Mexican ranches."

Ashe walked to a path that led up the mountainside. "The bracelet isn't tarnished, so it couldn't have been here long." Looking over his shoulder, he asked, "Do you want to check farther up the mountain?"

"Since the mountain is sacred, the Indians wouldn't make a campsite there. We might find proof that the Indians have run off with our horses already. I'm game if you are."

"You're sure you'll be all right?" he asked, mounting Rebel.

"Of course," she replied adamantly.

Nodding his head in dismay, he grinned at her and proceeded up the mountainside with Hallie close behind. The well-worn trail was steep and treacherous. Several times Ashe looked over his shoulder at Hallie, concern etched across his features.

Nearing the top, he stopped abruptly and whispered, "Do you hear anything?"

Hallie cocked her head, hearing only the familiar

sound of the birds and the rustling of small animals in the overgrowth of shrub bushes. "No, what am I suppose to be hearing?"

"Guess it was only my imagination." Shrugging his shoulders, he nudged Rebel and they continued upward.

A scream split the stillness, mingling with the frantic outcry of the birds as they flew from their haven in the treetops. Both horses' ears perked up nervously.

Hallie whispered, "That wasn't a bobcat's cry by any means."

"Tether the horses, and we'll walk the rest of the way," Ashe decided, dismounting. "I believe it was a woman crying out, but I could be wrong."

They walked as quietly as Indians, their rifles poised and ready. Ashe assumed a crouched position as they reached the crest, waving his arm behind him to warn Hallie to stay back. He crawled on his belly like a scout, and peered over the top. He remained there for several minutes, and Hallie became impatient. Ignoring his warning, she maneuvered her way up beside him and gasped when she saw what had held his attention.

A woman was stripped of her clothing and lying with her arms and legs staked to the ground. Two men—Mexicans, judged Hallie from their attire and dark features—walked in circles around her, taunting and jabbing her with the toes of their pointed boots.

From Hallie's prone position, she could see only the woman's long black hair whipping back and forth when one of the men bent and pinched her breasts.

The wind roared as though the gods were angry,

and the tall, thin pines bowed and swayed. The baggy pants of the men plastered against their legs, and their long, unruly mustaches blew haphazardly around their cruel mouths. Their voices carried on the wind to Ashe and Hallie's ears.

"Apache," the man said, and spat on her face. "You are not worth the spit I grace on you." When she said nothing, he grinned lewdly, showing broken yellow teeth. Kneeling down beside her, he picked up a pinecone and tossed it back and forth between his hands. His laugh was spine-chilling.

Bile rose up in Hallie's throat, and she clutched Ashe's hand as the Mexican rolled the rough sharpedged pinecone over the woman's breasts and continued the torturous journey over the woman's naked skin. The woman arched her hips in pain and thrashed her body in a vain attempt to escape.

Finally the man tossed the pinecone away and stood up to view the bloody scratches trailing over the woman's body.

He said to his friend, "What do you think, mi amigo? Would Sundog like the fertile seed of a Mexican in his sister's belly as a constant reminder to stay where he belongs?"

"Si," the other man replied excitedly. "Though she is only an Indian, she is a pretty one. We will show her how a real man feels inside her, no?"

"My God," Hallie exclaimed beneath her breath, "that's Sundog's sister, my friend Doe Eyes. Oh Ashe, no." Tears welled up in her throat, and she fought the urge to cry out.

As the man unbuttoned the front of his baggy trousers and bared his gorging ugly member, Hallie could bear it no longer. Ashe was ready to move in on them, but Hallie beat him to it. He attempted to grab her ankle as she scrambled forward, but she slipped out of his grasp.

"You yellow-bellied bastards," she shouted, pointing her rifle at the men.

Ashe lay back out of sight, his rifle propped on a ledge, his finger resting on the trigger. Hallie's action had diverted their attention for the moment. He had to think fast. If they thought this was a mere helpless woman at the end of the gun, they were sadly mistaken. But there were two of them, and by the way they were looking at her, they didn't know what they were up against.

"Madre de dios, where did you come from?" the man demanded, shifting his eyes around the camp.

"That doesn't matter. Cut her loose," Hallie snapped, motioning with the rifle.

"Ah, senorita," the man said, rising undauntedly to his feet, not bothering to rebutton his pants. "She is only an Indian, an Apache . . . a mean breed." Walking toward her, his leering dark eyes swept over her admiringly. "But you . . . you are *muy hermosa*, much woman." Casting a grin over his shoulder to his companion, he asked, "Is she not, mi amigo?"

"Stay back," Hallie warned him. "If you value your lives, you'll leave now."

"How do you plan to take the both of us at once? One of us will be a most fortunate hombre after it is all over. There will be two women to pleasure rather than one."

Hallie's eyes flitted from one to the other, weighing her chances. With Ashe behind her, she was not entirely helpless; but at this close range, she could take a fatal bullet from either way, if they chose to fire at the same moment. That she was a woman gave her a slight advantage, for they evidently had little faith in her ability with a gun. She had never killed anyone in her life, and the prospect unnerved her. But when she saw Doe Eyes gazing at her pleadingly from beneath long black lashes, she felt she had no choice.

As Hallie talked to the men, she moved cautiously, slowly, until the talkative Mexican was positioned between her and his friend. This was her only chance for survival. She could kill the one in front of her and block the gunshot from the other, giving Ashe time to shoot.

Her heart raced in her chest as she watched both of them ease their hands toward their holsters. They were challenging her, mocking her with their dark, evil eyes.

Oh God, Ashe, what have I done? was her thought as both Mexicans whipped their guns from their holsters in the same split second.

The next instant, everything was in confusion. One shot rang, and then another. All Hallie saw as she dived to the side was the Mexican pointing his gun at her prone body. For the first time in her life, she froze. His eyes were glazed in stunned disbelief as he gazed at the blood gushing through fingers that clutched his abdomen. He tried to laugh, but the jolt to his insides etched pain on his face.

Ashe raced forward; the blast from his rifle striking

the Mexican full in the face, and he fell backward to the ground.

Why doesn't the other man shoot? Hallie wondered, her mind befuddled as Ashe drew her into his arms. "Oh, my sweet, sweet Hallie," Ashe choked, his heart nearly bursting in the aftermath of the violence. "Let me hold you."

Doe Eyes screamed. Ashe shoved Hallie out of the way and rolled to his side. The injured Mexican had pulled himself up on one knee. His eyes blinked in rapid succession, and his hand trembled as he tried to focus his gun on Ashe.

Ashe fired. The blood spewed from the man's throat as he toppled forward, his dead weight relaxing across Doe Eyes' chest. She screamed, her bound body thrusting upward as she tried to free herself of his bulk.

Hallie and Ashe rushed to her side. As Hallie severed the ropes from her ankles, Ashe lifted the man from her body. He cut the ropes from her wrists, but Doe Eyes remained immobile, her head barely raised from the ground. Her eyes rested on her bloodsoaked breasts and stomach.

Moaning, she dropped her head to the ground and rolled to a fetal position. Hallie found a blanket that had belonged to the Mexicans and draped it over her.

Sitting down beside her, Hallie stroked the long, tangled hair away from her friend's face. "Doe Eyes, you're going to be fine now. My husband has killed your attackers. They'll never hurt you or anyone again." Then, when Doe Eyes did not respond, Hallie murmured almost to herself, "You don't remember me, do you? It's been many years, and I have changed."

Doe Eyes tilted her head, her swollen, half-closed eyes studying Hallie's features. Hallie removed her hat and unpinned her hair. She pulled the heavy silver chain and medallion from inside her blouse and held it out for Doe Eyes' inspection.

A tiny smile tugged at the corner of Doe Eyes' mouth and she reached up to touch the long curl that draped over Hallie's shoulder. "Bright Star Falling," she said in broken English, tears springing to her eyes. "The omen has proven true once again."

"What do you mean?" Hallie asked with a noticeable frown.

"Did you not see the shooting star one night ago?"

"No." Hallie looked at Ashe for confirmation. He shook his head.

"For two days I've been held captive by those animals. Last night, as I lay here gazing at the heavens, I prayed to the Great Spirit to release me from my pain and let me go in peace. A shooting star, like the one which appeared on that night ten years ago, swirled through the heavens. I thought that to be the answer to my prayer, yet I knew not how my deliverance would come . . . in rescue or in death."

A cold sensation permeated Hallie's body. The manifestation of Doe Eyes' deep spiritual beliefs combined with the howling wind on the sacred mountain seemed almost eerie.

Darkness was settling in, and Ashe was anxious to leave the windy crest of the mountain. Hallie found Doe Eyes' soft leather tunic which had been ripped down the front. Only a few strings of sinew held it together, but it covered her adequately and she slipped it on gratefully.

Ashe dragged the bodies of the two men beneath a tree. He piled rocks on their bodies, since he had no shovel to dig a grave. Then they hurriedly departed.

That night, as they camped at the base of the mountain, Doe Eyes told them how she had been kidnapped at the river where her tribe had arrived only two nights earlier. She and a few of the women were bathing in the river and had just finished dressing. She had misplaced her bracelet, and told them to go ahead without her. As she was searching the crevices between the rocks where she had placed her clothing, a blanket dropped over her, smothering her cries for help. Her abductors brought her to the mountain top, and began torturing her slowly. They planned to leave her barely alive, hoping that Sundog would find her raving mad from her violent ordeal.

"But why did Black Wing's tribe leave the reservation?" Hallie asked.

"Our people, along with other Apache tribes, were dying a slow death. Our rations were meager, and our fields were taken over by Mormon settlers. Some of our strongest warriors were made to dig coal from our own land for the benefit of the white man. So we left the reservation to go to the mountains where we knew we could survive and rebuild our lives."

"How far away is your village?" Ashe asked.

"Nearby. I was surprised the Mexicans did not take me farther away, but I think they wanted me to be found, and they knew my people would come to the sacred mountain."

"Do you have children, Doe Eyes?" Hallie asked quietly.

"Yes, two beautiful children, a boy and a girl."

"Ashe and I are expecting our first child," Hallie confided, looking happily up at Ashe. He smiled back, and then tactfully left them alone to talk while he saw to building a fire. Doe Eyes watched him, her eyes following his every move.

"You have a very handsome husband, Bright Star Falling. He is brave, too. Two strong people will make strong babies who will grow up to be brave warriors like their parents." Doe Eyes touched Hallie's cheek affectionately. "Even as a child you were more daring and clever than many of our braves. Today, you gave no thought to your own life when you came to my rescue."

"No, you're wrong, Doe Eyes, I did think about my life . . . and that of my unborn child. But I realized I could not live in peace with myself if I did nothing to save you. Especially since I would have died years ago in the desert had it not been for your brother."

They were so caught up in their conversation they didn't notice Ashe towering over them with an amused smile. "I hate to interrupt, but it's late. Tomorrow will be a long day, we need to eat and get some shut-eye."

Hallie didn't realize how drained she was until she lay down next to Ashe beneath his bedroll.

"Ashe," she whispered softly.

"Um?"

"I nearly killed a man today." For a moment she stared into the darkness, then added, "I don't think it would have bothered me, not after I saw what they were doing to Doe Eyes. How does it make you feel after you've killed someone?"

Ashe drew her against him, his warm, naked chest against her bare back. "I usually don't feel anything, but today I relished their deaths. Had you not shot that bastard when you did, you might have been the one I buried today."

"I hope I never have to go through anything like that again."

"You won't, love, if I can prevent it." He turned her to him and kissed her tenderly. "I wish we were alone."

"Does it matter?" she asked, and snuggled in closer to him. After quenching their need, they lay quietly, content with each other.

"Thank you, my love," Hallie whispered.

"For what?"

"For forcing me to marry you. I don't see how anything that seems so right could ever be wrong."

Ashe laughed quietly. "It's not. Go to sleep, love, before I decide to keep you up the rest of the night, exploring your exquisite body."

Nestling closer to him, she murmured sleepily, "Sounds terribly wicked," and she promptly fell asleep.

It was noon by the time they reached Sundog's camp. Doe Eyes rode a short distance ahead of them on one of her captor's horses. Several braves rode out to meet her. They talked briefly with her, and then Doe Eyes motioned for Ashe and Hallie to follow her.

As they rode through the camp, the Indian women ran from their wickiups, their small children following behind them, curiously scrutinizing the two strangers who rode with their princess.

A beautiful young woman stood at the head of the group, tears of relief running down her cheeks. Doe Eyes dismounted and they hugged each other. Bending down, Doe Eyes embraced the two youngsters who rushed into her open arms.

Hallie's eyes were misty as she and Ashe were introduced to Morning Dove, Sundog's wife. She nodded her head approvingly and invited them to Chief Black Wing's wickiup so that he might thank them for the safe return of his daughter.

The years of wretched reservation life had left its mark on the old chief's face: it was as parched and wrinkled as the sun-dried desert. He did not rise to meet them, for Morning Dove said his bones were weak and hurt him frequently. Hallie surmised that he suffered from arthritis, a common ailment among the Indians.

Reaching out a crippled hand, he took Hallie's hand and added another line to his face as he smiled and thanked her for the safe return of Doe Eyes.

They sat with him for several minutes, and in broken, clipped English, he recounted for Ashe the story of Hallie Parker's time with the tribe. Ashe listened with interest as the old chief described that part of Hallie's life that she had not yet told him about with this much detail.

In the midst of his narrative, they heard a commotion outside the wickiup. Morning Dove threw back the flap to see Sundog and his group of warriors rapidly approaching the tent.

Surprise and relief washed over his severe features as he saw Hallie and Ashe standing quietly behind Morning Dove.

"It has been many moons, Bright Star Falling. I never thought to see you again." He gazed with curiosity at Ashe, then back to Hallie.

"This is my husband, Ashe Barkley," she said, taking Ashe's arm. "Ashe, this is Sundog, of whom you've heard me speak many times."

Sundog regarded Ashe from beneath hooded dark eyes, giving no outward expression of his feelings about him. He wondered if this man was worthy of Hallie's love. He had often thought of Hallie and his desire to have her as his own, and the children they might have had together.

Ashe too was assessing the tall warrior before him dressed in buckskin britches with soft leather knee boots. His long, beaded tunic was belted, and on his hip rested a glittering scabbard with hammered silver embedded in the leather. His features seemed sculptured in bronze metal, lending him an air of shrewdness and austerity.

"Please... be comfortable," he said, motioning them to sit down. He took a seat on a large woven rug next to his father and drew his legs up in the Indian fashion.

Black Wing brought out a long clay pipe, and it was passed among the three men.

"Were you responsible for bringing Doe Eyes to her people?"

Ashe told Sundog the harrowing saga of the kidnapping, and the death of the two Mexicans in the end. Sundog's relief that Doe Eyes had not been violated was visible on his face.

"They were fortunate to have died quickly by your hand," Sundog said. "I would not have been so kind." He shifted his interest to Hallie, his eyes sweeping her in admiration. "Twice now I owe you my sister's precious life. There is no reward I can offer to you or your husband to repay this debt."

"It is not necessary, Sundog," Hallie said. "I owe you my own life, and this cancels the debt."

Sundog nodded, satisfied. "How is it you are so far from home?" he asked curiously.

Hallie told him about the wild white stallion and how they had searched the mountains and found no evidence of him or the mares.

"I have seen the white stallion. We had planned to capture him for our own, but our time has been spent in searching for Doe Eyes. How many horses has he taken from you?"

"A dozen. He chose well, leaving me with only a couple who are worth breeding."

"Would you know your own horses if we could capture the herd?"

"I know all my horses," Hallie assured him.

Sundog laughed, which was unusual. "Then perhaps I can show my gratitude in a small way by capturing them from the stallion."

"Thanks, Sundog," Ashe said, offering his hand to him. "Now, I think it would be best if we headed back to the ranch."

"You are welcome to remain here for the night," Sundog offered.

"Thank you, but no, we must leave," Ashe answered courteously.

Sundog rose with them, and after bidding Chief Black Wing farewell, they left the tent. As Hallie and Ashe mounted their horses, Sundog said, "Go in peace, my friends, and remember you will always be welcomed guests in my village."

Doe Eyes threw back the flap of her wickiup and walked over to Ashe and Hallie. "Goodbye, Bright Star Falling," she said, clasping Hallie's hand. "And thank you both for bringing me back to my people. I will pray to 'Usin,' and he will reward you for your kindness."

"Thank you, Doe Eyes, and I'll remember you in my prayers."

Ashe and Hallie rode out of the Apache campsite, each lost in thought.

Ashe was thinking over the old chief's story about the young girl the Apache had come to love as one of their own. Had it not been for the medicine man—who was now dead and replaced by another—she might have been the mother of the next chief in line after Sundog. He recalled how Hallie blushed when the chief referred to her as one of the most skillful and courageous young braves in the camp.

He wondered if she would have still possessed the same self-will and fortitude in the face of the ordinary day-to-day life of a Southern belle, had the war between North and South never happened. A smile tugged at the corner of his mouth. Yes, she was by nature strong-willed, though if she had been a protected young lady of society, she might never have been tested for valor. Her encounter with the Indians, her search for revenge, and her independence had influenced her character. It struck him anew that he had married an extraordinary woman. But did he, in all truth, completely possess her? He thought not. Her love, yes, and that was all that mattered.

Chapter 16

Stabbing the pitchfork into the ground, Hallie removed her handkerchief and mopped her brow. She had not lied to Ashe when she told him she did not have morning sickness, but she did find she tired easily, especially in the heat of the day. Perhaps she should cut down on her chores until the weather cooled off considerably.

Ashe had gone into town for supplies, and Juan had asked for the day off so he could help Luis mend his roof. She had just finished feeding the horses and was almost at the point of exhaustion. It might be nice if the man around the house helped out with the chores. But since they had been married, it seemed she had seen so little of Ashe they might as well not be married at all. The last time they had been together was when they went in search of the white stallion, and that had been weeks ago.

He had left the management of the stables to her and spent most of his time tending to the cattle. He had hired additional men and added considerably to their herd because he felt that was where the money was to be made.

Since Rebel had been reunited with his family, Hallie had intended to breed him with two of her choice mares. But that plan had been shelved when the white stallion ran off with them.

Hallie whimsically compared her own life with that of the stallion. She roamed the land with complete awareness of the perils that awaited her within its vast silence. She had never known loneliness as she rode her horse through the canyons and across the cactus-strewn desert, with its wild and unpredictable elements.

Would Ashe attempt to break her spirit and forbid her to run free? He didn't seem to mind her having her own way now, but after years of living with her as independent as she was, would he regret he married her?

There was only one thing he had been adamant about from the very beginning, and that was Stephen Bradshaw's presence in her life. He made her take Stephen off Ben's case, even though he didn't have the time to look into it himself with all the other chores he had to do, and that caused no small dissension between them. But Stephen had remained in town anyway and was courting Clara, so maybe it hadn't turned out too badly.

She heard a footstep behind her. Turning, she said,

"Ashe, I didn't expect..." She stopped, paralyzed, and she paled visibly.

"Hello, princess."

"B...Ben..." she stammered, fear clutching her. Running to him, she pulled him into the stall, afraid someone would see him. "Has...has anyone seen you?"

Ben stared at her dumbfounded. "Hell, gal, I don't know if they have or not. You act like you've seen a ghost."

Tears gathered in her eyes as she hugged him to her. "Oh, Ben, it seems an eternity has passed since you left. So much has happened; so much that I don't know where to begin."

She stepped back, and looked him over. His appearance had changed little, except for a marked difference in his eyes. They were laughing blue eyes, sparkling like a child's when presented with a new toy. He doesn't know, Hallie thought in consternation, and how am I to tell him? He was as handsome as ever, his hair more salt and pepper now.

"Now that you've inspected me, let me take a good look at you." He ran his eyes appreciatively over her. "There's somethin' different about you, princess... and for the life of me I can't figure it out. You always were a purty little thing, but...well, maybe I've been gone so long I'd forgotten just how beautiful you really are."

He took her by the hand to lead her out the door. When Hallie made no effort to move, he said, "C'mon, gal, got to go see my old buddies, Grady and Maria.

Is she still as ornery as she was before I left? And Sinbad? Is he faring well?"

"Grandpa's at the mine," she said rapidly. "Sinbad's the same as always." Then, taking a deep breath, she said, "I can't let Maria see you just yet, Ben."

Ben noted her concern, and his brow furrowed deeply. "What is it, Hallie? I've never seen you so jumpy."

Her heart bet a rapid stacatto. "Have you seen no one since your arrival?"

"No, I came straight here," he said, his eyes narrowing to slits.

Hallie breathed a sigh of relief. "Ben, we have to talk. You aren't safe here anymore. It's going to be as difficult for me to tell you this as it is going to be for you to hear it."

"Then maybe I'd better sit down," Ben said. "Guess this bed of straw will have to do."

Hallie sat down next to him, drawing up her knees and wrapping her arms around them. She stared pensively at the rows and rows of shelves across the room, her mind working furiously on how to begin.

She finally turned to face him. "Vern Hargrove is out to hang you, Ben, for the murder of his wife Sarah." When she saw pain take the sparkle from his eyes, she wished she had told him in a gentler way.

"Murdered? Sarah?" he asked disbelievingly. "Oh, dear God, no." He buried his head in the palms of his hands, and wept silently for several minutes.

Hallie allowed him this moment of mourning as she realized that there had been more to his relationship with Sarah than she had perceived. She had never seen ring on her finger. "Well, well, and what's this?" he asked. "Seems like there's something else you have to tell me."

"I'm... married now."

"Well, I'll be damned. I knew somebody'd melt your butter one day. What I'm wantin' to know is how he went about it and where he came from. You never did have nothin' to do with the local fellers."

Hallie laughed nervously. "You might say his overbearing arrogance and sheer determination left me with no other choice. I had to marry him in order to keep my sanity."

"I'd like to meet this daring young man," he said appreciatively.

Oh no you wouldn't, Hallie thought with fierce dread.

"What's his name?"

"Ashe Barkley. And I might as well tell you now, because you'll hear it sooner or later, he's everything a woman shouldn't marry: a drifter, a bounty hunter, a Yankee, and, worst of all, he worked for Hargrove."

Ben turned white as a sheet.

Hallie berated herself for her careless words and quickly added, "But he has no use for Hargrove." *He has no use for you either, Ben, but I can't tell you that.* Even now she wondered how she was going to rehire Stephen without Ashe's knowledge.

"The most important thing, princess, is: do you love him?"

"Regretfully, I do," Hallie answered with a smile. "I must add that I tried to prevent it, though."

"Where is he now?"

"He's probably at the Drinkalot trying to find some sober men who are willing to work. You won't believe all the changes he wants to make around here."

"Does it bother you having a man around, Hallie? You've always been such an independent little cuss, never asking for nobody's help even when you've needed it."

"As long as he sticks with the cattle and leaves me with my horses, we'll do fine together," she said laughingly. "But the minute he starts offering his unwanted advice, then he's in trouble."

"Yep, I'd say if he's been around you long enough, he learned that part of your character quickly."

Peeking out of the stall, Hallie asked, "Where's your horse?"

"Tied up in front of the house."

"Well, there goes my idea of sneaking by Maria." Flashing him a bright smile, she said, "Let's go tell her you are home. She's on our side, but I hate for her to be involved in such danger."

As they walked into the kitchen, they were greeted by Maria's back as she continued to crush hot peppers with a ferocity that belied her air of industriousness. "It's about time you came in. Are we having a guest for lunch?"

"Is that an invitation?" Ben asked sheepishly.

Sinbad heard his master's voice and squawked, "Ben? Ben? Is that you, Ben? Squawk...squawk."

A partially filled jar of crushed peppers dropped from Maria's hand and crashed to the floor. "Madre de Dios, no..." she whispered loudly. She turned, and her mouth gaped open and a hint of fear entered her big brown eyes. "Oh, Senor Langley, you have come home."

"Yes," Ben announced sadly, "but a trifle too late, it would appear."

Maria looked curiously at Hallie, her eyes speaking volumes.

"He knows, Maria. Would you mind packing all the food we have on hand? Ben can't stay here. If anyone saw him, they'd come here first."

Maria mumbled a stream of Spanish words and went quickly to the pantry.

Ben walked over to Sinbad's cage. "Well, Sinbad, seems you've been well cared for. Believe you've put on a little weight since I saw you last."

"Yes," Hallie said humorously, "as long as we keep his mouth full, he can't talk. If I didn't think he'd blow your cover, I'd let you take him with you for company."

"Yeah, me and Sinbad's traveled a lot of miles together, haven't we, old boy? I remember one time when I was so near to starving that I nearly skewered him over an open fire... but he talked me out of it."

After they had everything assembled, Hallie took Maria aside. "Don't tell Ashe anything, Maria. If he returns before I get back, tell him I had to go to the mission."

"Oh, mi niña, I hate for you to start out your marriage with deceit," Maria sighed, clenching her hands together.

"I don't like it either, Maria, but I have to this one time. I can't tell you why, but he mustn't know. You'll just have to trust my judgment."

Hugging her, Maria said, "I sometimes wonder if your judgment is always right. I pray for your sake it is this time."

Taking no chances on being seen, Hallie and Ben traveled a route through the foothills, weaving in and out of the high-walled canyons; it was a treacherous path, but necessary for Ben's safety. There was only one place Hallie knew of that would give Ben protection from Hargrove and Ashe—the place where she had hidden during her escapades as the bandit. Only Ashe was aware of its existence, but he would have no reason to go there now unless he discovered that Hallie was hiding Ben.

Once inside the quiet, protective walls of her sanctuary, Hallie asked Ben, "What do you think of it?"

"How in the hell did you ever find such a place?"

"Quite by accident, I assure you. One of my childhood discoveries. You have a pool to bathe in, and the water coming off the canyon wall is drinkable. I've seen jackrabbits, but I don't know if you should chance shooting one in case the shot might be heard. And there's only one way out, and that's the way we came in."

"Hallie, I appreciate this, but I'm worried about you. Are you telling Ashe what you're up to?"

Hallie hesitated. "No, it isn't necessary. He would try to stop me. As you said before, Ben, I am very independent in some ways. I'd better be getting back before he comes looking for me. I'll ride out every other day if I can slip away unnoticed. Maria's packed enough food to carry you through for a while if something prevents me from coming."

Ben leaned over in his saddle and squeezed her hand. "Take care, princess, and don't worry about a thing. Mother Nature and me have gotten along well over the years, so I don't foresee any problems."

On the way back to the ranch, Hallie took the same time-consuming route. She hoped Ashe would still be away so she wouldn't have to lie to him. Now, more than ever, she had to protect Ben from Ashe. Though Ashe had said he would help her find Sarah's murderer, she wasn't sure he would give Ben the chance to prove his innocence.

How long had Ben known Sarah? She had never asked him. He said he had loved her all his life, but that could have just been his way of expressing his love for her. Sarah and Vern had been in Prospect City for a few years before Hallie had arrived at age thirteen. Surely Ben and Sarah hadn't been lovers for that many years. How devastating it would be to love someone that deeply and know you could never be together.

She wondered if she should show him the letter from Sarah's lawyer. Had Ben known she had another lover and had borne a child? Would the knowledge make him so angry he might go after Vern Hargrove openly and damn the consequences?

How would she feel if she and Ashe were in the same predicament that Ben and Sarah had been in? There had to be a way to bring together the two men she loved without one destroying the other. If anything should happen to either of them, she didn't think she could endure the heartache.

* * *

That evening after supper, Ashe was busy, so Hallie took a stroll to the base of the foothills where her father was buried beneath a lone cottonwood tree. Sitting down, she leaned back against the tree and watched the sunset spread its tentacles in slow motion.

Longing for the presence of her father, she closed her eyes, listening to the plaintive wail of the coyote. A twig snapped, a jarring note among the familiar evening sounds, and Hallie opened her eyes to see a pair of long, muscled legs standing before her.

"Sorry if I'm disturbing you."

"You're not," Hallie said, her eyes full of love.

Ashe saw the rough hann-hewn tombstone and the name of her father etched into it. "Do you come here often?"

"When I seek peace."

Sitting down beside her, he drew up his knees. "I noticed you were unusually quiet tonight at supper. What's troubling you, love? Is married life so disagreeable?"

"No, it's not that," she said, laughing lightly. "Although I do think I saw more of you before we were married."

Ashe reached over and took her hand in his, and traced the contour of each finger thoughtfully. "That was before I had a ranch to run. I managed to find some men in town today who said they'd come out tomorrow and help me. If I could find a few who'd be willing to stay on, then we'd have more time together. What would you think of building a bunkhouse?"

"That would be all right with me... but, Ashe, that would require around-the-clock cooking. Maria could hardly be expected to take on all that responsibility."

"You're right. It was just a thought."

Not wanting to dismiss the idea entirely, she said consideringly, "It wouldn't hurt to ask her, though. I might also need additional help in the stables if I increase my stock. Of course, a lot of that depends on when Sundog finds my horses."

"I've noticed lately you tire easily, Hallie. It's not good for you to work so hard in that stable. Please take my advice... and Dr. Nelson's, and rest more often."

"I will, I promise." Then, changing the subject, she said, "We could build a dining room and hire a cook, too. Grandpa has always been so wrapped up in the mining business that he never gave much thought to his cattle. Of course, all this would take money, Ashe." A mischievous gleam sparkled in her eyes. "Since Hargrove has been so generous in the past, maybe..."

"Oh no, Hallie," Ashe said, clamping his hand over her mouth and easing her to the ground. "The bandit rides no more." Removing his hand, he replaced it with his mouth and kissed her thoroughly. "Do I make myself clear?"

"Perfectly," she murmured. "But, Ashe, where are we going to get that much money?"

"I have money, Hallie. You didn't exactly marry a complete pauper."

"Ashe, this may not be the appropriate time to bring up something like this, but I've thought about it often since I discovered Sarah was your mother." She noted how his back tensed as she stroked it with her fingertips. "I'm sorry... forget I said anything."

He relaxed, but a cold, sober expression crossed his face. "I know what you're thinking, love, and I've thought about it myself. Hargrove used my mother's wealth to get to where he is today. Of course, he cheated and hurt many other people, too. By rights, my mother's money belongs to me when Hargrove dies. I look at his damned gaudy mansion and all the expensive furnishings and it sickens me. If it were mine, I'd burn it to the ground."

"Will you ever confront Hargrove with the fact that Sarah was your mother?"

"When the time's right," he said grimly. "When that time will be, I don't know."

"Ashe, how did you know where Sarah was after so many years?" she questioned softly.

Ashe rolled over on his back and gazed at the moon breaking through the dying remains of the sunset. His mind swirled, unlocking the secret chamber of his heart where the sad memories lingered. "I almost didn't discover her whereabouts. I had hoped to find her in Boston. The information I gathered from several affluent people in the city was that Sarah had moved away with her husband, but they didn't know where. The church records had established Sarah and Vern Hargrove's marriage date, which did not coincide with my birthdate. If Hargrove were my natural father, why would my mother abandon me?

"On the eve of my departure, after I'd given up all hope of locating her, a man came to my room at the hotel. He identified himself as William James, Sarah

Hargrove's solicitor. He had heard that I was seeking information about Sarah Ashton. I did not attempt to conceal my identity, so he knew right away I had to be Sarah's son. James was the man who had recommended Ruth Barkley to Sarah; Ruth was to raise Sarah's child as her own, and, honoring Sarah's wishes, James saw to it that money was sent each year for the child's needs. Mr. James told me that before Sarah had left Boston with her husband, she had arranged for a sizable trust fund for me that I was to receive on my twenty-first birthday. Mr. James reached into his briefcase, and with a wide smile handed me my legacy in the form of a banknote. I told him that before I accepted a dime of her money, I would find her. I'd have none of her conscience money until she explained to me her reasons for giving me up."

Ashe laughed when he remembered the surprised expression on James' face.

"When I asked James if he knew their whereabouts, all he could tell me was that they were somewhere out West. So I drifted toward the western territory. The Reward posters in the towns I saw gave me the idea how I could make the money I needed to continue my search. Hargrove heard of my reputation as a gunslinger, and as luck would have it ... he sought me out and saved me the trouble of finding him. That's how I ended up in Prospect City in Hargrove's employ.

"When I arrived at Hargrove's home, the first thing I found out was that Sarah Hargrove was dead. All those years I had searched and killed in order to throw her conscience money back into her face had been for nothing." A muscle flexed tightly in his jaw. "You know, Hallie, I feel that I've fought a useless battle. The only thing good that came out of it was winning you for my wife."

Joy surged through her. He was revealing his deepest thoughts for the first time.

"I'm afraid I'll hurt you, love, with all this business concerning Ben Langley and my mother. You feel in your heart Ben is innocent," he continued, positioning himself on his side to face her, "but, damnit, I wish I could put that much faith in the man."

"Please do one thing for me, Ashe. Hear him out before you seek revenge."

"There's a chance I won't get to him first, love. Hargrove would kill him on sight; we both know it. I promise that if it is at all possible, I will hear what he has to say."

"And if he denies it?" she asked with a remnant of hope.

"Then I want to know why he disappeared that night. If he loved her, how could he leave her with a man like Vern Hargrove?"

Hallie had wondered the same thing. The next time she saw Ben, she planned to ask him. There had to be a good reason, for there was nothing false about Ben's reaction when she told him of Sarah's untimely death.

Hallie reread the letter from the solicitor and stuffed it inside her boot, praying she was making the right decision by showing it to Ben. The thought had occurred to her that Ben might know all about Sarah's past and why she had given up her child. At the very least, she was going to find out why Ben had left Sarah the night she died.

Ashe had told her earlier he would be gone until dinnertime. She hoped his meeting with Jeb Smith about the plans for the new bunkhouse would keep him in town overnight. She needed the time to talk to Ben.

She sensed his depression the moment she dismounted. He smiled, but it didn't reach his eyes. They had so much to discuss, but for a moment she considered withholding the letter and what it might reveal. No, she needed answers if she were to help him. Concern for his feelings had to come last.

"Brought you some more food," she said briskly, unstrapping a knapsack from her saddlebag.

"I've still got plenty. You needn't have bothered." He picked up a smooth, flat pebble and skidded it across the lake, rippling the still blue water. "I can't stand much more of this, Hallie. I'd just as soon confront Hargrove and get this whole mess over with. If I kill him or he kills me, what the hell does it matter?"

"Damnit, Ben Langley, it matters a whole lot to me."

Hallie dropped the knapsack and scowled at him. "Do you know how much trouble and money you've cost me already? Stephen Bradshaw was just about ready to leave town in defeat. When I told him how desperately we needed him, he agreed to stay and help us all he can. He's not even going to charge me a cent this time to do it. He believes in you as I do."

"Where'd you get the money, Hallie, to pay for

such luxuries as hiring a detective? Has my mine finally paid off?"

"No, but Grandpa has moved in up at the mine and is bound and determined to find silver if he has to dig his way to China. By the way, I haven't told him you've returned. The fewer who know, the better." Hallie hoped she had diverted his attention from the money.

"I'm sure you haven't told your husband about me, either. Evidently he doesn't believe me innocent, or he'd be supportin' you."

Hallie cleared her throat. "That's something we need to talk about," she said, reaching down into her boot and retrieving the letter. "I want you to read this, Ben. It may not be pleasant, but maybe it will explain why I've not told Ashe of your presence."

Ben took the letter from her hand and sat down on a boulder. Unfolding it, he read it with a sad smile crossing his face. "Sit down, princess, I have a long story to tell you, one that will answer many questions for you, but resolve little of my dilemma."

Hallie seated herself next to him and waited as Ben arranged his thoughts carefully before he began.

"As you know, many years ago, I was a sea captain. One of my ports of call was Boston harbor."

She knew the moment he mentioned Boston what he would say next, and a happiness she'd never thought possible welled inside her.

"I met a very beautiful young lady who was travelin' on my ship, and we fell deeply in love. Each time I'd come in, we would meet secretly, for she was a lady of high station and her father would have protested adamantly about her cavortin' with a seaman. Her name was Sarah Ashton." He paused, and watched the tears fill Hallie's eyes.

"I know, Ben, and I'm so glad it's you." Wiping her eyes with the cuff of her sleeve, Hallie said, "But what happened to cause your separation for so many years?"

"I had an important run to make, and after that we were going to elope and leave Boston. Well, needless to say, my ship never returned... due to a storm at sea. Everyone believed that my men and I drowned, until several weeks later a few of us were found on an island in the Atlantic."

"And Sarah married Hargrove in the meantime? But why?"

Ben sighed, and his shoulders sagged. "She was carrying my child, and Hargrove said he'd marry her and accept the child as his own."

"Mighty noble of him," Hallie commented with a touch of irony.

"Yeah, well, a saint he ain't. After they were married, he told her to get rid of the baby at birth—or an accident would be arranged."

"My God!" Hallie was horrified.

"She left Boston to have her child. The family she stayed with took him into their home to raise him as their own. Everyone in Boston believed the child died at birth, never knowin' that Sarah's grief was not for the death of her child, but knowin' she'd never be able to call him her son."

"Surely you looked for her when you came back."

Ben cocked his head in her direction and raked his

head through his graying hair. "The night she died was the night I learned I had a son." Then he continued. "I did look for her, but when I discovered she'd married another man so quickly after my disappearance, I was angry and hurt, feeling she couldn't have really loved me at all. I got me another ship and vowed never to love another woman. I never planned on seeing her ever again, but I think I was unconsciously looking for her everywhere I went. While I was in San Francisco, I read about Hargrove's big new house in Prospect City that he had built for his wife. Well, I know you thought I came here to find silver, princess, but Sarah's presence in Prospect City gave me another reason to come; I was searching for a treasure more precious to me than silver or gold. And then when I got here, I avoided her like the plague, but I watched her every movement. Finally one night she sent a message to me to meet her. Vern was out of town at the time. We became braver after that, meeting frequently, but she never told me about Ashe. I wanted to take her away with me, and that was when she finally broke down and told me about our son."

"Oh God, Ben," Hallie groaned, rising to her feet. "This is almost more than I can bear."

Ben stood up and took a deep breath. "We argued because she wouldn't come with me. She was frightened that Vern would track us down and kill us both. I finally understood her fear and told her I'd be back to get her after I found our son. I never knew that when I kissed her that night, it would be the last time."

Hallie went to him and buried her face against his chest. "It's just not fair," she cried.

"Hallie, we can't let Ashe know I'm his father yet. If something should happen to me before I'm proven innocent, I wouldn't want him to think his own father murdered his mother."

Hallie lifted her face. "But he thinks you did murder her and wants to get to you before Hargrove does. What if he... succeeds?"

Ben gazed at her with sadness. "If I am to die by my own son's hand, then let me die as Ben Langley, the stranger, not the father. He must not know the truth until I'm proven innocent."

"I know you are right, Ben, but it would hurt me deeply if Ashe could never know what a wonderful, kind man his father is, and how much he wanted to be with the woman he loved."

"Perhaps I will be with her, Hallie," Ben sighed wistfully.

His statement startled her. "Don't say that... please. You're talking to your daughter-in-law, Ben Langley, and she loves you like a father."

"Tell me about my son, princess." Ben again sat down, drawing her down beside him. "You said he was a bounty hunter, and it leads me to believe he's had a hard life."

Hallie told him about the war and how Ashe had searched all these years for his mother, only to find her dead.

"But tell me about the man himself, Hallie. Is he ruthless and cold-blooded as most gunslingers are?"

Hallie's laughter rang like a tingling bell. "He would like for you to think he is, but I know better... at least, now I do. Beneath that hard exterior is a gentle and loving man who protects those he loves with a vengeance. Since I have known him, he has killed five men; two were in self defense, and the others had threatened to kill me. Of course, I don't know about the men prior to his arrival in Prospect City. But I know he doesn't kill for the sake of killing."

Ben smiled. "You will be good for him, Hallie. You are the kind of woman who can bring out all the goodness that's buried within him." His words seemed wrenched from his heart, and he stared solemnly at the ground as he said, "You are so fortunate to be with the man you love. I came so close to having my love, but as you have seen by my story, fate is not always on our side."

Hallie kissed his sun-lined cheek. "Maybe fate is on your side this time, Ben. I'll leave you now, but I'll return in a couple of days. You just stay put and we'll get this under control. Stephen's coming with me the next time to talk to you."

"Maybe a rattlesnake'll get me in the meantime. Seen a few of the varmints basking in the sun," he said mockingly.

"It'll take more than a rattlesnake to get rid of you, Ben Langley," Hallie said, mounting Licorice and making her way to the entrance of the tunnel. She waved good-bye and began the journey home.

She knew she was taking a chance, but once she left the boulder-strewn canyon, she took a shortcut around the tip of Hargrove's property. It was late in the afternoon, and she knew there would be hell to pay when she got home. Ashe would be furious at her if she was late.

* * *

She didn't know where he had come from—probably rose from the burning pit of hell, she thought, oddly calm, but Vern Hargrove and two other men sat astride their horses waiting for her. Slowing Licorice to a trot, she could think of no alternative but to face her enemy. This time she wouldn't have Ashe to protect her, but even Hargrove wouldn't be stupid enough to harm her in view of his ranch hands.

The brisk tattoo of a deadly rattlesnake shattered Hallie's thoughts. Licorice reared, his screams ripping the stillness, his ears lying back as fear possessed his massive body. Hallie held on with one hand, reaching for her gun with the other. Pulling back tightly on the reins to control Licorice's sidestepping motion, she managed to pull the gun from her holster. Licorice paused only a brief second, all the time she needed to squeeze the trigger at the sidewinder that leaped at them from its coiled position. The snake slithered downward, its head a bloody pulp. Licorice calmed down, but she could still feel the quivering of his muscles against her legs.

For a second, she forgot what lay ahead—a different breed of snake, but just as deadly. She gathered her composure and watched Hargrove approach her. She gripped her gun tightly, her finger resting on the trigger.

The men who rode beside Hargrove were not ranch hands, as she had thought, but two enemies, Lem and Farley.

Lem looked at the dead snake and rubbed his hand over his scraggly beard in wonderment. "Ain't never seen no woman shoot like that afore in my life... and left-handed to boot. Why, you shot that critter whilst he was in midair."

Hargrove studied her with curiosity and narrowed his beady eyes. "Where did you learn to shoot like that?"

Hallie looked him squarely in the eyes, her heart hammering in her chest. She had never intended for Hargrove to witness her skill with a gun. "Just luck, I guess. You do what you have to when your life's threatened."

Farley dismounted and picked up the snake. Taking his knife, he severed the rattles and tossed the snake aside. Holding the rattles up to Hallie, he asked, "You want these for a souvenir?"

Hallie shuddered inwardly. "No, keep it for yourself."

"What are you doin' this far off the beaten track, Miss Parker... Mrs. Barkley, it is now, ain't it? You're trespassing on my property."

Hallie stiffened, and glared maliciously at him. "I'm aware of that, Hargrove, but I've done nothing to damage your property, so let me be on my way."

Farley sidled up next to her and boldly raked his eyes over her. "You sure are a purty little thing. Can't believe your husband would allow you to ride out here all alone."

"I believe you're sadly outnumbered," Hargrove intervened. "Now get down off that horse and gimme that gun."

"Why should I do that?"

"Just do as I say," Hargrove commanded.

Farley stepped closer. As Hallie swung her head toward him, she caught Hargrove's brief nod, and realized her mistake.

Farley grabbed her by the leg and jerked her from the saddle. She landed with a thud; her gun sailed from her hand, and Hargrove scooped it up in his meaty fist.

Trepidation coursed through her as she struggled to her feet clenching her hands at her sides.

"Now," Hargrove said, handing her gun to Lem, "tell me why you're out here, and don't gimme none of your smart lip."

Hallie remained silent, her back stiff and proud.

"I think we can take care of that," Hargrove said with a wicked chortle. "Farley, take off her shirt, I always did wonder what Mrs. Barkley was like beneath that spinster clothing. Seems like Barkley knowed somethin' we didn't."

Farley stepped forward, his fingers excitedly loosening the buttons on her shirt.

"Ashe will kill you for this, mark my words." She refused to cry and be humiliated still further. The warm desert breeze found its way through her open shirt, billowing beneath it to bare her full, creamy breasts to their lust-filled eyes.

Hargrove seemed uninterested in her nudity, but his eyes flashed in amusement as he watched Lem and Farley. "What have you got to say for yourself now, Mrs. Barkley?" he sneered.

"I say you're a coward, Hargrove. Aren't you man enough to do it yourself?" Hallie countered, feeling she had nothing to lose at this point.

She watched Hargrove twist the reins tightly around his hands, knowing it was her neck he was thinking of. Lem and Farley were stunned at her brazen comeback and waited for directions from their boss.

The saddle creaked in protest as he swung his beef-sized leg over it. He slid his booted foot from the stirrup, steadying his bulky weight when the saddle threatened to slide beneath the belly of the horse. Then he came toward her, the heavy denims encasing his legs rubbing audibly with each step he took.

"So you challenge me," he stated harshly.

He was so close to her face, she could see the tiny red veins threading across his large bulbous nose and puffy cheeks. His eyes were mere slits in his bloated face. His mouth dominated his features. His breath reeked of stale cigars and whiskey.

Clasping her shirt together, she pulled herself to her full height and stared at him defiantly.

Her composure made him angry. "How would you like to spend a few days alone out here, with no horse, no food or water, and stark naked?"

"Have you forgotten, Hargrove? If so, let me jolt your memory. I was thirteen years old when I first survived the perils of the desert. Leave me, and I will most assuredly endure it again, and you'll never live another peaceful moment. Someday you'll get your just reward, and I'll be there to enjoy it."

"Then maybe I ought to just get rid of you now," he snarled, pulling his gun from his holster.

Hallie didn't flinch. "Ashe won't need proof. He'll kill you if you talk to him in the wrong tone of voice, Hargrove."

Hargrove stood before her like a towering red butte, his facade beginning to crumble at the truth in her words. He had never trusted Ashe Barkley, and there was no doubt in his mind that Barkley would come after him. But he would be damned if he would let her get by with her threats. Pointing the gun at her, he said coldly, "Barkley may be a widow man sooner than he expected. Start by removing your boots, Mrs. Barkley."

Hallie's stomach plunged, thinking of the letter still hidden in her boots. Then she remembered Ben stuffing it into his vest pocket after reading it.

Hargrove had unwittingly given Hallie an opportunity to escape. Bending down, she ran her hand inside her boot, pretending to struggle as she removed it. She felt the hard handle of the knife she always wore strapped to her ankle and eased it out, keeping it turned toward the inside of her wrist.

"You wouldn't mind assisting me in taking these off, would you, Hargrove?" she asked, feeling wickedly good all over.

Hargrove's lips curled derisively. "This is one time I would be happy to oblige you."

She lifted her foot, and he bent down to grasp the heel of her boot. She placed her hand on his wide shoulder, pretending to balance herself, and gripped the handle of the knife. As Hargrove pulled her boot off and released her foot, she drew the length of the blade across his throat while he was still in a stooped position.

"I wouldn't even swallow, Hargrove, if I were you,"

she whispered, pressing the blade against his jugular vein.

Every square inch of Hargrove's body froze, and his blood curdled in his veins. He started to speak, but the cold steel at his throat numbed his tongue. He stifled the urge to swallow the free-flowing saliva that swamped his mouth.

"Lem, Farley," Hallie cooed softly, aware that they had no idea of what was happening since their eyes were riveted on her bared breasts. "Your boss is unable to speak for himself at the moment, but he would like you to empty the bullets from your guns and toss them over here to us."

Reaching into Hargrove's holster, she pulled out his gun and tucked it in the waistband of her pants.

"What's goin' on?" Farley and Lem asked in unison, wondering why Hargrove couldn't stand up.

"He doesn't want his throat sliced," Hallie said, putting slight pressure once again to Hargrove's throat. "Isn't that right, Hargrove? Now, Lem, I'll have my gun back, if you please."

Lem looked hesitantly at his boss, but Hargrove could only groan. Lem handed Hallie her gun, then he and Farley quickly emptied their guns and dropped them to the ground.

She removed the knife from Hargrove's throat, and backed off, keeping the gun trained on his stooped figure as she pulled her boot on and slid the knife back inside and buttoned her shirt with one hand. "You may stand up now, Hargrove." Hargrove's face was white as a sheet.

"I figure we're about twenty-five feet from the boundary line. So move it over, boys."

She followed them as they walked backward, stumbling over their feet in the process. "Now, you're on my property, and you're trespassing," she said, grinning from ear to ear.

She paced back and forth in front of them, seeming to give their situation great thought. "You may start by removing your boots, boys."

Glancing from one to the other, they quickly complied.

Hallie briefly looked at the sky. "It's a mighty hot day for walking. You might be more comfortable without clothes."

"What!" Hargrove shouted. "Now, I'll go along with the boots, lady, but you're carryin' this a bit too far!"

"Turn about's fair play," Hallie said. "Now strip!" The click of the gun sent them into action.

Hallie nodded her head, assessing each man slowly. She wouldn't call any of them a prime masculine specimen. Lem boasted a potbelly from consuming more than his quota of beer. Farley was so thin his upper torso reminded her of Sinbad's cage. Hargrove, well ... he looked like a great white whale, his excess fat spilling over the waist of his underwear down to the top of his legs.

"Well, what are you waiting for?" Hallie asked sharply. "I thought all men were boastful, and never embarrassed to bare all. Could it be you're ashamed of what I'll see?"

They eyed one another. No one made a move. The sun beat down on them, and rivulets of sweat ran down their faces and chests, mingling with the dust and grime.

"On second thought," she said disgustedly, "forget it."

She watched the blood surface to their faces. "Take your clothes and put them in your saddlebags, and then tie your boots onto the saddles. As for the guns, Lem, you can put them in my saddlebag."

After they had done what she asked of them, they once again lined up side by side, grateful they still had their underwear intact.

She went to the horses, slapped their flanks, and shouted. The horses took off at a flying gallop, leaving the three men staring after them with a mixture of astonishment and dread on their faces.

"You ain't leavin' us out here like this!" Hargrove yelled. "It's five miles back to my ranch."

"My walk would have been triple that, Hargrove." Looking at the sun's position, she said, "I figure if you start now, you may make it back by midnight... that is, if a rattlesnake or gila monster doesn't get you first."

She mounted Licorice, hearing Hargrove say as she rode away, "You won't get away with this, I promise you that, Hallie Barkley."

When Hallie reined Licorice into the stable, Juan was there to assist her. By his extreme nervousness, Hallie knew she should expect the worst.

"Is Ashe home?" she asked, seemingly unconcerned.

"You'd better believe he is, señora," Juan said, taking Licorice into his stall.

Remembering the gun collection in her saddlebag, Hallie said quickly, "I'll tend to Licorice. Will you tell Maria I'm back?"

"What about señor Barkley?"

"He'll know soon enough, Juan."

Leaving her, Juan walked back to the house, shaking his head, discouraged.

Hallie hid the guns at the bottom of an empty crate and scattered straw over them. As she was unstrapping Licorice's saddle, a shadow fell across her shoulder. She pretended not to notice, knowing to whom it belonged.

"Where the hell have you been all damned day?"

"Because of circumstances I couldn't control," Hallie said calmly while lifting the heavy saddle from Licorice's back, "I returned later than I planned."

Ashe took the saddle from her and put it in its proper place. He stood in front of her, feet slightly apart, his thumbs hooked into the waistband of his pants. "Would you enlighten me further on what these unusual circumstances were? I've been home for hours pacing the floor, worried sick that something had happened to you."

Hallie smiled coquettishly, and ran her finger down the center of his chest. "There's no need for you to worry about me, love. You should know by now that I'm perfectly capable of taking care of myself." Reaching up, she placed her arms around his neck, her blue eyes sparkling impishly. "But it's nice having someone worried about me."

Ashe removed her arms and held them down at her sides. "It won't work, Hallie."

"What won't work, love?"

"All this lovey-dovey display you're putting on. You've been up to something, and I want to hear what it is."

"Very well, if you insist. On my way home, I had the misfortune of meeting a rattlesnake ... a big one. I killed him before he could strike Licorice."

"What did you do, skin him and eat him?" he asked. "That shouldn't take all damn day."

"I thought you'd be concerned for my safety, but it seems I was wrong. I could be lying out there now dead." She started to stomp away, but Ashe's strong arm gripped her own, slamming her against his hard chest. His eyes glazed over in anger as he stared into her defiant face. There was only one way he knew to erase the smirk from her face. His mouth crushed against hers in a savage kiss, more in punishment than in desire.

Suddenly his tack changed. His hands enveloped the sides of her head, his fingers massaging her scalp and tangling in the thick mass of auburn hair.

He tasted drops of blood on her lips and groaned with despair at his brutality. "Hallie ... Hallie," he moaned into her mouth, his tongue lightly stroking the bruised, tender flesh of her lips. "I'm sorry, love, believe me I am."

"I asked for it," she answered softly. "You had a right to be angry with me."

"No, Hallie, brutality is for lawless men and murderers."

She held him close, thinking of Ben. "I hope you will always feel that way," she murmured with foreboding.

Chapter 17

Stephen and Hallie raced their horses down the rocky embankment from the cave. Stephen had questioned Ben at length about the last time he had seen Sarah, diligently seeking any clue that might help prove his innocence. They had talked a long time and Hallie was late. She knew that Ashe would be furious, and he would not be put off by any excuses. What could she tell him this time? Ashe was no fool, and he had begun questioning her many absences. If he got it in his mind that something was going on, he could worm it out of Maria with little effort. She couldn't go on like this much longer. The deceit was almost too much for her to bear.

Glancing at Stephen, she wondered if he regretted getting involved.

Catching her look, he smiled wistfully. "Don't torture yourself, Hallie. It'll work out, I'm sure."

"I hope you're right."

Without warning, three riders pulled into their path, guns drawn, pointing directly at them. Fear oozed through Hallie as she faced the one man she hated passionately. His henchmen, Lem and Farley, cocked their guns and trained them on her and Stephen.

"I told you we'd meet again," Hargrove said with a sneer. "Only this time you won't be gettin' the upper hand. Throw down your guns and toss down that knife ... easy. I know you've got one."

"What do you want from me this time?" she spat, tossing her weapons to the ground.

"Oh, just a little information." His beady eyes sent chills up her spine.

"I don't know anything of any interest to you."

"How 'bout Ben Langley's hidin' place?"

Hallie paled. "I don't know what you're talking about."

"Well, I think you do, and I mean to find out. I figure I got all the aces this time." Then, looking at Lem and Farley, he said, "Okay, boys, that old cottonwood looks like it'll serve our purpose."

Before Hallie knew what was happening, Lem had grabbed the reins of Stephen's horse and was leading it toward the tree.

"Wait," she cried, "what are you doing?"

"We're jest goin' to stretch yore friend's neck a little. Maybe that will loosen yore tongue," Hargrove growled, nudging his horse in the flanks.

"But I don't know anything."

"You're lyin' through your teeth. One of my men seen Langley the day he come back, and we've been watchin' you comin' and goin'. We just ain't had no luck findin' him. We've combed this range as far as the eye can see. You've got him hidden somewhere, and you'll either lead us to him or we're going to string up your friend." Glaring at her with hatred, he said, "Which is it goin' to be?"

Choking back the tears, she croaked, "I tell you, I don't know."

"String 'em up, boys," Hargrove bellowed.

Stephen sat astride his horse straight as an arrow, his gaze never leaving Hallie. I can't let them kill Stephen, her mind screamed. Dropping her head, she mumbled, "Okay, Hargrove, you win."

"No, Hallie, call their bluff. I don't believe they'll do it," Stephen implored.

As he was talking, Farley slung a rope over the large limb of the tree and fashioned a noose, then he draped it over Stephen's head. With a violent jerk, Farley tightened the rope.

"It's ready, boss. All I got to do is slap his horse on the rear and he's a dead man."

Hallie's composure collapsed. "Don't do it. I'll take you to Ben."

"Lead the way," Hargrove growled with satisfaction.

"Aren't you going to let Stephen go?"

"All in good time. If I let him go now, you're liable to change your mind. Langley first, then we'll talk about lettin' your friend go."

"But I thought..." Her words faltered.

"I told you I was holdin' all the aces this time," he said with a smirk.

Turning Licorice, Hallie hissed, "If Ashe finds out what you've done, you'll wish you had never played the game."

Hargrove shuddered inside. "Start moving, bitch. I ain't got time to listen to your idle threats."

"Don't worry, Stephen," she shouted as she spurred Licorice away.

Hargrove muttered harshly to Farley, "Give us time to get out of sight, then hang the bastard. We don't need no witnesses."

"You got it, boss," Farley replied with relish.

As Stephen's mounted figure receded in the distance, Hallie prayed that somehow Ben would hear them approaching and he would be ready to deal with this disastrous situation which might cost both their lives.

Stephen hoped Hallie had not heard Hargrove's parting words. He kept his face expressionless as he waited quietly. He was not going to give that son of a bitch the pleasure of seeing him suffer.

"It ain't nothin' personal, Bradshaw, you just oughta watch the company you was keepin'," Farley said assuringly and slapped the horse harshly, never hearing the gun blast in the distance.

Frightened, the horse leaped forward. Suddenly Stephen plunged to the ground, the wind knocked from him. Gasping for breath, he lifted his eyes to the tree. The rope had been shot through, its ends uncoiling like a snake.

Farley was as surprised as Stephen. He drew his gun quickly, pointing it at Stephen's head. Before he could pull the trigger, his gun went flying from his grasp. He screamed in pain, grabbing his hand in horror as the blood rushed down his arm. His index finger had been completely severed. Sinking to the ground, he cowered in fear as Ashe Barkley loomed over him.

"I'll ask you only once... where's Hallie?" The coldness of his voice surged through the air as deadly as the cocked gun he aimed at Farley's head.

Farley's tongue tripped over his teeth in his eagerness to answer, and his words came out incoherently.

"Hargrove's got her," Stephen supplied. "You might as well know the whole of it." Stephen rapidly related the story of Ben's return and Hallie's attempt to clear him. "She was afraid you would kill Ben before he could prove his innocence."

"I might have known it was something like that. Her absences, her preoccupation... Damnit, I should have paid more attention. My God, why didn't she come to me?" A muscle twitched violently in his lean cheek, a sure sign of his tension. "If Hargrove harms one hair on her head, I swear by all that's holy, I'll kill him."

Farley, taking advantage of their preoccupation, edged his good hand toward his other gun. Drawing it from his holster, he brazenly lifted it. For once he would be the hero. A puzzled expression fanned across his face. Heros didn't feel such pain... His eyes glazed over and blood trickled from the corner of his mouth as he fell forward.

Ashe reloaded his gun and spun the cylinder, making sure he had replaced the three spent bullets. Without another word, Stephen mounted his horse and they set out in pursuit of Hargrove.

Hallie jerked her arm from Hargrove's grasp. "I'm not going anywhere," she snapped.

"You're right, I'll see to that," Hargrove snarled, grabbing her arm, his fingers biting painfully into her flesh.

The commotion roused a sleepy Ben. He jumped to his feet, and stopped short when he saw Hargrove dragging Hallie into the cave entrance.

"I'm sorry, Ben, I had no choice," she choked out.

"It's all right, princess. I knew it would come to a showdown eventually."

"Well, I've finally found the murderin' sidewinder who killed my wife. And I aim to see justice done. Search him, Lem. I don't want no surprises."

"You lying black-hearted bastard, you know I didn't kill Sarah," Ben growled. Had Hallie not been in jeopardy, he would have tried to strangle Hargrove with his bare hands.

"Yeah, me and you know you didn't, but who's gonna believe you? It was so easy to pin it all on you. She was at your mine. You two were heard arguin'. Hell, it couldn't have worked out better if I'd planned it myself," he sneered with contempt.

As Ben lunged, Hargrove cocked his gun and aimed it point-blank at Hallie's head. "I don't think there's much chance that I'd miss this close up even if you managed to get me."

Hatred blazed from Ben's eyes as he reluctantly drew away.

"You gonna stand there, Lem, or are you gonna search him?"

Lem quickly ran his hands over Ben's rigid frame. "He's clean, boss."

"You make damn sure. I don't want him pullin' no pig-sticker the minute I take my eyes off him."

Lem searched him again, checking his boots and his pockets. "He ain't got nothin' on him, lessen he's got it stuck up his butt... and I'll be damned if I'm checking there."

"Let's get the hell out of here. She may have told Barkley more than we think," Hargrove said, pushing Hallie toward the entrance.

"What about Stephen? You promised to turn him loose. He has nothing to do with this."

"I'd say about now he ought to be trying to convince Saint Peter to let him through the pearly gates," Hargrove chuckled.

Choking back tears, Hallie swung wildly at Hargrove, her fist catching him in the folds of fat that layered his midriff. Her blow caught him unaware. Catching his breath, he grabbed her by the hair and jerked her until she was only inches from his face. "Another trick like that, gal, and I'll kill Langley where he stands. Now, move, damnit."

Stumbling, Hallie let herself be pulled along. Lem followed with Ben and his horse. As Hargrove propelled her from the cave, he looked around in astonishment.

"Nice little setup you got here. How in tarnation did you find this place? I never knowed it was here.

Sure would be a good place for a man who was hidin' from the law."

Hallie's blood ran cold. If Hargrove didn't add up all the clues pointing to her as the Poet Bandit, then he had less sense than she had given him credit for.

Lem bound her wrists roughly, and boosted her up on Licorice's back. Not taking any chances, Hargrove grabbed Licorice's reins, pulling the horse. Hallie clasped the pommel and whispered soothingly to Licorice, calming him after the unnecessary rough treatment.

They traveled as fast as Hargrove's laboring steed could go, with Hargrove continually watching over his shoulder. He was really scared of Ashe, Hallie thought, and the notion was comforting even though she knew how little chance there was that Ashe would start searching for her before it was too late. Whatever happened, she would not make it easy for Hargrove.

Evening shadows were lengthening when Hargrove reached his destination, a dilapidated lineshack with only two walls standing. Collapsed beams lay at dangerous angles, their precarious support the only thing holding up the remaining wall. This was to be their prison.

Hallie was hot and tired, her wrists on fire from the rope burns on her tender skin. All she wanted was to lie down in the soft luscious grama grass and shut her eyes for a few minutes.

Ben's features were blank; none of the anguish he was feeling showed in his face. His concern for Hallie was apparent only by the rage that emanated from him like a living thing.

They were tied roughly to a tree, the bark scarping Hallie's back with her slightest movement. Then Hargrove and Lem moved just out of earshot and started talking.

Hallie whispered to Ben, "If he was going to kill us, why didn't he do it back in the canyon? I don't understand his reasoning, unless he just wants to drag it out for his own enjoyment."

"Could be he's plannin' ahead like he did when he had your father killed. He's not one to pass up the chance of lining his pockets if he can make a dime. If he can manage to make our deaths look accidental, what's to stop him from ending up with your ranch? He's always wanted it—if for no other reason than to expand his kingdom. Grady would be crushed by your death, and Hargrove would be there like the bloodsucker he is, using any means to get what he wants." Ben's voice cracked as his mind played with all the possibilities. What means would Hargrove have used to keep an unhappy wife from leaving him? He was so consumed with his own importance that the thought of people knowing he couldn't keep his wife would have been an extreme humiliation.

Hallie's words interrupted his thoughts. "But, Ben, that wouldn't work. Grandpa doesn't own the ranch. The ranch belongs to me. If something happens to me, Ashe would own the ranch, not Grandpa."

"Hargrove doesn't know that, princess. His way of thinking would never consider that a woman could own anything."

Hargrove walked over to them and they fell silent.

"I'll be leavin' you two for now, but don't get it

into your head that you all will receive any leniency from Lem. He'd just as soon kill you as look at you. He knows there'll be a bonus in it for him if everything goes well." He left, satisfied that he had them at his mercy.

Burning sticks from the campfire crackled and fell, sending shooting sparks into the velvety darkness.

Since Lem had securely bound their bodies to the tree at the waist, he was willing to untie their hands so they could eat. Their ankles were also tied—so tightly that Hallie's feet had grown numb.

Their dinner was dried beef that was stringy and tough. Hallie could hardly swallow it past the lump in her throat. Then Lem brought them coffee that was surprisingly good, and Hallie washed the meat down with the hot coffee.

As Lem stooped to refill her cup, Hallie raised her hand as though to push her tangled hair from her face. Lem saw the gesture, and jerked from her side. The hot coffee sloshed from the pot, drenching his pants.

"Hot damn!" he screamed, hopping around, beating at his steaming pant leg. "What you tryin' to do, woman, scald me? Well, by Gawd, you done a good job of it. I bet my leg's as red as a hot poker. You might've branded me for life."

"It was an accident, Lem. You're the one who spilled the coffee." She didn't know if he heard her or not in his hurry to uncap his canteen.

He poured the cool water over his leg with an audible sigh of relief. She and Ben exchanged a satisfied glance. But this moment of triumph was short-lived; afterwards, there was nothing else to do but go to sleep.

But Hallie and Ben slept little, Lem had retied the ropes with a vengeance, and they kept twisting and turning, trying to loosen the knots so they could get comfortable.

As dawn broke, Hallie persuaded Lem to give her a few minutes to take care of personal needs. He agreed only after he made it clear that he would shoot Ben if she tried to escape. The same applied to Ben, and the feel of cold steel pushed against her temple brought home to her just how perilous their situation was. This was no clumsy fool, but a cold-blooded murderer.

Ashe and Stephen found the cave empty; they spent the rest of the day searching every other conceivable place, but there was no trace of Ben and Hallie anywhere.

They had returned to the ranch with sagging spirits. Ashe had little to say, and the firm set of his jaw discouraged conversation. Maria told what little she knew about Ben's return and watched Ashe's face darken as the story unfolded.

"I would have listened. Damn it, I would have," he stormed. Maria twisted her apron, and Stephen became unusually interested in the pattern of his coffee cup, while Grady shuffled through a worn deck of cards.

With a vicious curse, Ashe swept through the door. Had darkness not prevented it, he would have continued his search. His mind worked frantically, sorting through fragments of information. He had made two trips to Hargrove's ranch, each unsuccessful. No one seemed to know where Hargrove was.

Everything Hallie had told him about Hargrove surfaced. She truly believed Ben innocent of murder. The thing that puzzled him the most was—if Ben really was guilty, Hargrove should be bringing him in to stand trial. But if Ben was innocent, Hargrove wouldn't want him in court for fear of his being able to prove his innocence.

"Oh hell," Ashe groaned. Was he just grasping straws?

He had ridden out to the mine to check with Grady. Grady had broken down and cried like a baby when Ashe told him of Hallie's disappearance.

"Why do you think I work this damn sorry mine the way I do?" he sobbed. "It's for her. I wanted to leave her something worthwhile; see to it she'd never have to worry about losing the ranch."

"I'll find her, Grady, I swear I will," Ashe swore, his words filled with pain. "I need her, too. She's the very core of my being."

"You love her very much, don't you?" Grady whispered, looking strangely at the man he had once thought had no heart.

"She's as close to me as my next breath," Ashe confessed hoarsely.

Standing on the porch now, Ashe stretched his tired muscles. He was bone-tired, but he couldn't sleep. Every time he closed his eyes, Hallie loomed before him. He wondered if she was suffering. That thought sent pain shooting through his gut. Don't do anything foolish, love, he thought, knowing full well what a damnable temper she had.

Easing down on the steps, he placed his head in his hands, trying to ease the throbbing. Suddenly he heard a noise. He lifted his head abruptly; he could see nothing. Had he been so engrossed in his own thoughts that he hadn't paid any attention to the night sounds?

Drawing his gun, he placed it over his legs, prepared to wait. Whoever or whatever was out there could make the first move. He would be ready.

"Ashe," the voice called hesitantly.

"Yeah."

"It's me. Bart. Don't ya go shootin'. I need to have a few words with ya."

"Come on around, Bart, and have a seat."

Cautiously, Bart eased from the corner of the house. The moon shed its light brightly through the darkness, silhouetting his shabby figure as he approached.

"I seed ya at the ranch today, but I didn't dare approach ya. Hargrove would cut my tongue out if he knowed about our talks," Bart whispered fearfully.

"You know something that might help me find my wife, Bart? Hargrove took her. It may take me a while, but I'll find her." He rolled a cigarette and struck a match. As he brought the light to the cigarette, Bart drew in his breath sharply at Ashe's haggard appearance and the wild look in his eyes.

"I knowed somethin' was goin' on, the way Lem and Farley's been a sneakin' around. They hightailed it out yesterday mornin' with Hargrove. Then, 'bout evenin', Hargrove returned alone. He jest kept askin' after Farley, wantin' to know if he'd come back. I tole him I hadn't seen hide nor hair of 'em since they left. He wasn't none too pleased, but hell, that ain't my fault."

"Farley's dead."

"Can't say as I'm sorry. He was a low-down varmit if I ever did see one. I don't know fer shore where Hargrove might have your wife, but I know the general direction he came from when he returned."

Ashe thanked him for the information, and Bart promised to keep his eyes and ears peeled for anything else that might help.

Early the next morning, Ashe packed his gear and strapped his blanket roll to Rebel's back. Stephen agreed to remain at the house in case any word of Hallie was sent there. Ashe vowed silently that he wouldn't return without her. He headed in the direction Bart had told him and meticulously renewed his search.

Hallie was stiff and sore all over. She had dozed intermittently, but the sleep had not been restful.

Ben looked haggard, too. He blamed himself for placing Hallie in such danger, and for going along with her scheme to hide him.

Hallie, too, was wrestling with her own thoughts. She should have trusted Ashe with the information and sought his help. Why had she doubted him? Because he thought Ben had killed his mother, her mind screamed.

Hargrove rode into their makeshift camp, huffing and puffing as he dismounted.

"I see you've kept a close eye on our friends. It wouldn't do for them to escape yet. Maybe later we'll give them a chance. Too bad they'll be killed in the process. I'm sure the townspeople will mourn Hallie's passin', but once they learn she was tryin' to help a murderer escape, they'll revise their thinkin'." He chuckled evilly.

Lem began rummaging through Ben's saddlebags. Leaning over to Hallie, Ben whispered nervously, "The letter is in there. See if you can't divert Lem's attention."

"Lem?" she called urgently, but it was too late.

"Hey, boss, look at this. It might be somethin' important." Lem glanced at the letter curiously.

Hargrove glanced from his captives to Lem. "What is it?"

"Don't know, boss. I can't read."

"Must be something if Langley has kept it," Hargrove muttered, unfolding the letter. Scanning the contents, he paled slightly, and perspiration beaded on his brow. "Well, I'll be damned. So that bastard, Barkley, is her son. I told her to get rid of the kid; I didn't ever want to lay eyes on it. If she hadn't agreed, I assured her an accident would be arranged for the brat." He shook his head in astonishment. "Now don't that just ice the goddamn cake? Wonder why he waited all these years? I always wondered at his curiosity about her portrait. But, damn, I never dreamed it was because of anything like this."

Stuffing the letter into his shirt pocket, he said, "Okay, Lem, this calls for a slight change of plans."

Approaching Hallie, he said, "I want some answers, little lady. I've had it with secrets and half-assed answers. I'll have the truth now."

Although Hallie was very emotional, she had not, up to now, become hysterical. But Hargrove's discovery of the letter, and Ashe's identity, broke her defiance.

"Truth," she screamed. "You creep... you want truth." Her wild laughter sent chills over the men. Backing off, Hargrove wondered if she had lost her mind.

"Did you offer my father truth? How about Sarah? Did you offer her truth? Hell no," she ranted, "you killed them. God only knows how many others you've killed to add to your wealth. Oh, and I might add another one to your score of victims—Stephen Bradshaw."

"You don't know what you're talkin' about, you crazy bitch," he sneered.

"So now I'm crazy. That's where you're wrong, Hargrove. I saw your men kill my father in cold blood. ...I saw it, Hargrove," she stressed. "I know you killed your wife and then placed the blame on Ben."

"It don't matter none, because you'll never leave this place alive. But to set the record straight, Sarah's death was an accident. She brought it on herself. If she'd been at home where she belonged and not sneakin' around after Langley, she never would have died."

"So you played God," she spat, shaking her head in disgust. "Your sanctimonious attitude sickens me."

"Well, by God, since we're clearing the air, how about your robbin' me blind? Do you think I don't know you're the thief?"

At the sudden revelation, Lem swore loudly and

looked at Hallie with admiration. One sharp look from Hargrove quelled his outburst.

"I'll grant you, you had me fooled. That little trick you pulled the other day started me thinkin'. It all fit. Too bad you won't live long enough to stand trial."

"You wouldn't be able to prove your accusations. You'd be the laughingstock of Prospect City."

"We'll never know, will we," Hargrove jeered.

Ben had remained silent, searching for a way to help Hallie. His voice was undaunted as he spoke. "Let her go, Hargrove. It's me you want, and from the looks of things, you've got me."

"Hate to disappoint you, but that's no longer the case. That letter changed things. She's my drawin' card. I can't afford to have Barkley tellin' people Sarah was his mother. He's liable to get it in his head to lay claim to my ranch. It was his mother's fortune that bought the place. If he hired hisself one of those fancy forked-tongued lawyers, there's no tellin' what the outcome might be. I can't take that chance. I've worked too hard to have her bastard son take a share of my holdings."

"Ashe isn't like that," Hallie cried. "He wouldn't have anything your filthy hands have touched."

"I'm not goin' to have that threat hangin' over my head. Barkley must have gotten to Farley, because he's not shown up. He made two trips out to my place yesterday, so he knows I've got you. Only, he don't know I want him. I figure we'll just wait it out. He'll show up sooner or later, and when he does..." Pointing his fat finger and thumb to resemble a gun, he mouthed, "Boom."

"No!" Hallie screamed and collapsed against Ben's shoulder.

The fiery sun beat down relentlessly. Ashe's head pounded, and his eyes burned from lack of sleep, but he pushed on. His search had encompassed almost the whole of Hargrove's property. An old mining area that had never been proven worthwhile was the last hope.

As he cautiously approached, Rebel's ears perked up and Ashe could feel the horse's body stiffen. "It's okay, boy, let's take it real slow. We may have found something."

Dismounting, he led the horse, moving as quickly and quietly as any Indian. Excitement surged through him. Leaving Rebel in a clump of paloverde, he snaked through the scrub brush and mesquite, never feeling the sharp rocks that scraped and skinned his hands.

He came up behind a broken-down shack. He couldn't see any sign of movement, but he could smell the smoke from a campfire. Easing his knife from its sheath, he placed it between his teeth and crawled closer on his stomach.

He could hear Hargrove bragging of his plans, and the killer-lust shot through him like hot lava. He swore silently as he scanned the area.

He could see Hallie, and a man he was sure was Langley, bound to a tree. His eyes assessed her disheveled form. Her hair was loose and lay in tangles over her shoulders and her face was smudged with dirt. Her clothing was torn and dirty, but she was alive and that was all that mattered. His heart filled with pride. He would bet everything he owned that she had given as good as she'd gotten. Hargrove wouldn't get the best of her. Even bound up against that tree, Hallie's back was stiff as a rod, and her lovely blue eyes shot sparks that would make the meanest of men wary. He was sure Hargrove had felt the bite of her sharp tongue more than once.

Edging up behind Hallie, he stroked her hands. When he noticed her raw wrist, he gritted his teeth in anger, controlling the violence that whipped through him.

Hallie tensed. He knew she was aware of his presence. Quickly slicing through the ropes, he disappeared once again into the undergrowth.

Hallie and Ben exchanged relieved looks, but neither stirred, waiting for Ashe to make his move.

Hargrove, caught up in his own words, didn't at first believe his eyes when Ashe stepped from behind the shack, his gun drawn, the hammer pulled back and his Bowie knife hanging loosely in his other hand.

Hargrove stood stone-still, his courage fleeing. Swallowing rapidly, he stuttered, "Wh...where'd..."

Lem burst out, "My Gawd, where'd you come from?"

Hallie and Ben rapidly loosened the ropes from their hands and ankles. Rubbing their legs briskly to regain the feeling, they stumbled to their feet.

"You're at a dead end, Hargrove. Got any more tricks up your sleeve?" His shadowy eyes revealed nothing as he faced Hargrove. Turning his eyes briefly to Hallie, he asked, "You okay?"

"Now wait a minute, Barkley, you got it all wrong. This don't look like it really is. Langley here tried to kill Hallie. I was just lookin' out for your interest."

As he saw the blood surface in Ashe's eyes, his tongue picked up momentum. "I swear, he tried to kill her. Only way I could keep her safe was to tie her up with him. I knowed you'd get here; been waitin' for you. Ain't that right, Lem?"

"Yeah, boss."

"They're lying, Ashe. They've been waiting, all right. Waiting for you so they could make a clean sweep and kill us all."

"You lying bitch. Shut your damn mouth." Lunging forward, Hargrove shoved Hallie to the ground.

Lights went off in her head as her foot twisted at an odd angle beneath her. Ashe was beside her immediately, his attention diverted from Hargrove.

Lem, taking advantage of the opportunity, drew his gun. Hallie screamed just as Lem fired. With precise accuracy, Ashe threw the deadly knife. It found its mark, burying itself deeply into Lem's chest. Lem's shot barely missed its mark, leaving Hallie shaken.

In the melee, Hargrove grabbed Ben. Holding his gun to Ben's side, he shouted, "If you want to see him live, you'd best drop yore gun, Barkley."

"It matters little to me if he lives or not," Ashe retorted, his voice harsh and uncompromising.

Hargrove pulled the hammer back, a feral gleam in his eyes.

"He's your father, Ashe," Hallie screamed, the tears breaking free at last and streaming down her cheeks.

Surprise danced across Ashe's features. Hallie had heard how fast Ashe was with a gun, but nothing prepared her for the lightning speed with which he fired.

Hargrove's gun shattered to the ground. With one last mighty shove, he threw Ben sprawling into Ashe. It was a desperate chance, but the only one he had left. He grabbed Hallie, wrapping his thick arm around her neck; he dragged her along, using her as a shield to reach his horse. He mounted, and with superhuman strength, he pulled Hallie up into the saddle. With a vicious kick, he sent his horse racing off.

Hallie's foot throbbed, but she paid it scant attention in her attempt to remain astride. The horse's sides were heaving with exertion. When she tried to look back over Hargrove's shoulder, the side of her head met with a meaty fist. After that, she did nothing that would arouse his temper and she waited for a opportunity to unseat Hargrove.

Her hair fanned out, slapping Hargrove in the face. He pulled it back with a cruel jerk that brought tears to her eyes.

Suddenly the sound of thunder drew her attention. Scanning the cloudless sky, she wondered at the rumbling sound. Again she heard it, and this time it seemed closer. Hargrove heard it too. He turned in the saddle, thinking an army of men was on their trail from the cloud of dust in the distance.

Cursing profusely, Hargrove pushed his laboring mount on. Glancing over his shoulder, he yelled, "Oh God, no... you're holdin' me up, bitch. I can make better time without you."

With a reckless push, he unseated Hallie. She hit the ground with a dull thud as Hargrove raced on.

The ground shook and the air was filled with the sound of pounding hooves. Lifting her head, she saw what had frightened Hargrove. Hundreds of horses were headed straight for her, the white stallion leading the pack. Dust created a curtain of choking air. Hallie struggled to stand, but her foot wouldn't take the pressure. She couldn't even drag herself.

The horses were drawing nearer. She was certain death was imminent.

She could almost feel their energy as they raced toward her. Unexpectedly, she was pulled from the ground and tossed unceremoniously onto the back of a pony. Hanging on, she didn't question her rescuer. She had been saved from the stampede. She manifested her relief in a deluge of tears, burying her face against the naked back of her savior.

Hargrove urged his mount on with one blow too many. His cruelty had crushed the spirit of the animal. The horse heaved a choking breath and collapsed beneath him. Hargrove scrambled away. He had not made it this far to be crushed by his own lazy horse.

Seeing the gaping hole of a mine, he laughed hideously and scurried for its protection. Fate would not get the best of him. He had dealt a dirty hand too long to be outdone.

The timbers were marked with time and supported large families of insects that had weakened their strength. Clumps of earth and sawdust sifted to the ground, covering Hargrove in a layer of dirt. That was the first inkling he had that he should look for safer ground. But it was too late.

The pounding and shifting of the earth from the stampede broke the beams loose. Earth and stone crashed into the mine opening, burying Vern Hargrove. A few beams stuck awkwardly from the ground marking his grave. A moment later, all was silent, as if nothing had ever happened. Hargrove had played the last hand and lost.

Ashe swallowed rapidly, trying to dislodge the lump in his throat. Never had he felt so utterly helpless. He had seen Hargrove scrambling up the hill, but there was no way to know if Hallie had made it to safety. All he could do was wait for the horses to pass so he could begin his search. Ben drew up beside him, the anguish apparent in his features.

"I love her, too," he shouted.

"I know," Ashe said, fear welling inside him.

As the last of the horses passed and the air began to settle, Ashe blinked his eyes and rubbed a tired hand across them. The pain in his heart was choking him. He drew a shuddering breath, revealing his agony. As he peered intently into the haze of dust, he saw a rider approach.

Drawing closer, Sundog leaped from his pony, and lifted his arms up to Hallie. "My friend, I give you back the life you gave to me."

A huge grin spanned Ashe's face. Scooping Hallie into his arms, he kissed her soundly. "I accept, my friend, thank you," Ashe replied humbly.

Sundog left as silently as he had come. Jubilantly, Hallie nestled closely to Ashe as they headed for home.

With a bittersweet smile etching his face, Ben whispered reverently, "Sarah, my love, we have a fine son ... thank you."

Epilogue

Black acrid smoke billowed against a robin's-egg-blue sky. The desert wind fanned the remaining sparks to life. Charred and burning timbers groaned in protest, then plunged to the ground, as the flames completely consumed what was left of Vern Hargrove's mansion.

Ashe and Hallie Barkley sat astride their horses in the distance, their faces devoid of any emotion at that moment. A year had passed since they had gone to Hargrove's home to remove Sarah Hargrove's possessions from the house. After that, Ashe had left the doors unlocked, an open invitation to looters. And now, the last of Ashe's inheritance lay in ruins.

"I couldn't have done better," Ashe said dryly, "if I had started it myself."

Turning their horses, they headed back to their ranch.

This final disposition of the mansion also marked the end of Hallie's search for revenge. The silver mine

Hargrove had taken from her grandfather was depleted, a worthless holding. But Ben's mother-lode vein was discovered when they dug Hargrove's crushed and mutilated body from its caved-in depths.

"An appropriate ending," Hallie had said with satisfaction. "Hargrove was buried by his own greed."

Topping the ridge, Hallie tugged back gently on the reins and urged Licorice to a standstill. "Oh Ashe, please wait." Securing the long strands of auburn hair behind her ear, she gazed at the breathtaking view. "It's so seldom I get the chance to see the ranch from this angle."

Ashe sidled Rebel up next to her. Instead of feasting his eyes on the scenery, he feasted them on his wife's radiant beauty. "Yes, it is beautiful... everything about it."

Settled against rain-washed buttes, the sparkling white adobe walls of the ranch seemed to sprawl in every direction, and from their position on the hill, it seemed to merge with the new bunkhouse and enlarged stable.

A large herd of cattle looked like mere pinpoints in the east as they grazed on the fertile grass in the valley. Mile after mile of land was irrigated with water channeled from the river, a single blue thread woven into the earth-tone tapestry of the desert.

To the west, Prospect City seemed like a miniature painting surrounded by other prosperous ranches. Tiny windmills whirred in the late autumn breeze.

Their thighs brushed as Ashe leaned over and turned her head so that her bright blue eyes met the warm gray of his own. "I hate to wipe that radiant glow from your gorgeous face, love, but it's almost time for our son to wake up and protest loudly about his lack of nourishment."

Hallie laughed and kissed him lightly. "You're right. I'll race you back."

Halfway home, they saw Pascal Fritts in his worn-out wagon ahead of them, the large wooden wheels hitting all the ruts in the road.

Ashe reined in beside him, shouting over the rattling noise. "What brings you out here, Pascal?"

Pascal mopped the perspiration from his brow with a soiled handkerchief and pulled out a paper from his shirt pocket. "A telegram come fer ya; and being as you folks don't come in to town often, I decided to ride out and deliver it."

Hallie read it, and a wide smile pulled at the corner of her mouth. She read it aloud for Ashe: "It's a girl! As redheaded as her daddy. Bring Benjamin for a visit soon. Clara and Stephen."

Ashe laughed. "Sounds like they're matchmaking rather early, doesn't it?"

"Speaking of matchmaking," Pascal interrupted, "guess ya'll are coming in for the big weddin' between Martha and Doc, ain't ya?"

"Sure thing," Hallie said, laughing lightly. "I heard Doc say it was a sudden decision. Can you imagine that?"

"How's yore boy?" Pascal asked.

"Growing like a weed. He looks more like his handsome father every day . . . except he does have my blue eyes," Hallie said boastfully.

"Well, don't want to keep ya. One day when I have time I'll jest mosey on out fer a short visit. That is, if ya don't mind."

"Please do, Pascal. Come for supper some evening."

"Mighty grateful for the invite. Tell Grady and Ben I said hello." With that, he made a wide circle and headed back to town.

They tethered the horses in front of the house. Ben and Grady were waiting on the porch with a chubby bundle in Ben's arms.

"Damnation, Ben Langley, I know he said 'Grandpa.' It was just as plain as the nose on your face," Grady protested.

"Hell, Grady, you're just dreaming. He ain't but six months old," Ben argued.

Hallie and Ashe strolled up the walk. Hallie cast them a disapproving look. "If you two don't watch your language, his first word certainly won't be 'Grandpa.' If you don't behave, I'll have to make room for both of you in the pantry with Sinbad."

At her remark, Ben held Benjamin James Barkley in the air and jiggled him, bringing a delighted smile to his rosy mouth. "You hear those threats, lad? She'd do it, too, you'd better believe it."

Sitting down on a hand-hewn bench, Ben plopped Benjamin on his knee and bounced him up and down. Immediately Ben's smile changed to consternation as a dark wet circle appeared on his leg.

"Hallie, come here quick," Ben shouted.

Taking Ashe by the arm, she began walking in the

opposite direction, calling over her shoulder, "Not this time, Ben, he's all yours."

They continued their walk until they reached the stable. It too had undergone drastic changes. Several rows of new stalls had been added to the original building, and two new corrals had been built to accommodate the additional horses Sundog had returned after he captured the white stallion. All the ranch hands were eating lunch under the watchful eye of their new cook, Bart, so there was no one to interrupt them as Hallie purposefully drew Ashe into an empty stall.

Running her fingers up his chest, she eyed him coyly, unbuttoning his shirt with skillful fingers. "There comes a time when a busy mother has to work like the devil to find a minute to be alone with her husband."

Slipping her hands into his open shirt, she caressed his shirt, her fingers entwining in the crisp mat of hair. She smiled up at him mischievously.

"You haven't forgotten what happened the last time we were here, have you?" Ashe's hand circled her waist and pulled her slim body against his rock-hard frame.

"Why else do you think I sneaked you in here?" she asked coquettishly.

"What about Benjy? It's time for his lunch."

Hallie giggled. "And when, Ashe Barkley, have you ever been concerned about anyone's appetite besides your own?"

Ashe smiled crookedly and lowered her to the bed of straw. "Maybe Maria has a leftover drumstick bone from last night's dinner. That ought to keep him satisfied for a while."

"See, my love," Hallie said, drawing his mouth down to meet hers, "where there's a will, there's a way."